FLINTRIDGE

AHI KELEHER

ISBN: 1499221355
ISBN-13: 978-1499221350

DEDICATION

To my boys, Scout and Savvy.

CONTENTS

ACKNOWLEDGMENTS

I would like to extend heartfelt thanks to the following people for offering their thoughts, time and support: Barb, Kathleen, Linnea, Barbara, Bonnie and Chelsea. Without this team I would never have gotten this book completed in time.

CHAPTER ONE

Flintridge, 1842

The town of Flintridge is situated in the mountainous country west of the Iowa Territory. Scattered at the base of the foothills stand a handful of shacks that pass as houses, a dry goods store, a stable with attached smithy, and various other businesses necessary to sustain a standard of living. At the entrance to the town stands a constabulary, the youngest building in the newborn town.

A little over a mile from the town proper a river descends from the mountaintops, shrinking as it reaches lower elevations. Where it flows past Flintridge it is little more than a shallow brook. Regardless, the fresh water is the lifeblood that keeps Flintridge alive in an otherwise forbidding country. Sagebrush clings to the banks of the creek and its floodplain feeds a modest acreage of grass. Each year the stream is inundated with water from the snow melting off the mountains, necessitating the town to be placed some distance from the water source to avoid flooding.

Flintridge supports a population of fifty-seven souls, divided amongst a handful of families. Out of necessity the community is close-knit, but every town has its deviants. To handle these disturbances, a new sheriff was sent for.

Alexander Judge departed from New York on a Friday morning in August. He boarded a train. His horse, an elegant black Morgan-bred, had been loaded in a stock car. Together they were headed west, to embark on a new adventure in their lives.

Before stepping up into the third class carriage, Alexander adjusted his waistcoat. It was new-bought from the tailor, made from a modest but smart navy blue fabric. He shrugged into his coat and took a moment to ensure that the cuffs and lapels laid as they should. Though he had not come from a wealthy family, his father had served on the police force in New York for years and insisted that his only son maintain his appearance meticulously. Alexander was now in his twenty-sixth year, fresh out of law school, but his father's teachings still held firm in his mind.

Through his father's connections, Judge the younger had been appointed as the sheriff in the town of Flintridge, located in the rugged western territories. Personally, Alexander was not certain what to make of the commission but his innate sense of duty did not allow him to question it for long. Dutifully he had accepted and was eager to take up the reins of justice in Flintridge.

The fledgling sheriff found an unoccupied seat in the carriage. He stowed his travel case in the carrier above and settled onto the uncomfortable bench. The bench seat was without padding and the wood was worn so badly with use that it was beginning to splinter. Others crowded in, filling up the benches and squishing close together so everyone would fit.

A rather large man dropped onto the bench beside him and bumped into Alexander in the process. Judge squirmed on the bench, trying to find a more comfortable position. Try as he might he could not escape the bulk pressing against his right side, for he was barred in on the left by an elderly woman with a bad cough.

The train whistle sounded and the coaches lurched forward. Everyone was thrown against their neighbor as the train took off. Once the train had left the station and reached optimum speed the movement of the cars, though annoying, became more predictable.

Brushing a lock of ginger hair from his brow, Alexander reached into his coat pocket. He extracted his reading glasses and an envelope, the seal of which was already broken. Licking his lips, still discomforted by the close presence of strangers to left and right, he opened the letter and perused the contents again. He had read this particular missive at least a dozen times, but felt that once more would do no harm.

Mr. Alexander Judge,

I have heard that you have been appointed as the new sheriff of Flintridge. I am writing to express my congratulations and to wish you welcome as you make preparations to come west.

Flintridge is yet a very young town and I am pleasantly surprised that the government saw fit to send us a worthy lawman such as yourself. To give you some local history, the town grew around a homestead belonging to one Byrne Jameson. He came west some years ago, the exact number escapes my memory, and makes his living as a mustang runner. I have met him on only a few occasions - he is a recluse - but he seems to be a genuine, honest fellow.

Your quarters at the newly built constabulary are prepared, ready for your arrival. Our chief water source, a mountain river, is located about a mile without the town. There has been talk of putting in wells but so far the dream has not been realized. My hope is that one will be prepared before you arrive.

If, upon your arrival, you find yourself in need of anything at all please do not hesitate to call on me. My family and I live in the apartments adjoining the general store, of which I am the proprietor, and would be glad to lend you any assistance.

With most sincere regards,

Roy Fletcher

Postscript: As I am sure you are aware, the outlaw problem has been growing in Flintridge and the surrounding towns. It is my sincerest hope that you come fully prepared to deal with these barbarians.

Alexander appreciated the time taken by the general store owner to write him and bid him welcome. He looked forward to meeting this man and determined that he would stop in at the store as soon as he was settled in Flintridge.

Refolding the letter and tucking it safely back into his coat pocket, Alexander searched for another task with which to busy his mind. He knew the journey ahead of him would not soon be over.

Indeed it was a long, tiring journey. The incessant rocking of the carriage on the rails, the dust pushing through the cracks in the windows, the smell of bodies confined in a cramped, hot space for too long, all contributed to making the trip seem to last an eternity. Alexander spent the first few hours struggling to read one of his legal tomes but could not steady his hands for the jarring motions of the train car. He began to feel ill, suffering from motion sickness. Setting the book aside, he removed his reading glasses, loosened his cravat, and pinched the bridge of his nose.

"You look like you could use a drink," a male voice commented from across the car.

Alexander opened his eyes and searched the faces of those on the bench opposite, trying to determine which of them had spoken. One man, heavily bearded, raised his hand briefly and offered a grin. He tossed Alexander a ratty, stained wineskin.

Never having been the most coordinated person, Judge fumbled to catch it. "Much obliged, thank you." Reluctantly Alexander uncorked the drinking vessel. It was heavy, almost completely full. He felt the other man's expectant gaze on him. "Alexander Judge. Pleased to meet you, Mr. ..."

The bearded man shook his head. "I don't hand my name out willy-nilly."

"Though you seem willing to share your drink willy-nilly." Alexander took an experimental sniff. Over the powerful scent of goatskin and grime he could not smell the contents. He was loath to have to drink from the filthy, well-used wineskin.

"Are you going to drink or what?"

Not wanting to make an enemy over something as trivial as sharing a drink, Alexander took a small sip. He had to suppress a cough for the alcohol was potent.

The man across the car chuckled good-naturedly. "Where're you headed?" He scratched his beard and with a jolt of repulsion Alexander wondered if the owner of the drinking vessel had fleas.

"West. Flintridge." Alexander corked the skin and threw it back to its owner. Fortunately for him the bearded man was perfectly capable of receiving his poorly aimed toss. Otherwise it would have struck the slumbering woman to his acquaintance's left. "Thank you for the beverage." Judge was still suffering from a motion sickness headache and his stomach felt unsettled. The alcohol had not improved matters.

"I daresay you'll need to learn to handle your liquor if you're heading out that far," the stranger said with another kindly laugh. His next statement was more serious. "Coarse country out there. Lawless. What's sending a dandy like you out west?"

"I am bringing the law to the outskirts of civilization," Alexander answered, gaining some confidence from the familiar subject. He pulled back the lapel of his coat, revealing the silver star pinned to his waistcoat. The newly minted badge gleamed even in the weak light of the carriage; its wearer, likewise, was brimming with pride.

The train car lurched and the occupants all rocked into one another. Alexander's headache grew suddenly worse and he again pinched the bridge of his nose, letting his coat fall back into place over the silver star. The dozers slept on, undisturbed. Alexander envied them.

"Need another drink?" the observant man on the other side of the carriage asked. Though Alexander's eyes were closed he knew the other was grinning by the tone of his voice. His tolerance for being made sport of was beginning to slip away, chased by the pounding pressure in his skull.

"I think I've had all the drink I can stomach for now, thank you." Immediately he regretted his brusque tone. "Do forgive me, this headache is having an appalling effect on my manners." He waved his hand in the air dismissively. "Whither are you bound, sir?"

"Same place as you." The bearded man stretched his legs out as far as he could in the cramped space and leaned back, cradling his wineskin against his chest. A crude knapsack sat on the floor between his feet. His clothing was simple: an untucked long sleeve shirt, pants, wide-brimmed hat and overcoat, all of which had seen better days as evidenced by the holes that riddled the clothing. To further complete the picture of scruffiness and lack of hygiene, he was coated in a fine layer of sand.

Alexander looked askance at his own shoulder to determine if he had received a similar dusting from travel. Brushing the gritty dust from his coat, he responded to the other man's answer. "Really? From what you have said about it I was given the impression that you have a low opinion of the place." He pulled his coat off and folded it on his lap. The stale air in the carriage was growing hot. "What sends you to Flintridge?"

The man shrugged and drank from the wineskin. Alexander noted with some dismay that he had no issue tolerating the strong liquor. "No real reason. I've been out west before, lived in one small town or another. When I came back east I discovered that modern amenities in the big cities didn't suit me so well. So, I'm headed back out where a man can live a life of adventure." He took another swig. "Maybe I'll see you around town then."

"Perhaps we will." Alexander nodded in salute. He leaned against the backrest and closed his eyes, intending to sleep away as much of the miserable journey as possible. The ever-present sand continued to sift into the carriage, sticking to sweaty skin and damp clothing.

~~~~~~~~~~~

When he woke some hours later the bearded man was no longer sitting on the bench opposite. Alexander groggily surveyed those surrounding him. Most were asleep.

He worked his jaw, trying to get the parched feeling out of his mouth. To his great dismay he felt sand grind between his teeth. He glanced around him, suddenly self-conscious. He hoped no one had caught him sleeping with his mouth open.

With a sharp pang his bladder reminded him why he had woken in the first place and he stood. Stretching as much as the cramped space would allow, Alexander went in search of a water closet.

His search took him out of the compartment. As he stepped out onto the platform between cars he was startled to realize that he was not alone. The bearded man stood with his back to the door, smoking placidly as he watched the scenery go by. Alexander hardly took note of the fact that they were now well away from big cities. The train steamed over a tall grass prairie. Without sparing a second to acknowledge the bearded man he hastened on to the next compartment.

After he had relieved himself he took his time going back to his seat. Being up and moving around was such a relief after being seated for so long. There was a kink in his neck that he wished he could work out but despite his stretches it would not budge. He paused on the observation platform between cars. He was alone. After the cramped quarters inside the car the fresh air and solace was welcome.

Leaning on the rail for support against the jarring motion of the cars, Alexander watched the scenery go by. He did not know what part of the country they were now passing through but it was apparently uninhabited. As far as the eye could see were rolling hills blanketed in tall grasses. The wind rushed through the grass, giving the illusion of silvery waves rippling across the prairie. Splashes of color, golds and oranges, whites and pinks, broke the blue-green sea of grass. The immensity of it all, the complete emptiness, the pristine nature of the land took Alexander's breath away. High above, only a few puffs of white clouds floated across the brilliant blue sky. Judge inhaled deeply, savoring the variety of scents wafting from the grass.

A piercing metallic screech suddenly filled the air. Alexander threw his hands up to cover his ears, gritting his teeth and wincing against the horrendous noise. What he failed to realize was that the sound meant that the train was braking quickly. The cars lurched as the train gradually slowed up. Alexander spared one hand to hang onto the railing. The high-pitched whine continued to assault his senses.

White-knuckled on the rail, Judge leaned far out, trying to see what was causing the sudden stop. The platform jumped beneath his feet, threatening to pitch him over the railing. Alexander gave a cry as he was hurtled upward.

5

A firm hand caught hold of his coat and hauled him back to safety. Breathing hard, the young sheriff turned to thank his savior. It was the bearded man.

"Take care, Mr. Judge. Where you're going you'll need to keep aware of your surroundings."

Alexander nodded vaguely, shaking with adrenaline. He took in gulps of air, trying to steady himself. When he had got his breath back he realized that the train had started up again and was slowly accelerating. "What had happened? Why did the train stop so suddenly?" he inquired of his companion.

The bearded man shrugged. "They were stoppin' for something." He steady, wise, brown eyes were trained on the far horizon.

"Evidently." Alexander could not quite keep the sarcasm from his voice. He was finding his companion's habit of stating the obvious tiresome.

Gradually a lowing sound could be heard over the clatter of wheels on rail. Alexander's brow furrowed as the sound registered with him. He approached the rail again, taking care not to lean so far over.

Great brown beasts were seething away from the train. Alexander's jaw dropped as he stared at them, each individual taller than his saddle horse and far greater in bulk. Their shaggy chocolate-colored coats bobbed as they galloped heavily along, emitting their snorting, lowing cries. The combined sound of their hooves striking the ground drowned out even the sounds of the train as their carriage passed through the mob of beasts.

"What are they?" Alexander shouted, unable to take his eyes off the huge curved horns of the animals as they ran past. The whites of their eyes showed stark against their dark brown faces.

"Buffalo," the bearded man answered as a shout close to his ear. Fascinated, Alexander could only stare at the hulking beasts as they stampeded away from the train on both sides. "Welcome to the Wild West, Mr. Judge." The bearded man clapped him on the shoulder.

CHAPTER TWO

After a seeming eternity spent in the cramped confines of the third class carriage, Alexander was growing restless. The other passengers seemed to have the same restlessness about them; even the stoic bearded man took to pacing up and down the narrow corridor.

Finally the train pulled into a station. Alexander departed expectantly. As he stepped down from the carriage he stopped to take stock of his new home. Compared to what he was used to the place was barren. The platform was small, shielded from the elements by a simple awning. There was a small building attached to the platform, likely the ticket office.

Beyond, he could see the main street of the town. Buildings were arranged neatly along each side of the main drag. Some veins of the road branched off to structures set back from the town proper. Milling about the streets was quite a number of people and animals.

By contrast, wild, empty land stretched on for miles on the other side of the railway tracks. The new sheriff hardly spared the wilderness a thought, preferring to focus on the town which held his future.

Overall the town looked to be young but prosperous.

Alexander heaved a sigh of contentment. "Yes, I think this will do quite nicely."

His companion from the train ride came to stand beside him and followed his gaze with some curiosity. The bearded man looked at Alexander, then at the town, and back again. "Going to Flintridge you said?"

Alexander turned to face the other man. Satisfaction was written clearly on his face. "Yes I did."

"Ah." The man paused, nodding as if in contemplation. "You're not there yet." He brushed past Alexander, walked to the edge of the platform and jumped down, heading for the livestock cars.

Alexander did a double-take and then trotted off after the man, calling for him to stop and explain. Growing frustrated as the man did not obey, Alexander stopped and looked around. A sign stood at the entrance to the town, one that had been obscured by the station shack. It read 'Glenn Rock'. His jaw dropped and he had the overwhelming urge to beat his head against a wall. He had been so certain his grueling journey was at an end!

"How do I get to Flintridge?" Alexander asked of no one in particular, deflated and frustrated.

"There is a stagecoach headed out that way," a helpful passerby mentioned. By the time Alexander spun round to thank him and ask for more information he had disappeared in the bustle of departing passengers.

At a loss for how he would get to his final destination, Alexander stalked down the length of the train to collect his horse and belongings. Steam shot up from the train's smokestack and the whistle sounded. Alexander picked up his pace. The workers had unloaded most of the luggage and thrown it in a heap outside the train car. The bedraggled sheriff-to-be began the onerous task of finding his trunk.

As he was shuffling through the mishmash he saw his horse being led away by one of the railway employees. Tripping over scattered packing cases, Alexander chased after them. "Wait! Sir! You have my horse!" His shouts went unheard. He followed to where several other horses stood tied. Before his horse could be added to the herd he caught up with them and breathlessly announced his intention of claiming his animal.

"Of course sir. Ticket?"

"Ticket? Oh!" Alexander dug about in his pockets, searching for the scrap of paper he had received when he checked his horse in at the railway station in New York. While he was hunting for it another man approached the railway employee. Handing off his slip, he received the lead of a rather plain but stoutly built chestnut horse.

Finally Alexander produced the worn piece of paper and was given his horse's lead. He patted the gelding on the neck in greeting. For now the animal was his only familiar companion in an unfamiliar place. Alexander led the animal off to search for his trunk.

Once he had secured all of his belongings he cast a look about rather desperately for his next move. For a quarter hour he stood helplessly in the street, not knowing where to go. The crowd from the train dispersed to various inns, taverns and homes. The train whistle sounded again and the locomotive moved off, chugging slowly out of the station. Clouds of steam enveloped the platform.

The horse nudged Alexander with his head, bored of standing aimlessly in the street. He stamped a foot. It was just the motivation Alexander needed to decide on a course of action. He led the gelding to a hitching post outside the nearest saloon and tied him up. Retrieving his trunk, he dragged it to sit beside his horse. Alexander stood tall as he dusted off his coat one final time before pushing through the swinging doors and entering the tavern.

Within, voices sounded in revelry, some accompanying the piano player in the far corner. At the bar every stool was occupied and men wearing coats and dusters threw back shots or guzzled mugs of beer.

Taking the star badge off his vest, Alexander held it high for all to see and raised his voice above the din. "I am the new sheriff. Can anyone tell me how to get to Flintridge?"

Abruptly all sound cut out. Patrons turned to stare at him, most with disinterested expressions. Alexander's eyes darted about; he found that he was suddenly uneasy at being the center of attention.

One man stood and approached. Alexander had not even realized that the bearded man from the train was one of the patrons at the bar. Mug in hand, the bearded man sauntered over. "Put that down," he instructed easily, indicating the badge with a flick of his eyes. "Have a drink and we'll talk about how you're going to get to Flintridge. Barkeep, a, uh," he paused, looking Alexander over and then grinning. "A sarsaparilla for the sheriff!"

Activity resumed as normal. Feeling like a fool, Alexander pinned the badge back onto his vest and let his coat fall to cover it. He shuffled after the bearded man, following him up to the bar. The bearded man claimed his previous spot and at a nod from him the man to his right vacated his seat. Alexander took it at a cue from the bearded man.

"Quite the dramatist, aren't you?" the bearded man asked with an amused grin. The barkeep delivered the beverage and the bearded man tossed payment onto the counter. "Have a seat and relax. There's no getting to Flintridge until tomorrow."

Sheepishly Alexander took up his drink, hoping to cover the fact that he was blushing. "Tomorrow?" he asked belatedly as the statement soaked in.

"Yep. Stagecoach. Leaves at ten in the mornin'." The bearded man watched Alexander's response out of the corner of his eye. "I reckon you didn't make plans for the night yet."

"No," Alexander confirmed with a downward tilt of his mouth.

"Of course. You know lawman, you're a bit helpless. Finish your drink and I'll show you to a place to spend the night."

"Thank you," Alexander said, genuinely grateful for the guidance. "I should not bother to ask you for your name, I suppose, since you do not give it out willy-nilly." He was trying for a joke, though his annoyance at not knowing the name of the man who kept getting him out of tight spots brought a touch of sarcasm to his words.

"Never trust a man 'til you've shared a drink with him," the man replied as if quoting a well-known saying. He turned and extended his hand. "Byrne Jameson."

Alexander smiled and shook his hand. "Pleased to make your acquaintance officially." Then, belatedly, the name clicked with a memory. Alexander stopped shaking the hand he held and stared openly at the bearded man. "Did you say Byrne Jameson?"

"Yes," he replied slowly as he took his hand away.

"The very same Byrne Jameson that founded Flintridge?"

Byrne looked at Alexander closely, his eyes narrowing. Then he shrugged and gave a little laugh. "Now who went and told you that?" he asked as he took a drink.

"I read it in a letter," Alexander said, trying to be cagey. He threw back his drink, finishing off the nonalcoholic beverage.

Byrne finished his drink with a final swig and hopped off the stool. He did not seem to be too keen to follow up on his question. Alexander followed him to the door. Once outside Byrne paused and Alexander continued on to his horse.

He began to untie the lead but Byrne's voice stopped him. "Leave the horse. I'll send a boy to take them to the stable. We'll just take your trunk across the way." He pointed at a building and led off.

They each rented a room at the inn. True to his word, Byrne found a stable boy and sent him off to the stable with their horses. Exhaustion from the long journey overtook Alexander. He retired early and dropped off to sleep almost instantly.

~~~~~~~~~~

Next morning Byrne and Alexander met in the street outside the inn. Alexander had managed to drag his heavy trunk out into the street. His gelding stood tied alongside Byrne's red chestnut stallion. The stallion swished his tail as Alexander approached to untie his horse.

"So where are we to meet this stagecoach?" Alexander asked as he fought with the rope.

"The other side of town, I reckon. That's where the trail leads off."

Alexander stood on tiptoe to peer over his horse's neck. At the far end of the town, where the main road opened up into empty space, a track worn by countless wagon wheels could just be seen in the packed dirt.

"Tack up your horse. Less to cram onto the coach that way." Byrne took his own advice, throwing blanket and saddle onto his horse's back. Alexander followed suit though he took considerably more time at the task. He was thus distracted when the clatter of many hooves sounded at the far edge of town.

The sheriff consulted his pocket watch. "The stagecoach is here already?!" Alexander exclaimed. He tucked away the watch and fumbled with the cinch in his rush.

Byrne was just finishing putting his horse's bridle on. He looked to the end of the street upon hearing the clamor. The harnessed horses appeared around the far building, galloping full out. The coach appeared in turn, its driver leaning forward and whipping the horses on. Byrne took in the scene in a glance before swinging into the saddle. Alexander, too, had sensed that something was wrong and he circled his horse, frantically trying to finish putting on its tack.

Before the sheriff had finished his task, a series of deafening cracks rang out in the street, echoing off the buildings. The sounds stirred up a sense of sheer panic in the hearers. Alexander's heart began pounding as he recognized the sound of gunshots. Hanging off the side of the saddle he paused to turn and look up the street.

Following in the wake of the coach, a gang of riders appeared, all attired in dusters and western-style hats. Curiously for outlaws, which Alexander realized they must certainly be, they took no care to cover their faces. Even at that great distance it was clear that they were rough, ruthless men. Every one of them was armed with multiple guns and as they thundered into town after the stagecoach they fired shots at random.

Alexander tried to pull himself up into the saddle but his horse spooked at the myriad of sounds and the rapidly approaching coach. The Morgan reared, touched down, and reared again, rolling his eyes in fear. Only Alexander's hand on the reins kept him from bolting.

The coach swung a tight corner, threatening to tip clean over. The axles gave a worrisome groan before the outside wheels touched ground again. The coach barreled down the main drag. Pedestrians screamed and jumped out of the way as the rig barreled down the road. Some were faster than others; at least one was run down by the rig.

Byrne kicked his horse into a canter, riding toward the oncoming stagecoach. The bandits followed the rig into town and were gaining on it. Alexander scrambled into the saddle and drew his pistol. He let his horse run, directing him toward the approaching gang.

Once the local riders had passed the stagecoach driver was able to slow his team and pull them up. The horses were blowing and drenched with sweat, stretching out their necks to catch their breath. They danced in their tresses, unnerved by the sounds of gunfire. The driver turned round to watch the encounter with nervous interest. Likewise, the passengers within the coach peered cautiously out of the open windows.

One passenger grew skittish as the gang bore down on them. Flinging the coach door open, he jumped out and ran toward the nearest building. One of the random shots from the gang caught him and he fell with a scream.

Alexander held his badge aloft and fired one round into the air. He stopped his horse in front of the advancing gang and raised his voice. "In the name of the law, I order you to stop!"

The bandits continued to advance at a full gallop. Alexander willed himself to stand his ground though he was greatly unnerved by their charge. He fired another round into the air. "Stop!" he shouted again.

A shot answered and the sheriff flinched as he heard the bullet whiz through the air. It struck the tip of his badge, miraculously missing his hand, and the silver star went flying from his grasp. Alexander yanked his hand down, glancing at it to make sure no damage had been done. When he looked up again the gang was almost upon him.

Byrne came galloping to join the sheriff after having ensured that the stagecoach and its passengers were secure. The driver had his steeds back in control and the injured man had been dragged into a nearby building. The bearded man stopped his horse alongside Alexander and held his shotgun at the ready.

Byrne heaved a silent sigh of relief as reinforcements came. The Glenn Rock sheriff and his deputies came galloping over, adding to the defensive line. Most of them held shotguns and had pistols holstered on their belts.

The gang drew up at the last minute, spinning their horses in tight circles. The beasts neighed and snorted, protesting the rough handling. More shots were fired into the air.

After letting their horses dance in place for a time the leader of the bandits yanked his mount around and kicked it into a gallop, forcing through his own comrades and charging out of town as quickly as they had come. The others turned their horses and followed, leaving no evidence of their visit but churned dirt and a cloud of dust.

Alexander dropped his arms with a heavy sigh. He had been terrified throughout the ordeal and suddenly his body felt as if it were made of jelly.

Absently he wondered if he could stay in the saddle. He turned to his companion as if just noticing his presence. "Have you been there all the time?"

Byrne gave him a strange look, then turned his horse and headed back to the stagecoach. Alexander remained still for a long while, not trusting his ability to stay in the saddle if his horse should move. When he had regained his composure somewhat, he directed his horse to where the stagecoach still stood. The local authorities had split up, most to chase after the bandits and ensure they did not return, while one deputy got the story from the coach driver.

The coach horses had their heads down, working the bits in their mouths; foamy sweat covered their bodies. Byrne was listening to the conversation between the coach driver and deputy when Alexander dismounted and teetered over to them. The bearded man moved off as the hapless sheriff approached.

The deputy, still mounted, noticed Alexander approaching, leading his horse. The dazed sheriff paused as his boot clunked against something on the ground. Bending to retrieve his badge, he stared blankly at the divot left in the metal by the bullet.

"Hey, thanks for holding them up while we got our horses saddled," the deputy said, extending his hand. Alexander reached up to shake it. His grip was weak. "Gotta say though, you're a new breed of crazy, taking on a gang like that alone. What's your name friend?"

"Alexander Judge. I am headed for Flintridge to serve as the new sheriff." He paused for a moment, making sure he had answered every question posed to him. "I was not alone, though," he added, thinking of how Byrne had come to his aid.

"Oh, right, your deputy?" The Glenn Rock deputy cast about, searching for Byrne. "Where'd he go? He was here a minute ago."

Alexander looked around as well. He could see no sign of the bearded man. "Er, not my deputy. He is just a man I met on the train. As far as I know I do not have a deputy yet."

"Uh huh. Well if you're planning on pulling stunts like that on a regular basis I'd suggest you get a couple deputies to back you up. For starters, get the man that helped you today."

"Is there much trouble out in Flintridge?"

The deputy shrugged and laid the reins on his horse's neck. "No more'n any other town out here. You deal with the usual stuff: Indian raids, bar brawls, brothels, and of course there's the outlaws. Today you met the Hayes-Lawson gang. I reckon you haven't seen the last of them, either. They've been stepping up their game in the past several months."

Alexander stared at the deputy with a furrowed brow. All of a sudden he was feeling overwhelmed, dizzy, distraught. How would he, a single lawman, cope with the so-called 'usual stuff' of the Wild West? It was far more rugged and uncivilized than that to which he was accustomed.

The deputy must have noticed his change of expression for he let out a laugh meant to reassure and clapped Alexander on the shoulder. "Don't worry about it, help is just a two days' ride. Any time you need extra muscle send word back here to Glenn Rock. We're more'n happy to help out, at least until you get a posse of your own rounded up."

"Much obliged," Alexander said, appreciating the offer but unable to fathom being isolated so far from the next town. Two days' ride just to muster a posse? Undoubtedly any criminal would make a clean getaway in that time. "So what were they after?"

"Ha! What are bandits ever after? The coach was carrying a moderate payroll, some mail, the usual. Once we see that delivered to the railway and get fresh horses hitched up you can take the coach to Flintridge. Godspeed my friend!"

Alexander did not feel at all reassured.

The clatter of hooves sounded at the far end of town again. Alexander jumped round, ready to fling himself onto his horse and confront the bandits once more. The deputy was much calmer, merely glancing at the approaching hoofbeats. "Relax Mr. Judge, it's just our sheriff and company comin' back. Ah! Looks like they caught one of the devils!"

Sure enough, the lawmen rode in a circular pattern, surrounding one man on horseback. The bandit and his mount were in rough shape. The horse was limping, breathing hard and sweat-soaked. The rogue had lost his hat and sported a sizeable welt on the side of his face, apparently from the butt of a rifle. His hands were bound and anchored to the saddle horn.

As the posse drew nearer, the deputy got a better look at the captive's features and let out a whoop. "Got ol' Cliff Hayes I see! The Gravedigger hisself!"

"Stop your gawkin' and go get a cell ready. We'll be keeping a guard posted 'round this one at all times; you know the gang won't let him go to the rope easy," the man riding at the front, leading the prisoner's horse, barked. He had an obscenely large mustache and sharp eyes with a flinty quality. A sheriff's star shone on his coat, reflecting the morning sunlight as a blinding glint.

The deputy tapped his hat in farewell to Alexander and obediently trotted off. The posse brought their prisoner to the constabulary, dragged him from his horse and hustled him inside. He did not utter a single word, not even a shout of protest. Throughout the ordeal his weathered face did not show the least bit of emotion. Alexander thought that he was being very cooperative for an outlaw.

His attention was diverted as the coachmen traded out the horses in their rig for fresh animals from the livery stable. The bandit's lame beast, which had thrown a shoe in the wild chase, was led to the livery stable so the blacksmith could forge it a new shoe.

As it turned out, Alexander and Byrne, who had reappeared as mysteriously as he had disappeared, were the only two going on to Flintridge. They tied their horses to the back of the coach, stowed their belongings, and climbed into the carriage.

Very quickly Alexander learned that his traveling companion was not inclined toward conversation that day. His early attempts at striking up a conversation went ignored or, if he was lucky, elicited one-word answers. Something was clearly on Byrne's mind, distracting him. For most of the journey he stared vacantly out the carriage window. Alexander dozed fitfully. The jerking motions of the coach were far less tolerable than those of the train car had been. His motion sickness returned tenfold.

The day wore on, seeming never to end. The stagecoach stopped only a few times to allow the horses a brief drink and the travelers to relieve themselves.

When darkness began to fall the driver urged the horses onward, hoping to make a good campsite before the light went completely. The lanterns at the fore of the carriage were lit, providing necessary light as they traveled through the early night. Finally, to Alexander's great relief, the carriage stopped for the night. They had a quiet meal of canned foods, having no fuel to light a fire over which to cook. Lacking the warmth of a fire, all four men piled into the carriage and slept sitting upright on the benches within. Though the curtains were drawn down over the open windows, the cold night air seeped into the chamber. At dawn the next morning they set off again.

It was dusk when a shout from the driver roused Alexander. They had reached Flintridge. Suddenly filled with apprehension and excitement, the sheriff threw up the blind and poked his head out the window, trying to glimpse the town that would be his home for the foreseeable future. Byrne seemed disinterested, not even looking out his window.

When the journey was finally at an end and Alexander stepped from the coach, he had to suppress the urge to kiss the dusty ground at his feet. He would not be making another journey like that again for some time, of that he was certain.

Belatedly the sheriff realized that he looked a fright. Since the stagecoach windows lacked glass, dust had blown in and he was powdered over with brown grit. Hastening to brush it off, he glanced at his companion who seemed untroubled by his own grungy appearance. "So Byrne, what do you plan to do here in Flintridge?"

"Keep to myself," was the brusque answer. Still there seemed to be something nagging at Byrne, distracting him and preventing him from being social.

Alexander was a touch disappointed; he had been banking on having at least one friend in this new, forbidding world. He nodded, accepting the statement. "Well, best of luck to you."

"I'm not the one that'll need it." The comment had been no more than a whisper, probably not intended to be heard. Alexander had heard it, though, and the words sent chills through his body. He thought of the ruthlessness of the Hayes-Lawson gang and flinched at the sound of gunshots echoing in his memory.

Hoping to clear his mind, Alexander looked upon his new home town. Compared to Glenn Rock it was a sore disappointment. Only a handful of buildings comprised the town, all of them ramshackle and crude at best. Though night was fast approaching not a single lantern had been lit. In the dusky light Alexander could see that the nearest building bore a sign identifying it as the constabulary. "Well, at least home is not far away," he muttered to himself.

Lugging his trunk and leading his horse, Alexander made his way toward the constabulary at an awkward shuffle. Midway there he had to let go his hold on the reins. Not wanting to leave his horse unattended in the street, he put the strip of leather in his mouth and continued on. Very quickly he learned that he had to shuffle backward to move the crate most easily and avoid his head getting yanked round if the horse decided to stop abruptly.

Moving backward as he was, he could not judge the distance remaining until he reached his destination. His foot dropped into a divot in the ground, his ankle twisted, and he fell backward. The trunk slammed to the ground and his horse propped, startled by the sudden noise. Alexander looked at him with wide eyes. "No!" The reins dropped out of his mouth and the horse whirled, trotting some distance away. He stopped on the other side of the street, snorting, ears pricked and tail held high.

Alexander jumped to his feet and started toward the loose horse. His ankle gave out on the first step, dropping him to the dust again. Groaning and embarrassed, Alexander stood again and hopped toward his horse. The action only further upset the animal; he rolled his eyes as Alexander approached and threw his head up. "Stop it you ridiculous beast," Alexander growled as he seized the reins. Urging the horse on, he used him as a support, hopping along beside him.

"Is that your case, mister?"

The sheriff stopped abruptly, yanking his horse to a standstill along with him. He looked toward the sound of the voice, horribly embarrassed. "Yes. Yes it is." He spoke to the woman that stood on the covered walkway attached to the front of the constabulary. Her hand rested on the railing and the other clutched a shawl close around her neck. She was young, he guessed near to his twenty-six years, and not at all bad to look at. Realizing that his clothing was askew, he stopped leaning on his gelding's shoulder and dusted himself off. "Please forgive my appearance. It has been a long journey." He tried to step forward but his ankle wobbled dangerously, threatening to give. Alexander reached for his horse, catching hold of the rein and yanking down on the animal's mouth as he steadied himself. The gelding threw his head in frustration.

"Are you alright?" the woman asked, apparently just realizing that he might be injured.

"I think so. I merely twisted my ankle."

"Well stop pulling on that poor animal's mouth." She descended the two steps and approached him. "Here, let me help. Where are you headed?" She pulled his arm over her shoulders, offering her support. Regretfully Alexander allowed her to do so, feeling immensely foolish as he hopped along beside her. She was sturdier than she looked.

"There." He pointed with his free hand at the sheriff's office just ahead.

"What business can you have there? The sheriff hasn't arrived yet."

The moment Alexander had been dreading the most had come. After making such a fool of himself he now had to identify himself. "He has now. Sheriff Alexander Judge, pleased to meet you."

She stopped dead in her tracks and looked at him closely. "You are the new sheriff?" She spoke slowly, enunciating each word carefully, trying to reconcile her expectations with the rather disappointing man she was supporting.

Alexander cleared his throat, uncomfortable. He knew what a pathetic sight he must be, all travel-worn and clumsy. "Yes ma'am."

"Miss. Miss Emily Fletcher."

"A pleasure to meet you. I believe I can manage from here." They had reached the steps leading up onto the veranda. He was only a few feet from the door of the constabulary. Refuge was within sight.

"What of your trunk?"

"What of it?"

"Do you not wish to bring it inside with you?"

"Oh. Yes, yes of course." Alexander hobbled back down the steps and shuffled toward his packing case. Gritting his teeth he knelt and grabbed hold of the handles, hefting it with a great deal of effort. He took one faltering step. His ankle threatened to give way; he wobbled, but did not fall. He took another step. The trunk was very heavy. He regretted having brought so many books.

"Do you need help with that?" Miss Fletcher pressed. She stood at the base of the stairs, watching him with ill-concealed, friendly amusement.

"No, I can manage." Alexander's masculine pride was kicking in, refusing to accept a woman's help with a physical task. His voice was strained with effort and he began puffing, struggling to hold the bulky weight of the trunk. He made it up the stairs haltingly, each step an enormous effort. He was not the most muscular of men.

Once at the top of the stairs he could hold his burden no more. He half-dropped, half-lowered the trunk; it hit the wooden planks with a resounding thud. Alexander pushed it toward the threshold of the constabulary, desperate to hide himself and his blunders away for the night and thus minimize the damage to his reputation. Much to his frustration there was a lip of wood at the base of the doorway that stopped the trunk's progress. Climbing over the crate he lifted the one end and yanked it through into the room beyond.

His ankle chose that moment to give out. He dropped heavily on his rear, dragging the trunk with him. It crashed into his front and he bit back a cry of pain. Overwhelmed by vanity, he gained his feet and hopped to the doorway, looking out into the street. He sincerely hoped the attractive young woman - Miss Fletcher - had missed his most recent blunder. Much to his relief, the street nearby was deserted.

Remembering his horse, Alexander scanned the darkness for any sign of him. A black horse in a dark night, like a needle in a haystack! he thought to himself. The darkness was complete, far blacker than any evening in New York. Down the street a lantern or two burned outside the saloon, the only business open after dark in this small town.

A quiet nicker gave the horse's location away. Alexander carefully made his way down the steps and passed around in front of the veranda, feeling his way. When his hands touched hide he blew a small sigh of relief. He worked his way to the gelding's head, feeling for the reins. He followed the path of leather only to discover that the reins were wrapped round a hitching post.

Alexander stepped back, contemplating this. Obviously the horse could not have tied himself up. Reluctantly he had to admit that the only answer was that Miss Fletcher had secured the horse for him, had helped him avoid another inconvenience.

Between Byrne and Miss Fletcher he was beginning to grow tired of feeling like a helpless, incompetent charity case. Pounding a fist mildly on the hitching post, Alexander ran a hand through his hair. It was disheveled from his long journey and subsequent accidents.

The gelding gave him a nudge, reminding him that it was past feeding time. The sheriff was at a loss. It was so dark that he could not determine which building was the stable, where he might buy food for his animal. "Sorry Duke," he murmured, patting the gelding on the neck in consolation. The horse snorted.

Alexander fished his canteen out of his saddlebag and let the horse drink a few mouthfuls from his hand. He then unsaddled the gelding but left the bridle on to keep him tethered for the night. The sheriff lugged the saddle into the constabulary and deposited it in an out-of-the-way place. Yawning mildly, he went back outside to double-check that Duke was tied securely.

Quite abruptly the exhaustion from the long, bone-jarring journey hit him. Alexander wanted nothing more than to crawl into bed and sleep. He ascended the steps, each foot moving slowly and heavily. Once on the veranda he picked up his pace somewhat, eager to get in out of the chill setting in the night air.

He remembered the trunk too late. Alexander let out a cry as he tripped over the case and crashed to the floor. Lacking the energy to care much about his situation, he merely kicked the door shut and settled himself down to spend the night on the floor.

CHAPTER THREE

Next morning Alexander slept late. By the time he roused himself the sun was well up. Consulting his pocket watch, he was dismayed that it already read ten and some change. Running a hand down his face, he made a face. Stubble covered his countenance. He recalled that he had not shaved since before departing New York. That would need to be remedied.

Opening the trunk, Alexander rifled through his belongings in search of his shaving kit. The mirror had been cracked during the journey. Displeased, Alexander began the process of shaving. He was acutely aware of the fact that every muscle, every bone, every joint in his body ached. Again he promised himself that he would not endure such a grueling journey like that again for some time, if ever.

Once he had shaved and changed, making himself more presentable, he stepped down into the street. The townsfolk were out and about, already engaged in their daily chores. Women brought water from the centrally-placed well - which Alexander was pleasantly surprised had been constructed, since the tone of the letter he received had not led him to expect much - men stood around smoking or discussing business. Children chased dogs and chickens in the street. In the light of a new day the town did not look so dismal and the sheriff felt a new sense of hope welling within him.

Alexander went to untie his horse. The pothole, his nemesis from the night before, tripped him up again. This time he was able to catch himself before he hit the dirt. Hauling himself back to his feet using the railing as leverage, Alexander glared malignantly at the hole as if it would be affected by his anger.

Realizing there was nothing to be gained from glaring at an inanimate hole in the ground, Alexander turned to Duke. The horse was placidly munching on a mouthful of hay. A large pile of the coarse dry grass lay on the ground within the horse's reach, as well as a large bucket of water. Confused, Alexander took a step back and contemplated the situation. So far he had only met Byrne and Miss Fletcher. Since the bearded man had not seemed taken with him he very much doubted that Byrne would do him a favor like this.

Fletcher...Fletcher...the name kept spinning in his mind, trying to connect with a memory. He had heard the name before, of that he was sure. With a start he bolted back into the constabulary, intent on finding the letter he had read so oft.

Alexander returned with the worn piece of paper in his hand. He read the closing lines again. Roy Fletcher. There must be some relation between the letter writer and the pretty young woman; in this small town having the same name could not be coincidence. He recalled, then, that he had intended to call upon the general store proprietor.

Fetching the saddle and putting it on his horse, Alexander then untied the animal and mounted. His first stop would be the general store. Alexander had taken inventory of his new abode and discovered that it was an empty shell, devoid of furnishings and supplies. Intending to remedy this, he set a leisurely pace down the main road. He made a point of greeting everyone he encountered and introducing himself cordially. Mostly he was met with lukewarm responses; in the eyes of the townspeople he was just a stranger with a shiny badge until he had proved his worth to the town.

Alexander dismounted outside the dry goods store and tethered his horse. The gelding gave him a nudge, reminding him that he had not been allowed to finish his meal. Alexander patted the animal's velvety nose and made his way into the store.

Inside, the store smelled of a mixture of salted meats, leather, wood and flour. Dust hung in the air, making the environment stifling and breathing difficult. Barrels, sacks and crates were stacked to the ceiling several rows deep toward the back of the store. Near the front, behind the counter, the shelves were stuffed with product. For such a small town the general store was amazingly well supplied. A man stood behind the counter, forcing a smile at the newcomer.

"Good morning," Alexander greeted, sauntering over and trying to hide how sore his ankle was.

"Mornin'. New to town?"

"What gave it away?" The question was rhetorical, as they both knew, and it elicited a small laugh from the large man.

"Word has it you're the new sheriff. Allow me to welcome you to Flintridge, officially." He extended a burly, calloused hand which Alexander readily shook. "Roy's the name. Did you get my letter?"

"Alexander Judge. Yes I did, thank you. I see your little well project has been a success."

"I suppose you could say that. I do plan to put in a few more in the coming months, so long as I can find some men who are not afraid of a hard day's work. The last bunch wrung a small fortune out of me to get it completed in time." He gave a sneer of distaste at the memory of the bad business deal. "Pleasure to meet you. But I reckon you didn't stop in here just to shoot the breeze. What can I do for you?"

Alexander tipped his head with a small, strained laugh. If he had been hoping to negotiate prices the conversation was not starting in his favor. "I suppose you are right. That constabulary is emptier than a jail cell."

The shopkeeper laughed heartily. "Those railroad men are indeed cheapskates: willing to pay the wage of a new sheriff, aye, but they won't spare a penny to make their new lawman comfortable."

"I thought the government was paying my wage?"

"Oh, didn't you know? The railroad's interests are so important to the government that they've been allowed to control the policing out here, make sure their interests are protected to the full extent of the law. Sometimes even beyond it." The man watched Alexander closely, judging the effect of the words. Clearly he had given the young sheriff plenty to chew over. "But that's nothing to concern yourself with. Just so long as you get paid, right?" He grinned, enjoying his little joke. "Truth is we're glad to have any lawman in this town. It's not so bad out here compared to some places but lately the bandit raids have been picking up. Why just last week Mueller lost three heifers, driven past the point of exhaustion for the fun of it by that Hayes-Lawson gang."

"Hayes-Lawson?"

"Heard of them already, have you?"

Alexander nodded. A queer feeling was rising in his gut. "Actually had a run-in with them in Glenn Rock."

"Oh yes, I'd heard of that from the coachmen. After payroll, were they?"

Alexander shrugged, feigning nonchalance. He wanted to give the townspeople confidence in his ability to handle any situation calmly. "One can only assume so. You seem to be very well informed."

It was the shop owner's turn to shrug. "Small town. Everyone stops in here. I hear gossip, rumors, you name it. Ever you need to know something, just come for a visit."

"Thank you." Alexander filed the information away in his mind for future reference. "Say, would you happen to know who was good enough to feed and water my horse last night? I must confess I was a bit overwhelmed from the journey and neglected him."

"Oh I did that. My daughter mentioned that you were a bit disoriented."

"Disoriented?" Alexander repeated in a deflated whisper.

"No need to pay for the hay. Consider it a gift to welcome you to town. Going forward you might want to consider trusting his care to the livery stable."

"Thank you." The sheriff's voice was still subdued as he continued to think about the poor impression he made on Miss Fletcher and, indirectly, her father.

"Now then, what commodities would make that shack of yours livable?"

~~~~~~~~~~

Alexander led his gelding down the street. Hitched behind the high-stepping horse was a palette of sorts, loaded with various foodstuffs, bedding, small furniture and a shovel. The animal's quarters strained; he was fresh and wanted to run but his load was too cumbersome for his master to allow it.

Outside the constabulary Alexander tethered the gelding, who danced in his tresses. As Alexander passed him the gelding let out a whinny of protest. He was still hungry but his tether was not long enough to permit him to eat the hay lying just out of reach.

"Give me a minute, will you?" Alexander demanded of the beast. The horse snorted in answer.

The first thing Alexander unpacked was the shovel. Once he had finished with it he leaned it up against the railing and began unpacking the rest of his new belongings. His path in and out of the building took him over the fresh dirt with which he had filled the infamous divot that had tripped him up before.

Within a quarter hour he had moved all the dry goods into the constabulary where they sat in an undignified, disorganized heap. Deeming that satisfactory for the moment, Alexander pulled the door shut behind him and locked it before attending to his horse.

For most of the day Alexander attended to menial domestic tasks. He saw his horse settled in the livery stable, paid his care in advance. Next he lunched at the saloon, making awkward small talk with anyone who sat nearby or passed his table. By midafternoon he was back in the constabulary, moving furniture and organizing his new purchases to his liking. The larger items - table, bed frame, dresser - he had ordered through the town's carpenter and did not reasonably expect them to arrive for some time. His mattress, a crude conglomeration of burlap and straw, had been laid down in the miniature apartment that was situated above the jail.

The floor plan of the constabulary was a curious one. Upon entering a person found himself walking between holding cells, the iron bars fresh and black. At the back of the first level was the compacted dining area which could also serve as an office. Out back was the kitchen, merely a shed with a hearth. At one end of the dining room a stairway rose to the second level. Upstairs was a small sitting room and bedchamber. These spaces were open to one another; much to Alexander's dismay they afforded no privacy. He added one more project to his to-do list.

Abruptly the peace of the afternoon was interrupted. The ricocheting crackle of gunshots brought Alexander flying down the stairs at a run to the front of the constabulary. His heart was in his mouth as he looked out onto the street.

The townsfolk, apparently accustomed to the raids, had cleared out of the street, taking shelter behind closed doors. The sheriff fingered the silver star on his vest and chewed on his lip. He was not certain what course of action would best be taken in this situation. With a sinking feeling in his gut he realized that he had left his holster and gun in the bedroom. His horse was in the stables. Effectively, he was useless to stop the raid. Fear rose within him, smothering his ability to make rational decisions.

Without thinking of the consequences Alexander jumped down into the street. He ran blindly toward the charging gang, yelling incoherently as he went as if that would stop their advance. The horsemen drew their mounts to a halt, momentarily dumbfounded by the rash act. They stared at the foolish lawman in confusion. Their leader was mounted on a bay horse that Alexander thought he recognized from the original team that drew the stagecoach days before. Amongst the crush of horses he also thought he spotted the lamed equine on which the captured bandit had been brought to justice. All that he saw in a fleeting second before all his attention focused on the rider bearing down on him.

As he looked up at the sturdy chestnut horse, its eyes rolling white, and its rider, Alexander realized that he was going to die. Everything seemed to slow down around him, seemed surreal. He looked up at the bandit's face. There was an ugly bruised welt covering most of one side of his face.

With a start everything came together in Alexander's mind. The leader of the Hayes-Lawson gang had escaped, taking at least two horses with him. How? When? What had become of the Glenn Rock posse, his only form of backup? He desperately hoped that they were hot on the heels of the gang but a sinking feeling in his gut told him otherwise. Time caught up with him and returned to normal speed.

When his attention returned to the rider he found a pistol leveled at his head. Alexander closed his eyes tightly, tensed every muscle in his body, steeling himself for the shot.

What came instead was the furious pounding of hooves followed by a thud of flesh striking flesh and the scream of a horse. Something heavy struck him, throwing him clear of the melee. Alexander scrambled to his feet and got further away from the eight hooves churning the dirt. Squinting against the sunlight he tried to make sense of the scene.

Two men struggled atop their horses: the bandit and Byrne. The bearded man held a rifle and was using it as a club, harassing the outlaw and trying to unhorse him. A swift blow stunned the bandit. The rest of the gang stood some distance away, guns at the ready. None had a clean shot at the vengeful bearded warrior.

The gang leader broke free of the scuffle. He kicked his horse into a gallop. Turning in the saddle, he fired a few shots back at Byrne, who had his rifle up on his shoulder. His horse shuffled nervously as the shots whizzed by. The rancher fired, hitting the ground just behind the retreating horse's rear feet. The horse screamed in fear and bucked. The bandit kept his seat. "You haven't seen the last of us! You hear me?!" he shouted over his shoulder. He led his gang off at a gallop, leaving a cloud of dust hanging in the air.

Alexander stared at the spot where the gang had last been. His knees felt like jelly, he felt light-headed. Only willpower kept him on his feet and kept him from vomiting.

Byrne directed his horse up to the shaky-legged sheriff. He tossed his rifle over; Alexander fumbled to catch it. "Hang onto that, reload it, keep it handy. I won't make a habit of saving your hide."

The harsh words broke through the fog of shock that had enveloped Alexander after the encounter. "Why did you help me this time, then?"

Byrne did not answer. He urged his horse on, brushing past the sheriff. Alexander watched him go, perplexed. The man and his motives were a complete mystery to him. Alexander weighed the rifle in his hands, staring at it contemplatively.

"Having a good first day sheriff?" the barkeep called from the door of the saloon. He waved Alexander over and shoved a glass of whisky into his hand. "Good to see they won't catch you off-guard again." He indicated the rifle that Alexander held and led the way into the tavern.

Alexander followed him. He was pale and shaking so badly that he had spilled a good portion of his drink before reaching the bar. He threw back the remainder of his whisky. The alcohol revived him enough for him to hold a coherent conversation. Leaning forward on the countertop, he asked the question that was on his mind. "What can you tell me about that bearded man?"

"There are lots of men with beards hereabouts. I'm afraid you'll have to be more specific."

"The man who gave me this gun - Byrne. He just came into town with me yesterday." He laid the rifle on the counter. "Surely you can recall something of the newcomer?"

The barkeep glanced down at the gun and back up at the sheriff. The young lawman seemed to have recovered from his shock, at least enough to put on a stoic face. He was still pale but the hard set of his mouth told the barkeep that he was not leaving without information. The barkeep shrugged; he could be giving the story to worse sources. "Byrne Jameson is practically the father of this little town. Frankly I'm surprised it isn't named after him."

"Why do you say that?"

"Why? I wasn't here, mind, but local lore has it that ol' Byrne was the first one to come to this remote place. That shack up on the hill," he pointed out the window to their right, indicating a small hillock with an unprepossessing home built atop it. Wisps of smoke rose from the chimney. "That one's his. Supposedly the first structure built in Flintridge."

"Hmm. He didn't mention that to me."

"Likes to keep to himself, ol' Byrne. Can I get you another?" He indicated the empty glass which Alexander still held clutched in his hand. Alexander nodded, willing to pay the expense if it would garner him more information.

As the barkeep poured, Alexander formed his next question. "If he settled this town why would he not want a more active role in it? You saw what he did out there - why is he not the sheriff?"

The barkeep shrugged again, his favorite gesture apparently. "Byrne's a rare breed for certain. The way I read it, he's willing to take to violence to protect his own interests but he doesn't want that to be his all-consuming purpose in life. He doesn't want to have to have everyone else's back all the time. If he did, when would he have time for tending his livestock?"

"He is a rancher?"

The barkeep nodded. "Drink your drink."

"Where might I find him?" Reluctantly Alexander took another sip. He was not overly fond of whiskey.

"There's no telling where ol' Byrne will turn up. Like I said, he keeps to hisself."

"Hrm," Alexander murmured to himself. He had learned some things, but very little of actual interest. Leaving a few coins on the counter, he stood. "Well, thank you." He forced down a parting gulp of the whisky.

"You might try calling on him at his homestead," the barkeep pointed out the window again. "But don't count on finding him there. He goes into the mountains quite often. I think town life wears on him." The speaker laughed to himself, enjoying a private joke at Byrne's expense.

The barkeep eyed the glass skeptically as Alexander put it down on the bar, still over halfway full. Sighing in defeat after reading the judgment on the other's face, Alexander picked the glass up again and, grimacing, threw back the rest of the drink. He left the saloon, coughing and sputtering against the crude burn of the alcohol.

As he stepped out into the street the alcohol hit him hard. He began to feel sick. Forcing down the bile rising in his throat, he hastened to the constabulary. Despite the roiling feeling in his gut distracting him he was keenly aware that numerous pairs of eyes were watching him, felt their weight upon him. The townsfolk were only just growing bold enough to leave the safety of their homes again and he knew that they were judging their new sheriff.

Alexander tried to put that uneasy knowledge to the back of his mind. He had to put on a good front and right at that moment it meant getting home before he wretched in the street for everyone to see.

Once in the shelter of the constabulary he whipped up a quick dinner and shoveled it down greedily, hoping to quell the effects of the hard liquor.

When his stomach had settled somewhat he made for the livery stable. He determined that he would not be caught off-guard again.

CHAPTER FOUR

For the next week Alexander lived in a state of high alert. He kept his horse tied up, fully tacked, behind the constabulary. His holster with pistol was always strapped round his waist. The rifle was kept within arm's reach, even when he went to the outhouse. Aside from regular visits to the dry goods store and saloon for supplies and information he spent most of his time at the constabulary.

Late in the week a stagecoach dropped off a sack of mail. Alexander took charge of it and spent most of the day delivering letters and parcels. At the close of the day there were two pieces of mail remaining. One was addressed to the sheriff in formal block type. Tearing open the envelope, Alexander perused the bold typeset missive. At the top of the page was the official seal of the territory. As he read on, his heart began to sink. His worst fears had been confirmed.

Just a day after he had departed, the letter informed him, the Hayes-Lawson gang had attacked the Glenn Rock prison. The gang had assembled a force sufficient to easily overpower the lawmen, no matter what precautions they had taken against a jailbreak. The sheriff and most of his men were killed, their bodies dragged behind horses and eventually left for the desert scavengers, far from town. Only one man had survived, if it could be called that; he had been unconscious since the incident and was not expected to recover. Reading the horrifying details set forth in a clipped, unemotional tone made Alexander feel quite ill. His imagination began to run rampant and he found himself sticking on the fact that he was now alone, the only lawful influence for miles and miles. There was no one to back him up, no one to give him advice or counsel.

Wishing to put the sickening images from his mind, he turned his attention to the final letter. This one, though just as travel-worn as the previous, was in stark contrast to the message he had just set aside. The handwriting on the envelope was neat, homey, and decidedly feminine. The name to which the letter was addressed rather surprised Alexander. He leaned forward in his chair, peering out the back window. In the dusk a square of light glowed atop the hillside overlooking the town. He glanced at the paper he held in his hand. All week he had seen nothing of Byrne Jameson. He had been meaning to have a conversation with the mysterious man but until now he had had no reason to intrude on the rancher's homestead.

Laying the letters aside, Alexander picked up his lantern. He checked the bolts on the front and back doors, looked out the window to ensure his horse was settled for the night. The gelding stood placidly, one hind hoof cocked, chewing on his evening ration of hay. He was saddled, as he always was nowadays. Without and within, everything seemed to be in place.

Regardless, Alexander could not shake the paranoid feeling that had been plaguing him. He pulled his pistol from its holster and opened the chamber. He counted each bullet, making sure the gun was fully loaded. It had become a habit even though he knew full well that the pistol had not been fired since last he checked it.

Exhaling, Alexander took his light and weapons upstairs. He changed into his nightclothes and buried himself beneath the covers. He kept one hand on his pistol. His eyes watched the dancing flame under the glass of the lantern for a long while. Nothing in particular was pestering his mind and keeping him awake; he felt emotionally numb. Eventually his eyelids fell shut. The lantern flame continued to dance in his mind's eye.

That evening he slept fitfully, plagued by nightmares. Ghoulish horses screaming in ear-shattering tones and ridden by skeletal men cloaked in hellfire charged into the town, ransacking and destroying everything in their path. Alexander stood helplessly in the middle of the street, watching it all unfold but unable to stop it. A group of riders charged past him, dragging the bodies of the Glenn Rock lawmen.

When he looked up another rider with a huge welt on his ghastly features was bearing down on him, swinging a rope overhead. The lasso sang through the air, seizing Alexander round the neck. The sheriff tried to pull the noose off before the rope tightened but he found his hands tied by a snake, squeezing his wrists and hissing threateningly. As the rider galloped past, the rope drew taut. Alexander was yanked off his feet, falling backward in slow motion. The hoofbeats of the hellish horse were deafeningly loud.

Before hitting the ground, he woke with a start.

Alexander sat up, panting and soaked in a sweat of fear. A blanket had twisted round him as he tossed in his sleep. He ripped it from his neck and threw it aside. For awhile all he could hear was his own heartbeat and gasping breaths, echoing loudly in the small space.

Downstairs he heard a small sound. It could just be the house settling, he told himself, or a mouse in search of crumbs. His heart was still pounding though it had been almost a quarter hour since he had woken. Alexander ran his fingers over the stock of the rifle, assuring himself that it was still there.

He knew he would not get back to sleep. His mind was too disturbed. Fortunately for him the day was already beginning, dawn was lightening the eastern skyline. He changed quickly, shaved by the light of a candle, and had the breakfast fire going before the sun rose in earnest.

As he walked back toward the constabulary his gelding moved to block his path. Alexander looked at the horse, puzzled. The gelding had been tied up... His eyes followed the path of the leather reins where they dropped from the bit straight to the ground and dragged in the dust. "How did you get untied Duke?"

Alexander looked around, suddenly fearful that he was not alone. Who would untie his horse? Why?

Confused, the sheriff grabbed the reins, leading the horse with him as he looked around. He looked at the dust, hoping for some clues in the form of tracks, but all he could see was a jumbled mishmash of his boot prints and Duke's hoof marks.

Grabbing the reins with his other hand as well, he made a face. The leather was wet, slimy. He looked at his palm, grimacing. Duke nickered. "You did this?" Alexander asked, holding the wet leather at the animal's eye level. Duke threw his head up and down as if nodding in answer.

"A true horse whisperer, are you sheriff?"

Alexander jumped into the air at the sound of the voice. It was still quite early and he had not expected anyone to be out and about, much less paying social calls. As he realized that he knew that voice, he was thankful that he had already shaved and changed into fresh clothes. He could only wish that he had tucked his shirt in. Turning slowly, he put on a brave smile. "Good morning Miss Fletcher. Is there something I can help you with?" He subtly began stuffing his loose shirt into his waistband.

"My apologies for calling on you so early. I was on my way to the well and father had set me an errand for today; I heard you were outside so I thought I'd check that off my list."

"Oh," Alexander had no idea what she was talking about.

Sensing his confusion, Miss Fletcher elaborated. "Father wanted to give you time to settle in. If it is convenient for you, our family would like to invite you to supper tonight."

"I would be honored," Alexander replied formally.

"You know which house is ours, correct?"

"Yes."

"Very good. We'll see you about five o'clock then."

"Perfect. See you then." As she turned to go he felt as if he should say something more; conversing with her brought him a great deal of contentment, even if he felt like a foolish schoolboy. "Please send my thanks to your father."

"I will," she threw over her shoulder as she sauntered off.

Alexander turned back to his horse. "Now, Duke, what am I to do with you?" he mused. He was having a hard time believing that the gelding had released himself. Still, there seemed to be no better explanation. He really did not want to expend extra effort building a corral if it had been a fluke or an isolated incident. Following the only logical train of thought, he tied the horse up again and stood back to watch.

Duke turned his head to stare at his master but otherwise did not act.

Sighing in exasperation, Alexander turned away. He resumed the task of preparing breakfast, always watching the horse out of the corner of his eye.

Eventually, as he was eating the canned biscuit and scrambled eggs he had prepared, Duke raised his muzzle to the hitching post. His lip wriggled over the reins experimentally and then he bared his teeth, pulling on the leather ties.

"Aha!" Alexander exclaimed, hastily setting his plate aside and running up to the horse, waving his arms. Duke stopped what he was doing, threw up his head and snorted. The whites of his eyes showed and he spun around as much as he was able, trying to face the onslaught. The horse jumped into a half rear as Alexander grabbed hold of the reins. "Easy, easy." His hand stroking the ebony fur on the gelding's neck soon quieted the animal. "Apparently we need to come up with a new arrangement," Alexander mused.

The majority of his day was spent in constructing a small corral behind the constabulary. The task was interrupted just after lunchtime. Duke bored of watching and listening to the cutting and hammering; he untied himself while Alexander was not looking and went for a stroll. By the time Alexander missed the gelding he had to search half the town before finding the horse behind the livery stable, dragging down bales of hay and scattering them about with violent shakes of his head.

"Duke!" the sheriff shouted, at his wit's end. He intervened, trying to restack the bales despite Duke's efforts to the contrary.

It was while he was thus engaged that the stable manager stepped out for a smoke. Alexander froze, arms high above his head holding a bale precariously on the edge of the stack. "I am so sorry," he began awkwardly. He shoved the bale on top of the stack. "Of course I will pay for this." Duke stood off to the side, hovering over a bale, chewing on a mouthful of hay contentedly.

~~~~~~~~~~

Shortly after returning to Flintridge, his hometown for all intensive purposes, Byrne departed. He was riding out into the untamed countryside with only his mount and pack mule for company. The rancher, experienced in solo ventures into the wilderness, had loaded the mule with only the most essential supplies. He had to travel light, had to travel fast. After all, he was hunting for wild horses-- mustangs.

As he jogged his horse away from the frontier town, the sturdily-built chestnut pricked his ears and extended his stride. The mule plodded on, indifferent as always. Byrne knew why the stallion always grew spirited as they headed out to wild country and he could hardly blame him for the energetic pace he set. When the chestnut mustang would have broke into a joyous run for the canyon, Byrne reined him in. He patted the horse's shoulder, quieting him. Deep down a part of him hated what he did, rounding up wild things and denying them freedom, but it was the best way he knew to make a living.

As they left the town behind they passed over the swath of grass growing near the small river. The mule dropped his head and tried to snag a bite of the lush grass but the mustang dragged him along at an eager jog. Braying in annoyance, the tan mule picked up his pace.

Further from the river the grass dried up, giving way to hard, dusty earth. Sagebrush covered the ground, interspersed with the occasional cactus plant. Having been born and bred in the rangelands, the chestnut mustang knew exactly which path to choose through the sagebrush.

Just after noon they came upon a small stream. Byrne knew the country for miles around Flintridge well. He had come to the creek not only to refresh himself and his mounts but also to search for evidence of a wild herd. Dismounting, he knelt down and examined the ground carefully. Much of the creek bed was chips of shale, heavily overlapping sand. There were a few depressions but Byrne judged them to be too small to have been made by horses. Most likely a coyote or some Pronghorns had stopped for a drink.

Hopping back into the saddle, Byrne led his horses into the stream and let them drink their fill. He let them rest for a quarter-hour in the shade of a rock outcropping while he had a light midday meal. The whole time he lunched he was scanning the horizon, looking for a herd of horses.

At the completion of his meal he had no fresh clues. Pausing only to refill his water skin, he directed his sturdy mounts onward. They followed the stream for over a mile, hoping to come upon fresh tracks.

There had still been no sign of horses when they were forced to leave the creek bed due to rough, seemingly impassable country ahead. Byrne knew his mustang-bred could find a path through it but he saw no reason to risk laming his best horse over a shortcut.

The trio climbed out of the gently sloping canyon and set off at an easy jog across the flatlands. They encountered a mixed herd of antelope and mule deer. The wild beasts regarded them warily, and when they continued to approach the herd panicked and bounded away. The rancher paid them little attention.

Search though he did, Byrne had not seen fresh signs of horses by the end of the day. All he had come across were the bleached bones of a deer. He brought his animals to a stop in the shelter of some cliffs. He unloaded the mule, untacked his horse, and hobbled the pair for the night. Before preparing his own meal he made certain that the horses had been watered and fed some of the meager forage he had packed out for them. For himself he had brought equally poor fare: smoked meats and canned vegetables. He built a small fire from tinder collected nearby for warmth. Unrolling the wool blanket he had brought, he settled down, using the saddle for a pillow. A coyote called in the distance, a lonely, eerie call that echoed off the cliffs. Unperturbed, Byrne drifted off to sleep.

At dawn the next morning, after brewing and drinking his habitual cup of coffee, Byrne set off. He had another place he wanted to inspect that day, somewhere that he surmised the wild horses might be. Turning his mounts, he headed up into higher country.

As the slope grew steeper Byrne leaned forward in the saddle, resituating his weight to make the going easier for his horse. The chestnut was in fine form and took to the challenge eagerly. His powerful haunches propelled them up the rock-strewn slope. The mule did his best to keep up but was always on a tight lead.

Eventually they came to a level spot. Byrne dismounted and went behind a rock to relieve himself. Just as he was finishing, the chestnut stallion let out a whinny. Byrne jumped and buttoned his fly frantically, looking about for whatever had drawn his horse's attention. He caught a glimpse of a horse's tail, thrown up and lit aflame by the sun, vanishing around a shelf of rock further up the mountain.

Sprinting toward his horse, Byrne threw himself into the saddle. With fast, expert hands he untied the mule's tether from the saddle horn. He knew the beast of burden would stay put until he returned; he had trained it well. Releasing his lasso from its tie, Byrne took a tight hold of the reins. The stallion jumped in place, raring to fly off after the wild horse. Already he had broken into an excited sweat.

When he was ready, Byrne let his mount go. The tamed mustang shot up the hillside, quarters straining, breath blowing in frenzied excitement. He followed the strange horse's scent. It led them a merry chase across the rocky hillside. Always the wild horse was just out of sight; at most Byrne would see the swish of a silvery tail, the flicker of a golden ear, the flash of a solid hoof. Byrne kept his rope at the ready, waiting for his chance.

They rounded a corner and Byrne had to yank sharply back on the reins. The narrow path, no more than a goat trail, stopped abruptly. Had his horse not been able to stop they would have careened over a sheer hundred-foot drop.

The rancher looked around, puzzled. To where did the mustang escape? The chestnut danced in place, still eager to run. The scent of the other horse must be heavy in the air, driving the once-wild animal crazy.

Byrne eased his horse nearer to the edge, side-passing so he could look right down into the gorge. Immediately below, perhaps four feet down, was a ridge of rock. It was narrow, flat, and the only means of escape he could fathom. Behind and around him, sheer rock walls rose and fell away from the track. He studied the outcropping for some time, judging how best to reach it, wondering if it was worth the risk. Leaning as far out as he dared, he tried to see where the shelf led but it wrapped around behind a boulder, putting the exit out of sight.

Finally he determined to give up the chase. The jump down onto the rock shelf was a tricky one and he was not certain his mustang could do it, especially with a rider. They turned back to collect the mule and continue searching.

True to Byrne's expectations the mule was standing exactly where he had been left. He barely twitched an ear as the horse and rider approached. The chestnut stallion, however, stopped abruptly and threw his head up, scenting the air. He let out a low nicker, his nostrils quivering.

"Risky business leaving your pack mule, with all his trappings, alone in the middle of the mountains. Wouldn't you say, Byrne?"

Byrne's jaw tensed at the sound of the voice. He nudged his steed along. Only when he was right next to the mule did he see the speaker.

The other man sat on a lithe stock-type horse with a roan coat. He wore a dark gray duster and a well-styled hat pulled low over his eyes. In his hand he held a match and was in the process of lighting a cigar. Shaking the flame out, he tossed the matchstick away. He crossed his arms and leaned jauntily forward, resting his elbows on the saddle horn. "You know there are bandits out here, right?" He looked up and met Byrne's guarded stare with hard gray-green eyes.

"What do you want Derek?"

The outlaw took a drag on his cigar and blew the smoke out casually, a calculated, timed act meant to infuriate. "Can we not have a civilized conversation?"

"With you I doubt it would be remotely civilized." Byrne nudged his horse onward, grabbing the mule's tether and pulling it along with him. He made a point of taking an oblique angle away from the well-dressed rogue, never showing his back. Always he kept one eye on the trail ahead and watched for any movement from behind out of the corner of his eye.

When he caught a glimpse of motion from the dangerous man Byrne turned full in his saddle, dropping the reins on the stallion's neck. The horse continued to pick his way down the slope. Byrne glared at the outlaw, daring him to finish the act he had begun. Derek offered a sly grin as he leveled the Colt at the retreating rancher. "Come on Byrne, I just want to talk," he remarked around the stem of his cigar.

Rolling his eyes, Byrne reluctantly turned his mount back round and stopped him. The mule brayed in protest as he was yanked around. The rancher was watching tensely, fingering the pistol he kept with him for just such an emergency. In the back of his mind he knew he could not draw faster than the gunslinger could fire, but he would go down with a fight if it came to that. He sincerely hoped it would not. "Alright," he said in a hard, unwelcoming voice. "Start talking."

The outlaw gave his horse's flanks a small kick, urging him down the incline. He circled Byrne and his stock, eyes carefully calculating and memorizing everything the rancher had with him.

"I'm getting tired of your antics Derek. Speak your mind or leave me be."

"So rude," Derek chided. He stopped his horse behind the mule, blocking the easiest route of escape. "But since you insist, I'll tell you straight that the boss is of the opinion that you broke our little pact."

"How's that?" Byrne's fingers tightened on the butt of his pistol. Every muscle in his body was tense, the hairs on the back of his neck standing on end. He watched the outlaw's every action closely.

Derek swung the barrel of his pistol in a slow circle. He knew his motions made the rancher nervous. He wanted to keep it that way. "Suffering from memory loss now, are you? You saw what happened in Glenn Rock."

"That was none of my affair. Cliff shouldn't have been a fool and gotten his horse lamed." He paused, considering another tack. "Why are you troubling with me at any rate? Shouldn't you be proving your loyalty to your master by trying to spring him?"

"Oh, that's been done already."

"At the cost of how many lives?"

"All of them." The outlaw's voice was completely devoid of remorse. He grinned tauntingly.

"Do you stick at nothing? I would have thought, given your upbringing, that you would have some sense of compassion for others. You did once, at any rate."

Derek shrugged, unaffected. "An eye for an eye. It is the law of the West." His accent, though fading from years spent out West, was far more well-bred than Byrne's.

"Don't even think of threatening me, no matter how oblique the reference."

"Oh, using our big words now, are we?" Derek chuckled and tipped his pistol in salute at the rancher. "You are sharp Byrne."

"Have to be, out here."

"Aye. It is a shame you chose the wrong side; you would have made a wicked outlaw."

"I'll pretend that was a compliment."

"It was. Do you doubt my sincerity?"

"Look, if you're plannin' on killin' me I don't see what you're waiting for," Byrne spat out in exasperation. The tension was getting to him.

Derek glanced at him in mild shock. He looked at the rancher closely. "Now why would I waste my time in good conversation if I was just going to kill you?"

Byrne could not help but test the waters at the risk of escalating the situation. "Maybe because the only way you can have conversation of any sort is if you are using the threat of death to get the other person talking."

The outlaw seemed amused by the brash words. He smiled tightly, looking at the rancher from under the brim of his hat. "There may be some truth in that," he mockingly conceded, the grin broadening. "Since you like straight talk, I will put it simply: get rid of this new sheriff if you want our arrangement to stay intact."

"I wasn't expecting they would replace the last one so soon."

"Neither did we. Washington must be stepping up their game. Regardless, it is in our best interest that no lawman stays in Flintridge for very long. Indirectly, it serves your purposes as well."

"Meaning: if you have a lawless town in which to hide out you won't burn it to the ground?"

"If you do not want to mince words, then yes, that is the long and short of it. Your stead, in particular, we can guarantee will not be harassed."

Byrne bit his lip. He knew he was making a deal with the devil. He also knew that he had no way of making the new sheriff leave. Would he be able to hold up his end of the bargain? He would have to find a way. His livelihood, and that of his wife back east, depended on it.

"So what will you do if you cannot terrorize Flintridge?"

Derek smiled knowingly, showing a gold tooth. "That is for us to know, rancher. Do not concern yourself with superfluous facts." He steered his horse up alongside the rancher's mount. The chestnut pinned his ears at the unfamiliar horse and gave it a swift bite on the neck. Derek nonchalantly smacked the stallion's nose. "We'll be seeing you around." He clapped Byrne on the shoulder and started to ride off. "The sheriff must be gone within the month," he added, throwing the comment casually over his shoulder. "Do not forget."

"I won't," Byrne growled. "Believe me, I won't." He added in the smallest of whispers as a promise to himself.

CHAPTER FIVE

After corralling his errant equine, Alexander deemed that he had just enough time to ride out to Byrne Jameson's place to deliver the letter. Swinging into the saddle, he sent Duke off at a fast trot, wanting to make haste. It was nigh on half past three and he was not certain how long his conversation with the rancher might take. He felt they had a lot of ground to cover.

Once outside the city limits he let Duke stretch out in a canter. The Morgan's gait was smooth and the scenery flew past in a blur. Before long Alexander found himself standing on the porch of Byrne's home. He knocked on the door and waited.

He waited for a good half hour, repeating the rap on the door every now and again. Alexander slunk down the length of the porch, peering into each window. Within, all was quiet. No fire burned in the stove, no candle with flickering light sat on the table.

Eventually he conceded that the homeowner was not there. Turning his back in disappointment, he went to where Duke stood tied. He would have to try again another time. The sheriff kept the letter, planning to use it as his excuse to visit the next day.

As he rode back to town he pondered over the curious absence of the rancher. He had expected Byrne would still be about his homestead, tidying things up and fixing anything that may have suffered the effects of weather and time while he was gone. Then again, he conceded, he had no idea for how long Byrne had been traveling away from Flintridge. It could be as brief a span as a month. It could have been years. Regardless, he was surprised that the rancher would make himself scarce so soon after returning to town. He found it rather suspicious.

Duke pulled up so suddenly that Alexander, still lost in his musings, was almost pitched forward out of the saddle. Reseating himself, he peered over the horse's shoulder to see what had startled him. Lying curled in the dirt before them sat a snake, quite sizeable. It stared at them with beady, unfeeling black eyes. The forked tongue flicked out rapidly. Duke shuffled in place, nervous. The rattle on the serpent's tail crackled and it twisted round itself, readying to strike.

Alexander backed his horse rapidly, putting a safe distance between them and the rattler. As the horse skittered away the snake made a half-hearted strike, hissing and baring its fangs. The sheriff whipped out his pistol and took aim.

The shot rang out, echoing eerily across the plain and reverberating in the foothills. In town it must have sounded deafening. Feeling a trifle foolish, as if all eyes were on him, Alexander holstered his gun and directed his horse around the dead snake. They trotted into town.

People peered out of their windows, watching curiously for what would unfold next. They had heard the shot, no doubt of that, and were wondering what had caused it to be fired. Many feared the Hayes-Lawson gang had returned. Upon seeing Alexander, riding calmly into town, most left their posts, assuming whatever it was had been dealt with and would not trouble them. For the few that remained Alexander called out the truth, assuring them he had only had to dispatch a rattlesnake. Everyone went back to their tasks as if the shot had not sounded.

Alexander consulted his pocket watch. It was twenty minutes to five. Suddenly feeling the need to hasten, he swung Duke round to the back of the constabulary. He pushed the horse into the corral, closed the fence behind him and left him standing tacked while Alexander ran into the constabulary. He sprinted up the stairs and sought his mirror. Rapidly he made a change of clothing, slicking his ginger hair down and assuring himself that he was properly shaven and tidy. He had a passionate dislike of the freckles that marked his face but knew there was nothing he could do to lessen their appearance. Making one final adjustment to his costume, he took a deep breath and forced himself to descend with dignity. It would not do for the sheriff to be tearing through his house like a disorganized maniac.

So eager was he to arrive promptly that he decided to ride the length of town to the Fletchers' home. He tied Duke to the hitching post and walked up to the door. Before he could knock it was opened and he was ushered in by Miss Fletcher.

Alexander was led into the dining room. The space would have been generously sized except for the overly large table, big enough to seat eight, that took up most of the space. It could not be missed that, contrary to the modest look of the house from without, it was furnished very well, almost to excess. The table was heavy oak, with detailed scrollwork carved into the edge. The chairs, sturdy, adorned pieces, matched the style of the table perfectly. They were upholstered in a lovely burgundy fabric. A fancy grandfather clock stood in one corner, ticking away the seconds.

Roy Fletcher walked over to him and shook his hand heartily. "So glad you could make it Sheriff. I thought it was about time you got a proper welcome to our little town."

"I very much appreciate it," Alexander replied with a smile. A dinner party was, thus far, the only situation he had encountered in the West in which he did not feel completely out of place. Here his eastern charm and manners served him well. He greeted the women of the household gracefully and waited until they had assumed their seats before he took his place on the right hand of the host. Their small party took up only half of the table's length.

Alexander found himself looking across the table at Miss Fletcher. He tried not to stare, but with no conversation currently going to distract his attention he found it increasingly difficult to take his eyes off her. Light from the iron chandelier hanging over the table cast a comforting glow over the assembly. It caught in her golden-brown hair, giving it warm highlights and soft lowlights. Her hazel eyes met his and he hastily looked away, embarrassed to have been caught staring.

The awkward tension was relieved as Roy spoke up. "So, Alexander, tell us something about yourself." He slapped his huge work-roughened hands on the table to draw the sheriff's attention away from his daughter.

"Really Roy, that's not the best opener I've ever heard," his wife chided, bringing in bowls of soup and setting them before the diners. She was a kindly looking woman with just the faintest streaks of gray in her blonde hair. The family resemblance between mother and daughter was strong, but it seemed to the observant newcomer that the younger woman had the bolder character.

Alexander chuckled good-naturedly. "No, no, it is quite in his right to ask. After all, I am a newcomer to town. Thank you Mrs. Fletcher," he added as Roy's wife, Jane, set a glass down before him. He picked it up and took a sip, savoring the rich flavor of the red wine. After having nothing but water and whisky for so long it was a welcome indulgence. "I am afraid my story is not at all entertaining and quickly told."

"You're from out east, are you not?"

"New York, born and raised. My father wanted me to go into law but midway through my studies I found that I leaned toward the enforcement side of law instead of the dusty courts, mingling with old men." He chuckled, somewhat self-consciously. One thing he hated was telling his back-story; there really was very little of interest in it, he thought. "So I joined the police academy, learned what I could. Father was not overjoyed to learn that I was following in his footsteps instead of aiming for a better position, but in time he has come to accept it."

"And your family?"

"My father and mother remain in New York. My younger sister was just married last year."

"And yourself? Unmarried I take it, from the lack of a ring on your finger."

"Really Roy, don't be so personal. Can't you see you're making him blush?" The fact that Mrs. Fletcher had brought up his encrimsoned complexion made Alexander all the more uncomfortable. He felt supremely self-conscious.

"For how long did you serve in New York before coming out here?"

Alexander had been hoping that question would not be asked. He could think of no way of avoiding answering, and he did not want to build his reputation on lies. The truth was all that was left to him. "Four months and seventeen days."

All activity stopped for a brief moment as the admission sunk in. The Fletchers covered well, resuming their meal and drink and concealing their looks of shock.

Miss Fletcher was the one who came to his rescue. "I would not let that confession leave this room," she remarked with a kindly smile. "Some in this town might think you unequal to the task of facing the Hayes-Lawson gang. I am sure my father has every confidence in your abilities," she added, trying to soften the observation.

"Indeed." Roy's tone left some argument whether he agreed with the sentiment expressed by his daughter. "Well, Washington would not have sent you out if you were not up to snuff."

"That is true. I feel confident that, with a little help from loyal men like yourself, the Hayes-Lawson gang and all other outlaws will pay for their crimes and cease to exist."

"Let us hope so," Roy chimed in, raising his glass. The others at the table echoed the toast and they all drank. Alexander could not be sure, but he thought Miss Fletcher had glanced in his direction. "At any rate," Roy began again, drawing the sheriff's attention, "we are all grateful for a newcomer like yourself. Livens up life in this isolated place a bit. Also brings an eligible bachelor into the mix."

"Oh father," Miss Fletcher complained almost before the words had left his mouth. Apparently the subject of marriage was often discussed between father and daughter, and the topic worn out in the opinion of the latter. Alexander wondered absently why she was not already wed. She had to be at least twenty years of age.

His musings were cut short as conversation resumed. The topics covered in the latter half of the evening were less personal, more general: weather, politics, local news and the like. A second bottle of wine was opened and consumed.

After the most general topics had been exhausted, Alexander ventured to ask about Byrne Jameson.

"Why wasn't he at home?" Roy echoed in response to his question. "That young rascal is hardly ever at home. When he's not eating or sleeping, he's out tending someone's cattle herd or his horses."

"Horses? I was under the impression that he had only the one," Alexander remarked.

"For now that's all he's got, aside from the mule," Roy agreed with a nod of his head. "That's his business, though, going out into the wild country and picking a few mustangs he thinks will do well at auction. So far he's made a good run of it, I think, always picks the prettiest colors and the horses with the best conformation." He took a drink of wine. "Heck, I'd almost buy one of his, except that they're all mad, even once tamed."

"How do you mean?"

"They're mustangs! Born and bred. Once wild, they stay wild even if they may act like normal beasts."

"I see."

Alexander leaned back in his chair, imitating his host's casual posture. The ladies had retired to the kitchen and were cleaning up after the meal. The men smoked languidly.

Footsteps on the veranda interrupted their quiet conversation. The men looked toward the door in some surprise. The hour was late, past the time for new visitors. The footsteps were heavy and slow-moving. They sounded unusual.

"If I didn't know better I'd say a horse was about to knock on our door," Roy remarked with a laugh. Blowing out a cloud of smoke, he put out his cigarette and stood. "Wonder who it could be at this hour?"

Fletcher's words had awakened in Alexander a vague foreboding. He could not quite put his finger on it due to the effects of the wine he had consumed.

When the host opened the door and let out a shout of surprise Alexander shot out of his chair. He knew then why Roy's comment had unsettled him. Standing and rushing toward the front door, Alexander pulled up short. He leaned on the doorframe for a moment, simply unable to process what he was seeing.

The dark shape of a horse loomed, almost completely filling the doorway. Alexander heard a familiar equine voice and just barely suppressed the urge to beat his head against the wall. "Duke," he grumbled under his breath.

"Father, what do you want me to do with--" Miss Fletcher cut herself off and could not quite contain her mirth upon seeing the horse. Alexander wanted to crawl into a hole. Duke shoved his head in through the open door.

"I'll just take him home," Alexander murmured, keeping his head down so his face, red with embarrassment, would be harder to see. "Thank you for your hospitality." He had almost forgotten his manners in his rush to escape the humiliating situation as quickly as possible.

"Any time," Roy replied with a smile in his voice. Clearly he was far more entertained by Duke's antics than was the horse's owner. "And be sure to bring your trick horse again!"

Alexander forced himself to laugh, tried to sound somewhat genuine. It was through no fault of the Fletchers that Duke had gotten loose. It was not their fault if they found his incompetence amusing. At least they were sweet, not malicious, when laughing at his expense. He knew he would never forget the sound of Miss Fletcher's laugh.

~~~~~~~~~~

Byrne directed his mustang steed back down into the valley. The encounter with the outlaw had unsettled him and his mind roiled with one thought after another. He let his horse have its head as his mind wandered.

At least the gang had sent Derek to deliver the message. That so-called 'gentleman amongst thieves' was the only man in the gang that had a modicum of sense. He was the only one Byrne could tolerate speaking to, but even then it was a near thing.

Anger flared within him. They were being completely unreasonable, expecting him to manipulate the politics of Flintridge and even influence the decisions of those beyond the small frontier town. At the end of the day he was only a rancher, a stockman, and his opinion meant nothing to those in higher stations.

Years ago, when others had moved further west and established a small town near his homestead, everything had been ideal. Everyone worked toward mutual survival in the harsh landscape. There was no reason why one man should be wealthier than another, no reason why anyone should possess more than their neighbor.

As the population grew things began to change. Suddenly the town was large enough to merit a name and the services of businesses. First the general store moved in, supplying the townsfolk with simple conveniences that seemed like the most posh accoutrements after the hardships they had hitherto endured. The equilibrium which had existed was altered. The clever man that had established the dry goods store soon began to grow far wealthier than the common man in Flintridge.

Others followed his example and moved their businesses further west. The saloon opened, providing a new distraction to those who had grown bored of scratching out a living. A carpenter offered his services and a stable opened to accommodate the increasing number of horses being brought to Flintridge.

Byrne had watched the changes take place. He had seen raw, untouched wilderness molded into a budding town. No longer could he look out his window and see empty plains. The challenge of surviving by his wits and resourcefulness had been diluted.

The rancher, the unofficial founder of Flintridge, was not the only one to take notice of the changes sweeping across the West. Men who wanted adventure, a life outside the law, moved out into the wilderness as well. They began leeching off the growing wealth of newborn towns. Payrolls were robbed, mail stolen, livestock slaughtered, influential persons kidnapped and then ransomed. Utter chaos broke out.

Washington took note of this unacceptable state of affairs in its new territories. Lawmen were sent in force to counteract the activities of the outlaws. This initial strike against crime seemed to work, tempering the frequency and ferocity of raids.

But then the outlaws seemed to grow more intelligent, calculating their attacks. Robberies were still common, the ransacking of towns still occurring. Some outlaws had been captured and hanged but their general population remained unaffected. They took to hiding in the hills, striking when it suited them and vanishing again. Some would argue this new breed of rogue was uncatchable.

When Flintridge was hit not once but thrice within a very short time, Byrne took it upon himself to protect his interests. Thus far the growing town had not been assigned a legal protector. Byrne had lost almost a dozen cattle and one horse in the last raid. He knew things had to change.

That night, as the residents of Flintridge tried desperately to put out the fire set by the brigands in the livery stable, Byrne jumped on his trusty mustang and followed the outlaws into the foothills.

It had not taken them long to realize they were being followed. Byrne confronted them, firing rounds meant to frighten rather than kill. They had encircled him, their firearms at the ready. Their leader, Cliff Hayes, also known as 'the Gravedigger' had asked Byrne to give him one very good reason why they should spare his life. That was when the rancher had made a game changing bargain with the outlaws.

How he regretted that night now!

Shaking off his unsettling encounter with Derek Ward, Byrne took up the reins and directed his horse through the foothills, towing the placid mule along with him. He had set out on this excursion with a specific purpose: to capture wild horses. He would be darned if he returned empty-handed. Since he had sold off his meager cattle herd the mustangs were his only source of income. The fleeting image of the copper palomino he had pursued earlier in the day filled his mind, tempting him on.

The sun was already past its zenith as he turned his stallion back up the mountainous incline. Ordinarily he would have kept to the flats so he could spend the night in the shelter of the cliffs on level ground. He had not paused for a midday meal; he had only stopped long enough to give the horse and mule a quick drink and handful of oats before pushing onward.

They climbed steadily for hours. Even the hardy mustang, though perfectly willing, was growing sweaty, his breath blowing and muscles tiring. The mule was far less willing. The saddle horse was pulled up mid-jump as the mule decided he had had enough travel for one day. Planting all four strong hooves, the mule balked. Byrne turned in his saddle to coax the beast on. The mule stared back with calm eyes. It simply refused to move.

Reluctantly, Byrne consented to stop for the night. There was little else he could do. He hobbled the equines and made camp. The rocky landscape offered no tinder for a fire. Byrne consumed his meager meal and spent a long, cold night beneath the stars, surrounded by the bare bones of the earth.

In the morning he set off again. The course he set zigzagged back and forth up the face of a steep hill. He hoped that this would bring him round to the back of the cliff over which he had lost the mysterious palomino the day before. Whether or not he would be able to find a way down, he had no way of knowing until he got there.

The sun was almost at its noontime high when Byrne finally started downward again, making his way carefully down the steeper backside of the hill. Skirting around cliffs, they made better time on the decline. The mule voiced several protests of the rough terrain but had little choice other than to follow.

Eventually they happened upon a narrow track, little more than a goat trail. Byrne's heartbeat quickened. A worn path, however minute, proved that animals used the track frequently. He turned the chestnut onto it and the mule grumpily came along behind.

The trail swerved through the mountains, threading around boulders and hovering over hair-raising drops. Byrne had every faith in his mount's sure-footedness and knew that the mule could hold his own in the dangerous terrain.

Finally the rocky walls that had pressed in along the trail opened up. Sunlight flooded over the sandstone cliff to which Byrne's animals clung precariously. The rancher took in the new scenery with interest. His breath caught as his eyes followed the streamlet below. The line of water, sparkling in the sunlight, flowed through a small valley. Green grass carpeted the rocky ground. Grazing peacefully, unaware of the human looking down on them, was a herd of horses. Byrne counted eight in all. Standing at the head of the canyon, perched on a small knoll, was the palomino stallion, gleaming in the sunlight.

Seeing the horse in his entirety for the first time, the rancher took a moment to fully appreciate the beauty of the wild animal. The stallion was well-built, strong and not overly tall, with heavy fetlocks that could withstand speed over the roughest terrain. His golden palomino coat was dark, almost the same shade of copper as a new penny. In contrast, his mane was a light cream color and seemed to reflect the brilliance of the sun's rays. A large star on his forehead complemented the snip of white on his nose. Byrne ran an expert eye over the rest of the herd. Four mares grazed, two with foals at foot, and a two year old stood a little away from them. All in all, they were a decent looking bunch.

Pulling back on the reins, Byrne stopped his mount to give himself time to evaluate the situation. He searched for any outlet, any means of escape open to the herd. To his dismay the only exit to the valley was directly behind the stallion's knoll. The rancher determined that there were two options left him. He could try to find a way to drop into the narrow chute behind the stallion's lookout post, thereby cutting off the herd's escape. However, he knew that when he moved in to round up the horses they would all funnel out through the outlet anyway. Therefore, he took the only option left to him.

Releasing the mule's tether, Byrne spurred his mustang down the slope. The chestnut stallion leapt eagerly off the trail. His neat, hard hooves dug into the scree of loose rock chips and sand on the hillside. Byrne leaned back in the saddle, positioning his weight so the stallion could move freely. He gave the horse its head, knowing he would find the best way down, if there was one to be found. The ring of hoof on stone echoed in the small canyon.

The wild horses threw their heads up and turned to look at the small rockslide, at the center of which was a horse and rider. Cries of fear and warning rose from the mares and foals. The stallion screamed his defiance. For a while all they did was stare at the whirlwind of rocks charging down into their hidden valley.

Then the stallion called them and they took off, tails flagging high. Byrne did not rush his mount. He hoped that the foals would slow the band up and give him time to catch up to the herd. It would be stupid to force the chestnut to descend any faster and risk injury to his best horse or to himself.

Finally the tame mustang's hooves struck the canyon floor. Here Byrne spurred him on, pointing him toward the narrow opening through which the herd had vanished. He could still hear their thundering hoofbeats on the hard ground ahead. As the chestnut stretched out across the thin grass, the mule brayed high above.

Byrne's horse picked up speed as he galloped through the winding fissure in the rocky terrain. His ears were forward, his breath quick, every muscle tense with excitement. Sweat was darkening his coat beneath the headstall and saddle but Byrne was not fooled, he knew his horse was still fresh enough.

The rancher let out a sharp whistle and leaned low on his horse's neck. "Let's get 'em," he murmured, getting caught up in the thrill of the chase.

They turned around a rocky outcropping and ahead spotted the fleeing herd. Grinning with determination, Byrne reached down and untied the coil of his stock whip. As the chestnut emerged into a more open space, the rancher cracked the whip. His horse had been trained not to be bothered by the whiplash but the unexpected, unfamiliar sound drove the wild horses crazy with fear.

Ahead, many of them whinnied uneasily as they ran. As Byrne had expected, the foals were straining to keep up with their mothers and already showed signs of tiring. He had been lucky that there were some late summer babies with the band. The adults would never leave them behind and the little foals lacked the stamina to gallop straight-out for long.

Eventually the rocky corridor opened up. The herd spread out, running more abreast than single-file. Byrne continued cracking the whip, urging them on. He wanted to push the foals close to exhaustion; if the little ones pulled up their mothers surely would too, and the stallion would not leave his mares unattended.

The chestnut's breath was beginning to rasp. He had been working hard for days with limited food and water. The oats he had been fed, however, gave him energy enough to race with the fresh wild horses.

One of the foals caught a hoof on a stone and fell, rolling in the dust as a tangle of gangly legs. It gave a squeal of terror as the tame mustang barreled down on it. As Byrne had hoped, the foal's mother turned back to protect her offspring. She stood watch over the exhausted little horse. As Byrne approached she rolled the whites of her eyes and tossed her head, even jumping into half-rears. She would not leave the foal. The little horse lay at its mother's feet, blowing hard. Sweat stood out behind its ears, on its chest and haunches. The mare was breathing heavily and sweating as well. It had been a long, hard chase.

The palomino stallion whirled back, screaming in rage. He charged at the chestnut and its rider, teeth bared and ears pinned to his neck. Byrne's horse pinned his ears in response and trotted in place, held back by the rancher's restraining hand on the reins. As the palomino approached the chestnut struck out with a foreleg, squealing in response to the unwelcome advance.

The wild stallion pulled up at the last second, rearing so that his hooves flailed in Byrne's face. Gritting his teeth, Byrne cracked the whip several times, trying to drive the wild mustang a safe distance away.

Byrne let the whip fly once more, catching the furious wild horse on the shoulder. Though the tail of the whip landed with very little force, the wild mustang jumped back, snorting in fear. The mighty palomino tossed his head, flinging his creamy mane into the sunlight, and stared at the rancher. He pawed the ground defiantly. Despite his bold actions he knew the foals could not go on, knew the mares would not leave them, knew his family was caught.

Noble creature that he was, he refused to leave them.

~~~~~~~~~~

Days later Byrne drove his hard-fought-for band of horses before him to his dwelling just outside of Flintridge. He had had to rope the stallion, who was proving to be quite a handful. The mule looked askance at the palomino that fought madly at the end of his line, bucking and rearing, bolting in every direction, screaming and striking out at the very air. The poor mule received more than one blow and did its best to keep its distance from the mad horse. The desperate stallion's energy was infectious; over the days of travel, the tamed chestnut stallion was growing increasingly unmanageable. Byrne was eager to get the herd home.

CHAPTER SIX

Alexander had been keeping an eye on the mountainous horizon, awaiting the rancher's return. He felt it must be soon. How many supplies could one pack out on a single mule?

He spotted the cloud of dust raised by the band of mustangs and their new owner. For awhile he contented himself with watching them approach, losing his sense of urgency as he watched the mustangs canter so fluidly over the plain. They were a rangy bunch of horses, nothing like what he was used to seeing in the city. Their coats were mostly dull earthen tones, lacking the shine of a groomed domestic horse.

Looking the herd over, Alexander wondered how the rancher would care for so many animals. He often found it hard taking care of his single tame horse. When his eyes lighted on the stubborn beast being dragged along at the end of the procession, he started in his chair. The mighty horse fighting and straining against its lead was a flashy copper palomino with a nearly white mane and tail. Though its coat was roughed and dirt-stained, it was a truly magnificent horse.

When the horses neared Byrne's homestead, the sheriff shook himself out of his thoughts. Donning his coat, he left his home, locking the door behind him. He tucked the letter addressed to Byrne in his saddlebag, mounted, and set off.

By the time Alexander arrived the bearded rancher had opened the gate to the corral and was herding the wild horses into the pen. Alexander held Duke back and the pair watched the proceedings with interest. Duke let out a loud whinny, excited by his first encounter with wild horses. He stood with ears pricked and neck arched, every muscle poised to spring, dancing in place. The sheriff was too consumed with watching the expert handling of the mustangs to bother trying to discipline his excited Morgan horse.

Lastly Byrne dragged the fierce, fine-looking palomino into the yard. The wild stallion fought every step of the way, even going so far as to rush at Byrne's mount, trying to knock the chestnut off his feet. Byrne kept his calm, laying the whip across the stallion's neck. As the tail wrapped round his neck the wild horse screamed and jumped away, unintentionally backing into the corral.

Byrne drew his knife and cut the rope, leaving a noose and tail hanging on the palomino's neck; he had not been able to put slack in the rope due to the stallion's desperate pulling. The palomino stud tore across the pen, plowing through his mares and foals. His headlong charge was stopped by the sturdy fence rails. Screaming in anger, frustration, and terror, the stallion cantered along the rails, bucking and snorting, searching for a means of escape. Byrne watched him for a long while, sitting perfectly still in the saddle.

His attention was distracted as the sheriff rode over and hailed him with a wave of greeting. Byrne shot a glance his way and then immediately looked back at the band of mustangs. The stallion was chewing on one of the rails, trying to pull it down. The nails held the board firmly in place.

The conversation Byrne had had with the outlaw whizzed through his mind, unsettling him. How was he to keep his word with the rogues, short of cold blooded murder? Violence had never been to his taste.

Belatedly he realized that the sheriff was speaking to him, probably trying to make polite conversation. The rancher forced himself to pay attention.

Alexander dug in his saddlebag and produced a travel-stained envelope. Byrne took one look at the missive, saw the elegant hand in which it was addressed, and snatched it from the other's hand. Alexander recovered from his initial surprise at the rancher's unexpected, somewhat rude, action. "Good news I hope?" he ventured, forcing what he hoped was a friendly smile.

Byrne had eagerly torn the envelope open and was intently reading over the contents. A rare, warm smile turned up one side of his mouth and his brown eyes softened as they perused the neat cursive writing. Partway through he chuckled to himself at something on the page, seeming to have forgotten the other man was there, watching him. The last paragraph sobered him quite quickly. The words, though they should have been good news to a lonely man on the frontier, made him unreasonably nervous.

"Not so good news?" Alexander prodded, reading the other man's rapid change of expression.

Byrne snapped out of his musings and looked at the sheriff as if just realizing he was still there. His face was once again impassive, the expression impossible to read. "Never you mind," he growled. Taking one last glance at the captured herd, which was calming down, the rancher turned his horse. "Thank you for the mail delivery." He urged his horse into a trot. As far as he was concerned the conversation was at an end.

Alexander followed on Duke. "That is a fine batch of horses you brought in," he remarked, repeating his original attempt at generalized conversation. He turned his head to unnecessarily indicate the band in the corral. Alexander felt certain the rancher had not heard him the first time. "What do you intend to do with them?"

"What else do you do with wild horses?" Byrne responded, asking a rhetorical question which he then proceeded to answer himself. "Break 'em and sell 'em." The rancher did not stop to talk. He rubbed his bearded chin contemplatively as his thoughts turned back to the letter.

Alexander could not stop staring at the stallion, the only one in the band that was still prowling around the pen restlessly. "That palomino is a nice looker. If you can tame him I would be willing to purchase him from you. Just name your price."

The rancher shot him a bemused, dismissive look. "You'd buy a horse based on looks alone?" He shook his head, laughing a bit. "Stupid city slicker," he added under his breath.

"What was that?"

"He's not for sale. I'll be keeping that one."

As if on queue the palomino stallion screamed at a mare that was in his way and gave her a swift nip. She bolted out of his path.

Alexander was disappointed that his offer of friendship had been rejected without a thought; he had been hoping that the rancher would warm up to him if he was perceived as a potential client. He would have to go back to the drawing board, try a new tack. In the time he spent trying to come up with a new conversation starter, the rancher was moving further away. Throwing planning to the wind, Alexander trotted after him. "Byrne - Mr. Jameson - wait!"

The rancher turned to face the approaching rider with ill-concealed annoyance. He had already dismounted and his horse was drinking deeply from the water trough. "Look, sheriff, I've only just got back. I'm tired and dusty and have quite a lot to do before the light goes."

Alexander sunk in the saddle, foiled. He could not ignore such a blatant dismissal. "I completely understand. Perhaps I will just call on you another time?"

"If you must." Byrne turned his back, not even bothering to say goodbye or see the visitor off his property.

Dejected and burning with curiosity, the sheriff turned Duke back toward town. He was kicking himself for having been so ineffective at getting information from the strange rancher. He was displeased to realize that he was leaving with more questions than he had when he came.

~~~~~~~~~~

For the next couple of weeks things were quiet and peaceful in Flintridge.

Alexander finished the alterations he had planned for the constabulary, even completing the privacy wall between the common room and bedroom upstairs. The carpenter finished his orders and delivered them. The living quarters above the cells were beginning to look like a proper bachelor's apartment.

Manual tasks aside, Alexander found that he had very little to do. In his official capacity all he had done was to chastise the local drunk for making a ruckus in the saloon one night. Some petty thefts had been reported but so far no one had come forth with any suspects. Determining that the only way to identify the thief was to catch him in the act, the sheriff kept his eyes open and patrolled the town often.

While not occupied with professional issues, Alexander did his best to get to know the people in the small town. For the most part they were reserved with the newcomer, but in time they opened up to him. All but one.

Try though he did to establish friendly contact with the rancher, Alexander made very little progress on that front. Byrne kept mostly to himself, staying primarily on his homestead and rarely coming into town. Each day he spent a good portion of the daylight hours working with the wild horses he had captured. The mares and foals got the bulk of his attention. He had built a separate pen in which to house the stallion, who seemed every day to grow madder and ferociously wild. It did not go unnoticed by the sheriff, watching from his window, that the palomino's pen was built much sturdier and had much higher rails than the one in which the mares and foals were kept. Apparently Byrne was taking no chances of the magnificent stallion escaping.

~~~~~~~~~~

Every morning Byrne prepared his morning cup of coffee and stood at his front window, gazing across the dawn-stained expanse of country at the close-built structures of Flintridge. Each morning his conversation with Derek Ward, the right-hand-man of the Hayes-Lawson gang, filtered through his mind and a chill of trepidation ran through his bones. That morning was no exception.

He had still not determined how he would go about convincing the sheriff to leave. He found it a bit curious that he had not heard from the gang; the defined grace period was almost up. Perhaps they had given up on corrupting Flintridge, found another hideout, or been captured or killed? He could only hope.

Also on his mind that morning was the pending arrival of the stagecoach. His heart leapt in his chest and he felt alive with excited energy. Glancing at the letter he held clutched in his hand, he perused the elegant script again and smiled longingly. Today the coach was due to arrive and on it would surely be his wife. Glancing at the sun, he hoped desperately that the conveyance would arrive early.

As he set about tidying the interior of his shack his mind wandered over the fond memories he held of his wife, Ivey Jameson. He had not seen her since moving westward seven years ago. At that time the West was not a suitable environment for a young southern belle such as his Ivey. The rancher admitted to himself that he questioned whether things had truly improved. Byrne had left her in the south with her family out of necessity. He could not get a job to stick in the city since he lacked the personality to be contented with sitting at a desk day in and day out.

To fill in the long years spent apart they had exchanged letters regularly. Byrne kept her up to date with his livestock business and the rapid growth of Flintridge. She, in turn, relayed information about her family, local society, friends and distant relatives.

Recently she had been growing ever more insistent about joining him on the frontier. He had tried to discourage her, to convince her that life was rough out West. In his mind she was so delicate, something that needed to be protected. Yet her headstrong personality had finally won out and she had purchased her own ticket West. Byrne had no other choice but to await her arrival and try to set up a comfortable home for her.

Finishing his coffee and indoor chores, Byrne stepped down into the yard. His trusty chestnut had been drinking at the water trough. The horse threw his head up and whinnied eagerly, knowing breakfast was soon to come. Water dripped from his muzzle, reflecting the pinkish early morning light.

Byrne tossed some hay into the pen of wild horses, causing them to scatter nervously. He fed the wild stallion and his very presence set the mustang to cavorting around his corral, screaming, bucking and kicking at the air. Having grown accustomed to the untamed beast's behaviors, Byrne pointedly ignored them. Once his task was complete, he turned his back on the temperamental mustang and approached his tamed equines.

"Mornin' Cowboy," he greeted, rubbing the wide blaze on the chestnut mustang's forehead. The stallion nickered, pricking his ears and bobbing his head. He knew what the rancher held behind his back. The mule did too; he came right up to the fence and, twisting his head sideways, nibbled at Byrne's plaid shirt. Chuckling at their antics, the rancher produced the bucket laden with oats and poured it into the feed trough.

He crossed back to the feed shed and returned with an armload of hay, which he pitched over the fence for his favorite horse and helpful pack mule. For a quarter of an hour he stood at the rail, arms crossed atop the wood plank, watching both the domestic horses and captive wild herd. The only one he refused to look at was the wild stallion.

When he felt that the horses had had a reasonable amount of food with which to start the day, he pushed himself off the rail. He had to find an outlet for his excited energy, had to find a way to pass the time. Filled with off-season spring madness, he sought out a knotted rope headstall, whip and lasso, and approached the palomino stallion's corral.

His approach was heralded by a loud scream of rage and the thundering of hooves on the churned terrain. The stallion charged madly around the corral, trampling even his hay. Byrne spoke softly to the insane animal, standing at the gate and looking in, watching the maddened stallion's movements closely.

Captivity had not dampened the beast's spirit; in fact it had strengthened it, whetting it to a razor-point. There was an indomitable fire in his eyes, a pride in his every movement. His coat, though roughened from a prolonged lack of communal grooming, was still striking, his knotted mane and tail still catching the sun's light.

"Easy," Byrne cooed as he unlatched the gate. The headstall hung casually over his shoulder, the whip and lasso in his hands. He kept his eyes trained on the unpredictable, violent horse as he slipped into the pen and closed the gate behind him.

For a while the stallion stood frozen in place, staring at the bearded human in consternation. His ears flicked to and fro, every muscle of his body tense. His hooves seemed barely to rest on the ground, so tightly wound was he; it seemed he would bolt at any second. Byrne waited him out.

When the mustang did move, it was in an explosion of action.

Throwing his head high with a wild cry, the stallion reared, dropped to all fours, ran in a tight circle, kicked vaguely in the rancher's direction, turned back toward the fence, found himself still trapped, and tore off down the fence line. Byrne jumped, hauling himself up onto the highest rail to avoid being trampled. The stallion's hoof, raised in a mad buck, just clipped the rancher's thigh.

Byrne's temper flared. He dropped to the ground, pulling out the whip and lasso. He cracked the whip and the horse propped, spinning back in the other direction. In the other pen the mares and foals shuffled about nervously.

As the palomino feinted a charge at the rancher, the man cracked the whip and the horse spun round on his haunches. They continued this for some time. Each time the stallion got it into his head to try and run his captor over, the whip intervened, snapping in the air over the wild horse's head. Rarely did it need to touch the golden hide.

Eventually the stallion gave up his aggressive charges. He still ran, turning in tight circles, snorting and wild-eyed. Even when he turned his back on the human he kept his magnificent golden head cranked round so he could see what the rancher was up to.

As the stallion wore himself down with spinning uselessly in the far end of the pen, Byrne determined that he could proceed. He stepped away from the rail, his best escape route should the mustang attack, and sauntered unobtrusively toward the blowing horse. Again he felt the mustang's eyes on him, felt the sheer electric current emanating from the muscles tensed beneath the coppery hide. Reaching the center of the pen, Byrne lifted his head and locked eyes with the wild horse.

The stallion flinched once, twice. He threw his head, undecided what to make of the human's strange, rather calming actions. With a loud snort he broke into a nervous trot. He went round and round the pen, stretching his strong legs out and lifting his knees high in an animated gait. Always he kept his head turned toward the rancher, wary of any movement from that source.

Byrne let the horse work himself. All he did was continue turning, keeping his shoulder in line with the palomino's hindquarters, pushing the horse on exclusively with body language. His stare, which he kept locked with the horse's white-rimmed gaze, was almost predatory and kept the horse moving at a swift trot. Sheer nerves made the horse's skin quiver.

The tension built to a bursting-point and the palomino threw his head, breaking into a fierce, slanted canter. His hooves drummed on the hard-packed dirt, threw up clouds of dust and the random small stone. Byrne lowered his gaze, taking the invisible pressure off the mustang. Though it took awhile for the stallion to realize this, he did eventually slow up, dropping back into an animated trot. Without the rancher's constant gaze he got distracted and stopped, putting his head way up, trying to sling it over the top rail. He called to his mares. A few of them answered.

The whip cracked in the air, drawing the stallion's focus back in an instant. Byrne was staring him down again and the horse started off, cantering heavily. The stare dropped away and, after a delay, the horse slowed to a trot.

For over an hour they played the strange game. The stallion picked up on the concept quite quickly. Eventually he just kept up a trot no matter what the rancher did.

Byrne wanted the horse to stop. He was growing hungry and thirsty, but he could not get to the gate and through it before the horse made another circuit of the small ring. Using the only method he knew, he dropped his steady gaze and turned his back on the stallion.

The hoofbeats slid to an abrupt stop. He felt the horse looking at him, could imagine him wiggling his ears in confusion.

Keeping his back turned to the horse, letting the whip drag in the dust, Byrne side-stepped toward the gate. First one step, then another, and another...and he stopped at a sound he had not expected to hear. Hoofbeats, slow, hesitant, sounded behind him. He held his breath. Presently he felt hot breath touching the back of his neck, felt a huge, solid presence behind him. The horse's shadow engulfed his.

Byrne knew he should simply get out of the pen. He had achieved his goal; the horse had come to him for company. That was enough for the day. But for the rancher, always wanting to push the boundaries, he had one more test in mind. Slowly, so as not to alarm the skittish horse, he stretched his left hand backward. He heard a snort, heard the hooves shuffle in the dust a bit. The stallion did not run away.

The rancher kept moving his hand slowly back, not daring to risk even a glance to see where, exactly, the horse stood. His fingers moved through the air, seeking hide.

Swift and silent, the horse snaked his head down and bit at the fingers. Byrne yanked his hand back, tearing the skin of his knuckle open on the strong teeth. He swung round, ready to hit the temperamental beast, but the stallion was gone, already running to the safety of the far end of the pen. He whinnied, the sound almost mocking.

Byrne glared at the horse. He knew nothing would be gained by violence. Glancing at his torn knuckle, he could see that the wound was not serious, only annoying. Sucking at the blood welling on his fingers, he spat it out at the horse. The stallion snorted and went cavorting about, always keeping to his end of the pen.

The rancher slipped through the gate, latched it, and went to clean up at the well he had dug on his property. The sun was rising ever higher in the sky, warming the dusty ground, the rocks, and everything in sight. Though he was still fuming over the mustang's trick, Byrne could not help but feel light-hearted. The stagecoach would arrive soon, very soon. He had a few more preparations to do before then.

~~~~~~~~~~

Byrne set off for town astride his chestnut mustang. The mule he led in tow; it was hitched up to a small cart which bumped over the uneven terrain, slowing them up.

That day he had spent a great deal of time and care over his appearance. He wore his second-best clothes (after all, he reasoned, he would be moving packing cases which could prove to be a dusty task) and had even gone so far as to shave off his growth of beard. Looking in the mirror, he had hardly recognized himself. His brown eyes had seemed brighter and the lower part of his face looked pale since it had been covered by the dark beard. He comforted himself with the knowledge that it would soon tan even with the rest of his skin since he spent so much time out of doors.

The only fault to be found on him was the bit of cloth he had used to bandage the scrape on his hand. The injury had been stubborn; it would simply not stop bleeding as every movement of his fingers caused it to reopen.

In addition to his own appearance, he had spent hours cleaning the leather tack for both animals, even washing out the bed of the small wagon. Both Cowboy and Frank the mule had been given a thorough brushing so their coats were relatively dust-free and shining.

Once he entered the city limits he began to feel self-conscious. Everyone who was about did double-takes, stopping their tasks to stare at him. The consternation on their faces led him to believe that they were struggling to place who he was. They had all seen him in good clothes before, but only on Sundays, which that day was not. None had ever seen him clean-shaven. The women looked on him with more favorable eyes. Cleaned up he looked far more respectable, even handsome, as compared to his usual rough bushman appearance.

Reaching the far end of town, where the stagecoach road passed, he stopped his horses and dismounted. There he stood for an indeterminate amount of time, distinctly aware of the stares leveled at him. Uncomfortable as he was, he kept his eyes trained on the eastern horizon, squinting against the glare of the sun. The celestial orb was high, the temperature rising. Mirages danced along the line where sky met land. Often Byrne mistook one of these apparitions for an approaching coach, but each time he was disappointed.

When the stagecoach finally came rattling into view Byrne could scarcely contain his excitement. He left the mule and cart on the edge of town and urged Cowboy on to meet with the conveyance. As he neared he waved to the drivers. To his shock he realized that one had a pistol trained on him.

"Whoa, easy there!" Byrne swung Cowboy wide, hoping to throw off the other's aim in case he had an itchy trigger finger. He pulled his hat off and waved it in a gesture of goodwill. Reluctantly the driver lowered his weapon, though his eyes remained suspicious.

Byrne directed his mount to run round the back of the stagecoach and come up alongside the far side of it. Cowboy settled into an easy lope as he kept pace with the conveyance.

The rancher switched the reins to his right hand, leaned to the left out of the saddle and knocked on the door of the carriage. Presently the curtain was drawn and the face he had been waiting so long to see appeared. It took a moment for realization to dawn on her but then she smiled, showing her perfect teeth, her blue eyes sparkling. She waved at him and mouthed something; he could not hear her over the rattling of the trap.

The rancher settled his hat more firmly on his head and let Cowboy stretch out his gait. He kept his eyes on the woman in the stagecoach and she continued to stare at him. Only when the coach pulled up and Cowboy continued to run on with his rider did Byrne return to reality. Reining his horse in, he turned him back around and waited for the carriage to come to a complete stop and have the blocks put in to lock the wheels.

The coach horses lowered their heads, breathing heavily after the long run. One of the drivers held the heads of the leading pair while the other opened the door for the passengers.

Byrne was off his horse and running to the carriage door when his wife stepped out, assisted by the hand of the driver. The rancher caught her up, lifting her off the ground and spinning round, holding her above him. She laughed, a sound that almost brought tears to Byrne's eyes; it had been so long since he had seen her last.

When he let her down he pulled her close, kissing her passionately, heedless of the prying eyes of the townsfolk. To him they no longer mattered, for his whole world was in his arms.

Their moment was interrupted as the driver insisted they collect their belongings. Byrne released his wife and went to retrieve her luggage. When he returned one of the other passengers was speaking with his wife, handing something off to her. The way they were standing, the stranger's body blocked his view. His wife thanked the stranger and the latter moved off.

Byrne almost dropped the packing cases in his shock. "Ivey, my dear, what is that?" he asked in a strained voice.

She turned toward him, cradling the puppy as she might hold a child. "I would think you could recognize a dog when you see one, Byrne," she teased in her southern drawl.

Despite himself, Byrne smiled. He was not angry, not really, only surprised. It would, however, be one more mouth to feed...

He looked at the puppy and it looked back at him, eyes alight, floppy ears pricked and tail wagging. It was not of any breed he could identify but he had to admit it did have a peculiar kind of cuteness about it. The unusual intensity of its - *her*, he corrected himself, looking the critter over - bicolor stare gave him a notion of its lineage. Perhaps she would prove a useful herding dog someday.

He reached out to pet the young dog's head. She tipped her head back and stuck her tongue out, ready to lick his hand even before he had touched her. Ivey saw the bandage over his knuckles and took in a sharp breath. "What happened there?"

"Oh, nothing, nothing really," Byrne answered, stroking the puppy's silky-soft ear. She licked him giddily, wriggling in Ivey's grasp. The woman adjusted her hold on the puppy, tucking her under one arm. The small dog continued wiggling and pawing at the air with her forepaws as if she could swim to Byrne. "Shall we move along?" he asked, giving her a bright smile. He slipped an arm around her waist and landed a quick peck on her cheek.

Once Byrne had retrieved the packing cases he led her to where the mule and Cowboy stood, waiting patiently, as they had been trained to do. "These are yours?" Ivey asked of her husband, having never seen the animals before. Her husband nodded in the affirmative. "What happened to Star?"

"My dear, Star was old. She didn't last long out here. I'm sorry." He spoke of the horse he had traveled west with, a bland brown animal with lackluster conformation. She had been graying at the muzzle when he started out but she had got him all the way to where Flintridge would eventually grow. After such an effort she had gone downhill rather quickly, but not before he had been able to capture Cowboy when the colt was a two-year-old. The mule he had bought at auction. "So what have you named our new dog?" he asked, wanting to change the subject to happier things, to the future.

"Sadie," she replied without a second's hesitation.

"Sadie," Byrne repeated, testing the name. It was not what he would have chosen, but he knew better than to say as much. "And where did you pick her up?"

"Oh, I don't know," Ivey replied whimsically. She caught her husband's disbelieving look and rolled her eyes with a smile. "Alright, alright, I'll tell you. It's a funny story, actually. I was just about to board the train back in Tennessee when this adorable creature came gamboling across the platform with one of the rail men in hot pursuit. I could not stand to see the poor thing running loose where she might get run over by a train so I took a chance and called her. It took a few tries but before I knew it she ran over to me and I was able to catch her. When the worker came to claim her I asked if he knew to whom she belonged. He told me she was a stray, at which point I corrected him and told him that she was mine."

"Oh you did, did you?" Byrne asked slowly, running his hand down his face. He had to cover his mouth to stifle a defeated laugh.

Ivey gave him a playful pat on the arm. "You like her and you know it," she remarked with a smile against which Byrne could not argue. "What is this handsome boy's name?" Ivey asked, running her free hand down the blaze on the stallion's face. The puppy stretched out her nose and sniffed the horse curiously. Cowboy sniffed her back and then snorted as if he did not like what he smelled. Sadie whimpered and pressed tight to Ivey's body.

"This here's Cowboy," Byrne answered, patting the chestnut's neck proudly. "Took him off the range and broke him myself. He's solid as a rock and gentle as this here pup. The mule's Frank. Now, I'll play the gentleman and let you ride back if you like," he added, jerking a thumb at Cowboy.

Ivey glanced down at her armload of wriggling fur. "What about Sadie?"

"Put her down. She needs to learn to stay close and run alongside the horses anyway." He saw his wife's look of uncertainty. "Don't worry, Cowboy is used to the town dogs. He won't step on her."

Ivey still seemed reluctant. She continued to hold the dog close. Byrne extended his hands toward her, making an imploring face, trying to convince her. Slowly she gave in and handed the squirming puppy over. Byrne set the dog gently on the ground, ruffled her ears. He cupped his hands, standing at Cowboy's side. "Come on Ivey," he invited.

As Ivey paced over she kept an uncertain smile on her husband. He had a mischievous streak, but she did not think he would let her get on a horse that was not completely docile. She had been raised in the south and was used to the airy gait of southern-bred stock. A mustang off the range might prove an unwelcome challenge to her horsemanship skills.

Ivey set her dainty little foot in Byrne's calloused hands and let him assist her into the saddle. Cowboy stood still as a statue, unperturbed when she settled her volume of skirts and wriggled to correct her seat. She adjusted as best as she could, but in the end the simple fact was that the rancher's western-style saddle was not suited for sidesaddle riding. However it would be far too unladylike for Ivey to ride like a man - that is, astride the saddle - so she made do and hoped that Byrne's homestead was not too far away.

Byrne handed her the reins. Hesitantly, Ivey took them. Riding a horse with which she was entirely unfamiliar seemed a daunting task but she had faith in her husband. Giving Cowboy a final pat on the shoulder, Byrne set off, leading the mule with its loaded cart.

"Byrne, Sadie!"

The rancher stopped his beast of burden and looked around. The dog, at first, was nowhere to be seen. He put his fingers to his mouth and whistled. He did so again. Finally the puppy appeared round the corner of the saloon. She was sniffing about, not seeming to care much about where her human parents were. Byrne whistled again. The puppy looked up, ears pricked. The rancher called her by name and waved, trying to communicate with gestures that he wanted her to come to him. It took some coaxing before she broke into a gleeful bounding run toward them. The mule flicked his ears, unamused, as the energetic puppy wove round his legs. Byrne stooped in order to pet and praise the pup before setting off on their path back home.

Several times on their journey through town, as Byrne was pointing out the local landmarks to his wife who set an embarrassingly slow pace on the chestnut mustang, they had to stop in order to call the puppy back from some adventure or other. The rancher had to give her credit; she was a sharp little creature, for each time he stopped to call her she returned just a little more quickly. He hoped that by the time she was old enough to start working horses she would learn to stick around.

As they neared Byrne's rather plain homestead, his wife let out a breath. "What is it?" Byrne asked, suddenly fearing that she would think the place too coarse or uninhabitable.

"It's so beautiful. Is it really yours?" Her eyes were traveling over the small, unimpressive house with its porch and chimney, back to the scenic mountains that rose blue-purple behind the structure, dwarfing it into irrelevance. To the left, the vast plains and desert stretched out away from the river.

"Ours," Byrne corrected in a quiet voice.

Finally her eyes lit upon the stock corral containing the collection of mares and foals. "More horses? What are we to do with them?"

"It's what I do for work now. Cowboy and I round them up off the range, break them, and take them to auction once a year. Actually I'm just back from one such sale. Took two mares and a stud colt back east."

"How much did you get for them?"

"Not exactly what they're worth," he admitted. When the auctioneer had mentioned that they were mustangs off the range many interested parties had dropped out before the first bid was cast. It was a shame, and set a bitter tone with Byrne. After all the effort he had put into training the horses they were better behaved than many of the blue-blooded lots he had seen at the sale. "It's a living, though."

"May I see them?"

"Of course." Leaving the mule standing, Byrne walked alongside Cowboy over to the mares' pen. The wild horses eyed him warily. Their initial terror at the sight of man had abated as they identified him as the source of food and water. Still, none of them ventured anywhere near the rail. Cowboy whinnied as he approached, creating a stir amongst the herd. His call was echoed by a far meaner scream off to the right. Byrne shot a glare in the direction from which the sound had come.

"What was that?" Ivey asked, suddenly afraid. Everything out West was wild, untamed and unfamiliar. She had heard so many horror stories, many of which encouraged her to stay in the safety of the familiar east. Her desire to be with her husband had overwhelmed her fears and prompted her to make the journey.

Sadie stood by Cowboy's hooves, looking in at the wild horses in interest, her tail wagging furiously.

"That was the new stud I brought in with these mares." Byrne's voice was hard, dismissive.

Ivey looked at him in surprise. "Is there something wrong with that horse?"

"I guess you could say that." Byrne raised his hand, showing off the crude bandage which was already out of place and stained with dirt. "He's the one that did this."

His wife looked at him with pity in her azure eyes. "Does it hurt much?"

Byrne gave the typical masculine answer. "No." In this case it also happened to be the truth.

"Can I see him?" she asked, looking down at Byrne from the saddle.

"Of course. Just don't get within striking distance of the fence. He's a bit unpredictable." Byrne led the way over to the corral holding the fierce wild stallion. He stopped Cowboy a safe distance from the pen.

Ivey leaned forward, peering eagerly through the rails. The sight of the striking copper palomino with silvery mane and tail took her breath away. "He's absolutely gorgeous!" she exclaimed, clapping her hands together in delight. "Oh Byrne, do keep him!"

"Don't worry dear, I plan to," he answered. There was a hard quality to his voice. A rivalry had sprung up between the rancher and the palomino mustang, a contest of wills that had to be seen through to the end result.

"What will you call him?"

"The Hellion."

"Byrne! No!" She was trying not to laugh, recognizing that his ill humor toward the horse stemmed from the little wound. Ivey sincerely doubted that even her husband, who was admittedly rough around the edges, could stay angry at such a beautiful creature. "That name is far too unkind for such a beau."

The rancher grinned, his mood lightening. "Are you French today, my dear?"

Ivey shrugged, toying with Cowboy's mane. "Depends on the weather," she joked, smiling winningly. The blonde curls of her hair cascaded over her shoulders and framed her face to dazzling effect. "But that'd be a good name for him."

"What's that? Weather?"

"No," she said through a laugh. "Beau."

Byrne looked at her, eyebrow raised. "Really?"

"Really."

The rancher sighed, shaking his head. "Well, Beau it is then. I know better than to try and name him anything else - you'd only ever use the name you picked."

Ivey laughed, acknowledging the truth of his statement. She leaned down to give him a kiss.

CHAPTER SEVEN

Over the next several weeks Ivey settled in to the cabin-like abode that Byrne had built so long ago. She rolled up her sleeves and gave the place a thorough cleaning. She shopped in town, buying inexpensive items that would help to bring a woman's touch to the rough structure. The southern girl took on the typical role of a housewife, cooking and sewing, cleaning and doing any small project for which her skills were suited.

Byrne spent the majority of his time outside, working with the horses. As time went by he grew absorbed in domestic life and his work. The conversation he had had with the outlaw became a distant memory, one that hardly troubled him. The deadline had expired and he had heard nothing from the Hayes-Lawson gang. Last he had heard they were raiding more prosperous towns further east. The situation to the east had been getting so out of hand that Alexander had been called from his post in Flintridge to provide assistance. With the sheriff gone there was no one to interrupt the happy existence the rancher led with his wife and their animals on their rustic homestead.

While the lawman was absent the saloon owner acted on an idea that had been at the back of his mind for no little amount of time. He penned a missive and sent it with the stagecoach driver on the very day the sheriff left town. Then he began renovations on the saloon, building rooms at the back of the establishment. Those in town watched what he did, expected that they knew what it meant, but said nothing.

The town's population was growing rapidly; news had spread that the railroad was coming. Workers were being shipped by the dozen to the western frontier in preparation for the frantic construction that would lay steel rails across the wild landscape. Due to its location, Flintridge was a prime place for stationing railway men.

It was approaching the end of the calendar year. October had already begun. The days, while still long and sunny, had lost much of the inherent warmth of summer. A chill was in the air, the promise of colder weather to come. The horses sensed it and they grew frisky, bucking and cavorting about in wild play, confined by the limits of their pens. Even Cowboy was not immune, as his owner discovered one day.

Byrne took the chestnut stallion out for a ride to let him burn off some energy. They trotted away from the homestead and the rancher was annoyed to learn that he had to hold his normally controllable horse back more than usual. He patted the mustang's shoulder, trying to calm him down.

At the touch Cowboy snapped, breaking into a headlong gallop across the plains. He was a complete runaway, ignoring Byrne's hands pulling back on the reins. The rancher continued to apply pressure on the mustang's mouth, pulling the horse's chin in toward his chest. Still Cowboy charged on, never slackening his pace. He bucked, protesting the rancher's attempts to curb his speed.

Eventually Byrne conceded that this was not his battle to win. Cowboy was growing ever more rebellious, kicking up his heels and swerving madly around cactuses and sage patches. The rider put slack in the reins and settled in the saddle to go along for the ride.

They crossed a vast expanse of ground. The wind was brisk as it brushed against Byrne's face and ungloved hands. He let the mustang run until the horse burned his excess energy. When Cowboy had finished his run and slowed to a trot Byrne turned him around. They had travelled far out into wild country.

Byrne returned home, feeling a bit foolish, but Ivey only laughed and told him that he and Cowboy had been very picturesque as they went charging across the prairie by the river.

The first frost came a week later. Winter was coming in early, threatening everything with an icy cold grip. The horses nosed through their hay, huddling together in the early morning chill. All at once they threw their heads up, all gazes trained on the far horizon. They stood tense, ready to flee at any second. Byrne followed the direction of their stares but could see nothing. Ignoring their curious behavior, Byrne pulled his coat collar up and continued with his chores.

As he passed the wild stallion's corral he paused, looking in at the palomino. The stallion had begun to grow his winter fur, darkening his coat to a deeper copper. His mane and tail were growing lighter in color, becoming almost white. Like the mares, Beau was staring at the horizon, seemingly oblivious of the rancher's intent stare. Belatedly Byrne wondered if they were missing their home country or were feeling the need to move to their winter grazing grounds. It was clear that all the wild horses were restless.

Byrne entered the house and sought out Ivey. She was in the kitchen preparing breakfast for them. He walked up behind her, putting his arms around her waist and rested his chin on her shoulder. He had neglected to shave for two days and his short whiskers tickled her cheek. She put aside the utensil she had been holding and turned into his embrace. "Good morning to you, too," she whispered with a smile. "What's on your mind?"

"I intend to break that hellion mustang before winter."

Ivey gave him a measured look. "Do you think that's wise? He's no tamer now than he was when I arrived in town."

Byrne shrugged. "It's got to happen sometime. I'm not feeding him and keeping him alive for nothing."

Ivey gave him a quick kiss on the lips. He caught her when she would have drawn away and pulled her in for a longer embrace. "Just be careful," she whispered against his lips. He held her for a long while.

Suddenly she pushed away from him. "Do you want your breakfast to burn? Go set the table, please."

Chuckling under his breath, Byrne did as he was told.

~~~~~~~~~~

Byrne shrugged out of his coat and laid it over one of the fence rails. The palomino stallion threw his head up, a few strands of hay hanging from his mouth. His ears were pricked forward, nostrils dilated, eyes keen. A chilly wind blew, streaming the great stallion's mane and tail out. "Today's the day," Byrne told the horse. He unlatched the gate and stepped into the corral, whip and rope in hand.

The stallion had not quite given up his habit of charging anyone who dared to enter his pen. Byrne was ready for him and cracked the whip as the mad horse approached. The tail of the whip sailed through the air just inches from the horse's face. The stallion pulled up, throwing his head and snorting.

"No more games," Byrne told him sternly. "Either you learn to play by the rules or there'll be a bullet with your name on it." He stepped toward the horse and the stallion stood his ground. "I've no reason to keep a useless renegade horse."

The mustang tried to charge him again but was once more driven back by the crack of the whip. Byrne backed the beast until he was pressed up against the fence rails. Ears pinned, the wild horse reared, flailing his hooves threateningly at the rancher. Byrne traded tools, uncoiling his rope. Swinging the lasso overhead, he threw it and caught the mustang around the neck.

Screaming in rage, the stallion bolted. He shouldered past the rancher and thundered over the cold ground. Propping at the other end of the ring, he swung around and made the short gallop around the perimeter. The rope biting into his neck was driving him to unreasoning madness.

Byrne jerked hard on the rope, pulling the mustang momentarily off balance. The horse squealed, digging his toes in and leaping in a desperate attempt to escape. Byrne yanked again, whipping the animal mercilessly around once more.

Nostrils flaring red and eyes wild, the stallion charged once again. He moved so fast that the rancher was unable to crack the whip in time. He tried to sidestep the advance but the mustang veered and succeeded in ramming the man with his broad shoulder. Byrne was knocked to the ground. The stallion's flailing hooves sailed past, narrowly missing his head.

The rancher was scrambling to his feet just as the huge horse planted his feet and whirled around. Teeth bared and ears pinned back on his neck, the palomino charged again. This time Byrne hit him as he flew past. Enraged, the horse turned again and made one more pass.

Byrne was ready for him. Holding the whip pointed down, out at his side, he flicked it at the golden legs as they passed. The whip's tail wrapped around the stallion's off foreleg and in the next stride he came crashing to the ground. Screaming and pawing at the ground, the stallion tried to stand. The whip had gotten wrapped round his limbs and prevented him from gaining his feet. Furious, the stallion writhed ineffectively. The whip held him fast.

The rancher backed up to watch the drama unfold. He was not certain of the outcome, but he did gain a small amount of satisfaction as he watched the magnificent, ill-tempered horse struggle. The stallion lifted his head and slashed at the air with his teeth. Unable to get his feet beneath him, he was almost defenseless.

Minutes passed and still the stallion continued to struggle. Even if Byrne had wanted to release him he could not approach, knowing that the horse would injure him if given the chance. The rancher leaned against the fence rails, waiting.

As time continued to drag by and the wild horse continued fighting with no indication of giving up, Byrne decided to leave him for awhile. He slipped out of the pen, chased by the stallion's mad screams. Patting Cowboy as he passed by, he approached the pen holding the mares and foals.

There was one little mustang, not quite a yearling filly, that was more gentle than the rest of the wild horses. He approached her and slipped a rope halter over her ears. She followed him although she stopped often to stare at her sire, brought to heel but still fighting valiantly. "Come girl," Byrne coaxed, pulling gently on the lead. The filly shook her mane and followed.

As Byrne put the young horse through her paces he kept one eye on the palomino stallion. He had been fighting the restraint for almost an hour and was finally tiring. The magnificent horse subsided onto his side, breathing heavily. Occasionally he would burst into a flurry of activity, trying once again to break free. Each time he failed. Finally he tucked his legs and rolled onto his belly, letting his head droop. His muzzle brushed the ground. Byrne watched him carefully, contemplating his next move.

The rancher finished with the filly, gave her a good rubdown and put her back in the pen with her family. He approached the palomino's pen, expecting a violent reaction from the stallion. Much to his shock the horse merely raised his head and looked at the rancher. There was a distinct change in the animal: all the fury was gone from him, his mouth was not pinched with anger. Beau had given up his fight for freedom, deeming it an unachievable goal. He seemed resigned as the rancher approached, showing no signs of aggression.

Byrne circled around the horse. He felt safer approaching the unpredictable animal from the side back, knowing the beast could strike out with a leg at any time. The stallion turned his head, watching the rancher closely. The close presence of the human had awoken his old spirit somewhat; he was not yet willing to trust the man who had stolen his freedom.

Boldly, Byrne came up behind the wild horse. He reached out and for the very first time was able to run his hands over that gorgeous golden hide, unraveling the tangles in the stallion's mane. Beau threw his head, snorting uneasily. He tried again to stand but was still trapped. Exhaling heavily, the stallion tolerated the touch of man.

Seeing the miraculous effect that disabling the wild horse had had, Byrne determined to leave him thus for awhile longer. Once again he stepped out of the pen, leaving the stallion tied up and helpless.

Sadie was waiting for him outside the fence. She tipped her head and whined, examining the downed horse curiously.

"Come girl," Byrne said to her, patting his leg. She trotted after him toward the house.

Sipping on the hot coffee Ivey had prepared for him, Byrne looked out the front window. His eyes rested on the pen and the palomino stallion within, watching the horse for any sign of distress. The large animal simply continued to lay where he had fallen, dejected. When Byrne had finished his drink he went back outside and loosed the stallion.

Beau heaved himself gratefully to his feet when the restricting whip had been removed. He tolerated Byrne's touch as the rancher slipped the lasso from around the horse's neck. Though Beau threw his head and took a few steps, eventually Byrne was able to slip a rope halter onto the stallion's head. He patted the mustang on the neck. "I knew you'd come around."

~~~~~~~~~~

Alexander returned to Flintridge early in the winter. Autumn had come and gone and the cold had claimed the land. The wind blew frigid, buffeting against the drawn curtains of the stagecoach. The sheriff shuddered beneath his heavy wool coat and pulled the collar tight around his neck. No snow had yet fallen, but the land was frosted over, the air stunningly cold. He had lost track of the time, as so often happened to him whilst traveling. His familiar traveling companion, motion sickness, also plagued him.

His adventures back east had been numerous. He had been invited to Dunnstown to assist the local lawmen in combating the attentions of the Hayes-Lawsons and other outlaw gangs. The railway had suffered enormous financial losses to the greedy, predatory bandits. Wanting that trend to end, the railway offered a bounty on all rogues and brought in lawmen from everywhere.

While Alexander had not been able to collect any of the reward money, he had gained some valuable experience in the field. Most of the time they had ridden out blindly, hoping to happen upon the outlaws by chance. They shadowed the railways and coach lines, but rarely did they see any bandits. When they did spot suspicious characters, the bandits would take off running and lost the lawmen who were not familiar with the terrain in the foothills.

Only a couple of men who lived outside the law were captured in the push to hunt them down, and the prisoners were low-ranking members of any given gang. The leaders always managed to evade capture. Despite the best attempts of the lawmen the outlaw numbers were virtually unaffected. So, with disappointed expectations and empty pockets, many of the men who had been called in to assist in the effort were sent home.

The sheriff of Flintridge was returning to his post under such circumstances. He had been away for months and was not certain what he could expect upon his return. It was with apprehension that he stepped down out of the coach and looked upon the town that he considered to be his.

At first glance it seemed that very little had changed. Then, belatedly, he realized that the saloon had been given an addition and that there were new barracks built staggered back from the main road. He was relieved that everything seemed to be in the same state of peace as he had left it.

Alexander took Duke to the livery stable and paid Cody Harris, the quiet farrier, to care for the horse. After long exposure to the cold the Morgan horse was shivering.

After stowing his belongings in the constabulary, which he noted needed a good dusting, Alexander went across town to the saloon to mingle and announce his safe return. Upon entering he took a deep breath, grateful to be back in familiar surroundings.

Belatedly he noticed that the pub was far more populated than he remembered it ever being and there were many more women there than in the past. He had heard talk of the railroad coming further west and assumed that the increased number of patrons had something to do with that.

Finding a table proved to be a challenge and he ended up in a far back corner, out of sight of many of the people in the main room. He noted that the wall behind his table was relatively new, the wood lighter in color and less weathered than that of the original structure. The stuffed head of a pronghorn antelope hung low above the table, staring down at him with unblinking glass eyes. Alexander looked at it and felt his skin crawl; taxidermy had never appealed to him.

Turning his chair so his back was facing the dead animal, he sipped at his watered-down whiskey and surveyed the room. Many rough-looking men were scattered about the space, some smoking, some playing at cards, but every one of them drinking. Women mingled with them, some in plain, dull garments and others in more colorful costumes. Alexander wondered what the occasion could be.

A hand gripped his shoulder. The touch was light but it commanded his attention. Turning his head, he was surprised to find that one of the more flamboyantly dressed women stood beside him and it was her hand that rested on his shoulder. He could not stop himself from blushing; women rarely paid him any attention. "Good evening," he greeted. "I do not believe we have met before. I am Sheriff Alexander Judge."

She extended her hand in a casual motion. He took it and respectfully kissed her knuckles. "May I have your name?"

"Chastity. Look, are you interested or not?"

"Interested? In what, may I ask? I am interested in the pleasure of your conversation," Alexander said slowly, uncertain. He was confused by her brusqueness and apparent disinterest. After all, she had been the one to approach him.

She scoffed and her features twisted into a sneer that tainted her beauty. "Are you kidding me?"

"No, Miss Chastity, I assure you I am not. May I buy you a drink?"

"I never turn down a free drink." She grabbed an unoccupied chair and sat down. Crossing her legs, she pulled a cigarette tin from her corset. Alexander diverted his gaze but could not quite hide his shock at her bold actions. "What, never seen a girl smoke?"

Alexander looked up, eyes wide. He was finding himself entirely out of his depth. "No, I, uh,"

"Oh shuddap and get me that drink. Tarantula Juice." She shooed him away with a wave of her hand.

The sheriff stood quickly, forgetting about the antelope. His head bumped against the animal's chin and he cringed. Crouching so as not to repeat the experience, he made for the bar. He was not sure what exactly the drink she had ordered was, but he assumed the barkeep would know.

By the time he returned Chastity had lit her cigarette. She had her feet up on his chair, one ankle crossed over the other. Her skirt, shorter than was proper, slid back almost to her knees. " 'bout time," she remarked as he handed over her drink. She threw it back in two gulps and dropped the empty glass on the table.

As he looked at her uncertainly, unable to sit down because her feet were in the way, Alexander realized that she was much older than she had originally appeared. She wore a great deal of makeup, literally painting her youthful looks on. Belatedly he began to suspect her reason for being in the saloon. He blushed crimson.

"Now then, are we going to do this or not?" Chastity asked.

"Ah, er, forgive me but...to what do you keep referring?"

The fancy woman, for now Alexander was fairly certain that was her occupation, let out an exasperated sigh and stood. "When you figure it out, little man, you come and let me know. Chastity will show you a good time. I might not even charge full price for the sheriff." She had put her hand on his chest and slid it along his collarbone, giving him one last chance to change his mind before she moved on. Alexander was too dumbfounded to respond. He was beginning to understand that her pseudonym was a sick joke.

The barkeep had been watching the proceedings. As Chastity moved off he winked at Alexander knowingly. "She out of your league?"

Still dumb with shock, Alexander took his glass to the bar. Chastity had claimed another man and Alexander took the vacated barstool. After consuming most of his drink he regained his composure enough to whisper: "Is this now a brothel?"

The bartender laughed heartily. Taking a drink from his stein, he locked eyes with the sheriff and nodded, smiling. "You're catching on," he remarked with another laugh.

"Wh-when did this start?"

"A month or so ago," the barkeep lied. It had started, at least in concept, before the sheriff had ever left town.

Should I be putting a stop to it? Alexander asked himself, and caught himself before he spoke aloud. Of course he had heard of brothels springing up across the West--he was not *that* naive--but he never expected to find himself the unknowing patron of one such establishment. Every bit of his sensibility was repulsed at the very concept.

He felt that it may lie within his official capacity to put a stop to the immoral business. For the life of him, however, he could not fathom exactly how he would accomplish that. He determined to think on it and act later.

Alexander finished off his drink and was about to beat a hasty retreat when he was approached by another of the so-called 'ladies of the night'. He shifted uncomfortably, wanting to run for it. However, no matter her place in society, he could not be rude to a woman. He greeted her cordially, if a little awkwardly, and tried to excuse himself.

"What, sheriff," she began, running her fingers over the metal star on his lapel, "you're not really going to leave without having a little fun first?" This one was more aggressive than Chastity had been, leaning in close to him and running her hands down his torso suggestively. Her perfume was cloyingly sweet. Alexander could not suppress a cough. "Whaddya say big boy?" she teased, pulling on his vest.

"Excuse me," Alexander stuttered, pulling away from her. So embarrassed was he that he was not thinking clearly. He climbed up onto the bar and stood, drawing his pistol from its holster.

"What are you doing?!" the barkeep demanded indignantly, sliding glasses out of the way of the sheriff's boots.

Some of the nearby patrons had noticed the strange actions of the sheriff. They ceased their conversations and games to turn and look. Alexander pointed the pistol at the ceiling and looked around at the crowd, his chest heaving. His blood was high, his morality insulted, his mind blank.

He fired, bringing down a small shower of splinters. The saloon fell instantly silent, all eyes turning to him. Alexander stared back at them, stunned, suddenly realizing that he had no plan of action.

"What's all this about, sheriff?" one of the men called. "Is it important or can we continue our game?" He gestured at the cards and coin lying on the table.

Alexander stared dumbly at the crowd. When several seconds passed and he had not spoken, activity returned to the room. The sheriff worked his jaw, furrowed his brow, but could not think of anything to say. Still, he had made a spectacle of himself and thus he felt he must say something.

"Ahem," Alexander began uncertainly but loudly, drawing attention back to himself. He flushed beneath the intensity of several pairs of eyes. "I just want to say that this...this..." He cleared his throat. "This den of iniquity is indecent, completely devoid of morals, and possibly even unlawful. You all are showing your disregard for common decency by patronizing this place."

"Are you done yet?" a jeering voice said from close by. He looked down and met the piercing eyes of the second harlot that had approached him earlier in the evening. She, too, had a great deal of makeup plastered on her face. Her outfit left little of her figure to the imagination.

Embarrassed, Alexander lowered his weapon and holstered it. "That is all," he finished, trying to uphold his pride and dignity. He haltingly climbed down from the bar. Once his feet were on the wooden floorboards he straightened his clothing and held his chin up. He brushed past the prostitute without a second glance and left the saloon.

As soon as he was out in the night air he heard activity resume in the tavern behind him. He shook his head and exhaled heavily.

Running a hand down his face, knowing he had just opened a can of worms and questioning the necessity of having done so, Alexander plodded back toward his home. His boots left marks in the thin layer of new-fallen snow. He could see his breath hanging as a cloud in the air before him. He felt warm yet, still burning with embarrassment.

Because he proceeded with his head held down he did not see the other walker until he was almost upon her. He stopped abruptly and looked up, his breath coming a little faster. He had not seen Miss Emily Fletcher for months, not since he had made his last visit to the general store before leaving Flintridge. She had not spoken to him then since she had been helping another customer.

She looked much the same, he thought, but then how much could change in a few months? Miss Fletcher was bundled up against the cold of the chilly night. A curled lock of golden-brown hair escaped from beneath her hood and framed her face. Her breath, too, could be seen in the air. Alexander tried to slow his breathing, growing conscious of the clouds of breath hanging in the air before him.

"Sheriff," she remarked in some surprise. "Are you not cold?"

This was not the question Alexander had expected. He glanced down at his costume and belatedly realized that he had discarded his coat when he went to the constabulary. He had left it there in his eagerness to rejoin the townsfolk of Flintridge. His embarrassment had hitherto kept him from feeling the cold. As he walked it had worn off and the chill began to seep in. "Not terribly," he bluffed with a forced smile. "It is very nice to see you again, Miss Fletcher."

"You as well. Where have you been? I heard the rumors, but one can never believe everything they hear in this town."

"I would be very happy to tell you all about my travels. May I suggest that we go back to the constabulary, get out of the weather." Snow had begun to fall again, small drifting flakes. The chill in the air was eating through the sheriff's clothing. Their breath hung in the air, intermingling as they conversed.

"That sounds very nice," she answered.

Alexander, still a gentleman at heart despite all he had witnessed in the past few months, offered her his arm. At first she gave him a quizzical look but then she took it and they proceeded up the street in close proximity. The sheriff could not help but notice that she pressed closer to him as the wind began to blow. It had to be for warmth, but he hoped there could be other reasons for her actions as well.

He admitted them to his modest abode and closed the door against the blowing cold. "May I take your coat?" he offered.

Miss Fletcher wrapped her arms around herself, trying to rub warmth into her body. "It's no warmer in here than it is outside," she remarked quietly.

"Oh, yes, forgive me," Alexander stuttered. He hastened to the back room with its simple table. A stove sat in the corner and he hastily set about building a fire. "I have only just got back into town, you see, and I have not had a chance to settle myself. Please excuse the dust," he added apologetically.

He was such a pathetic, neurotic sight that Miss Fletcher could not help but take pity on him. "I don't want to put you to any trouble, Alexander. We could go over to the saloon and--"

"No!" Alexander composed himself with a great deal of effort and lowered his voice. In his excited reaction to her suggestion he had completely missed that she had used his Christian name. "I am sorry. No, that saloon is not—well, it's—"

"I know what kind of business is run there."

"And you are still willing to patronize the place?" He could not keep the shock and judgment from his voice.

"Your tinder is alight," she remarked.

The sheriff jumped and shoved the burning material into the stove, beneath the tepee of wood he had built. Closing the door, he stood and turned to face her, brushing his hands together to remove the soot.

"Of course I still go there. We can't afford to be all that choosy in a town such as this."

"I suppose, but…"

"I don't like it any more than you do, sheriff," she said hastily, not wanting to tarnish her reputation in his eyes. "But in a way I do understand it. Most of those women have lost their husbands to Indian attacks, mining or railroad accidents, even snakebites. They have little choice but to do what they are doing, just to feed themselves."

"You've spoken with them?!" His voice conveyed his shock and abhorrence of the notion.

"I wish they had some other alternative. If I could find a way to help them I would, but in the meantime I cannot condemn them for what they do. Chastity, in particular, has quite a good sense of humor, considering what she has been through."

Alexander could not force his jaw to close. He was staring at her, too shocked to fret about his manners. His freckles were standing out in stark contrast to his suddenly pale skin.

"I see I may have shocked you," she remarked with a wry smile.

"Oh, no, no," Alexander blundered, trying in vain to hide his bewilderment. "It's just…you've spoken with them?!" He simply could not get past the fact. It just seemed so wrong to him, the daughter of an upstanding merchant associating with fallen women.

"Men can be so small-minded at times," Miss Fletcher said with a sigh. She turned her face away, looking out at the cold night beyond the windowpane.

Alexander was not so far lost in bewilderment that he did not realize that he may have insulted her. He closed his jaw with an audible click and put what he hoped was a pleasant smile on his face. "I suppose we can be," he agreed handsomely. "That is very kind of you, to take pity on those unfortunates and offer the honor of your friendship." As the look on her face changed, growing still darker, he realized that he had misspoken. "Er, that is to say…" He could think of no recovery.

"Perhaps it was a mistake that I came here tonight. I should have kept my opinions to myself. Please forgive me." Despite her placating words her voice was hard. She refused to look at him, though he tried to catch her gaze.

Alexander heaved a sigh borne of exasperation, at himself and at her stubbornness. Mostly at himself. "I do beg your pardon. I should not have been so judgmental. Will you remain here awhile longer if we change the subject and I tell you about my travels these past few months?"

Finally she turned her hazel gaze on him once more. She regarded him for a long moment, enjoying watching him squirm. He was such a silly creature, noble and bookish, not at all the rough-and-ready type that one usually found out West. For just a moment she considered…but no, she told herself, it was not her place to make the first move. If he wanted her hand, (assuming he had an interest in her, she reminded herself,) he would have to work for it.

"That would be nice," she said finally, ending his uneasiness.

Alexander let out the pent up breath he had been holding in expectantly. Feeling a little self-conscious yet, he began his tale. He told her anecdotes as he thought of them, told her of the men he met and worked with, of their wild chases through the prairies and deserts and mountains. Encounters with wild animals and outlaws alike featured, though he did his best to leave out the more frightening or violent moments.

When he did slip, mentioning one of the men who had been shot brutally, Miss Fletcher surprised him yet again by not batting an eye; evidently she was more hardened to western life than he had expected. A couple of his stories elicited soft, musical laughter from her and his heart skipped a beat. He had suspected it for awhile but now he was certain that he was falling head over heels for Miss Emily Fletcher.

"Is that all you have to tell me about your time away?" she prompted after he had fallen silent.

Alexander started, realizing that he had trailed off and was staring at her with a stupid, contented smile turning up one side of his mouth. He blushed and leaned back in his chair, distancing himself. "I am afraid that is all I have to tell. I can think of nothing more that might interest you." He glanced at his pocket watch, needing to take his eyes off her for just a moment. He had caught himself on the brink of making a very foolish admission. "My goodness!" he exclaimed, sitting up straight. "The hour is late. I am terribly sorry to have kept you so long. I do hope your father will not be cross."

He stood and she did the same. Alexander retrieved his coat and, donning it, ushered her out into the cold. Again he offered his arm and again she held onto him, walking pressed close to him for warmth. Though the night was chilly and growing colder they did not rush to the Fletcher residence.

The snow was drifting down around them, silvered by the shafts of moonlight filtering through the clouds. As before, their breath hung in the air before them as they conversed in low voices. Their tracks were the only ones to be found in the new-fallen snow, for all others had already been filled in by the peaceful but persistent snowfall. The wind had died down, leaving the night crisp and silvery white.

Alexander saw her home and apologized to her father for keeping her out so long. Emily bade him a good evening and slipped past her father into the house. Alexander could not be entirely sure, but he thought she had thrown a wistful look at him just before she passed out of sight. Emotions stirred in his heart, pressuring him to act. He opened his mouth to speak but when Mr. Fletcher's gaze lighted on his face he lost his nerve. Letting his breath out in a defeated sigh, he bade the merchant a good night and turned for home.

As Alexander trod through the snow he reflected that suddenly, without her by his side, the night was bitterly cold and held no joy for him. The moon had disappeared behind the clouds, which suddenly seemed much heavier and darker. Wind kicked up, biting into his exposed skin. He bowed his head and pushed onward. The snow seemed so much deeper, the going harder alone. He missed the warmth of her body pressed to his side, missed her sweet voice and cheerful presence.

Mentally he was kicking himself for not asking of her father the question he longed to ask. Once again, for the umpteenth time in his life, his mild nature had cost him an opportunity. He let out a frustrated sigh. The exhaled breath hung as a translucent cloud on the air for an instant before he stepped through it, lengthening his stride out of sheer irritation with himself.

A beam of cold, silvery light cut across his path as the moon emerged briefly from behind a cloud. Alexander stopped there in the cold, silent night, and looked up at the frozen bluish-silver orb. Snowflakes drifted down around him, landing on his hair and shoulders, dusting him with white.

~~~~~~~~~~

Byrne looked out his window the next morning, a hot cup of coffee in hand. His wife stood beside him, wrapped in the sheltering embrace of his arm. Snow had fallen in the night and everything outside wore a fresh coat of white fluff. It looked so very silent, peaceful, as if any sound would be deadened by the smothering blanket of snow.

Only one set of tracks broke the even white surface: those of Sadie, who had gone out when her masters woke. She trotted back and forth through the snow, at times sniffing curiously and alternately bounding gaily through a spray of white crystals. Her joyous barks sounded without, muted by the wooden walls and panes of glass that sheltered the humans.

"What shall we do today?" Ivey whispered.

The rancher sipped his coffee, enjoying the warmth of the liquid more than the flavor. His eyes passed over the snow-covered ground and lighted on the palomino stallion's pen. The great horse stood with his rear turned into the wind, head down, apparently asleep.

"I imagine you'll want to stay inside where it's warm," he remarked. He was not being judgmental or catty, merely making an educated guess.

"You guessed correctly," she answered, hugging his arm as if trying to steal his warmth. "And you'll be outside at some task or other I imagine?"

"I was thinking it'd be a good day to break that mustang."

Ivey looked up at him, eyes wide. "No Byrne."

He glanced down at her out of the corner of his eye and smiled. "Don't you think I can do it?"

"Of course I do. Just, not today. Don't try it yet. Wait for spring."

"And let him have the winter to grow wild again? Not likely." He kissed the top of her head, then her lips. "Don't worry, I know what I'm about."

After changing his clothes and donning heavy coat and hat, he pushed open the front door and stepped out into the cold. Sadie came flying across the white plain, barking excitedly and kicking up a spray of snow behind her. She met Byrne a few feet from the porch and danced around him, jumping and whining happily. Absently the rancher patted her bobbing head as he walked toward the shed containing his tack.

The horses noted his appearance and raised their voices in the morning chorus of greeting. Even the palomino stallion raised his head in anticipation of breakfast. When Byrne approached the pen with a saddle slung over one arm and a bridle dangling from his shoulder, Beau eyed him warily and retreated to the far side of the corral.

Byrne moved casually, keeping his motions quiet. He approached the wild stallion and slipped the bridle on, the bit into his mouth. They had practiced this before. While Beau still disliked the procedure, he acknowledged the human's dominance and tolerated it.

However, when Byrne came at him with saddle and blanket in hand the stallion backed away, snorting. He tossed his head, flicked his ears. There was a quirk to his mouth that indicated he was tense, ready to strike out if he perceived danger. So determined was the rancher on his task that he either missed the warning or chose to ignore it.

He maneuvered the stallion so that he was pushed up against the fence rails, contained as much as the corral would allow. As if it were nothing at all to saddle an untamed mustang, Byrne placed the saddle on the animal's back. When Beau tried to bolt the rancher's firm hand on the reins held him back. The palomino fidgeted, throwing his head in a circular fashion, blowing nervously.

Byrne managed to tighten the cinch single-handedly, having to keep one hand on the reins to prevent the stallion from running. Inevitably he came to the point wherein he had to use both hands to secure the saddle. Throwing the reins over the horse's neck so they were within easy reach as he stood just behind the animal's shoulder, Byrne yanked the cinch strap tight.

With a scream of rage and terror the stallion leapt forward. Byrne made a grab for the reins but was too late. The stallion went cantering along the rail, throwing up clods of snow. The rancher chased after him, determined not to let him get away with such behavior.

He caught hold of the reins and planted his feet, swinging the crazed animal around. Beau screamed again and charged blindly, kicking up his heels in a desperate attempt to rid himself of the saddle. Byrne dodged and managed to get alongside the beast.

Holding the reins taut with one hand, he vaulted into the saddle. He yanked the mustang's head around, making him spin in a tight circle to prevent him bolting, bucking or rearing. For a time the infuriated horse simply turned around and around.

When the stallion began to slow up, getting dizzy, Byrne let him stop. The rancher jerked his body weight to one side, trying to reposition the saddle which had slipped off-center during his frantic mount. The sudden movement stirred the mustang to a frenzy again.

This time Byrne could not get him circling in either direction. The horse was mad, ignoring the metal bar pulling on his mouth.

Beau bolted forward, dipping and making abrupt turns of direction as he bucked and bucked and bucked, desperate to get the weight off his back. The horse was making guttural snorting sounds and working very hard to remove both rider and saddle. Byrne still had the reins but they gave him absolutely no control. He held onto the saddle horn tightly, trying to compensate for the animal's frenzied, unpredictable movements.

The stallion slid to an abrupt stop, got his quarters beneath him, and reared almost vertically. The rancher leaned forward, grabbing fistfuls of the coarse mane to keep himself from falling backward. As soon as Beau's hard hooves touched ground he was off again, plunging and twisting down the short length of the corral.

Byrne felt the saddle slide beneath him. As the horse twisted right the saddle slid still further. Using his grip on the horse's mane, Byrne tried to lever the saddle back into place and tried to stay on. If the horse threw him now the animal would think it a victory and be all the more unmanageable in the future. Byrne gritted it out.

Just when he thought the mustang might be resigning himself to defeat, the mustang summoned a final burst of energy. Screaming, Beau swung his hips in a hard buck. The cinch came loose, the saddle slid, and Byrne was catapulted off the horse's back.

The rancher hit against the fence rails hard, getting the wind knocked out of him. He slumped to the ground and lay there, unmoving, while the horse threw a tantrum, charging around the pen.

Sadie had been watching the flurry of activity with interest. She was at her master's side in an instant, barking furiously at the horse to keep it at bay. The stallion regarded her uncertainly. She did not move towards him, she only stood in front of Byrne with legs splayed out and teeth bared, gnashing. A low growl of warning rumbled in her chest. Beau moved off, keeping to the far end of the corral, not wanting to be near the creature that, to him, was not a wolf but awfully similar.

The loyal young dog barked loudly, directing her voice at the house. She dared not leave her master lying there, injured and helpless, but her instincts told her that raising her voice might bring help. So it proved to be.

Ivey was in the kitchen, washing the breakfast dishes, when she heard Sadie's barking. At first she was prepared to dismiss it as nothing out of the ordinary, but then she recognized a tone in the bark that she had never before heard. When she heard the ferocious growling she knew something was amiss. What could make the sweet-natured puppy sound like that?

Going to the front window, she looked out. The palomino stallion stood at the far end of the corral, steam rising off his sweaty body. She did not see Byrne. Just around the bend of the pen she saw Sadie's fluffy banner of a tail; it was not wagging. The frantic barking continued.

Throwing aside the towel she had been using to dry her hands, Ivey raced for the door. She stopped only long enough to throw a shawl over her shoulders and stuff her feet into a pair of Byrne's boots - the only footwear in immediate reach.

Heart pounding, she threw open the door and jumped from the porch into the ankle-deep snow. Floundering more than running, she made her way to the pen. The stallion saw her coming and snorted in alarm at her sliding, jerky progress. Byrne's boots were far too large for her feet and the snow slowed her up.

"Byrne!" she called breathlessly. Sadie swung around the outside of the pen, always keeping an eye on the palomino horse. She met her owner and tugged on her skirt, pulling her toward the spot the dog had just left. Ivey's blood ran colder still at seeing the nervous look in the dog's eyes as she watched the wild horse askance. The fur on her scruff stood on-end.

When Ivey rounded the bend of the fence line she got her first good look at the scene. Byrne lay sprawled out in the snow on his back, his head and shoulders propped up against a fence post. He was not moving, not even breathing as far as she could tell as she came trippingly along through the snow. There were dark spots in the snow around him: blood which had turned a dark, almost brownish, color as it fell into and stained the snow.

Reaching him from the outside of the fence, Ivey dropped down to her knees in the snow. Sadie stood nearby, growling and gnashing her teeth at the wild stallion who, out of curiosity, had begun to approach.

So many questions and thoughts and fears raced through Ivey's mind that for a second all she could do was stare at her husband's body. Then common sense kicked in and she grabbed hold of him under the arms. Carefully but quickly she began to pull his heavy, dead weight through the fence, guiding it through the narrow space between the horizontal planks. Despite Sadie's warning barks the palomino inched closer.

Finally, after much hard work and struggle, Ivey fell backward, breathless. She had managed to pull Byrne out into safety and, exhausted, she sat for a moment, cradling his head in her lap. Feeling something sticky in his dark hair, she brought her hand up and was horrified to learn that the blood she had seen in the snow had come from some injury on his scalp. She leaned over him, hugging him close, desperate to learn if he lived or not.

She got her answer as he opened his eyes blearily, looking around as if confused by what he saw. Ivey stifled a cry of relief.

Byrne, typical stubborn man that he was, insisted that he was perfectly fine. The head wound, to him, was nothing to be concerned about. Despite Ivey's protestations he sat up, gingerly, and would have stood immediately if she had not intervened.

"Don't you dare," she spat in equal parts anger and concern.

"Why not? The snow is an awfully cold place to sit and have a conversation," he remarked, wincing at a stab of pain on the back of his skull. He tried to smile at her, to get her to relax, but she was in such a state that none of his reassurances would calm her.

Belatedly he noticed that her skirt was darkened, wet with melted snow. She had very little on to protect her from the cold, only a shawl wrapped haphazardly around her shoulders. "Ivey, please, let's go inside." The look she gave him told him she was not inclined to move. He was not sure what course of action she would recommend but he knew they would both catch cold if they stayed sitting in the snow. "If I let you baby me once we're in the house will that convince you?"

After a long moment she half nodded. "I will be fetching the doctor as well."

Byrne heaved a sigh. "Alright. Completely unnecessary, but if it makes you feel any better…"

"It does."

Smothering a groan of discomfort, not wanting to upset her further, Byrne pushed himself to his feet. Pain shot up and down his back, momentarily paralyzing him. He clenched his teeth, unwilling to let the pain win out. As he forced himself to stand completely still, the stabbing flares of pain subsided to a fierce throb, but one he could deal with. Opening his eyes, he was disconcerted that everything around him seemed to be spinning while he stood in place.

Ivey tucked herself beneath his arm, pulling it across her shoulders. She was significantly shorter than him and thus rather ineffective as a support, but Byrne knew better than to comment. Stumbling through the snow, both encumbered, they slowly made their way to the house. Sadie, throwing a final snarl at the palomino stallion, trotted after them and followed them inside.

Ivey plopped Byrne into a chair at the kitchen table and ordered him to remain there while she ran into town. "Just let me assume proper attire and I will go as quickly as I can," she assured him, stepping into their bedroom and digging through the chest of drawers.

"Take Cowboy," Byrne instructed.

"No, no, I think this family has had enough of mustangs for awhile," she remarked. "Besides, I cannot ride without a saddle and putting tack on the horse would take time. I will walk."

"That will take longer, be more dangerous," the rancher pointed out.

"I will take my chances without a horse." Her tone of voice brooked no argument. Donning her heavy winter coat, she left the house and started off.

For the first quarter hour Byrne felt restless. He worried about his wife, so fragile and unaccustomed to the roughness of the country out West. The wind was blowing again, sweeping the snow in sheets through the air. The trek into town on foot was a long one and if the snow got to blowing too thickly she might lose her way. He wished desperately that she had taken Cowboy; even if she were to get lost, the sturdy mustang knew his way home in any weather and he would be able to break trail through the snow far more easily.

He squirmed in the hard-back wooden chair, uncomfortable. The pain in his back was still there, his head still throbbed. Leaning one elbow on the table, he rested his chin in his hand and waited impatiently. Without him realizing it, sleep crept up on him.

When Ivey returned with the doctor in tow, they found Byrne slumped over the kitchen table. Ivey ran to him and shook his shoulder violently. The rancher made a sound in his sleep but did not wake. His wife persisted and eventually succeeded in rousing him.

Byrne stared at her blearily, blinking frequently, unaware of the reason for her frantic behavior. His vision was a little blurry as he looked past her at the other occupant of their small kitchen. He knew he had seen the other man before but his foggy mind was having trouble placing a name with the face.

The physician introduced himself as Lucas Simmons and greeted the patient briefly before starting his examination. Byrne was too foggy, sore, and sluggish to voice much complaint as the doctor looked him over. The wound on the back of his head was found, examined, and passed off as painful but not life-threatening. When the rancher complained about the pain in his back, the physician duly took a look but could find nothing clinically wrong. He prescribed a concoction that he claimed would dull the pain and recommended that Ivey keep a close eye on her husband for the next several days. The fact that he had been so slow to wake was a little concerning.

Feeling not much relieved, Ivey thanked Doctor Simmons. As she was going to fetch payment for services rendered, the front door opened. Byrne leaned back in his chair to get a look at the newest interloper. His eyes opened wide as he recognized the sheriff stepping into his house.

Alexander blew out a shuddering breath, rubbing his hands and stomping his feet. "It is frightfully cold out," he remarked conversationally.

"What are you doing here?" Byrne spat out, too out of humor to bother being polite. He stood, swayed in place and caught at the back of the chair to steady himself.

"I saw the doctor driving out this way and thought something might be amiss. Therefore, I stepped out and offered my assistance, which was readily accepted. This lady," he indicated Ivey with a polite tip of his head, "explained to me about your accident. You really gave her a fright, you ought not have been so foolish with that mustang."

"Well, thank you for that nice sentiment," Byrne said with heavy sarcasm. Belatedly it occurred to him that the sheriff had only just entered the house, when he had supposedly travelled with the doctor and Ivey. "What have you been up to?"

"I was out of town on business-"

"No, not that. Just now. You came with Ivey and the doc, didn't you?"

"Indeed I did. I did not want to crowd in the house where I would be of little use, so I stayed in the yard to see if there was anything I could do. I picked up the saddle and blanket, even managed to get the bridle off that insane beast. Almost lost a hand to those teeth of his." He noticed Byrne's expression of impatience. "At any rate, I put them away in one of the sheds out back."

Byrne wanted very much to order the annoying sheriff to leave, but even he could not be that rude. He knew the young man had done him a favor, acted in his interest, and deserved at least the courtesy of a thank you. "Thank you," he ground out, trying not to sound as gruff as he felt. His head was pounding and he felt very tired. All he wanted was to be left alone.

The rancher's wishes were granted as a large black formed moved across the snow, visible through the front window. Alexander's face fell as he realized what it must be. "Please excuse me," he said, hastening toward the door. As he stepped out onto the porch he raised his voice. "Duke! Get back here!"

Despite his pain Byrne could not help but chuckle.

CHAPTER EIGHT

That winter was a quiet one in Flintridge. The snow fell frequently, laying a thick blanket of white over everything in sight and making travel difficult. The stagecoach line scarcely traveled out that far, but when one did stop it was cause for celebration. The wind blew bitterly cold, rushing across the snow-bound plains and biting straight to the bone. Those souls who dared to brave the weather and go out only did so for the briefest of intervals before returning to the warmth and shelter of their homes or businesses.

The saloon saw an upswing in business of all kinds, as the railway men were unable to lay ties and unable to travel home. Essentially they were stranded in a far-flung frontier town with very little to do for entertainment.

The harsh travel conditions also meant that outlaw gangs did not visit the sleepy town. They could not get far, as their mounts would have to break trail through the deep, deep snow and would tire very quickly. The brigands, too, were trapped, but they spent the winter further east. Byrne hardly gave a thought to them.

The rancher had made a good recovery from his accident, though his back still twitched with pain every once in awhile when he moved a certain way. His vision and dizziness had cleared up and he felt fighting fit, which proved to be a great stressor to his wife. Ivey watched over him like a hawk, even long after he was out of danger. The incident had given her a great fright; she did not know how she would survive on the frontier without her resourceful husband to care for her and show her what to do. Her comfortable southern upbringing had left her ill-prepared for the hardships living out west presented.

Respecting his wife's wishes, Byrne did not try to ride the palomino mustang again. She allowed him to do groundwork with the horse and in those sessions the animal did seem to tame up - or maybe his docile behavior was due to the fierce grip of winter, which seemed to subdue even the boldest spirits. The rancher was allowed to work more with the mares and foals and in the course of those cold, foreboding months, he managed to break two of the mares to saddle.

"You can have your pick of the new lot of horses," Byrne remarked energetically to his wife at dinner one evening. "The sorrel is coming along quite nicely."

Ivey rolled her eyes at him. "I'll take a nice southern gaited horse instead," she said as sweetly as she could manage. She reached across the small table and placed her hand atop his to soften the words.

~~~~~~~~~~

That whole winter Alexander stayed mostly to himself, holed up in his empty constabulary. Since he had come to Flintridge not a single one of the cells had been occupied. Rumors and complaints of the small-time thief persisted and Alexander felt incompetent for not succeeding in solving the mystery. With the new influx of residents to Flintridge it was difficult to single any one person out as the culprit. But then he reminded himself that the small thefts had been occurring before the railway men began arriving in town. That narrowed the pool of suspects significantly.

Of those who had been living in Flintridge when Alexander arrived, he had met perhaps three-quarters of them. Naturally he had seen everyone at one point or another but usually just in passing. It was somewhat difficult to strike up conversations with people who were busy with other tasks.

On one of the warmer days - meaning the mercury was above zero - Alexander heard a ruckus out back. Over the course of the winter the sheriff had grown less skittish, feeling confident that outlaws could not break trail through the snow all the way to Flintridge. He casually looked out his back window and saw Duke in the small paddock, throwing a fit. Confused, the sheriff donned his coat and boots and went out into the chilly morning.

Duke cavorted about the pen, throwing his head and kicking up his heels. He charged up and down the short fence line as if possessed. When Alexander approached, the horse turned to look at him with head held high, ears pricked, breath blowing out through his nose and hanging in the air.

"What is wrong with you this morning?" the sheriff asked of his equine.

His voice seemed to add to the fire of energy within the horse for Duke kicked up his heels in Alexander's general direction, clods of snow flying into the air. As Duke trotted off, prancing with tail held high, Alexander noticed that the horse was limping. Frowning, the sheriff entered the pen to investigate.

Duke permitted his master to put his halter and lead on and stood more or less still as Alexander examined each hoof in turn. Although the horse behaved himself, he was quivering with raw energy. The day, though cold, was warmer than the previous week and the horse was seized with pent-up energy.

Finally Alexander's examination yielded results. When he picked up Duke's white-socked foot he discovered that the horseshoe was missing and a chunk of hoof wall had been torn out by the nails.

With a sigh the sheriff let the horse's foot down. He stood and rubbed the back of his neck. Another expense. He had to have a sound horse. He led Duke, still prancing and limping, out of the corral and into town. He took the excited animal to the livery stable where the town farrier, Cody Harris, was based.

Upon entering he found the blacksmith at his work. The farrier was holding up the foot of a large draft horse, paring away at the sole with his hoof knife. Alexander stood by, watching as the hoof was trimmed and filed.

Harris let the foot down and moved to his workstation, a forge and anvil, and set about shaping a new shoe for the enormous hoof. The pattern of heating the steel, hammering it into shape, cooling and fitting it was repeated until the shoe matched the shape of the draft's hoof.

The farrier heated the shaped steel once more and, holding it securely with a pair of tongs, approached the draft. The large animal stood sedately, accustomed to the scents and sounds of this procedure. Cody applied the hot shoe to the bottom of the hoof, burning off any excess tissue so the shoe fit flush to the hoof.

Alexander curled his lip and blinked at the unpleasant stench. It smelled like burning hair.

Tossing the horseshoe into a bucket of water to cool, Cody Harris stood and stretched. Belatedly he recognized that he had a new customer. "Mornin' Sheriff," he remarked in his deep, solid voice. He was not a man to mince words, as Alexander had learned from previous encounters, but he seemed an honest person. From years of working with horses the rather short man had built up quite a bit of muscle. Though he had to be approaching fifty years of age he looked younger. Only the sprinkle of white in his brown hair hinted at his real age.

"Good morning Mr. Harris," the sheriff greeted in turn. "Duke seems to have thrown a shoe," he explained. "Do you have time to put a new one on him?"

"Sure," the farrier replied as he leaned down to retrieve the draft's shoe from the water pail. "Just gotta finish with this guy here. Jesse will see to your horse until I'm ready for him."

"Jesse?"

"My nephew. Tall wisp of a thing, hardly suited for this kind of work. But, he's got to learn a trade."

"Indeed. I do not believe I have met him."

"He came out a few months back when his parents died of consumption. Why they sent him to me I'll never know; hadn't ever met the kid before."

"Well I'm sure if you give him a chance he will take to the work."

"Don't count on it," Cody remarked as he picked up the draft's hoof. He had grabbed his hammer and nails and was positioning the new shoe. "Got a wild streak, 'e has, always looking for some new adventure. Foolishness, if'n you ask me." He placed the first nail and began hammering.

"How old is he?"

"Fifteen. I think." Another nail was hammered in. "Jesse!" The farrier's shout, quite unexpected, made Alexander and Duke jump. The Morgan horse trotted forward and his owner pulled him around. It took a few tight circles before the black gelding settled down and stood still.

Finally the sullen youth made his appearance. "Yea, what?" he grumbled at his uncle. It was clear the pair did not get on well. Jesse was a lanky youth, his hair an unkempt mess of blonde locks. He slouched as he approached, hands in his pockets.

"Take da Sherish's 'orse 'ere," Cody remarked around the nails clenched in his teeth. He pounded two more nails into the draft's hoof and let it down. He stepped back to look at the leg head-on, to be sure everything was as it should be.

When Cody looked up again, Jesse was sitting on a hay bale, disinterestedly picking at his fingernails. "Didn't you hear me?"

"I heard you."

"Then git goin'!" the farrier snapped, giving the boy a shove off the bale. Reluctantly Jesse slunk toward Alexander and accepted the lead of the spirited black horse.

"Right then," Alexander said, more to himself. "I will be back in a few hours Mr. Harris."

"Cody," the farrier corrected.

"Goodbye Jesse," Alexander said before departing, extending his hand. The youth looked at it with a surly expression and refused to return the gesture. He pulled Duke along behind him, heading for the line of stalls. As the boy turned away Alexander noticed a peculiar bulge under the back of his shirt. Knowing it was not his place to inquire about it, he left the stable.

~~~~~~~~~~

Whilst he was waiting to go and claim his mount, Alexander spent the time checking the functionality of the locks on the cells, oiling them where necessary. He checked the strength of the bars, ensuring the cells were suitable. What spring might bring no one knew - but everyone looked forward to it - and he wanted to be prepared in case the worst should happen.

In a way he was grateful for the small-time thief plaguing Flintridge. It gave him something to focus on, a way to take his mind off Miss Emily Fletcher. Since that night he could not stop thinking about her.

Alexander sat at his little table with pen, inkpot and paper. In school he had always found it useful to analyze situations by putting the facts down on paper and that is was what he intended to do with this case. He set down the details he did know: who had been robbed; what had been stolen; the dates and approximate times of the thefts; and any other information which he thought pertinent.

The sheriff sat back, stretching his hands, and reviewed the resulting document. He examined each line individually and then took them as a whole. A pattern was suggested by the data.

"Sundays," Alexander mused to himself, brow furrowing as he continued to examine the list. "Sunday mornings. Small, easily transported items." He leaned back in his chair, rubbing his chin thoughtfully. "Suggests a single person, likely on foot. Sunday mornings."

The sheriff stood and paced. How unusual! Flintridge was a small town, the residents were God-fearing folk. Undoubtedly they would all be in attendance at church on a Sunday morning. Who then was left to steal the items?

Alexander stopped before the mirror, staring blankly at his reflection as he tried to work out the problem. His own hazel eyes stared back at him, lacking a ready answer. As his mind wandered he realized that his appearance was absolutely unacceptable. His ginger hair was disheveled, his skin pale, and there was a smear of black ink on his chin. Scrubbing at the stain with his fingers, he only succeeded in making it larger.

Inspiration hit him. There was only one way to catch this thief. He consulted the list again, averaging the frequency of the thefts. The criminal did not strike each week, but every few weeks, and had not stolen anything for the last two weeks. The odds were in favor of another theft occurring on the coming Sunday. Alexander determined that he would skip services that day.

~~~~~~~~~~

In fact Alexander did attend church services on the Sunday. He had amended his strategy. As he mingled with the crowd before the sermon began, he was making a mental checklist of who was present and who was missing. The vast majority of the residents were there, packing tightly into the small church.

Alexander approached one family whom he knew to be missing a member. "Good morning Mr. Dorham, Mrs. Dorham." He nodded to each of them in turn respectfully.

"Good morning Mr. Judge," the man of the family returned.

"Where is your mother this fine day, may I ask?" He sincerely doubted that an eighty-year-old woman was the culprit, but every lead had to be followed.

"She stayed home with a bad cold," Mrs. Dorham answered. Her voice was quiet, sad, as if she expected the worst outcome from the illness.

"I am sorry to hear that. Please give her my best wishes," Alexander remarked. With a nod he stepped away to converse with the next person on his list. "Ah, Mrs. Chensy, a pleasure to see you again."

"Hello Mr. Judge," she returned in a wavering voice that suggested she was on the verge of tears.

"I was so looking forward to seeing Mr. Chensy and your son...Billy was his name, yes?"

His words proved to be the breaking point for Mrs. Chensy. She broke out in a fit of hysterical sobbing. Alexander was completely taken aback as she wrapped her arms around him and hugged him tight. She was a large woman and her grip was crushing. Her face was buried against his chest, her tears dampening his clothing. Confused and a little alarmed, Alexander looked about for someone who could intervene.

Awkwardly he patted the inconsolable Mrs. Chensy on the back. "There, there," he murmured, turning beet red with discomfort.

Finally a kindly person drew Mrs. Chensy off, speaking soothingly to the large woman. Alexander straightened his clothing and brushed at his lapel. He made a face when his hand found the wet patch where her tears had fallen.

"Shame on you, upsetting poor Mrs. Chensy so!" one of the women chided him in passing.

"I am sorry. What happened, may I ask?" He spoke the last quietly, not wanting to upset Mrs. Chensy any further.

The woman turned on him and spoke tartly. "Her son fell in the river. Mr. Chensy went in after him. They both caught pneumonia and died not two days past."

"Oh," Alexander replied, feeling very stupid.

"Have some common decency why don't you?"

"I truly am sorry, I had not heard."

"Hmph," the woman said with a dismissive turn. She went to console Mrs. Chensy.

Alexander hurriedly removed himself to a far corner of the room. He was about ready to abandon his grand scheme. So far all he had succeeded in accomplishing was to upset a grieving widow.

Taking a deep breath to steady his nerves, he determined to see the first phase of the plan through. After all, only one missing person remained on his list.

Turning around, he bumped into that very person. "Oh, do excuse me, Mr. Harris—Cody." Alexander extended his hand and smiled.

Cody shook it, his grip like an iron vice. "Mornin' Sheriff."

"Thank you for shoeing Duke so quickly the other day. What would this town do without you?" He laughed in a friendly manner.

"Just wouldn't put shoes on their horses is all." Cody did not seem to catch the spirit of the joke.

"Say, where is your nephew this morning? I have not seen him yet."

Cody snorted derisively. "The little wretch refused to come, was complaining his stomach hurt. I say he's makin' stuff up but if he wants to shun his spiritual health in favor of a physical ailment that's his business."

"Oh." Alexander really did not know what to say to that.

"I've half a mind to send the whelp packing. He's been no help at all around the stable."

"Give him time," Alexander advised, trying to sound as if he knew something of dealing with errant youths.

"Hmph." Brusquely the farrier moved off.

Alexander found himself alone in a sea of people. He had acquired the information for which he came and deemed it a good time to duck out, before the service began. Making a beeline for the door, the sheriff slipped out of the church, found Duke where he had left him tied, and headed back into town.

Instead of going straight to the constabulary and seeking the warmth of his little stove, the sheriff rode down the street toward the livery stable. He did not have an exact plan.

Dismounting, he led Duke into the stable and called out. "Hello? Cody? Jesse?"

"Cody's not here," the youthful voice replied. He did not sound at all ill.

"Jesse? Is that you?" Alexander asked, knowing full well that it was.

"Yea. I'm sick. Go away."

"I am sorry to hear that," Alexander replied, trying to keep the sharp tone out of his voice. "I was hoping to settle my account with Cody. Could you come help me with that?"

Jesse poked his head around the corner. His brown eyes were narrowed, suspicious. "He's at church. Why aren't you?"

"Why are you not at church?" Alexander countered. The boy's behavior was rubbing the sheriff the wrong way, making him cynical. He crossed his arms as he regarded the youth.

"I'm sick."

"Really? You certainly look and sound fine to me."

"I'm feeling better." The lie was unconvincing. Jesse knew it and turned away. He picked up a pitchfork and poked at some straw. "Look, I've got work I should be doing. Come back later when Cody's here. He doesn't let me handle the money."

"Alright then," Alexander replied. He sensed that pushing the youth further would not yield results. He had accomplished his goal: to see if Jesse were at the stables or not.

The sheriff left the livery stable and returned to the constabulary. He kept an eye on the street from the front window of his apartment. The angle did not afford him a good view of the stable, but if Jesse left it he would surely see him in the deserted street.

His vigil did not last long. Not thirty minutes had passed before Jesse appeared in the street, moving furtively. Alexander watched him for several moments. The boy ducked down an alley which the sheriff knew was shared by two homes.

Leaving his post at the window, Alexander descended to the street. He walked down the thoroughfare casually, as if with no real purpose. He approached the alley into which Jesse had vanished. The boy was nowhere to be seen, but the window of one of the houses stood open. Alexander leaned against the far building, watching the window intently. Within the house he heard rustling and other muffled sounds.

Before long a form appeared at the window. Alexander knew who the culprit was even before Jesse climbed out the window. The youth dropped to the ground, his arms full of small trinkets taken from the abode. He closed the window, turned around, and froze in his tracks. He stared at Alexander with wide eyes.

"Sick, are you?" Alexander asked accusingly, his voice and eyes hard.

Jesse straightened up, trying to act as if nothing was amiss. "I told you I'm feeling better."

"Evidently. Come with me." The sheriff took hold of the youth's arm and dragged him, plunder and all, out of the alley and into the street.

"Really, this is not what it looks like. I—"

"Why do you not save your tales for when your uncle joins us at the constabulary? I feel certain he will not want to miss out on hearing them."

Jesse dug in his heels, stopping them both. "No! Please. Don't tell Cody."

"Why should I not? He is your guardian, like it or not, and he must be informed. How he chooses to discipline you is none of my affair." Alexander was being harsh, he knew it, but there was no reason why the youth should have taken to stealing. The sheriff tightened his grip and pulled the resisting boy along.

"Please. No. Please, can't we wait for him at the stable? I'll confess to it all, I swear, just please don't lock me up."

Alexander heaved an exasperated sigh. The youth's plea did have one thing in its favor, namely that the sheriff would not have to leave the constabulary to fetch the farrier back after services. "Alright," he agreed tightly.

They went straight to the livery stable, found two bales of hay to use as chairs, sat down and waited. Jesse tried to make small talk but for once Alexander was not in a chatty mood.

He should be happy, he thought to himself, for he had solved the mystery of the petty thief. Now that his mind had finished with that puzzle it was inundated with thoughts and memories of Miss Fletcher. Alexander had not seen her for quite some time; in fact he had been avoiding her. He, himself, was uncertain as to why he refused to see her again.

His musings were disrupted by the return of Cody. The farrier stopped and looked at the pair in some surprise. "Sheriff," he greeted, his eyes going from the stern face of Alexander to Jesse's subdued countenance.

"Jesse," Alexander began, his voice hard, "is there something you would like to tell your uncle?"

Cody's features darkened. Jesse looked up at his uncle, his eyes glistening with unshed tears. No longer was he defiant, for he knew Cody was the only one who might yet side with him. "I've been stealing things."

The farrier exhaled heavily, furious. "Why would you do that? Do I not feed you? You have a roof over your head, clothing, a job - why would you need to steal? That would be more than enough for anyone else! What have you taken?"

"Small things," Jesse replied meekly. He could barely speak through his fear and embarrassment.

"I have a list made," Alexander chimed in, beginning to take pity on the repentant thief. "I will see it all safely back to the rightful owners. So long as everything is returned and Jesse gives up this habit—"

"I will, I swear!" the youth jumped in, eager to clear his name. A hard look from Cody silenced him.

"—then I see no reason to hold him." Alexander rose, having said his piece. He left the pair to sort out their differences after telling Jesse he would be back shortly to collect the stolen items.

The sheriff left for a brief time. He did not want to witness any punishment Cody felt appropriate for the boy. He took his time hitching Duke up to the small cart he kept at the constabulary.

When Alexander returned he found that Jesse was even more subdued, his face reddened with tears. Without a word the boy handed the items over and Alexander inventoried the haul to make sure everything reported stolen was present.

Cody watched the proceedings with a stern stare fixed on his nephew. Once everything was loaded into the cart Alexander drew the boy aside.

"Now, do I have your word that you will not steal again?" he asked seriously, trying to get the youth to look him in the eye. Jesse nodded vaguely, refusing to meet the sheriff's gaze. "Chin up lad, it cannot be all that bad," Alexander said in a lighter voice, trying to encourage the youth. Clearly he had had punishment enough and he seemed genuinely sorry for what he had done.

"I got one hell of a hiding," Jesse remarked sourly.

Cody approached and cuffed him upside the head. "Watch your language or you'll git another." The farrier turned his attention to Alexander. "I'll keep him in line, Sheriff. I appreciate you letting him off easy."

Alexander nodded, feeling a bit uncomfortable. Without another word, feeling that no more need be said, the sheriff took the stolen items to the constabulary. He would sort them and spend the balance of the day returning the items to their owners.

CHAPTER NINE

In the following days, having settled matters surrounding the petty thefts, Alexander found himself with a surplus of time. Daily he maintained the cells, oiling the locks and testing the hinges. He reasoned that spring was just around the corner and he might soon have use of the iron-bar cells.

In truth the manual work, the daily routine of checking the cells, was to keep his mind occupied. The night he had spent talking with Miss Emily Fletcher played over and over in his mind. He knew he wanted her for his wife, to have and to hold. He suspected that she regarded him as a fool, a useless bookworm, hardly suitable to be her husband. Due to this last thought he had kept well away from her, forcing himself to be lonely. He told himself he was doing her a favor, giving her the chance to find a suitable husband that would keep her safe from the dangers of the frontier.

But as the winter drew on, one endlessly white day after another, he began to grow restless. He grew bitter at himself for avoiding her, felt that he deserved better than the lot he had picked for himself. Getting up his meager courage, he determined to go out next day and speak with her father.

Assuming one of his best suits, Alexander regarded himself in the small mirror he used for shaving. The outfit suited him well, made him look professional. He had cut himself shaving that morning, as his mind had been racing with what-if scenarios. Though he had done his best to conceal the nick, it was all he could see in the mirror.

Trying to push that to the back of his mind, he found his best coat - though it was not his warmest - and a smart hat. The final touch was to wrap a gray wool scarf around his neck, muffling up against the cold. With a hard ball forming in his stomach he stepped out into the frigid day.

The snow was far deeper than he remembered. As soon as he stepped off the veranda he sunk up to his knees. Immediately he felt the cold, wet snow soak through his pant legs. Suppressing a groan he pushed on, stepping high to avoid floundering in the deep, deep snow.

The going was very hard and he found himself gasping for breath before he had gone far at all. Looking over his shoulder, he was depressed to see that he had only made it about fifteen feet from his front door. Heavy-hearted and wondering if he would make it all the way to Fletcher's general store without having a stroke, he forced himself to continue onward.

Fortunately for Alexander, as he got nearer to the center of town where more activity had taken place, the snow was packed firm and provided better walking. The only thing he needed to fear were those spots where the wind had blown persistently and polished the snow to glossy ice.

He found one such spot by sheer bad luck and only realized it once he was on his back in the street, trying to get his breath back. He had fallen right on his tailbone and it hurt a great deal. Feeling all the more a fool, with snow-soaked pants and an aching bottom, the sheriff carefully got to his feet. As he delicately continued, mindful of his sore rear end, he was much more cautious about avoiding suspicious looking spots of glassy snow.

Finally, after several misadventures, Alexander made it to his destination. He checked his pocket to ensure his billfold was still there; he did, after all, need to purchase a few supplies.

"Good day to you, Mr. Fletcher," Alexander greeted warmly as he entered the store.

"Alexander, how many times do I have to insist you use my first name?" Roy asked with a laugh.

"Chalk it up to old habits," the sheriff returned. He browsed, selecting what items he needed, and waited until the only other patron had completed his purchase and left before approaching the counter. Trying to sound casual about it, as if just making polite conversation, he asked after the shop owner's family.

"Jane is recovering from a cold, but otherwise doing well, thanks for asking." Alexander nodded politely. The shop owner continued to write up the receipt. "I don't suppose you'd heard, else I expect you would have been 'round before now with felicitations, but Emily has been pledged in marriage."

The news came as a punch to the gut. All the blood drained from Alexander's face. It took him some time to form an answer, a pause of which he was certain Roy took notice. "No, I hadn't heard. When did this happen?"

If Roy caught the odd tone in the sheriff's voice he did not mention it. He was not looking up and so missed the sudden change in the other man's complexion. "About a month gone."

"And who is the lucky man?"

"One of those railway men, actually. A foreman. He's a bit rough around the edges, but I think he'll do well for my little girl. After all, in this town there's hardly better prospects," he added with a laugh.

Alexander tried to echo the sentiment but only succeeded in miming a laugh; he was too heartbroken to mimic the sound. After paying for his goods and taking the burlap sack handed to him, he stepped out into the blindingly bright day.

He was so numb that the cold could not touch him. The sun shone, reflecting brilliantly off the snow. Blindly he stumbled his way back home, his mind blank. The trudge back through the deep snow did not even register with him. Only did he come back to himself when he was safely within the walls of the constabulary.

Then, his temper exploded.

In an unthinking rage Alexander tore through the small abode. There was little he could do in and around the cells aside from slamming the doors violently. That proved insufficient to quell his outburst of emotion.

He stomped into the dining or office area and whipped the chairs about. Accompanying the violent actions were his screams of despair, which he produced at the top of his lungs. One chair suffered a broken leg, the wooden spindle rolling across the floor. The infuriated man did not even notice the damage.

He overturned the table with some effort and then stood over it, chest heaving with each intake of breath. His screams had died out due to lack of breath. Despite the cold from which he had just come his blood was up sufficiently to make him sweat. His face was beet red, his features contorted with raw emotion.

Gradually common sense began to penetrate the veil of fury and self-loathing. Panting, Alexander subsided to his knees and sat back. Everything seemed so overwhelming, from his seemingly foolish posting in the outskirts of civilization to his depth of emotions. He had fancied himself in love, had thought the girl might feel the same. Why had he not acted sooner?

Pressing his face into his hands, Alexander tried to stifle the flood of emotions threatening to conquer him. It was not to be stayed. He began to sob bitterly.

For over a week the sheriff refused to come out of his home. He stayed in the apartment above the constabulary, watching life through the window. He took less to eat and drink, in part because of his misery and in part to ration what he had so he would not have to make a trip to the general store.

There was at least one fight in the saloon during this time. The railway men were growing restless, wanting to get to work and complete their contracts. Alexander could not be bothered to settle the dispute, which resulted in one man being toted off to the town doctor for treatment.

Byrne had been a witness to the fight. When it had started to grow beyond control, involving more than the original two as their friends took sides, the rancher had been the one to break it up.

Irritated, he looked toward the constabulary. Why had that fool of a sheriff not done his duty and intervened? The rancher intended to find out. It was not his duty, but he did not want to be the one to settle petty arguments when they had a sheriff in town for that purpose.

Swinging into the saddle, he turned Cowboy down the street toward the constabulary. Byrne rode slowly, not really wanting to initiate a social encounter with the awkward sheriff. He reminded himself that in the long run it would benefit him more than it would prove a detriment, and so he forced himself to continue onward.

As he neared the building he looked at the upper story, though he knew not why. Outlined in the window stood the form of a man; he assumed it was Alexander. The glare of sunlight on the glass made it a trifle difficult to make out details. The man saw him approaching and stepped away from the window, vanishing into the dark interior.

Leaving Cowboy ground tied outside the constabulary, the rancher stomped up the few steps onto the veranda. He knocked on the door once, assuming the sheriff had withdrawn in order to answer the door. Minutes passed and his knock went unanswered. Byrne tried again, knocking louder and more insistently. The cold wind was blowing, cutting through his coat and pants. His fingers were growing numb.

When more time passed without an answer, Byrne slammed his fist against the door and shouted. "Alexander! Get down here and open the door! I know you're in there!"

After a moment he heard hesitant footsteps within. There was a rattle of the chain being pulled and then the door opened a crack, only wide enough to show half of the lawman's pale face. "Yes? What is it?"

"Let me in, we need to talk."

"Is it really that urgent? I am in the middle of something-"

"Bull," Byrne spat. He shouldered through the door, throwing the slender man off balance. "I'm not standing out in the cold, nor am I coming back later to address this." He turned round to face the sheriff, who was resignedly closing the door against the cold. Curiously, the lawman kept his hand on the latch and did not turn around to face the other man.

"Please be quick and state your business," Alexander said in as even a tone as he could manage. His voice was rough, uneven as if he had not spoken for a very long time. Byrne noted that the sheriff's manners had been left by the wayside.

"I just broke up a fight in the saloon. That's your responsibility. Look to it in the future."

"Oh," was the only response the sheriff could muster. He still would not look at the rancher. He opened the door again, encouraging the unwanted visitor to leave.

Byrne was about to acquiesce when he got a glimpse of the other man's face. Alexander was a mere shadow of who he had been. Now he was perilously thin, the skin around his eyes dark and sunken. His clothes were ill-kempt, stained and crumpled. It was clear that he had not shaved for some time, as stubble covered the lower half of his face. The facial hair only partially hid his too-prominent cheekbones. "Are you ill?" the rancher found himself asking. Mentally he kicked himself and reminded himself that he really did not care about the sheriff's personal life. Asking the question had opened a door, a fact that Byrne realized too late.

Alexander's eyes brightened marginally as he finally met the other man's gaze. Until then he had been too ashamed to show his face; it had been an accident that the rancher saw his countenance in the first place. Still, he was glad it had happened. Here, perhaps, he might find a sympathetic soul. He closed the door, trapping Byrne in a situation in which the rancher did not want to find himself. "Have you a few minutes to spare?" The manners were back, but his voice was not quite up to par.

Byrne squirmed, shifted from foot to foot. "I do not," he began but it was as though the sheriff did not hear him or would not have his answer.

Alexander closed the space between them and seized the rancher by the arm. He stared at him with wide eyes as though possessed. Byrne tried to free himself but the smaller man's grip was shockingly strong. "All is lost!" the seemingly deranged sheriff moaned pitifully.

"Whatever it is, it can't be as bad as all that," Byrne replied, uncertain of the other's mental state. Had the sheriff gone completely mad in the course of his first winter on the frontier?

"But it is, *it is!*" Alexander insisted forcefully, shaking Byrne's arm to emphasize his words.

The rancher saw no way of escaping except to see the conversation through to the end. "Alright then, tell me what's happened." The last thing he wanted to do was waste his time being a counselor to a fool who had come to the boundaries of civilization only to find he could not cope with the isolation, the elements, or any number of facts of life out there. However, he found he had little choice.

Alexander dragged him down the narrow hall between the cells. Pushing his guest toward the only chair at the table, he began to pace to and fro in great agitation.

Byrne looked around, hoping to find an escape. Once more he was chagrined to realize that the crazed man was between him and the door. He knew he could overpower Alexander if need be, but he did not want to be charged with laying violent hands on the sheriff. Reluctantly, the rancher settled on the chair and waited for Alexander to begin his tale.

Much to his relief the tale was quickly told. "I will confess to you, man to man, what plagues my mind: the woman I love is engaged to be married."

"Congratulations?" Byrne replied after a moment, puzzling through the brief statement. His face held an uncertain expression.

"Not to me!" the sheriff exclaimed violently, whirling on his captive guest. His eyes were wild, bloodshot.

Byrne recoiled. He had never dealt with a madman before. "Oh," he managed. "I'm sorry." In truth, he could care less. All he wanted was to get back to his homestead and never deal with the sheriff again.

Alexander turned in a tight circle as if he had no idea what to do with his energy.

"How long have you been moping about in here?" Another stupid question.

"Since I found out."

"And when was that?"

"Not sure. Maybe a week ago, maybe two," he was calming down, his voice becoming very sad. He looked about as if searching for somewhere to sit down. The only unoccupied chair stood in the corner, cockeyed, one leg broken off.

"What's her name?" Maybe if he kept the sheriff talking he would calm down and Byrne would be able to leave.

"Miss Emily Fletcher." The sheriff, obviously smitten, pronounced her name with a sickeningly sweet, whimsical tone. His eyes got a distant look in them.

"Roy's girl?"

Alexander nodded. His eyes were vacant now, lacking the feverish fire they had held moments before. His whole frame seemed to stoop as if he was exhausted, the fight gone from him. The rancher hoped this was the beginning of the end of their strange conversation.

"So, you say you love her?"

"With all my soul."

Byrne bit his lip to keep from laughing at the ridiculously sappy answer. He very much doubted that a man of Alexander's limited experience knew the true passion of love; to him this sounded like a case of puppy love gone bad. Still, he could relate in some respect, for all men go through that first touch of madness they think true love to be. "Well then why are you moping about this shack? Have you told her father of your intentions?"

"By the time I got up the courage to do so he informed me that some railway man had already asked for her hand."

"But did you tell him anyway?"

"No, I never did get that far."

Byrne leaned back in his chair. Some part of him was actually enjoying the conversation, enjoying picking apart the puzzle of emotions. Considering the sheriff had brought it upon himself by beginning the discussion, Byrne allowed himself to enjoy the fact that he was opening Alexander's emotional wound afresh. "The more fool you," he remarked.

"What do you mean?" Alexander's voice was suddenly defensive. Apparently the man did have some fight left in him.

"Meaning, I would think any clever gentleman would prefer a sheriff as a son-in-law to a common railway worker."

Alexander stopped and shifted his weight. He was beginning to see the point of the other's argument. "If she is already spoken for it is too late."

"I see. You're not willing to fight for her. Well then, she can't mean all that much to you." Byrne did not know, himself, why he was poking the proverbial bear. He had no investment in the matching of Sheriff Alexander Judge and Miss Emily Fletcher. Why he was playing matchmaker, he had no idea.

The sheriff's blood rose at the other's dismissive tone. He took a firm step forward, waving his finger in the air threateningly. For a moment he was so choked with emotion that he could not speak. Then, he found his voice. "I love her."

"So fight for her," Byrne replied evenly, slowly, keeping his eyes locked on the other man's, watching for any sign of violent intent. He very much doubted Alexander would try to strangle him, but the man was in an unpredictable state of mind and could not be trusted.

Alexander heaved a deep sigh as if collecting himself. He closed his eyes for a long moment and when he opened them again he seemed more composed. "You are right. I was a coward. A real man would fight for the woman he loves."

The rancher nodded slowly. He hoped he had not put violent thoughts in the other's head; surely the sheriff would not attack a man because he had unwittingly been engaged to the woman that was loved by another.

"Go to her father, tell him your mind." Byrne risked standing, hoping that his counsel had been well received and that he could now make his escape. As he stepped around the sheriff, the slender man did not try to stop him. "Good day."

"Good day," Alexander replied vacantly, his mind already wandering elsewhere. Byrne had almost made it to the front door when Alexander rushed up behind him and stopped him again. "But what can I possibly say?"

Byrne rolled his eyes, exasperated. He had been so close. "Just say what comes naturally. Lay out the facts. Prove to him that you are the best match for his daughter, if you can."

"Are you certain? How can I possibly do that?"

The rancher tipped his head in a semblance of a nod. "Fairly certain. It's worked for men in the past, I reckon it can't do you any harm."

"But what do I say?"

"Don't get so hooked up on what to say. Just get the guts to go and do it. You'll figure out the exact words when you share what's on your mind. That's what I did and it worked out alright." The rancher bit his lip. He had said more than he intended. He hoped the last sentence would go over the sheriff's head, that he would be too absorbed with his own dilemma to catch it. "Now, I must get going," he added hastily, pulling free of the other's grasp and making for the door.

Alexander would have thrown questions at him indefinitely but Byrne was firm in his actions and made good his escape into the cold day. Feeling abandoned, the sheriff closed the door without watching the rancher mount and ride away. Byrne had left him with much to think over.

~~~~~~~~~~

Acting on the rancher's advice, which Alexander took to be sound, the sheriff made his first public appearance in a long time on the following Sunday. He had bathed and shaved. His clothes had been given a thorough washing and now were fresh, clean, and wrinkle-free. There was little he could do to improve his complexion and figure in so brief a time but he made his best effort. He took regular meals and went for rides out into the deserted countryside even on the coldest of days for a change of scenery and a bit of physical activity. Duke was spirited, having had so little work to do, and it took all of the sheriff's concentration to keep the gelding in check.

Before departing for church Alexander went over his appearance in minute detail in the mirror. His eyes and cheeks were still a bit sunken but there was nothing to remedy that. Aside from his face, he decided that the rest of his person would pass inspection. He was wearing his Sunday best, right down to the brightly polished star on his dress jacket.

He had tacked Duke before getting dressed in his best, and so when he stepped out the back door his black horse was waiting for him, ready to go. Climbing into the saddle, Alexander turned his mount toward the church which was situated outside of the town proper to provide enough land to house the cemetery.

Making sure to tie the reins so securely that he felt confident that even his escape artist of a horse would not be able to free himself, Alexander entered the church. He was punctual and had ample time to mingle before finding a seat and settling down for the sermon.

In due course the Fletchers arrived as well. Roy escorted his wife, Jane, to their customary seats which were just across the aisle and a few rows ahead of where the sheriff had seated himself. Emily came in after them on the arm of a coarse-looking man, assumedly her fiancé.

As the family passed by Alexander greeted them, tipping his hat respectfully. Roy and Jane returned the gesture cordially. Emily gave him a look that confused him; he thought it was a small smile of acknowledgement but it seemed far too sad an expression.

Seeing her with another man made Alexander feel physically ill. Anger rose within him, though he had no real grievances with the other man. The railway man had simply been the faster to act. For a moment Alexander considered abandoning his mission. He wanted nothing more than to leave immediately, pack up his belongings and leave Flintridge forever. He knew that seeing her on another's arm would always cause him pain.

Then, he remembered his conversation with the stoic rancher and the events which had led up to it. He refused to allow himself to fall back into that state of pitifulness. Summoning his courage, Alexander sat through the service and awaited his chance.

Throughout the whole sermon he was on the edge of his seat. Not because the preacher's droning voice held any great interest to him, but because his blood was thrumming. He wanted to speak his mind, to get the whole awful business over with.

When the service finally ended Alexander shot out of his seat. He had to wait for other patrons to file out before he could turn up the aisle and approach the Fletchers. He greeted the family with as genteel a manner as he could muster, engaging in general conversation. The fiancé was introduced to him as one Budd Stevens.

"It is a pleasure to meet you, Mr. Stevens," Alexander lied, smiling, though the expression did not reach his eyes. The sheriff was intensely aware of Miss Fletcher's eyes resting on him. She seemed very shy that morning, saying only a handful of words, almost none of which were addressed to him.

As conversation continued Alexander's prejudice against Emily's fiancé grew and grew. The man already made a point of referring to Roy Fletcher as 'Pa' and his conversation was as coarse as he, himself, looked.

The family was saying their goodbyes when Alexander got the confidence to speak. "Roy, excuse me but might I have a moment's conversation in private?"

Roy looked at his family to see if any of them were in any great hurry. Seeing no reason to rush, he nodded. "Well, sure." Alexander drew him aside to a spot that he hoped was out of earshot of the others. "Mr. Fletcher, please do excuse my impudence but I absolutely must speak my mind."

"Of course sheriff, what can I do for you?"

"It is in regard of your daughter, sir. I realize that I am too late, yet I must speak. Your daughter is the most beautiful woman I have ever seen. She is a tender-hearted girl, a true gem. Without her I feel my life would be empty and unfulfilling. I know that I was a fool to not seek your blessing earlier and now I have lost my chance. But I am begging you to reconsider this marriage engagement. If you were to break it off with Mr. Stevens I would ask your permission to court Miss Fletcher and eventually wed her." He paused and took in a deep breath, having blurted his speech out rapidly.

Roy stared at him, dumbfounded. The burly man could not help his bearded jaw hanging slack, the sheriff's pronouncement had been that unexpected. Alexander licked his lips and furrowed his brow, suddenly worried that he had spoken horribly out of turn.

When Roy laughed and hugged him, Alexander hardly knew what to do. "Thank God you spoke up boy," the shopkeeper said. He held the sheriff at arm's length and regarded him; as compared to the man currently lined up to be his son-in-law this specimen was all one could ask for. "If you really mean all that, she's yours."

"You will not even consult her? Who is to say she feels the same about me?"

"The only reason Emily agreed to the preposterous arrangement she is in at present is because you were not making a move. She feared she would become the town spinster and that drove her to seek out a husband, no matter how unsuitable he might be. I wish she had approached you from the get-go but I guess all's well that ends well. Budd!" He turned around, addressing the man attending to his daughter.

"Yes Pa?"

"The engagement's off. Stop calling me 'Pa' and get yourself back to the saloon where you belong." Though Roy's voice was friendly enough, his words were impossible to soften. Budd looked absolutely crestfallen. However, he realized he had little choice. He noted how Miss Fletcher's face brightened at hearing the announcement and it crushed his pride. Though his feelings may have been unrequited, he had felt some degree of love for the fine young woman.

"Yes sir," Budd muttered, forcing himself to step away from her. As soon as he was out of arm's reach she took off, running over to her father and the sheriff. Dejectedly Budd Stevens turned and left the church.

Disregarding all sense of propriety, Emily Fletcher threw herself into Alexander's arms. She hugged him tight around the neck, burying her face into his shirtfront.

Dumbfounded by her bold actions, Alexander took a moment to recover his wits before hugging her back. He lifted her off the ground and spun her round, smiling like a daft fool. She was smiling too, her face absolutely shining, tears of joy in her eyes.

Alexander stopped spinning her and held her in a close embrace. She turned her head up and snuck a kiss, heedless of the fact that her father was watching them closely. The sheriff blushed, having received his first proper kiss. Smiling goofily, he turned to look at the man that would soon be his father-in-law. "Thank you," he managed around the knot of emotion in his throat.

Roy nodded, a smile turning up the corner of his mouth. He put an arm around his own wife and Jane gave him a kiss on the cheek.

"Thank goodness," she murmured. Jane warmed to the idea of Alexander as a son-in-law far more readily than she had to Budd.

"Well, since we're in church already we may as well consult the preacher," Roy suggested.

"Thank you father, thank you!" Emily chirped ecstatically. She trotted over to him, gave him a quick peck on the cheek, and then returned to Alexander's side. He offered her his arm, which she took and leaned close to him. She was to have the husband she had dreamed of since the day he had come to town.

Alexander went through the proceedings in a fog of insuppressible joy; he had taken a gamble for once and it had paid off. The preacher's services were engaged, general plans were laid, and a date was set. They were to be married the first day of spring.

The next day Budd Stevens saddled his horse after having spent the night in the saloon, drinking away his woes. He kicked the unfortunate animal into a gallop, heading nowhere in particular. Those that watched him flee noted that he was horribly drunk, yanking his horse this way and that as it ran.

That night a blizzard came up. The land was smothered in a blanket of snow and a bitter wind blew. The citizens of Flintridge kept to their homes that night, for the cold was bone-numbing.

Alexander ate dinner with the Fletchers while the snow piled up in the street. Outside only the howling wind was to be heard. Emily picked halfheartedly at her meal, glancing often at the frosted window.

"A penny for your thoughts," Roy said finally, wanting to break his daughter out of her melancholy.

Emily started, almost dropping her fork. "What? Oh. Nothing really, father," she lied unconvincingly.

Alexander was watching his future bride with a furrowed brow. He was very concerned at her unusual silence and wanted to do anything he could to lighten her mood. "Please tell me," he implored in a gentle voice.

Emily bit her lip, thinking over whether or not she should speak. Finally, she decided on honesty. "I was thinking about Budd Stevens," she remarked tentatively. When the others only looked at her, encouraging her to continue, she did so. "I heard he raced out of town this morning, riding hard and very drunk. They said he was headed toward Glenn Rock. As far as I know he has not returned to Flintridge. Could he be out in this weather?"

"He might be," her father answered in a level voice, never one to soften the truth.

Miss Fletcher gave a small gasp of worry and went back to moving food around her plate with her fork. Alexander reached over and laid his hand upon hers. She glanced up at him, her beautiful hazel eyes glazed with unshed tears. "I just can't help but feel it is my fault. It was rather callous of me to throw him off so."

No one at the table had a good response to offer. It had been a brash move for certain, enacted in a moment of intense emotion with no regard for Stevens' feelings. The meal continued in silence. Alexander kept his hand on Emily's, offering her silent comfort.

Days later, when the weather started to break and construction was able to continue on laying the train tracks, Budd Stevens did not report for work. As far as anyone knew he had perished in the blizzard that came up not long after his departure. Optimists, like Alexander and his soon-to-be family, hoped he had at least made the shelter of Glenn Rock before the storm overtook him.

~~~~~~~~~~

Spring came and saw Miss Emily Fletcher wed to Sheriff Alexander Judge. She took his name with great joy. The ceremony, the most lavish ever seen in Flintridge, was the talk of the town. Roy had financed it, feeling that nothing was too good for his only daughter. Alexander was welcomed into the Fletcher family warmly.

The sheriff wrote home, eager to share the wonderful news with his family.

He received several letters of congratulations from his parents, distant relatives, and former associates from law school. These he dutifully shared with Emily, including the missive from his mother welcoming the young woman into the Judge family.

As the world began to thaw, recovering from the stifling grip of winter, ground was broken on a parcel of land owned by Roy Fletcher but set a way off from his main lot. His wedding present to the couple was to be a new house, one they could call their own. He did not feel that the cramped quarters above the jail were suitable for his daughter and her new husband.

Alexander was speechless with appreciation. While they waited for the house to be completed they stayed in the constabulary apartment. Often they would spend a day at the Fletcher residence when Jane proclaimed that she missed having another woman around.

With work commencing on the railroad and the town's population growing constantly, Alexander found he had more to do in his professional capacity. Emily took advantage of her husband's absence to spend time with her mother and father, apprenticing at the general store. Roy Fletcher had insisted that his daughter learn how to run the business so she and Alexander would have something to fall back on should the sheriff's salary fail.

With the snow leaving the country travel became easier. The stagecoach line was running swiftly, delivering mail and payroll regularly. Life in Flintridge was booming. No one stopped to consider that the warmer weather also meant that those with nefarious purposes could travel more readily as well.

CHAPTER TEN

Early one frosty morning a pair of rough looking men left their rooms at the inn and sat down at a table in the saloon. They were holed up in Lame Deer, a town devoid of the influence of the law. Even at such an early hour they were not alone in the saloon: men who had taken too much to drink the night before lay passed out in chairs and underneath tables.

The younger of the pair ran his hand down his stubbled face, his fingers habitually tracing the scar that ran across his left cheek. He was shorter than his companion but seemed more substantial than the older man, having more muscle and flesh on his bones. His brown hair was disheveled, testifying to the fact that he had just woken. "Why'd you get me up so early, Gravedigger?" he asked groggily. He had partaken in much drink the night before and was suffering the effects of it. His nearly black eyes were heavily hooded.

The Gravedigger, alias Cliff Hayes, regarded his friend - if Pistol Lawson could be called that - with a level gray stare. His darkly tanned skin, weathered almost to the consistency of leather, was taut on his thin face. Hayes leaned back in his chair and nonchalantly pulled back his long black hair, tying it with a strip of leather. "We're leaving town today," he informed the younger man in a gravelly voice.

Lawson perked up at the unexpected pronouncement. He blinked rapidly, trying to get his fogged mind around the idea. "But it's too cold."

"The weather's changed, idiot," Hayes informed him harshly with a sneer. Not for the first time he regretted taking on another co-leader after the last one left.

"Where're we going then?" Pistol asked. He was not offended by the older man's harsh words, having grown accustomed to them over the last few years. The youth yawned and stretched.

"Flintridge."

Lawson cracked one eye open mid-stretch. He could see that Hayes was serious. Heaving a sigh, knowing better than to argue, he nodded. "Alright. I'll go round up the boys." Snatching his hat up off the table, he planted it on his head and shuffled to the back of the tavern.

Cliff Hayes watched him go disinterestedly. Pistol had a quick temper, as his name implied, but the wizened bandit felt certain he had the youth well in hand. He had had many years of practice commanding a band of ruthless outlaws.

At the back of the saloon Lawson could be heard pounding on door after door. "C'mon boys, let's go! White! Travis! Get your sorry carcasses out here! Jarrod Cooke, set your whore aside!"

The commanding shouts brought about a flurry of activity. The bandits stumbled out of their rooms, half clothed, in response to the summons.

Jarrod appeared with a scantily clad woman hanging onto his shoulders. "This had better be good, Pistol," he growled in a thick voice. He was still drunk.

Zack White rubbed sleepily at his balding pate. "What's the ruckus?" He was a large man, burly with much hair on his chest. His wits were not as strong as his body.

"Pack up boys, we're moving out," Pistol announced in a voice far louder than necessary.

"Why?" Travis Brown asked, genuinely curious. He was a scrawny individual and had a habit of being jittery under pressure. The prospect of leaving their comfortable inn to break trail through the snow did not appeal to him. His pale blue eyes darted about nervously as he realized that by speaking up he may have inadvertently challenged Lawson's authority. He brushed a clod of greasy blonde hair off his forehead, licked his lips and shuffled from foot to foot.

Instead of berating the young bandit, Pistol turned to Hayes as if to pass the question on to the primary leader. The structure of the gang was an interesting one: Cliffs Hayes was the brains of the outfit while Pistol Lawson was the outspoken public face. The ambitious youth was not entirely content with the setup but even he could not deny that the old thief was far cleverer than he.

Feeling the weight of several gazes on him, Cliff Hayes steepled his fingers. He bided his time, knowing that withholding information made the listeners all the more eager to hear it.

Just as Hayes was opening his mouth to speak, Derek Ward emerged from his room. The so-called 'gentleman bandit' was attired in his usual fine clothing, his blonde hair slicked back beneath his smart hat. He tucked his pocket watch away as he joined the group.

"We're going to Flintridge," Hayes began, repeating that bit of information for Ward's benefit. "Lame Deer is as disinteresting as the name suggests. There is nothing here for us, no wealth to be stolen. It's a dried up hole in the wall, good only for wenching and drinking."

"Who needs more?" Jarrod interrupted, laughing heartily at his own joke. The others, except Ward, joined in too.

Hayes silenced the interruption with a sharp, steely look. "Flintridge, on the other hand, has only a pathetic man posing as a sheriff to protect it. With the railroad coming there is bound to be a lot of money heading that way. I say we strike before the snow is gone, strike when they least expect us to come."

"Our horses will drop dead before we get there," Derek remarked quietly, crossing his arms. A frown turned down the corners of his mouth. "Flintridge is too far and, unless you have information we do not, there is no trail broken through the drifts."

"There's the stagecoach road," Hayes reminded him.

"We would be sitting ducks," Ward scoffed. His gray-green eyes were hard as he looked at his leader, narrowing his eyes as he tried to guess the reasoning behind the unexpected move.

As Hayes stared Derek down he seemed to see something in the other man's demeanor that displeased him. The Gravedigger stood and covered the ground between them in a few long strides. Before reaching Derek, Hayes had a knife drawn, was clutching the handle and pointing the blade back toward his arm. He caught Ward's shoulder and pressed the knife to his throat. "Come again?" he whispered in a ragged voice.

Derek stared hard at him, unmoved. He had known Cliff Hayes for many years and knew that this was a show put on for the impression it would make on the duller members of the gang. Derek knew his part to play and, not wanting to meet an early end, played it. "Nothing. Never mind."

"Thought so." Hayes snapped the knife away, sheathing it in one fluid motion. He turned his back on Ward and addressed the rest of the men. "Saddle up, we leave in an hour!"

He turned to Derek Ward, the gang's right hand man, and added in a whisper: "See if you can't find a few more men to add to our numbers. We have some unfinished business with Byrne Jameson."

~~~~~~~~~~

Byrne took full advantage of the nice weather. Daily he worked with each of his horses, even the nasty palomino. His back was greatly improved, almost returned to normal strength. Rarely did the injury cause him any pain. Still, Ivey kept a close eye on him and if he even thought of putting a saddle on the wild mustang stallion she put him in his place.

There was an auction upcoming in a town several days' ride east of Flintridge. Byrne informed his wife that he would take the mares and halter broke foals to this sale to try and bolster their income. Though he had had offers, he refused to sell them to the railway, knowing they would be worked hard, possibly to death. He wanted better for the animals he had spent so much time with.

So, he saddled Cowboy one fine spring morning and tied the horses to be auctioned in a line. He had tamed them sufficiently and was fairly confident that they would not try to run away, but he would take no chances; they were living gold to him. There was no telling what feelings or memories of freedom the open plains might arouse amongst the herd.

Ivey watched him go with a heavy heart. She was plagued with a sense of foreboding. Before he left she had told Byrne as much; he had laughed kindly, kissed her, and assured her it was all in her head. He would return within the month and their lives would be much easier, as he would have money in his pocket.

The southern girl was left alone on a ranch on the frontier with only a dog, a mule, and an untouchable palomino mustang for company.

~~~~~~~~~~

The house Mr. Fletcher was building for his daughter and son-in-law was nearing completion in late April. It was to be a fine structure, only a single story but plenty large enough to accommodate a young couple just starting out. In his free time Alexander helped with the construction of the house and outbuildings, including a corral for Duke. He knew he could still keep the horse at the constabulary but he felt it would be more convenient to have him at the house, just in case.

Since marrying a local girl, the sheriff had received a warmer welcome from the townsfolk. He was now considered one of them. No longer did he get strange looks when he entered the saloon or strode down the main street, waving at everyone he saw.

Regarding his duties as sheriff, he had even given up his notion of ending the saloon's shady side business. After all, he reasoned, they were just trying to make a living like the rest of them.

Then, one spring night, everything changed.

Alexander and Emily were settling down to dinner with their parents. Jane Fletcher had gone to a great deal of trouble in preparing the meal, as she always did when her daughter and son-in-law came to visit. Though they had assured her such effort was unnecessary, she persisted in putting out the best food her cooking skills could offer.

Roy was just cutting the beef roast when a horrible ruckus sounded from without. It sounded like a stampede. Hooves pounded the earth, screams both human and horse rose into the air, shots were fired. The smell of smoke filtered into the small house, raising dire forebodings.

"Jane, Emily, get under the table," Roy instructed in a strong voice that left no room for argument.

At once the men were on their feet. Roy went for his shotgun while Alexander fingered the pistol he kept holstered on his belt. As one they went to the front door, instructing the ladies to stay put.

Using the muzzle of his rifle, Roy pushed the curtain at a front window aside and peered out into the early night. Dusk still permeated the land, lending a strange light to the proceedings. Alexander ducked his head below the rifle stock and looked out the window as well. Out in the street it was sheer, bloody chaos.

The sheriff counted six - no, he corrected himself, eight - horsemen charging up and down the main drag. They held their guns raised, firing shots left and right indiscriminately. Already a few bodies, some dead, some merely injured, lay in the street. The light was not strong enough to offer identification at that distance.

Further down, nearer to the saloon, one house was alight. Flames licked along the framework, creeping toward the roof, threatening to consume the structure. Though the residents had escaped into the street they now faced the danger of the outlaws' guns.

Without a thought for their own safety, Alexander and Roy pushed through the door out onto the porch. The sheriff was in the lead, his pistol in hand. His usual cowardice had drained away in his desperate need to protect the woman he loved. Now ice water ran through his veins, giving him a clear purpose. Leveling his pistol, he knocked a passing rogue clear off his horse with a single shot.

The action did not go unnoticed by the rest of the gang. They mustered together, riding hard toward the veranda on which Alexander and Roy stood. Roy hoisted the rifle, settling the stock against his shoulder, and fired. He was not a good shot, but the bullets striking the ground did spook one of the horses in the front of the pack. The animal screamed, rearing, and toppled over. The other riders had to swing quickly to either side, breaking off their charge. The fallen horse regained its feet and took off at a gallop, kicking up its heels in fear as it went. Its rider lay stunned for a moment.

Alexander leapt off the porch, gun ready, intending to finish the outlaw off. So focused was he on the fallen man that he failed to realize the approach of the riders. He pointed the pistol at the man lying in the dirt, who in turn pointed his own pistol at the sheriff. The riders bore down on the pair of them.

"Good luck firing before I do," the man on the ground sneered. "Or before one of the gang takes you out."

"Judge!" Roy shouted, trying to warn his son-in-law.

Alexander looked up. The approaching riders were almost upon him.

Pistol shots rang out, peppering the ground around him. Instinctively the sheriff jumped about, doing a foolish dance, trying to avoid being hit. One bullet grazed the side of his calf but his adrenaline was pumping so hard that he did not feel the wound. Alexander looked up, taking his gun off the man at his feet.

The horses charged around them. The outlaw on the ground raised his hands to protect his head and hoped he would not get stepped on. With his fellows around him, confusing the sheriff, he was able to gain his feet and squirm out of the tangle of horses.

One rider aimed to have his steed trample the sheriff, but Alexander managed to twist and turn and avoid being hit by the massive equine shoulder. Numerous sets of hooves churned the ground around him as Alexander ducked and weaved between horses, trying to stay out of shot of the riders. In the melee he was trapped and confused, hardly able to see anything more than the haunches, flanks, or shoulders of horses.

One of the bandits swung his rifle stock like a club, landing a glancing blow to Alexander's head. The force was sufficient enough that the sheriff fell, stunned for a few seconds. In those seconds the outlaws organized themselves, encircling him and aiming their guns at his chest and head. Blinking, Alexander realized that he was going to die.

Bullets whizzed through the air, drawing the attention of the gang. Instinctively they turned and fired back at the source. Alexander watched Roy fall amidst the barrage.

Shocked, unable to comprehend what he had witnessed, the sheriff gained his feet. He stumbled through the confused mass of horses, somehow avoiding the attention of the gang. When they turned back to finish Alexander off, he was not where they had left him.

The bandits looked around, shouting to each other. None of them had seen where the lawman had got to. They spread out, searching for their quarry. Their shouts to each other echoed in the otherwise silent street.

The house continued to burn, now a lost cause as the flames had reached the entirety of the structure. The fire was already reaching toward the surrounding buildings. Sparks flew into the air as the inferno burned.

Alexander had no time to think about anything but his own survival. Still dizzy from the strike to his head, he only could think of getting to safety. Sneaking from behind the mob of horses, he sprinted toward one of the narrow alleys between buildings. He tucked himself into the shadows and watched with a pounding heart as the outlaws began to search for him.

"Come on out sheriff! Die fighting!" one of the bandits screamed, waving his gun in the air. The group laughed, their cackles sounding eerily like a pack of coyotes.

The lawman ducked behind a stack of barrels as one of them rode by his hiding place. Alexander watched warily, fearing he would be found out. Belatedly it dawned on him that he had seen the man in the saddle before. Searching his memory, he tried to put a name to the face. When he did, his blood ran cold. It was Budd Stevens, the man to whom Emily had first been engaged, the man who had ridden out into the wilderness and was presumed dead in the blizzard that followed hard upon. Alexander let out a pent-up breath as the man passed by without discovering him.

As his breathing evened out, his sense of duty returned to him. After all, he was the law in Flintridge, it was his responsibility to confront and defeat the gang of outlaws. Adding to his intent, solidifying his purpose, was the fact that the gang had struck down his father-in-law. He wanted to learn how Roy fared; perhaps he had only been wounded. Alexander had not been able to tell where the older man had been hit. He reloaded his pistol.

Creeping out of his hiding place, Alexander looked up and down the street. There was no outlaw immediately nearby. They all seemed to be looking in any direction but at him. Perfect. The sheriff slunk along the fronts of the buildings, using any cover he could find as he worked his way back toward the Fletcher residence.

When he was on a parallel to where Roy's body lay further out in the street he paused. He looked about again, hoping none of the bandits were nearby or looking in his direction. It was a miracle he had not been discovered thus far; going out in the open would really be tempting fate.

Again, the coast was clear.

Alexander crawled on all fours out from beneath the promenade. He hastened across the dirt, ignoring the small rocks and pebbles that jabbed into his palms and knees. Reaching Roy, he grabbed the older man's shoulder and pulled his weight around so he could see his face. The shopkeeper's eyes were wide open, staring unseeingly up at Alexander. The sheriff shuddered all the way to his bones and released his grip on the body. That dead, vacant stare only confirmed the strong hint of the enormous bloodstain that encircled the body.

Alexander took a shuddering breath, suddenly feeling very ill. He feared he would retch then and there. For him, there was but one more thing he could do. He picked up the rifle lying beside Roy's body and cracked it open, casting off the used shells. Taking the extra ammunition off the corpse, he reloaded the weapon.

"Well, look what we have here," a cruel, heavily accented voice drawled. Alexander heard a pistol cock. Taking a shuddering breath, he slipped the last cartridge into the rifle, snapped it closed, and swung the gun up, aiming at the source of the voice. The bandit scoffed. He was leaning forward in the saddle, holding the pistol steady. His eyes were a flinty color, his weathered face contorted in a sneer. "I know you. Seen you before."

The sheriff held the rifle as steady as he could. It was difficult to control the furious trembling in his limbs. "Then you will know that as sheriff of this town I can place you under arrest."

"Oh, can you now?" The man sneered. "That'd be a neat trick." It took a moment for Alexander to remember who he was, what role he played in the gang. It was not reassuring to come to the realization that he was talking with one of the most bloodthirsty killers in the land: Cliff Hayes. His skin began to crawl.

While he was having a stare-down with the gang leader, other members of the gang surrounded him. Once again Alexander found himself in the center of a circle of guns. His body trembled uncontrollably. This time there would be no friendly shots to distract the outlaws. This time he would surely die.

He closed his eyes, mentally kicking himself. If he had just stood down perhaps he could have avoided this. Perhaps he would have lived to watch over his new wife, perhaps his father-in-law would not have died trying to protect him. He felt so stupid.

"Don't faint on us now, sheriff. Not again. Once was embarrassing enough," another coarse voice said. "There's no honor in killing an unconscious man."

Alexander's eyes snapped open. He knew the instance to which the outlaw - in this case, Pistol Lawson - referred. It had been an unfortunate incident when he was out east helping to hunt the outlaw gangs. His posse had cornered the Hayes-Lawson gang in a gully jutting off the mountain range. They thought it was a done deal, that there was no possible way for the gang to escape.

At that time the Hayes-Lawson gang had numbered only five. To this day Alexander was not certain how they had managed it. There had been an explosion, chaos ensued, and while the lawmen were calming their steeds and taking stock of their condition the bandits had slipped away. Alexander's horse had taken off instinctively after the fleeing horses belonging to the bandits. When they realized they were being pursued they had swung back. Shots had spooked Duke and he had thrown his rider. Alexander had been shaken by the whole episode. His knees had been so weak that he could scarcely stand as he confronted the bandits. Hearing their weapons primed had been the last straw for the sheriff's strained nerves and he had collapsed. Help had arrived in the knick of time, then, and the outlaws were forced to flee.

"There is no honor in an unfair fight, either," Alexander replied in a harsh tone of voice. "Drop your weapons and come along quietly."

The thieves all chuckled. Pistol Lawson holstered his weapon, still laughing maliciously. "I like your spirit, sheriff. Question for you though: when's the last time you got paid?"

"I cannot see how that is any concern of yours," Alexander replied coolly.

"How about the mail? When did that come in last?"

"Stop your pointless questioning."

Lawson reached into his satchel and Alexander tensed. He did not know if the bandit had another weapon. Much to his surprise the object that emerged clenched in the man's grimy fingers was an envelope, badly stained from excessive travel. "I only ask because we held up a stagecoach awhile back and found this little gem. Here, it's for you." He tossed it onto the ground at Alexander's feet.

Alexander glanced down at the filthy paper. Reluctantly, slowly, he stooped to pick it up, always keeping his gun leveled at the bandit leader. Once he had retrieved it he drew himself to his full height and adjusted his grip on the rifle.

"Aren't you even going to read it?" Lawson taunted.

"And give you the chance to shoot me while I am distracted?"

"Nah, we're not going to kill you, Mr. Judge."

"What?!" Budd Stevens barked indignantly.

"Not so long as you do the smart thing, that is," the leader allowed with a stern look at the man who had interrupted him.

"How do you define the 'smart thing'?" Alexander wanted to know. Cynicism was creeping into his voice.

"Read the letter."

Again Alexander found he had little choice but to do as he was told. He noticed that the envelope was already opened, the letter having already been read. Feeling that he was giving in, abandoning his cause, he lowered his rifle and unfolded the letter.

At the top of the paper was an official-looking seal. The sheriff began to read, extremely conscious of the guns still pointed at him. Very quickly, however, he became absorbed in the text. The expression on his face changed rapidly from disbelief to consternation to depression.

"Rather changes the rules of the game, now doesn't it?" The triumphant grin on Lawson's face was mirrored in his voice.

Alexander's jaw quivered. He could not fathom the enormity of what he had just read. The rifle fell from his slackened grip, raising a cloud of dust where it landed. When he finally looked up his eyes were sad and defeat was written in every line of his body.

Lawson narrowed his eyes as he regarded the sheriff. He glanced at his co-leader, on his right, and The Gravedigger nodded. "I take that to mean you're surrendering."

"Never." Alexander's voice was barely a whisper, hoarse and miserable. He was trying to hold back tears. He took a shuddering breath and glanced at Roy's body, lying in the street.

"Our terms are really quite reasonable, Mr. Sheriff," Pistol Lawson said, twirling his pistol round and round. "You get to live. We get this town. You can even continue to stay here if you like, just not in any official capacity since you don't have one no more." He chuckled, showing off his silver tooth.

Alexander's chest felt as if it would burst. His mind was in a fog, unable to process all that was happening in so short a time. The letter that quivered in his grip was a missive stating that it was becoming too costly to continue to keep lawmen posted in far-off outposts such as Flintridge. It stripped him of his commission and informed him that no further payments would come to him from the government for his services. Flintridge was to be left to thrive or fail on its own. If private interests chose to hire public defenders it would be on their dime.

None of it made a lick of sense to Alexander.

"We're waiting on your answer sheriff."

Choking on silent sobs, Alexander glanced again at the body of his late father-in-law, lying in the dust just yards away. One of the horses had apparently run over it for it lay twisted and broken, not as he had last seen it. Had everything they had built out there, everything they had accomplished been for naught? According to the letter, it had.

"Alright," Alexander conceded finally, feeling his soul break as he said the words, "you win."

The gang let out whoops and cheers. They kicked their horses to action, trotting them round and round the ex-sheriff of Flintridge. Behind them the house they had set fire to was collapsing in a loud rumble of charred timbers. Flames licked at the structures on each side of the devastated house. Frantic owners ran to and from the well, tossing buckets of water in an effort to quell the fire.

Alexander flinched as the outlaws fired their guns into the air. They circled him, whooping and hollering with their sick joy.

Dejected, he looked for a hole in their formation. He dashed out between two horses and stalked with head bowed toward the Fletcher's home. He passed by Roy's body and gave it a silent promise that he would see the noble man received a proper burial. That was the last thing he knew he could do right.

~~~~~~~~~~

A great feeling of oppression fell over Flintridge in the ensuing days. The gang gave their fallen comrade, the one Alexander had shot at the beginning of the engagement, a burial. They paid little heed to propriety, digging a random hole in the poor, sad graveyard attached to the outlying church. The body was unceremoniously dumped in and covered with dirt. They then went promptly to the saloon and drank themselves silly. They did not pay so much as a penny toward their bill.

For Roy Fletcher a more traditional funeral was planned. Alexander had refused to let the women of the house see Roy's body before it had been cleaned up and prepared by the local physician. Everyone in town, excluding the outlaws, attended the service, overflowing the small church.

As they stood beside the grave, watching the coffin being lowered into the ground, Alexander had a comforting arm around his wife and mother-in-law. He felt as sad as they; he had truly respected and loved Roy as a father. He owed the man a great deal, he reminded himself, tightening his hold on his wife. If not for Roy's straightforward character he would never have won the hand of the woman he loved more than life itself.

Immediately after the funeral there was another disturbance caused by the gang. As the attendees were returning to their homes they came up against a line of horsemen. The Hayes-Lawson gang sat on their horses, forming a horizontal line that barred the entrance to town.

For a long time, no explanation was given. Alexander kept a firm hold of his wife and mother-in-law, ready to rush them out of harm's way if necessary. He watched the gang with narrowed eyes, hatred burning in his heart.

The three men at the center of the configuration leaned across their horses to consult with one another. Alexander recognized them as being Cliff Hayes, Pistol Lawson, and Derek Ward, the gang's right hand man. Hayes jerked his thumb in the direction of the nervously mulling crowd and spoke to Ward. The blonde-haired bandit pushed his hat down further on his head and nodded. He, like the others, wore a stoic, almost cruel look on his face.

Derek Ward whistled and waved his arm in the air, signaling others of the gang to move. Three others joined him as he trotted his horse out toward the crowd of townsfolk. Derek drew his pistol and fired a shot into the air, causing generalized panic.

As the townsfolk seethed first one way and then another, the horseback riders blocked their escape routes. Trapped, the townspeople turned in a tight mass, pressing together for communal safety.

"Now that I have your attention," Ward shouted, raising his voice to be heard over the din. "We have but one question for the lot of you: where is Byrne Jameson?"

The gang had found it strange that Byrne had not interfered in their raid, as he had done so often before. The unofficial founder of Flintridge was also its most fierce protector and the gang was taking no chances. They had to discover his whereabouts.

Ivey Jameson was amongst those who had attended the funeral. She kept her head down, avoiding making eye contact with the bandits. She did not think they would know her identity, but there was no sense in taking a chance.

"He's not here," one frightened woman announced in a shrill voice.

Derek pointed the pistol in her direction and she ducked with a terrified cry. "Where is he?" the gentleman outlaw demanded. The woman had subsided into a fit of hysterics and did not give any more information. Ward let his gun travel over the mass of bodies, seeking another individual who could be persuaded to talk.

"He's out on the range!" a man finally offered. He ducked into the crowd to hide, suspecting he would become the focus of the outlaw's unwanted attention.

"No you fool, he's in Glenn Rock!"

"He went back east."

"Dead! He's dead!"

"Auctioning mustangs I heard,"

"At his ranch."

Derek looked over his shoulder to where his bosses sat on their horses. He raised an eyebrow. "Which story do we believe?" he asked in a low voice.

Ivey lifted her head, curious to see what action the outlaw gang would take next. Her blonde hair had fallen loose from its knot and hung in disordered strands around her face. She brushed it behind her ear absently, all her attention focused on the trio of outlaws.

One of the leaders spoke, but his voice was so quiet that Ivey could not hear it over the din of the crowd. Ward nodded and turned back to the townsfolk. "Right. We'll need all the men to step forward."

The crowd stared back at him, wide-eyed and uncomprehending. Terror ran like wildfire through the townspeople, making them all stupid. Derek fired another shot into the air, which at least got them moving. "Now, please."

Using their horses as if they were cutting cattle, the three outlaws that had been corralling the people began separating the men from the group and pushing them toward the remaining string of bandits. As each one passed by, Derek made him stop and look up. He knew the features of the man for whom they were searching.

Even after looking each man over, he had not found Byrne Jameson. "He's not here," he reported to his superiors. Turning his horse away from the crowd of men, he looked to Cliff Hayes. "What do we do now?"

"Isn't it obvious?" the leader returned in his gravelly voice. He explained his plan to Derek. The younger man nodded his understanding.

Ward turned back to address the crowd as a whole. "Alright, first person who spots Byrne Jameson when he returns to town, come and tell us. We will pay well for information!"

"What do you want with him?" Ivey started, realizing belatedly that she was the one to have called out the question. She found herself looking at the barrel of Ward's gun.

"Just to talk. Don't worry yourself, pretty little thing," he remarked, his gray-green eyes softening a bit as he looked at her. He lowered the weapon. "Oh, and where's our famous ex-sheriff?" Ward's hard stare traveled over the collection of men until he spotted Alexander. "Ah, there you are. Do us a favor and move out of the constabulary. From now on that building is off limits."

Without another word the gang of bandits moved off, led by Cliff Hayes and Pistol Lawson. The other thugs filled in behind their leaders and Derek Ward took up the rear of the procession.

~~~~~~~~~~

Following the orders of Hayes and Lawson, Alexander and his young wife vacated the constabulary. The gang did not want the one-time sheriff getting any ideas about filling those cells. So, the young couple moved back to Emily's ancestral home, keeping their mother company in the midst of her grief. Work stopped altogether on their wedding present. Without Roy's guiding hand Alexander felt unequal to the task, and there was no telling what harassment they might receive from the gang should construction continue. The situation was far too unsettled.

The fire set by the gang when they entered the town had been put out before it completely destroyed the houses left and right of the structure that had burned to the ground. Still, those buildings were in bad need of repair, sporting blackened holes in the siding and roofs. Those homeowners were allowed to make repairs without interruption whilst the gang celebrated their victory.

Looking at the sky one morning, it was evident that they would need to work quickly. Rain was coming.

What Alexander and other newcomers to the West could not have known was that each year rain fell in torrents, often for days on end. This annual rainfall renewed an otherwise dusty life on the plains. It refilled the small river, greened everything up. For a short time it would make growing crops a plausible notion. Such a system of storms was on its way.

Alexander looked at the far horizon. It was nearly black with heavy, terrifyingly dark clouds. He went back inside and told the women to look out the window. When they had done so, Jane assured him that the rain was coming and it was a normal occurrence. Alexander ducked outside, hoping to finish the corral he had begun building for Duke.

The ex-sheriff was unable to finish his task before the rain started. At first it was a few heavy drops plopping down here or there, nothing too intimidating. As the clouds rolled in, looming overhead and darkening the day so it looked like dusk, the drops began to multiply.

By the time Alexander had put the last rail in place and loosed Duke into the structure, the rain was falling in sheets, driven by the wind. Alexander sprinted for the house, his boots slipping in a slimy layer of mud. He rushed through the door, slamming it shut against the elements.

Emily came to him immediately, ordering that he take off his boots and strip out of his wet clothing. She found him a blanket with which to dry off and then sought a fresh set of clothing for him. His mother-in-law was good enough to make herself scarce as he began to peel the clinging, soaked fabric off his body.

CHAPTER ELEVEN

As the storm was beginning in Flintridge, Byrne was making his way home. He and Cowboy trotted along the stagecoach track.

The sale had been more of a success than in the past. Ranchers were beginning to recognize the potential of mustangs as breeding stock, for their prized qualities of sure-footedness and incredible endurance. The mares had been handsome things with decent conformation. While he had intended they be bought as working saddle horses, he did not mind that they were to be used for brood. Stockmen still did not trust full-blooded mustangs, feeling them to be too wild no matter how well trained. Watering down the wild blood through breeding would give them the traits they desired without the attitude. The yearlings did better; since they were young, people were inclined to think them less wild. Ranchers willing to work them into proper ranch horses bought them.

Ahead, dark clouds hung over Flintridge and stretched for miles in each direction along the horizon. The spring storms had come again. These rains were both a blessing and a curse to life out on the range. Byrne had spent enough years out there to know what to expect. He urged Cowboy into a gallop. He wanted to beat the rain home.

Before he even got close to town the rain began to pour down mercilessly. The drops hit the parched ground with such force that they rebounded. Cowboy kept running, sensing his master's urgency. Byrne pulled his hat down low to keep the stinging rain out of his eyes. From far off, thunder rumbled through the skies.

Very soon the ground became too slick for even the sure-footed mustang to keep up his pace. He was forced to slow to a trot and then finally a walk, picking his way through the mud with care. Byrne allowed this, understanding that haste could end in disaster.

The rain continued to hammer down on him, drenching both horse and rider to the bone. It was not a warm rain and Byrne soon began to shiver underneath his sodden coat. Cowboy snorted; he was as miserable as his rider. He shook his head to free it of rainwater. The chestnut's strong legs were splattered with mud up past his knees, mud had even splattered on his belly when he had been running.

Byrne's pant legs, too, sported muddy spots.

Finally they turned off the stagecoach track and into Flintridge. Byrne did not even look at the buildings as he passed by. His entire focus was on getting home. When they did reach his homestead, he looked to his mount immediately. He rubbed the worst of the mud off Cowboy's legs and belly, untacked him, cleaned the tack and stored it. Going to the feed room, he pulled an extra ration of oats for the tired chestnut stallion. He threw hay to the mustangs and the mule and then finally took himself inside, out of the driving rain.

Ivey was at the door to meet him, having been watching for his return. She was in quite a state of nerves as she greeted him. "Get inside!" she exclaimed, seeing him mud-stained and sopping wet. Byrne would not have thought of doing anything else.

Once inside, he slipped off his boots with their thick coating of mud, setting them aside to be cleaned later. Ivey helped him to peel his jacket and shirt off, discarding them in a sopping heap. The wet clothes squelched as they hit the floor. Byrne was shivering, his skin cold to the touch. His wife fetched a blanket and wrapped it around his shoulders.

Wrapped in the blanket, shuddering for warmth, Byrne moved away from the door. His damp pants clung to his body, making motion uncomfortable. He stopped beside the wood stove in the dining area, pressing close to it for warmth. Ivey followed after him, wringing her hands. He noticed that she glanced often out the window as if worried by the heavy rains.

"It's just a little rain," Byrne said with chattering teeth, trying to reassure her. "It will let up soon enough."

"Oh, I know all that," she replied vacantly, her eyes empty as if looking far beyond their immediate surroundings.

Byrne's brow furrowed. "What's wrong?" He turned to face her, extending his arm as if to take her into his embrace.

She looked at him with a bemused expression. "We need to get you some dry clothes first." Tapping him lightly on the chest as she passed by, she disappeared into the bedroom and found him a suitable wardrobe.

As Byrne was pulling his shirt over his head he asked again, "What's wrong?"

"Oh it's almost too horrible to put into words."

Byrne yanked the shirt into place and looked at her with an intent, defensive stare. "Has someone mistreated you?" His mahogany eyes sparked with an angry fire at the very thought.

"No, no," she said quickly, wanting to calm his indignant anger. She then launched into the tale of how the Hayes-Lawson gang had come into town. Ivey relayed how the bandits had ransacked the city, burning buildings. She told him how Roy Fletcher had been killed, along with other civilians, and about the deal Alexander made with the outlaws after learning that he would no longer be paid for his services as sheriff. The government had abandoned Flintridge as a lost cause and would let it fend for itself. Now the gang had the run of the town and everyone had been treading on eggshells for fear of angering them. She finished by adding that the gang was offering to pay anyone who would inform them of the rancher's return.

As he listened to her brief but descriptive story, Byrne's jaw tensed. He gritted his teeth and his eyes took on a determined, angry quality. Almost before she had finished he stalked toward the door.

"Byrne! Where are you going?"

The rancher picked up the rain-stained leather satchel he had carried in with him. He handed it to his wife as she followed him. "Take this. Hide it somewhere safe, where no marauder will ever find it."

"What is it?"

"Our money. From the sale of the mustangs," he explained tersely. "You'll need it someday."

Ivey's blood ran cold at the tone of his voice. He brushed past her and went looking for his rifle. He had had to buy a new one after giving his over to Alexander.

She trotted after him, trying to catch at his arm, trying to stop him. "Byrne. Byrne!" She succeeded in getting in front of him and blocking his way. He could not proceed without picking her up and moving her out of his path. "What are you going to do?" She laid her hands on his shoulders, trying to catch his eye. He would not meet her gaze.

"Only what needs to be done Ivey," he answered gruffly. He slipped past her.

She was after him in a second. "But why does it have to be done? Why do you have to do it?"

"Because this is my town. I can't let a band of mangy curs destroy it."

"You know they've got you outnumbered. What if you're killed?"

"You'll have money enough to see you back home," he replied. The words chilled her to the bone.

Toting the musket and making sure his pistol was loaded and strapped to his belt, Byrne made for the door. "Oh, and if something happens to me - it won't, but *if* - please release the mustangs back onto the range." He shoved his feet into his muddy boots.

"Your coat," Ivey reminded him, handing the sodden article over. Her voice was choked with emotion but she knew she could not stop him, no matter what she did. Something about this place - about the town - held him body and soul. Even she recognized it was a bond that could not be broken. Just as she could never ask him to move back east, she knew she could not force him to sit idly by and watch his precious town suffer under the bloody rule of the outlaws.

Byrne smiled grimly as he accepted the slicker. He caught Ivey in a one-armed hug and kissed her. It was a fierce but lingering kiss, telling her without words all that she meant to him. She pressed close, enjoying the warmth of his body and the strength of his arms. *Don't go*, she wanted to whisper. She knew they would be wasted words. Instead she murmured "I love you" against his lips.

The rancher shrugged into his coat, pressed his hat upon his head, and ducked out the door. Ivey watched him cross the yard in the rain, clinging to the threshold for support. Her whole world might come to an end that night. She prayed it would not.

Byrne disappeared around the corner of the house and came back seconds later with Cowboy's bridle in hand. He slipped the headstall over the chestnut's ears and then pressed the bit into his mouth. He led the mustang out of the paddock and locked the mule in when he would have followed. Standing at the horse's shoulder, facing backward, Byrne grabbed a fistful of mane and swung himself onto the mustang's bare back. Taking up the reins with the rifle tucked under one arm, he clucked to the horse and they set off. As they got clear of the muddy puddle that was collecting in a low part of the yard he gave Cowboy a kick and the sure-footed mustang took off, spraying up mud behind him.

They rode hard for town. Byrne's hand on the reins was firm, his knuckles white as he gripped the stock of the rifle. Cowboy took a particularly sharp turn onto the main street and slid in the mud. The mustang fumbled to keep his feet beneath him. Byrne allowed him to slow up, reasoning that he did not need to announce his approach to the gang. The footfalls of a galloping horse might be heard through the pounding rain, but those of a walking animal would be covered by the sound of the storm.

Leaving Cowboy ground tied outside the saloon, Byrne crept toward the building. The rainwater fell heavily, forming a sheet as it rolled off the slanted roof. The rancher endured one more soaking before he made it into the shelter of the overhang. Try as he did, he could not conceal his approach. His boots sounded loudly on the hollow deck. The front windows of the saloon were large, affording a good view of the street, and the swinging doors did little to conceal an approaching person.

Realizing he would not have the element of surprise no matter what he tried, Byrne opted to rush in with guns blazing - so to speak. Putting the rifle to his shoulder, he pushed through the doors and rushed into the saloon. It took a moment for the customers to notice his intimidating entrance. When they did, the saloon girls screamed and tried to make for cover. The card players dropped their hands and fingered their holstered guns. The barkeep started to reach for his rifle, tucked under the bar.

Confused, Byrne began to lower his rifle. He did not see any members of the Hayes-Lawson gang.

Rough hands gripped his arms suddenly and wrenched the gun from his grasp. Byrne let out a cry of surprise and anger and began struggling madly to escape the sinister hold.

Even against his furious energy the hands held firm. At least three people had hold of him. Byrne jerked hard to one side, hoping to break at least one of their grips. He received a cuff upside the head as a reward for his actions.

Shaking his head furiously, Byrne tried again and again to escape. His strength proved unequal to the task of breaking away from three strong pairs of arms. Regardless, he continued to fight, hoping luck would be on his side. If he could just get a hand on his pistol...

One of the rogues stepped around the struggling men and rammed a fist squarely in Byrne's gut. The rancher doubled over, gasping. The men holding him forced him to stay on his feet when he would have sunk to the ground. There was a twinge in his back which grew to a jolt of pain when he was forced to stand upright. Breathing heavily, he looked at the man who had punched him. His back ached severely.

The man standing before him was dressed well, better than most of the townsfolk. All his clothing was black, there was not a speck of color in his wardrobe. He wore a pair of ebony leather gloves and had a coarse scar which marred one cheek. "Thought you'd get the better of us rancher?" Pistol Lawson asked with an unkindly laugh.

Byrne coughed, unable to hold the sensation at bay any longer. He refused to answer the rhetorical question posed by the outlaw leader.

Lawson reached down and snatched Byrne's pistol out of its holster. The rancher struggled feebly against his captors. They laughed, adding to his fury and humiliation. Byrne rolled his eyes, trying to catch a glimpse of the men holding him. He recognized one as Jarrod Cooke, who was part of the original Hayes-Lawson gang, but the other two had to be newer members, unknown to him. In the background he spotted Derek Ward, the gentleman robber, seated at a table. The outlaw noticed his gaze and gave a small, sarcastic wave.

The gang leader turned Byrne's pistol over in his hands, judging the weight and quality of the firearm. He looked from the weapon to its owner with hooded, almost black eyes.

Byrne felt very foolish. He had lost before the fight had even begun. Suddenly overwhelmed with his own failure, he bowed his head and attempted to catch his breath.

Lawson shoved the barrel of the pistol beneath Byrne's chin, forcing his head up. Byrne's lip twitched in pure hatred as he stared into the ugly face of the other man. Boldly, the rancher spat in Lawson's face.

As he had every reason to expect he got a backhanded slap in response. His head was snapped to the side as Lawson whipped the butt of the pistol across Byrne's face. The rancher winced hard, shaking his head in pain. He spit out a mouthful of saliva and blood.

"What'd you hope to accomplish in coming here tonight?" Pistol Lawson asked, leaning down close to the subdued rancher.

Byrne's jaw stung so much he was not sure he could answer even if he wanted to. When he was too slow in answering he received another smack. Reeling, Byrne dipped his head low, trying to escape the pain. The men holding his arms bore him up. His back was spasming with pain, which fueled his fury.

Finally Byrne had organized his reeling thoughts enough to form a statement. "Get out."

"What was that?" Lawson leaned in close to hear. He twirled the gun in his hand threateningly.

"Get out," Byrne repeated, biting off each word. He met the other's gaze with a hard stare of his own.

Pistol Lawson broke out laughing. "You hear that boys? It seems we've outstayed our welcome!" The gang echoed his mirth.

"He's no threat to us, Pistol," Cliff Hayes drawled from his seat at a nearby table. He and Derek had been playing at cards with some other men.

"We don't know that Cliff," the man holding Byrne's gun retorted to his comrade.

"What can one man do?" Derek asked casually, laying down a card in the center of the table. "It is your move, Gravedigger."

Without even looking to see what the other player had set down, Cliff threw down a card. He kept his squinty stare trained on Byrne. The rancher was supremely uncomfortable. As the two villains stared at him from different directions the first hint of fear began to seep into his mind. Until then he had been too full of adrenaline and pious rage to give consideration to self preservation. Now, with his injuries throbbing and killers on all sides of him, he felt supremely alone and vulnerable. His eyes kept darting between the two outlaw leaders.

"It's better not to learn the answer to that question, Derek. Leave no one behind that could one day stab you in the back." Cliff drew a knife from his belt and planted it in the tabletop to emphasize his point. The blade and handle wobbled from the force of the strike.

"Wait Cliff, didn't you just say he was no threat?" Pistol countered, genuinely confused.

"For the moment he daren't act. He knows what we can do to him, to his town...to his wife. Don't you Byrne?" Hayes was not even looking at the rancher as he spoke slowly; instead he was reviewing his hand of cards. "But then again, if you're the man I knew all those years ago, you have a streak of stupid pride in you. Still got that flaw, Byrne?"

Byrne narrowed his eyes, watching the knife sway. His gaze shifted about nervously.

"You're worried about a rancher? Really?" Derek scoffed with a bark of laughter. He put his cards face-down on the table and stretched. His coat pulled back, showing the Colt strapped to his belt.

"Take him out back and teach him a lesson, boys." Having spoken, Cliff Hayes turned his full attention back to his card game. He yanked the knife out of the table, scraped it on the tabletop to clear off the splinters, and sheathed it. "I don't much care if he lives to tell the tale."

"Aw, really boss? Out in the rain?"

"Can it, Budd. Do as you're told."

"But it's raining!" Budd complained. He was standing behind Byrne, to the left. The name was vaguely familiar to the rancher, though he could not place it with what he knew of the Hayes-Lawson gang. He narrowed his eyes, searching his memory. Even if identification continued to elude him, the mental exercise kept his mind off the beating that was to come.

"You're too new to the outfit to have an opinion," Derek drawled quietly, just loud enough for those close by to hear. He and Cliff were continuing their game without the other players. Coins clinked together as they were wagered, the cards rustled as they were set down on the table. Quiet conversations had resumed halfheartedly in other parts of the saloon but Byrne was intensely aware that all eyes were subtly still on him.

"Stop whining and get on with it," Pistol snapped. "If you're going to be wimps about the weather just do it in here. I enjoy a good show." He settled into a chair, holding Byrne's pistol as if it was a prized possession. The outlaw kicked one foot up on the neighboring chair and leaned back, grinning insolently. "Get on with it!" he ordered sharply when the men holding Byrne failed to act.

Spurred by the rebuff, the bandits jumped to action. One held Byrne on his feet while the others administered blows. The rancher did his best to take the assault with a brave face but even his will broke down under the sheer force and pain. Before long he was bruised, bleeding and breathless, unable to stand on his own two feet, unaided.

Finally the one holding him tired of supporting his weight. He let Byrne drop and the rancher crumpled to the ground, wheezing. He was only half conscious, his vision badly blurred from all the punches he had received.

Dazed, Byrne hardly registered the point at which the outlaws left him lie, laughing raucously as they walked to the bar to refill their drinks. He seemed to drift in and out of consciousness, losing track of time. Every time he tried to move, tried to get his feet beneath him, pain shot through his body and he stayed where he had fallen. He was vaguely aware of the weight of several pairs of eyes on him but even that knowledge could not move him.

He lay there for a very long time, only half aware of his surroundings. The muted daylight waned into dusk. The chatter in the saloon, which had started up again to present a feeling of normalcy, was quieting down as patrons left to go home to an evening meal with their families. Eventually even the gang retired to the rooms at the back of the saloon, some with prostitutes on their arms.

Byrne woke as a hand was laid gently between his shoulder blades. He tried to open his eyes, tried to react, but managed only to open one eye a crack - the other eye had been struck during the fight and was swollen shut. The rancher moaned in agony as he was rolled over. Every muscle had stiffened, his bruises were keenly sore. All he wanted to do was lie still, for it hurt far less when he was not moving.

"Easy Byrne," a voice whispered. He thought he recognized it but he could not be certain. The voice had been furtive, intentionally only just audible; the speaker feared being overheard by the gang. They would not take kindly to someone helping the man that had tried to undermine them.

Having no strength left, Byrne could only groan as he was lifted and held between two men. His bearers took him out of the saloon, back out into the rain. Byrne did not remember the journey that brought him to the surgeon's office. Next thing he knew he was getting poked and prodded, all his injuries aggravated. He cursed and then instantly regretted the action for the pain that flared in his jaw.

"You're lucky they took it easy on you, Mr. Jameson," the doctor, Lucas Simmons, commented upon completing his examination. Standing against the wall on the far side of the room stood Ty Jennings and Mick Geller, allegedly the ones who had brought the rancher to safety.

Byrne could not stifle a derisive laugh. "They beat me within an inch of my life from the feel of it," he managed to remark.

"Yes, but they did leave you with your life," the doctor reminded him. "Since they came to town, other men have not been so lucky."

Byrne heaved a sigh. Yes, he hurt, but the doctor was right that he should be grateful to still be alive. The thought of others dying before him, victims of the gang's lust for blood and murder, was sobering. Though he had been defeated this time, the gang had left him alive. Byrne made a promise then, to himself, to Roy's spirit, to the very town itself, that he would make the Hayes-Lawson outfit regret their oversight.

He spent some time in the doctor's ward gaining his strength. Ty ran across the road through the rain to fetch the rancher's horse. Mick Geller, notorious drunk that he was, waddled through the downpour to return to the saloon and the comfort of drink.

Byrne had to get a leg up from Ty in order to get onto Cowboy's back. It was an interesting prospect, for the young railway worker was lanky and had to kneel low in the mud to get his cupped hands at a level where the rancher's foot could reach. The chestnut horse was soaked through and through, miserable. The rainwater on his back made his coat slippery and difficult for the rider to stay seated. To further complicate matters, his master's jerky, uncertain motions made the horse nervous and he refused to stand still.

Byrne was just about to set off when Ty produced his hat and handed it up to him. The rancher stared at the hat for a long moment before taking it and planting it firmly on his head. He gave the doctor and railway man a nod of thanks and set off. He made a mental note of their kindness; of all the people in the tavern only a few had dared to act.

Already a plan was forming in the rancher's mind.

CHAPTER TWELVE

In the following months Byrne kept his head down. Ivey had had quite a shock at seeing him when he had returned from that fateful night. In hindsight he was not sure if it had been his physical appearance that had so frightened her or if it had been the shock of seeing him return alive; undoubtedly she had feared he would never return from confronting the infamous gang.

Quietly and so subtly that even the paranoid gang leaders were oblivious to it, Byrne began to expand his circle of friends in town. Most days he still kept to himself, working his ranch.

On occasion he would make a venture out into the wilderness in search of mustangs but he was too concerned for Ivey's safety to be gone for long. He still feared that the gang would retaliate against him by harming her. But when he returned from each venture to find his homestead and family unmolested he began to think the gang viewed the score as settled. He wanted to keep it that way, to lull them into a sense of false security.

If he happened to run into a member of the outfit while in town he forced himself to be pleasant or neutral. He wanted them to believe that he had given up his fool's errand of running them off or killing them all.

So, Byrne continued to quietly make pacts with other men in town. He felt them out, trying to judge which of them would be best to have on his side and how they felt about the gang's occupation of the city.

Rather to his surprise, many of the men seemed to resign themselves to the new order of things and felt that they would rather keep their heads down then have them shot off. These men seemed to miss the potential power to be had if all the townsfolk were to band together against the gang.

Byrne continued to search for like-minded men.

The rancher kept a mental list of all those sympathetic to his cause. Alexander Judge, of course, being the ex-sheriff, was one on which the rancher thought he might rely. Happily the doctor, Lucas Simmons, was fed up with dealing with the casualties brought on the town when the gang was in a rowdy mood, bored, or just looking to have a little fun. Byrne knew it would be important to have the skills of a medical man, for what he proposed was a risky venture.

Others on the list included: Cody Harris, the soft-spoken but firmly opinionated farrier; Ty Jennings, one of the first men hired on by the railroad and who had made Flintridge his home just before the Hayes-Lawson gang had taken over; Mick Geller, who was a known drunk but had helped Byrne after he was beaten by the gang; and Tanner Lee, a man of whose morals the rancher was skeptical. It was a motley assortment, sorely lacking any quality fighting skills, but Byrne knew that even untrained men with a purpose could be dangerous.

Thus far he had not fully entrusted any of those on his list with the truth of his intent. He knew that anyone could be compromised if pressured the right way. If his plot were discovered before it was put into action it would mean certain death, not only for the rancher but for his wife, his animals, and the town he held so dear. Thus he only hinted at his displeasure at the gang's presence in private with his most trusted allies. His comments encouraged the others to share their sentiments.

As they sat idly by, unable to run the gang off on their own, they began to grow bitter. Hatred for the outlaws simmered in their minds.

Then, one day, Byrne received news that forced his hand prematurely: Ivey was pregnant. Byrne was elated, terrified, and disappointed all at once. He had never before been a father, since he and Ivey had spent so much of their married lives apart. It was a thrilling prospect that he should have a child to which he might someday leave his legacy. However, amidst the joy in his heart there was also the knowledge that he did not want his child to grow up under the thumb of an outlaw gang. The Hayes-Lawson outfit must be driven away or, better yet, destroyed before the child was born.

It was with this frame of mind that Byrne rode into town one day in the early summer. He still sported scars on his face from the beating he had received from the gang. It was a sore point for him, an ugly reminder that he had lost. He promised himself he would never lose again.

The rancher rode to the livery stable. "Oy! Cody! Come out here a minute will you?" he called, loud enough to be heard halfway across town. Byrne hopped out of the saddle and dragged one rein along with him, bringing Cowboy closer to the open barn door.

Almost immediately the farrier came rushing out, red-faced and breathing heavily. Upon seeing Byrne and no imminent disasters, he heaved a sigh. "Take it easy Byrne, I was shoeing a horse and it durn well near kicked me when you yelled."

"Sorry about that," Byrne said, and meant it. "Say, I wonder if you could take a look at Cowboy. He's been a bit sore up front and I'm wondering if it isn't time to put shoes on him." The rancher threw an arm around the shoulders of the farrier and directed him back inside where they could talk in private. Once they were in the barn, Byrne shot a surreptitious look around. It seemed as if Cody's other customer had taken himself off while his horse was shod. The scene was set for Byrne's scheme.

The rancher stopped and tossed the rein he held casually over Cowboy's neck. The mustang snorted and shook his head but stayed where he was.

"He doesn't look at all sore to me," Cody remarked slowly, wondering if he had missed something. His professional eye, granted knowledge by thirty years of dealing with horses, rarely missed a thing.

Byrne patted Cowboy on the wither. "He's sound as a rock," the rancher assured the farrier. "I just needed an excuse to come and talk to you."

Cody shot a quick, furtive glance around. He, too, was very paranoid about spies.

Byrne leaned in close. What he had on his mind would not take long to say. He hoped he had judged the farrier's personality aright. He opened his mouth to speak, thought better of it, and changed the story he had intended to tell. How could he be certain that no one was hiding around the corner listening in? It would be better to have a confidential conversation elsewhere, where they could be positive that no one was eavesdropping. "I'll be riding out tomorrow to round up some mustangs. I'd be much obliged for some help. Think you can spare the time?"

The farrier looked at him, uncomprehending. He had thought the conversation would go in a different direction. The way the rancher had been talking, he had been about to propose a mutiny.

Byrne locked eyes with him, communicating silently. He continued to stare intently, seriously, as he spoke, hoping the other would catch the underlying message. "Just after dawn tomorrow, meet at my ranch. Bring a sturdy horse and enough supplies for a couple days' journey. I'll pay you for your trouble, of course," he added. "And if you could look Cowboy over real quick, just to make sure he's up to the journey."

Cody was not the quickest thinker but even he could not help but pick up on the hints. "Sure thing Byrne," he said almost a little too quickly and a little too loudly. The rancher signaled for him to tone it down, which he did.

Approaching the mustang, whom he had known since Byrne brought him in off the range, Cody ran his work-roughened hands over the animal's legs and quarters, searching for any sign of unsoundness. Byrne stood by, watching, feigning interest. He knew his mustang was sound to a fault, even if he was getting a little on the old side for a working ranch horse. Byrne would not have traded Cowboy for anything.

Finally the farrier straightened up, having completed his examination. "Looks alright to me Byrne, I can't find anything amiss."

"Much obliged," the rancher returned, shaking the farrier's hand. "See you tomorrow mornin' then."

"Tomorrow morning." The farrier repeated with a nod.

"What's tomorrow morning?" A youthful voice inquired, stopping Byrne as he was about to lead Cowboy out of the stable. Gritting his teeth, the rancher turned around to face the voice. Standing a few feet away, leaning casually against a support beam, was a young man. His face was blemished and his clothes were threadbare. Byrne recalled having seen the boy before but did not recall his name.

"Nothing to concern you, boy," Cody retorted sharply. "All you need to know is that we're closed for the next couple days while I lend my friend here a hand."

"Doing what?"

"Doesn't matter. Just hold down the fort."

"What should I tell folks when they come around looking for you?"

Cody was losing his patience. "Tell them that your master is away on business. You can accept new boarders if we have the room, just no farrier work until I get back. Got it?"

"Mhmm. 'Sorry mate, but the boss is away on some mysterious business. Don't know where he's gone or when he'll be back. Sorry.' " The boy grinned cheekily, shoving his hands in the front pockets of his pants.

"Listen Jesse—" the farrier began, his patience spent.

Byrne put out an arm, trying to calm the annoyed farrier. He knew that men in a temper were prone to saying stupid things. "It's no secret. Cody here is going to help me track down and round up some mustangs. It'll probably take a few days but we're hoping to be back by week's end."

"Fair enough," the boy said, appreciating being treated as an equal by someone older than himself. After a beat he added, "Can I come with you?"

Byrne and Cody shook their heads simultaneously. The farrier crossed his arms and pinched the bridge of his nose. The rancher looked at the youngster skeptically. "How old are you boy?"

"Fifteen. Sixteen next month," he added quickly, hoping to improve his chances of going along.

"Too young," Byrne said dismissively, hoping that would be an end to it. It was a lie, for Byrne himself had been out on his own since he was twelve and had done alright. The truth was he did not want someone so young getting caught up in the town's dark politics. "Better luck next time boy."

Jesse crossed his arms, pouting. The rancher led his steed out into the warm sunlight and swung into the saddle. "See you tomorrow Cody," he said in farewell, tapping the brim of his hat in salute before trotting off.

His next stop was the dry goods store. Leaving Cowboy at the hitching post, he climbed the stairs and entered the business. As he had expected, Alexander stood behind the counter. Since he had been decommissioned he been without a source of income. After Roy's death the dry goods store, the very heart and lifeblood of the town, had been closed. That state of things had lasted only a few days, for Alexander reluctantly took over the business. It was the most logical solution, for he needed money and the town needed the general store. The ex-sheriff knew very little about retail and so he had received a great deal of coaching and help from Jane and Emily. Now, weeks later, he was beginning to get a handle on things.

By sheer good luck there was only one other customer present and he was one of the men with whom Byrne wanted to speak. Ty Jennings, the youthful man who had come out to work for the railroad, was leaning on the counter, having a casual conversation with Alexander. When the rancher entered they cut their chat off and looked at the door, as if they had something to hide. Seeing that it was only Byrne who had entered, not one of the gang's flunkies, they started back talking after offering a wave of greeting.

Ty brushed stray bits of blonde-brown hair out of his face. He seemed to perpetually be due for a haircut but enjoyed keeping his hair a bit longer than was fashionable. His skin was tanned bronze from endless hours spent working in the sun; though he was a tall, thin man, his arms were strong and well-muscled.

Byrne did a bit of browsing whilst waiting for them to conclude their discussion. He did have a list of supplies in mind and so he picked those up in the meantime. Because he knew exactly what he wanted, he was done selecting his items before the other two were done talking.

The rancher stood awkwardly by. He wanted to speak with them both, to get it over with. Each minute that he tarried he became more and more nervous that his plan would be discovered by the bandits, even though he had not yet given breath to his intentions. Even Ivey had not been let in on the secret.

Belatedly the conversing pair realized that Byrne was ready to make his purchases. Ty slapped his hand down on the counter and backed up. "Sorry Byrne, we've been yappin' away."

"Not to worry," the rancher replied, forcing a congenial smile. He set down his selections and dug in his pocket for cash.

As Alexander wrote up the bill, Byrne looked out the window, feigning casualness. Outside, the day was bright, sunny and warm. Business went on as usual in Flintridge, or at least it was normal by recent standards. Since the Hayes-Lawson outfit had moved into town folks were afraid to be about. They scuttled quickly from place to place, afraid of being seen by the gang in case the villains were in a dark humor. No one stopped in the street to hold friendly conversations as they had done so often in the past. They ventured out of their homes only on the utmost necessity.

"Say, I'm heading out in the morning to try and round up another band of mustangs. It'd be a much easier task with the help of other riders. Either of you be interested in coming along?"

"If I can borrow a mount I'd be game. I'm in need of a change of scenery, if you get what I mean."

"I do."

"How long's the job?" Ty asked, following up on his previous statement.

"We'll be back before week's end," was the answer. "As for a horse, talk to Cody. He's agreed to come along and I'm sure he has a spare mount you can borrow." Byrne paused, looking the railway man up and down. "You can ride, can't you?" He laughed and clapped Ty on the shoulder to prove it was a joke. Ty joined in his mirth. Alexander continued writing, focused on that task alone and seemingly oblivious of the conversation.

"How about you Judge?" Ty asked, leaning on the counter again. He received no response, no acknowledgement. Pretending to be irked, Ty slapped the counter near to where Alexander was writing. The shopkeeper jumped and looked up, adjusting his spectacles. "You going to ride out with us?" Ty repeated, looking down his nose at the other man.

"Oh. Uh, no, thank you. Very kind of you to offer though. Best of luck." He ducked his head and returned to his task.

Byrne rolled his eyes tolerantly. "You're not afraid of the wild west are you?"

"No I am not." The shopkeeper had not taken the bait. His pen scratched across the ledger paper. He announced how much the rancher owed for his goods and Byrne duly paid up.

"Shame you're not inclined to come with us," the rancher remarked as he shoveled his purchases into his saddle bag. "I was going to pay for the help. But, if you have other things you'd rather do I understand. Not fair to leave the ladies in charge of the store for a few days." He nodded, as if agreeing with himself. Turning for the door, he paused to shake Ty's hand. "Appreciate your help though, Ty. See you at my place at dawn tomorrow. Oh, and remember to stop by and talk to Cody at the stable. Tell him I sent you."

Ty nodded his understanding. "Will do. I'll be there."

" 'Til tomorrow, then." Byrne went to the door. "We'd have loved to have you along, Mr. Judge," he remarked quietly over his shoulder before he stepped outside.

Alexander glanced up over his spectacles but did not answer. He turned and set to dusting and reorganizing the shelves.

Since the upheaval in Flintridge had begun, people had been keeping to themselves. With them buying only on the direst necessity, business at the general store had dried up, leaving the Fletcher-Judge family strapped for cash.

When the rancher had mentioned the opportunity of a paid job, even a temporary one that would take him away from his family when they needed him most, Alexander had been sorely tempted to take it. Of course they had Roy's savings to live off of, but stashed money could only last them so long. He decided he would bring the topic up at dinner.

CHAPTER THIRTEEN

Byrne emerged from his house just before dawn the next morning. He had assured Ivey the night before that she need not see him off. All that he would need was packed and left in the feed shed next to Cowboy's saddle.

Byrne had taken great pains not to wake his wife as he slipped out of bed and got dressed. Before he had left he had gently tucked the blanket closer around her to ward off the morning chill. He wanted very badly to kiss her once more before he left but he did not want to be late in keeping his appointment.

Stepping out into the yard, he took a deep breath of the morning air. There was a slight chill in the wind but it was nothing to be concerned about. The sun was creeping up on the eastern horizon, painting the scenery in a blush of pink light. The horses mulled in their pens, just stirring to greet the morning.

With a sudden start he realized that he had not partaken of his morning coffee. Mulling it over, he acknowledged this would have to be one of those rare days when he went without. Already he could see dark specks crossing the buff plain from town. Given the early hour, he knew it could only be his comrades.

Kicking himself to action, Byrne jogged around the house to the feed shed and grabbed oats and hay for the animals. He quickly fed Cowboy and the mule and threw Beau his ration of hay. The palomino mustang had given up running away from people and even allowed himself to be patted through the fence, but he was still a royal terror if one tried to put a saddle on him. At least his ground manners were coming along, Byrne mused to himself. He entered Cowboy's pen with the saddle and blanket slung over his arm.

As he was setting the tack onto the chestnut stallion's back, Ty and Cody came trotting up. They brought with them a pack mule, loaded down with everything they thought they would need on the adventure. Byrne greeted them while he tightened the cinch. Cowboy tossed his head and looked around at his master. He was chewing a mouthful of oats, some of which fell out from between his lips. He snorted and went back to eating.

Byrne eyed the miserable-looking mule which his companions had brought. To the rancher's experienced eye it looked overloaded. "We're going to be gone for less than a week," he remarked, "do you think you brought enough?"

Ty looked back at the mule and laughed self-consciously. "That's my fault. I want to be prepared for anything I guess." He lifted his hat and ran a hand through his hair in the same motion before settling the hat back on his head. "So," he began, dragging the vowel on, "we ready to get going?"

"Just lettin' Cowboy finish breakfast and I need to settle ol' Frank," Byrne answered. He was already heading for the small pile of supplies. With swiftness borne from years of practice the rancher strapped all the supplies onto the mule's back, ensuring that everything was weighted equally so the beast of burden could move most easily.

Just as they were setting off they spotted a rider approaching. Byrne, in the lead, halted his mount and the others stopped as well to turn and look at the newcomer.

A fine black horse and his rider approached the group and reined in alongside Byrne. "Still looking for an extra hand?" Alexander inquired, grinning. He had been in need of an adventure, something to break up the tedium of his new job and the misery surrounding his father-in-law's death. When his wife and mother by marriage had granted him permission to go, assuring him they could handle the business for a few days, he had eagerly packed a small satchel and ridden out.

"Glad to have you."

The outfit started out again, turning their horse's heads toward the far-off mountains which were stained purple-grey in the early morning light. At first the men were inclined to chat amongst themselves as they rode along, often in pairs. As the morning wore on and they got further and further from civilization they exhausted their conversational topics and fell to silence.

The great enormity of the terrain that surrounded them seemed to command quietness. To either side and behind them the plain stretched out endlessly, seeming to be devoid of any living thing but themselves. Nothing stirred on that vast expanse of land save for the dust raised by their horses' hooves. The air was clear and fresh, the only scent being that of sage wafting on the breeze. They rode on toward the rocky foothills.

As they approached, a coyote cried high up on the rocks. Duke was the only horse to react skittishly to the sound.

After the wild dog's call the men were more uneasy, having been reminded that there were dangers in the wild country which they did not encounter in the safety of their town. Byrne was the only one unaffected, for he had spent a great deal of time in the wilderness. They kept their eyes focused on the land ahead. They did not look over their shoulders as they were miles from Flintridge.

As they began to climb higher, approaching the cliffs, the sounds their group made became distorted. The creak of the saddle leather seemed to be amplified and the clop of horse hooves on dry ground impossibly loud.

One more sound broke the stillness so suddenly that the men all drew their horses to an abrupt halt. "How much longer we gonna be ridin' for?"

The men turned rapidly in their saddles, jaws dropped. Only one of them had recognized the voice without seeing who had spoken.

"Jesse Wright," Cody said slowly, deliberately controlling himself to keep from yelling, "what the hell do you think you're doing here?"

The fifteen-year-old shrugged with a grin. Already his face was burned bright pink where the sun slanted past the brim of his hat. "It sounded like fun."

Cody pinched the bridge of his nose, at a loss for words. He had known taking on an assistant would prove challenging but he had no idea how to deal with a stowaway nephew.

"How did you find us?" Byrne could not help asking.

"Not that hard. I've been following you since you were a mile or two out of town."

"What of the stable?" Cody asked accusingly.

"It's all taken care of boss," the boy answered with a big, defensive gesture. "I closed the barn door and put up a sign. Says 'closed'."

"Stupid, stupid, stupid," Cody muttered, beating his forehead with his fist. Finally he left off his self-punishment and ran a hand down his face. "Go home. Now." The farrier spoke slowly and firmly, enunciating each word.

Jesse gave his master a confused look. He shifted his inquiring gaze to Byrne, whom he recognized to be the leader. He tried to look imploring, widening his brown eyes.

Byrne shook his head. "No. No. You're far too young for this. Besides, four men is more than enough for this job."

"Aw c'mon Byrne, let the boy live a little," Ty said lightly.

"No, this is too dangerous. Go home, boy."

"My name's Jesse, not 'boy'," the youth said disdainfully.

Byrne rolled his eyes. His patience was at an end. For his plan to work they had to proceed quickly. He could only see the boy as a hindrance.

Yanking Cowboy around, he was upon the boy before Jesse could move his mount. Byrne grabbed the reins of Jesse's horse just below the bit and, kicking Cowboy onward, began to tow the reluctant horse and rider back the way they had come. "Now, I really don't want to do this, but if I have to drag you all the way back to Flintridge and lock you in one of those dusty cells in the old jail I will." He let go the reins and slapped the horse's rear as it passed by. "Now get your ass back to town."

Jesse reined in his horse and shot a defiant look over his shoulder.

The rancher pulled the bullwhip off his saddle and let the tail drop to the ground, emphasizing his order. "Best get on your way." He jerked his chin in the direction of town.

Throwing a kicked puppy look over his shoulder, Jesse nudged his horse onward, head bowed. He was obviously disheartened.

Byrne tried not to be drawn in, knowing the boy would not be crestfallen for long. He turned Cowboy and rejoined the group. "C'mon," Byrne murmured as he led off into a canyon.

The rancher led them deep into the gorge, which wound through the foothills. As they travelled, the cliffs on either side of them rose higher and higher, growing ever steeper. The three men who had never before been in such country looked up at the dun-colored rock walls in awe. They marveled over the reddish and lighter tan stripes that ran through the stone in decorative bands, as if they had been painted in by the brush of God.

The riders rounded one last bend and Byrne's companions pulled up their horses abruptly. They cast looks around the narrow space, confused.

"Uh, Byrne?" Ty began, looking up and around as he spoke. "Where are these horses you've been telling us so much about?"

"Not here obviously," Cody remarked as he turned his horse around.

"Hold up a minute Cody," Byrne said quickly, his voice holding a commanding note that made the other man stop his horse. Cody twisted around in his saddle. Byrne suddenly found himself uncomfortable under their collective stares. He figured it was best to get it over with. "I apologize for misleading you but we are not out here to hunt mustangs. Not really. I need all of you to swear to keep what you're about to hear in the strictest confidence. Have I your words on that?"

The men nodded soberly.

"Thank you. The long and short of it is that we need to run the Hayes-Lawson gang out of town. That, or kill them all. Frankly I don't care which, I just want them to leave us - our families - in peace. Do you agree?"

Again, he received nods. All their faces were intent, grim. Apparently they had been thinking along similar lines for some time.

"How do you plan to do it? The four of us can hardly hope to overpower them," Alexander remarked quietly. Though they were out in the untouched wilderness they all feared being overheard. It seemed a silly concern out there but they kept their voices low none the less, just loud enough for each to hear the other.

Byrne launched into a description of his plan, all the details he had thus far worked out. Admittedly there were several holes and flaws in the plan, all of which his comrades were not afraid to point out. Byrne did his best to address their concerns and offer plausible solutions. The one thing none of them could get past was their lack of numbers.

"There are a few others I hoped we might recruit to our cause," Byrne offered slowly. He told them the last three names on his list.

Alexander shook his head. "Simmons is too peaceable. He would help us if one of us were to get injured, but do not count on him to carry a weapon."

"Mick Geller is a notorious drunk. In his stupor he'd be just as likely to shoot one of us as one of the Hayes-Lawson gang," Ty pointed out.

"I don't trust the likes of Tanner Lee," Cody remarked bluntly. "The only way he would commit to a cause is for money and in that case he could very easily be bribed to join the other side."

"Don't all of you jump with excitement at once," Byrne remarked a little harshly. He was smarting from having all his options shot down so immediately. "Have any of you a brilliant notion? Can you think of anyone else?"

All around, each man's expression offered little hope. Their mouths were all downturned. Byrne dropped his gaze, staring vacantly at the top of Cowboy's neck as he searched his memory for any alternative possibilities.

The hoofbeats of a trotting horse sounded round the curve leading into the canyon. Instinctively the men tensed, expecting that they had been followed. Those that had pistols with them reached for their weapons.

They all turned their horses to face the approaching rider, fully expecting to find that the Hayes-Lawson gang had suspected them, followed, and was now arriving to finish them off. Byrne directed Cowboy to the front of the pack; he would lead them into any trouble since he was their leader.

The head of a horse rounded the bend and they all tensed. As the rest of its body appeared with rider in tow, they let out a collective sigh of relief. It was only Jesse, the stable boy.

"I just saw a whole herd of mustangs take off across the plain. What are you brilliant horse hunters doing in this piddly little canyon?" The fifteen-year-old looked at them with a bemused grin, quite proud of himself for having spotted the wild horses first. Then, remembering that the animals had been moving at a good clip, he swung his mount around and made back the way he came.

After a few strides he realized that the others were not following. Turning in the saddle, he gave them a quizzical look. "Best be gettin' a move on if we're to catch 'em." He urged his horse on a few more steps. "Well, you comin'?" he prompted.

"Sure, just a minute, just have to find my...uh...rope."

"Isn't that it there?" Jesse pointed to the coil on Alexander's saddle.

"Oh yes, there it is," Alexander said slowly, pretending to be surprised at finding the item so close at hand. Jesse saw right through his pathetic act. The fact that none of the others had moved to follow him aroused his suspicions further.

"What? You lot afraid to go after some wild horses?" Jesse's tone of voice made it clear how he felt about that.

Byrne cleared his throat and nudged Cowboy forward. "Lead on boy," he remarked, pulling his lasso free of its tether. Jesse looked at the older man through narrowed eyes, trying to learn the secret the group was trying so hard to keep. The rancher's face was strictly impassive. Coming up empty, the youth shrugged and led on.

Letting Jesse set off at a rapid trot, Byrne held Cowboy back a bit so he could ride with the rest of the group. Together they trotted back through the canyon, always keeping the youth in sight but lagging quite a ways back from him so he would not overhear their whispered conversation.

One thing upon which they all agreed was that their mission was too dangerous to include an excited youth like Jesse. They agreed they must get him off their trail, but most of the plans they came up with were not practicable. Cody insisted that he could not order the boy to return to Flintridge, knowing Jesse would not obey. Byrne sat silent through most of the conversation. His eyes traveled over the horses surrounding him and Cowboy. He shot a glance ahead at Jesse and the short-legged stock horse he rode. "I think I have an idea," he murmured. The others leaned in their saddles to hear him out as he explained his plan.

Jesse often stole glances back at the group of men. They were all leaning in close together as they rode, obviously planning something. He wondered what they were up to. He wanted to be part of it.

Before any of them knew it, they were emerging from the canyon. Jesse was still staring backward as he unconsciously reined his horse in. The mousy brown horse with short legs and a stocky body pricked his ears, surveying the wide-open country.

The group of men emerged from the shadow of the canyon and reined in abruptly to avoid colliding with the stopped horse. Suddenly remembering himself, Jesse whipped his head around, pretending he had not been trying to listen in. He narrowed his eyes and raised his hand to shield them from the sun's glare. Visually scanning the horizon, he searched for any sign of wild horses.

The men had noticed his attempt at eavesdropping and hoped he had not heard anything. To redirect the youth's attention, Cody rode forward and spoke up. "So boy, where are these horses you've told us so much about?"

Jesse made a frustrated noise. "They were here. If we hadn't wasted so much time in the canyo—ow!" His exclamation came as Cody gave him a warning cuff upside the head.

"Don't be rude Jesse." The farrier turned his attention to scouting for the wild horses. After several minutes he turned to their leader. "I think they made a clean getaway Byrne."

The rancher, being more experienced at hunting wild equines, shook his head minutely. He worked his jaw as his eyes traveled over the buff hillsides, the wide-open expanse of pale, baked earth, the muted green scrub. Finally his eyes found what they sought.

Loosing a sharp whistle, he gave Cowboy an abrupt kick. Ever-responsive, the chestnut mustang threw his head in excitement and leapt forward. The stallion's energy spread like wildfire amongst the other domestic horses: they threw their heads, danced in place, and squealed. Their riders let their reins out and the small herd charged off after Cowboy.

The saddled horses stretched their legs out, black, bay, chestnut, dun, and gray. Their hoofbeats sounded as a rising tide of rumbling sound. The men leaned over their mounts' necks, making no move to check their steeds' pace.

They thundered away from the hills and out onto the open plains in pursuit of the wild band. The domestic horses reveled in the chance to stretch out and run like the wind. They ran with their nostrils flared and mouths open, gulping in great quantities of air to keep up their breakneck pace. Behind them was left a lane of trampled, churned earth.

Cowboy and his rider held the lead easily. The mustang, once wild, was in peak condition while the other horses had grown a bit heavy on feed and minimal exercise. Each mighty stride brought the mustang closer to his brethren. Before too long he was charging along just a few horse lengths behind the mob. The other riders were a several lengths behind him.

Byrne raised his lasso, twirling it over his head and feeding the noose. He nudged Cowboy to the right, around the trailing mustang. The wild animal rolled the whites of its eyes at the chestnut thundering along beside it with a man on his back. The wild horse squealed in fear and jumped to the side. Byrne let it go. Terror was flooding through the band of mustangs and they pushed themselves to an even more frantic pace. Eagerly, Cowboy matched them without waiting for his master's command.

Much to the domesticated mustang's surprise, Byrne coiled his rope and drew Cowboy back. The chestnut threw his head, unwilling to give up the chase. Stubbornly, the rancher held him until the others had caught up. The mustangs continued on, leaving the riders in a cloud of dust. Cowboy snorted forcefully; Byrne pulled his bandana over his nose and mouth. As the others came up alongside he saw that they had done the same.

While the men took care to slow their mounts to match Byrne's, Jesse urged his stubby-legged steed on at full speed. In his eagerness to chase down the wild horses he did not register that the men had slowed considerably and given up the chase.

Taking advantage of the situation, Byrne jerked his horse's head to the right and kicked him back to full gallop. The other men followed, leaving Jesse to his hopeless pursuit of the crazed wild herd.

Eager to put as much distance between themselves and the overly inquisitive youth as possible, the men forced their mounts to run hard and fast. The horses were blowing, already tired from their wild chase after the mustangs. Sweat streamed down their necks, down their flanks, and foam dripped from their mouths and spattered their chests.

They rode until their horses slowed, winded and heaving. Byrne patted Cowboy's neck and let the mustang walk on, stretching his legs and cooling down after the long, hard run. One of the other horses snorted and yet another coughed. They were all exhausted.

The rancher looked over his shoulder at his group. He counted three men; there was no sign of Jesse. Byrne suspected the boy would find himself lost for a time, long enough for them to get clear away. Eventually his horse would take him home.

As Cowboy plodded on, Byrne took a moment to survey the surroundings. It took him a while to recognize the terrain through which they were passing. Finally it matched a memory and he recalled their location. They had followed the mustangs much further north than he had intended. They would need to cut around an outcrop of rocky hills to get back on a path heading due east, toward Glenn Rock. First, though, he must find a source of water. Looking at some of the other domestic horses, it was clear they could not go much further without a drink.

He led nearer to the rocky hills, trying to get the party into the shade of the bluffs. The sun was still high, burning down on the parched land mercilessly. Try as he might, Byrne could not recall if there was a source of water that they could reach in time. He bit his lip, trying to force his mind to recall any possible solution.

Eventually he did what he realized he should have done a half hour earlier. He laid the reins on Cowboy's neck and gave the mustang his head. The chestnut, having once been a wild resident of this land, must surely know where to go to find water.

Cowboy stopped as the leather straps touched his neck. He lifted his head and looked about, seemingly confused. Find it boy, Byrne whispered in his mind, willing the mustang to follow his survival instincts. The band stood stopped for a long while.

"Byrne, what is the plan?" Alexander asked. He could not keep the worry from his voice. Even a city-slicker like himself could not help but realize their predicament.

"Wait," the rancher murmured in answer.

Cowboy took in deep, rapid breaths, scenting the air. With a small nicker he turned abruptly and walked with a determined stride. As they passed the others,

Byrne encouraged the men to give their horses their heads and let them follow the lead stallion.

They walked for another twenty minutes, wending their way through the wild frontier. They passed the bleached bones of some unfortunate animal. The horses waded through thickets of briars and sage scrub, even passing by a rare stand of cactus. Cowboy led on up one rock-strewn hillside, shimmied along the face of it, and finally dropped into a valley buried between two rises. The vale would have been hidden from view if they had not made the treacherous climb.

Miraculously, deep in the cleft, there stood a pool of water. Eagerly Cowboy trotted down the rocky hillside and waded into the water. The other horses followed, each going in up to their knees and drinking greedily of the cool, clear water. The men dismounted and scooped up handfuls of liquid, drinking as desperately as their steeds. They dunked their heads in the pool to cool their reddened, sweaty skin.

Once everyone had had their fill and replenished their water skins Byrne swung into the saddle. "Let's get back on track."

The others mounted as well and Cowboy led the way out of the hidden valley. The sun had sunk lower on the horizon. It was still hot but now the sunlight came at a slant as compared to pressing down with smothering ferocity.

The water had cooled and refreshed both men and horses. Feeling no immediate rush and not wanting to press the horses to utter exhaustion, Byrne led on at a sedate pace, heading back to the line that would lead them to Glenn Rock.

They stopped beneath a wind-twisted dead tree. The sun had set, making travel over the uneven terrain treacherous. The last thing they could afford was for a horse to go lame, or worse, break a leg.

They unsaddled their horses and tethered them to the tree for the night. Cody built a small fire over which they cooked their meager meal. Conversation was sparse, tempered by the fact that they were all tired after the long day's ride. They all slept soundly until dawn.

At dawn they woke to a great surprise.

Somehow, in the night, Jesse had caught up to them. He lay fast asleep at the feet of his trusty little horse, his torso draped inelegantly over the saddle he used as a pillow. The mousy chestnut horse nodded his head, waking with a start as Cody approached his nephew in the brisk dawn. The farrier regarded the youth for a long moment, thoroughly impressed that the lad had found them. He could not for the life of him figure out how the brat had done it.

"How did he find us?" Alexander asked in amazement as he joined the farrier.

Cody shrugged and gave the boy an unceremonious tap with the toe of his boot. Jesse moaned and rolled over, turning his back on the nuisance. It took a more forceful kick to wake him.

"What's the big idea?!" the boy snarled as he sat up. He glared blearily up at the men, his eyes hazy with sleep. "Oh. Mornin' Cody. Thought you could leave me behind, huh?"

The farrier groaned. "We were hoping you would wise up and go back to town."

"Hah, nice try," the pert youth said as he stood and stretched. He picked up his hat and planted it back on his head. "I knew you boys were up to something. I want in."

"It's nothing that concerns you. Go home." Byrne had spoken from across the camp and his tone brooked no argument.

Regardless, Jesse was one to argue against strict orders. "Aw c'mon rancher, let me ride with you." He walked into the midst of the men as they were packing their gear and preparing for the day's ride.

"You're too young," Ty answered in Byrne's place.

Jesse regarded Ty, only a few years older than himself, with an upraised brow and a look of consternation. "You're kidding, right? I'm sure I'm more skilled than you are, bud. After all, I found you lot in the dark and I was riding all alone." He sounded very proud of the fact.

"You followed the light given off by our campfire," Cody said dismissively. "You were a fool to ride at night in this country. It just proves that you're not ready to join us in this." The farrier took a fistful of the boy's shirt and dragged him toward the short-legged chestnut. Jesse made quite a ruckus, kicking and shouting and trying to dig in his heels but his scrawny frame was no match for the strength of the well-muscled farrier.

Cody tossed the boy at his horse. Jesse caught himself by latching onto a fistful of the animal's mane and just barely avoided falling flat on his face in the dust. Regaining his feet, he straightened his shirt with a brusque motion. He glared at Cody, his face turning crimson with anger. "This isn't fair! Let me help!"

"Go back to Flintridge. Take care of the stables, like you were supposed to do. Make sure you give your horse there an extra ration; he's had a rough time of it." As far as the farrier was concerned the conversation was at an end. He turned his back on his nephew, expecting to be obeyed, and walked toward his own horse.

"Can't very well give him extra when we don't know how long we'll be on the trail."

Cody stopped dead in his tracks and let out a frustrated groan. He turned on his assistant and raised a fist. Advancing on the youth, he threatened violence. Jesse winced, ready for the blow he was sure would come. He knew he deserved it, at least in part, but he wanted so badly to ride with the men, to feel he was doing something important with his life, that he was willing to accept the consequences of his actions.

"Let him follow if he wants," Alexander said suddenly. The men turned judgmental looks on the ex-sheriff. "No reason to hurt him, the boy is only doing what he thinks right." He lowered his voice so only the others of the posse could hear. "We will be traveling for awhile and I reckon he will grow bored and turn back before we reach our destination."

"Don't count on it," Cody grumbled, "the boy's like a dog with a bone." Having said his piece, he stalked over to his horse and began saddling it. Before swinging into the saddle he followed his usual habit of checking the horse's feet one by one, removing any stones and testing for loose shoes. Feeling the need to busy himself and take his mind off his errant nephew, he checked the other horses as well.

The frustrated actions of the usually calm farrier did not go unnoticed by his companions. Being men, they felt the best course of action was to leave him to his own devices until he cooled off. They still had to deal with Jesse.

Byrne took command. He looked Jesse up and down, judging his fitness and determination. "We will be on our way. You are not welcome to ride with us. I will not spare one a man to take you back to Flintridge, so you are on your own. Follow at your own risk or do the sensible thing and go home, it makes little matter to us. If your bones bleach out here I will offer your memory no sympathy."

Alexander and Ty seemed to think the rancher's pronouncement a bit harsh. The ex-sheriff glared disapprovingly at Byrne as the elder brushed past him to tend to his horse. "Mount up," Byrne ordered in a bark when they lingered still.

Jesse gave Alexander and Ty a pleading look, willing them to take his side and gain him admittance to the unique group with the mysterious purpose. Alexander gave him an apologetic look. He wanted to take the side of the underdog, for he understood Jesse's desire to be part of a cause. Still, the ex-lawman had to acknowledge that Byrne and Cody were in the right: the boy really was too young to risk his life taking on a bloodthirsty outlaw gang.

As Alexander turned his back on the hopeful youth, Jesse turned his pleading eyes on Ty. The older boy shook his head with a bemused smile and turned to join his companions. Jesse raced to saddle his mount as the men completed their preparations and began to ride off. He looked up from fumbling with the cinch as hoofbeats sounded, going past him.

"Good luck kid," Ty said cheekily. He tapped the brim of his hat in a mock salute, turned his horse, and trotted off after the others.

Jesse watched them begin to shrink as they rode away. The early morning sun was rosy, casting a deceptively warm glow over the landscape. The dust roused by the passing horses glowed pink as it floated through shafts of sunlight.

For a brief moment Jesse felt a great sense of indecision. Should he follow the men against their strict orders? Who were they to order him about? Should he obey his uncle and return to Flintridge? What adventure would he miss out on if he took the safest course of action? His youth and natural craving for adventure very quickly brought him to his final decision.

Turning back to his trusty little brown horse, Jesse tightened the cinch. The horse tossed his head, attuned to his master's sudden rush of energy. The young boy jumped into the saddle, took up the reins, and urged his horse on after the retreating posse.

All day the men kept up a rapid, determined pace. The horses easily maintained the trot demanded of them. Every few hours Byrne stopped the group to rest. It was during these stops that he had a chance to survey their surroundings and ensure there was no one watching them from hiding places on the hillsides.

The only follower they had was Jesse, on his short-legged horse. Because his steed was so short he often had to push the little chestnut faster than a trot. It seemed clear that the horse had not recovered from the previous day's exertions, for he was crabby and reluctant to speed up. Jesse was just as stubborn, desperate to keep close to the group but knowing he could not ride amongst them. So he hung a half mile back or so, always visible, always on the minds of the men.

As Byrne watered his horse he looked back at the shadowy speck trailing behind them, its figure distorted by waves of heat rising off the parched ground. He could not help but be impressed by the boy's dogged determination. It was foolish, illogical, and downright strange, but the rancher recalled with a smile that he used to be the same way. Although, he reminded himself, he had not outgrown his own reckless streak, as evidenced by the task he had laid out for himself and his comrades.

Still, he could not quite convince himself to let the boy join in on a cause to which he had no claim. There was nothing tying Jesse to Flintridge. He was not born there, so he had no reason to join in the fight to free the town from the oppression of the Hayes-Lawson gang. All Jesse wanted was an adventure; a hot-headed eager youth would be a liability in the fight that was sure to come. The boy simply could not be allowed to join them. They would have to find a way to detain him in Glenn Rock when they got there, if the youth persisted in following them all the way.

Mustering the others, Byrne led them on their way. Throughout their travels that day Jesse was always following, forcing his unhappy little horse onward.

When the light began to fade they made camp. Cody again lit a fire using what little tinder could be found on the barren plains. The men cooked and consumed their meal, making small talk amongst themselves. They were all tired and were ready to turn in as soon as they had finished eating.

Instinctively Alexander looked over his shoulder, where the speck that was Jesse and his horse had hovered all day long. They were closer than they had been following all day, but still far-removed from the men's camp. The boy had not lit a fire. He and his horse were just dark blotches against the velvety blackness of the night terrain. The ex-sheriff's brow furrowed. The air was already growing chill and he was concerned for the lad's safety.

Shooting a glance at the others he noted that they were all pointedly not looking in the youth's direction. Alexander was rather disappointed in them and wondered how they could be so unkind.

Deciding to act, he slapped his knee and stood. The others watched as he stomped purposefully away from the fire, out into the darkness, toward the younger man and his horse.

Far off a coyote called, breaking the stillness of the night. The men around the fire exchanged guilty glances. Secretly they were glad that Alexander had gone to bring the boy into their circle. No telling what might befall him alone in the desert at night.

The ex-sheriff returned minutes later, followed closely by Jesse leading his chestnut horse. The small equine looked quite tired as its master tied it with the other horses. The horses touched noses, sniffing each other to reacquaint themselves.

Without comment, Jesse was allowed to join the circle around the fire. He was handed a ration of food and ate it with ravenous hunger. He barely spared time to breathe as he bolted the meal.

When Jesse had finished he handed the plate back to Alexander. "Thank you," the boy said with genuine gratitude. After several minutes passed in silence, with the men keeping their eyes downcast, Jesse dared to ask the question burning in his mind: "So, where are we headed? Really?"

The men flicked their eyes at him, suddenly wary of him again. Much to his surprise, he got an answer from Byrne. "Glenn Rock. We need to get some supplies."

"What kind of supplies?"

"Food for us and the horses."

"Hm. Why not go back to Flintridge for it? That would have been closer."

"It's special food, too fancy for lil' old Flintridge."

Jesse could practically taste the lie. He knew better than to press the stoic rancher, however. "Alrighty then. When you feel like telling me the truth I'll be here. Mind if I ride along with you tomorrow instead of following like a stray dog?"

The men exchanged glances. They all shrugged, seemingly indifferent about his presence on the next day's ride.

"Get some sleep, we ride out at dawn," Byrne remarked. Taking his own advice he rose and went to his makeshift bed. Pulling the coarse wool blanket up to his neck, he rested his head on the saddle and was asleep almost instantly. The others very quickly followed suit after extinguishing the fire.

Throughout the night coyotes called at random intervals, disturbing those men who were unaccustomed to camping in the wilderness. The horses shifted restlessly when multiple canine voices sounded.

Dawn seemed to come far too soon for the exhausted travelers.

Tired and disinclined toward conversation, the men made their preparations. Jesse was very stiff, as was Ty, since neither of them was used to spending much time in the saddle. Another full day's ride was not an appealing thought, but they knew better than to complain.

Without a word passing between them the posse saddled their horses and set off. Byrne pressed the pace, wanting to make it to the town before night fell.

Due to the insistent pace and few breaks they took, Glenn Rock rose into view on the horizon by late afternoon. They rode into town and hired a room for the night. The horses were left in the stables and given a full ration of oats and hay. The tired beasts were able to lie down on warm straw bedding and relax after their journey. Likewise, the men were able to rest their bones in the safety of an inn room, even though most of them slept on the floor.

The structure muted the howls of the coyotes without. In the dead of the night the coyotes banded together, combining their voices in a cacophony of yelping, barking and crying. The sound cut through the men's sleep, giving them fitful dreams.

The next morning the men found themselves faced with a tricky proposition: they had to neutralize Jesse's interest in their purpose, get him off their trail, and, if possible, find a way to leave him in Glenn Rock. In the end it would be for his safety as well as theirs. As Byrne drank his morning coffee he mulled over the challenge facing him. The others were absent, each tending to their own purposes. The coffee was weak, more water than actual flavor. Regardless, the drink warmed his bones and helped his mind to function.

The rancher drummed his fingers on the table and sipped at his beverage. His face was lined with worry, his brow furrowed in deep thought. When the barmaid delivered his plate of eggs and ham he scarcely noticed its arrival. The plate sat, steaming, for a long while as the rancher turned one thought after another over in his mind. He finished his coffee and the cup sat empty.

Finally the aroma of good food broke through his musings and his stomach grumbled. Byrne shrugged out of his brown study and began consuming his breakfast. *It's not like Ivey makes it*, he mused silently as he chewed a mouthful of scrambled eggs. The thought, though fleeting and immaterial, made him suddenly very sad. Thinking of his wife, alone in a town governed by ruffians, made his heart race. A knot formed in his stomach as fear for her well-being flooded through him.

The strange melody of coyote calls from the night before flooded into his mind, increasing his anxiety. Suddenly he felt a strong sense of urgency; he had allowed them to waste far too much time. Setting his fork aside and tossing some coins on the table to pay for his meal, he rose and strode briskly out of the establishment.

Without even bothering to find the others he hastened through the town until he found the store for which he had been searching. He ascended the few steps to the veranda and entered.

Within, a few people loitered about. Some were leaning against crates or barrels, talking amongst each other about such bland topics as the weather, crops, and the like. Others were engaged in serious shopping, browsing the shelves for supplies.

Byrne's eyes searched for one thing only. Eventually he found a set of them, propped against a wall in the far corner. The rancher made his way toward them, swerving around other patrons and stacks of cargo.

He picked one up, testing the weight of it, examining the craftsmanship. The rifle felt sound and heavy in his hands, the stock was sanded smooth and varnished, the metal of the barrel cast without flaw. He judged it to be a decent weapon for their purpose.

Taking the gun to the front of the store, he laid it on the countertop. The clerk gave him a brief look. "How much for this?" Byrne asked, indicating the weapon.

The clerk, an older man who seemed to be weary of everything in the world, adjusted his spectacles and looked the rifle over. "We don't sell many of these," he remarked, picking the gun up to get a better look at it. He named a price.

"Is there any way we can barter lower? I'm looking to buy them in bulk if that makes a difference."

The shopkeeper raised his bushy gray eyebrows. "How many are you lookin' to buy?"

"How many do you have?"

"What on earth do you need that many guns for, sir?"

Byrne shrugged and realized he was showing too intense an interest in the conversation. He leaned back, feigning indifference. "Got one heck of a coyote problem back home. The boss wanted me to pick up some guns so we can exterminate the vermin. Do you have smaller arms as well?"

Unfazed by the sudden change of topic and apparently accepting the excuse as valid, the shopkeeper ducked under the counter and came back up with a pistol in his hand. "This about what you're looking for?"

Taking the gun into his own hands, Byrne nodded slowly. He opened the chamber, examined it, snapped it shut and spun it. The motions were fluid and he felt confident the pistol would not jam. "How many of these do you have?" The shopkeeper answered and gave him a price per piece. "Any bulk discount?"

"You really do hate coyotes," the older man said with a laugh, subtly deflecting the question.

Byrne took that to mean that no discount would be given. He nodded thoughtfully, silently wondering how much money his posse had amongst them. He very much doubted it would be enough for all the weapons they would need to take on the Hayes-Lawson gang.

He drummed his fingers on the counter, staring blankly at the guns. In his pocket he had only enough to purchase one pistol. Each of the men would need at least one gun, although the preference would be two pistols each and a rifle. Then there was the cost of extra ammunition, food for the journey back...the list continued to grow longer and longer in his mind. Byrne let out an involuntary sigh. There was no way they could afford all that. He decided to chance repeating his question. "So you can't make me a deal on these? Not even for the most up-and-coming rancher moving west?"

The look given him by the shopkeeper was withering. Byrne took the hint and did not question the pricing further. Reluctantly he dug in his pocket and laid some coin on the counter. "Alright then, I'll take one of these pistols and some extra bullets."

"How many bullets d'you want?"

"As many as my money can buy, good sir," Byrne replied, trying to keep the sourness he felt out of his voice.

Without further comment the shopkeeper processed his order. Byrne left with just one coin left in his pocket. But in his hand he carried the pistol, its chamber loaded with bullets. The rest of the bullets, the two extra he was able to afford, rattled in his pocket as he walked. Tucking the gun into the waist of his pants - he had nowhere better to carry the weapon - he went searching for his comrades. They would have to pool their resources to make their act of rebellion work.

CHAPTER FOURTEEN

Miles away, back in Flintridge, Ivey sat at the front window of the home her husband had built. She sat in the rocking chair, slowing rocking back and forth. Her azure eyes, sad and worried, stared out the window, praying for a glimpse of her husband returning. Absently she laid her hand on her stomach, where the baby bulge was beginning to grow. Sadie lay at her feet, chin resting on her paws, half-asleep. The dog had proven herself a good companion and served to banish at least some of Ivey's loneliness.

A loud whinny from without commanded her attention. The horses were reminding her that it was feeding time. Her eyes flitted over the paddocks. The equines stirred restlessly, as they always did when the hour approached a mealtime. "Come Sadie, let's go out," Ivey murmured, pushing herself out of the rocking chair.

She opened the front door and the dog charged out into the yard, barking gleefully as she cavorted about. Ivey followed more slowly, immensely conscious of the burden she carried. She had never before been pregnant and she was taking no chances with this first child.

The rancher's wife went to the feed shed and pulled out the rations of hay and oats for the horses. Dutifully she tossed the food over the fence and the horses fell on it as if they had not eaten for weeks. She knew it was nonsense, since she had fed them breakfast that morning. Ivey smiled as she watched the horses tuck into the hay.

Ivey was about to go back inside when Sadie's shrill barks cut through the air. They were not the playful barks that Ivey had come to expect from the dog. She turned to look in the direction of the sounds with a furrowed brow. The sun was setting, casting a blinding gold light at a sharp angle across the land. It made it nigh on impossible for Ivey to see whatever it was that was upsetting the dog. She brought her hand up to shield her eyes from the blinding light.

Through the slanting rays of liquid gold radiance she finally was able to make out a form. A horse and rider approached. Excitement rose in Ivey's heart at the sight.

She hastened across the farmyard, past the horse pens, and finally had to stop, winded, at the edge of the property. Sadie had run along at her heels and now came to a stop beside her. The dog held her brindle and white head tipped to the side, ears pricked inquiringly.

As the horse and rider drew closer, the dog leapt in front of Ivey, holding her head low and growling in an unwelcoming fashion. The fur on her shoulders stood on end.

"Sadie, what are you doing? That's Byrne!" Ivey chastised, taking hold of the dog's crude rope collar.

The sun was still blinding, obscuring the face of the rider, the details of his costume, even the color of his horse's coat. Still, Ivey was so desperate to see her husband that she believed it must be him. After all, no one had come to visit since he left, so who else would it be?

Her hopes were defeated when he drew near enough to speak to her. "I have not seen the rancher about lately. What did he do, just up and leave and leave you to tend the farm in his absence?"

Ivey stopped short. Immediately she took exception to the voice. It was a well-bred voice, but the words set her on edge. She stood tall, releasing Sadie, and raised her chin, showing herself as the fine lady she had been brought up to be. "I hardly see what concern it is of yours," she said haughtily, refusing to be intimidated.

The strange man swung down from his horse and dropped a rein, ground tying the equine. The horse cocked one hind foot, recognizing that it would now be allowed to rest. It hung its head and sighed. The rider stretched languidly and cast his gaze around the yard casually.

"State your business or be on your way," Ivey remarked in what she hoped was a firm voice.

"Is that how you treat guests?"

"That is how I treat strange men who barge onto my property," was the curt answer.

The strange man stepped closer to her. Ivey stood firm though her instinct was to move away from him. Sadie growled and raised her hackles. He stepped around the pair, slowly circling. Ivey refused to turn to keep her eyes on him, instead determining to stand firm. She noted that he was well-dressed, which was uncommonly seen in Flintridge outside of Sundays. One of his teeth was gold-capped and it glinted in the afternoon light.

She flinched involuntarily as his hand landed on her shoulder. "Where'd he go?"

Ivey spun to face him then, her skin flushed with indignant fury. She opened her mouth to scold him but the words stuck in her throat. His eyes were mesmerizing, like a snake's. She swallowed tightly, unsure what to do next. She knew she could not physically force him off the property. Maybe if she told him a convincing fabrication he would choose to leave. "He went mustang hunting."

"When?"

"A few days ago."

"How long before you expect him to return?" He began pacing around her again as if it helped his thought process. His hand slipped off her shoulder, for which she was very grateful.

Ivey shrugged, trying to act calm. "One never knows how long it will take."

"Did he go alone?" He put his hand to his chin, contemplating her answers. She knew he was examining her every word, eager to see if she was lying.

"He invited some of his friends along. Is that a crime?" Her voice was rising. She was growing more on-edge as the seconds ticked by. When he stopped abruptly she felt her heart start beating even faster. She wondered if her heartbeat was audible to him.

"It might be," was the smooth reply. Though his voice was light and seemingly conversational, it concealed a threat. "You seem to know very little of his activities. I find that odd. Does he not trust you with information?"

Ivey merely glared at him, unwilling to grace him with an answer. Without warning he stepped closer to her, invading her space. She tried to shrink back but his hands gripped her arms and held her fast.

Ivey struggled in his grasp, shocked at his impertinence. "Release me at once!" she commanded in a somewhat shrill voice.

Sadie snarled ferociously and bit the man's leg. He shook her off with a sneer and once she had been loosed he kicked her hard in the ribs. With a yelp the dog backed down, slinking around the pair with wary eyes. Her fur stood on-end.

When the man turned his attention back to the woman he held, she met his gray-green eyes with a hard stare. She swallowed tightly, terrified. "Why have your masters sent you out here?"

"They are not my masters," he replied with some vehemence, shaking her in his sudden rush of anger. Catching himself, he offered her a mildly apologetic look; his eyes softened marginally.

The man tipped his head nonchalantly. He grinned, showing off his gold tooth. "The bosses sent me out to check up on your husband, make sure he was comfortable with the changes to the social order hereabouts." He looked down at her with narrowed eyes, checking to see if her expression would give away her thoughts. "Hmph," he chuckled quietly. His breath fluttered her hair.

"Who are you?"

"Oh, please do forgive me for not introducing myself. How rude of me." He released her and backed away. Apparently, though he was an outlaw, he was not completely devoid of manners. "Derek Ward, at your service Mrs. Jameson."

Ivey thought she might press her advantage and her luck. If the man had manners enough to go through an introduction, perhaps she could shame him into leaving. It was worth a shot. "And who are you, Mr. Ward, to be trespassing on my husband's property?"

He pretended to be unfazed by her strong words but he shuffled back a step, giving ground. Emboldened, Ivey pushed on. "You should be ashamed of yourself; it is clear that you are not a common man. You were raised in a good family, I am sure of it, but where has your sense of decency and respect for others gone? My husband will not appreciate your actions today. I recommend that you leave immediately." She stepped forward, trying to push him back even further. He backed up once more. It seemed her words had held some sway with him for he did not invade her personal space again. For the first time he broke off eye contact.

"I am just doing my job, Mrs. Jameson," he said with his suave, well-bred voice. "You cannot blame a man for that, now can you?"

"I can if it violates the rights of honest folk," she snapped.

"Oh, I am sorry, you seem to be under some misconception: out here, in the West, there are no rights. Especially in this town. The rules are that there are no rules and no one to enforce them. My bosses' will is the only law, and is only such because they have the muscle to back it up. Your husband knows this."

Ivey's blood began to rise. "Only a coward would sneak onto his property when Byrne is not home to defend it."

Something snapped in the man. She had made a mistake, had pushed him too far. Derek stepped up to her and grabbed her arm, holding it in an iron grip. No matter how hard she tried to pull free, he held her firm.

She lashed out and slapped him with her free hand smartly. He worked his jaw. Their eyes met for a brief second before he turned, dragging her along with him. She fought every step of the way.

"I thought something was amiss here," he remarked in a cold, dry voice. "Come along, Mrs. Jameson, the bosses will want to have a few words with you."

Ivey screamed and flailed but her efforts were futile. He dragged her over to his horse. As they progressed, Sadie grew bold in her desire to protect her mistress; she chased after the man and latched onto his leg again. Again he shook her off. She jumped aside before he could kick her and went in for another bite. It took a good deal of Derek's concentration to ward off the enraged canine.

He flung Ivey toward his horse and she slammed up against the docile animal's shoulder. The horse merely turned its head and snuffled inquiringly at her. Derek picked her up and tossed her into the saddle. He swung up behind her and took up the reins, his other arm holding her fast about the waist.

As they rode off, back toward the town, Sadie chased after the horse. She nipped at its heels. She ran round and round it, trying to force it to stop. The horse had been well-trained; while he did throw a half-hearted kick at the dog, he was otherwise unfazed by her aggression.

Finally the determined mutt had to admit defeat. Her pursuit tapered off as they reached the property line. She stood in the yard, watching with sad eyes as her mistress was carried off.

Ivey did not give up so easily. She pounded her fists on the arm that held her. Derek grimaced in pain. She was much stronger than her petite form would lead one to believe. Still, he held her. The horse galloped on.

Her next tactic was to try and get the reins away from her captor. She grabbed hold of the leather straps and pulled on them with all her might. Derek was able to hold on, though the leather slid through his gloved hand just a bit.

Ivey leaned forward suddenly, looking to take control of the animal nearer it's mouth. Derek caught onto her plan and pulled her back but not before she got hold of one rein. As she pulled back, the leather tightened on one side of the animal's mouth, drawing it around sharply. The horse let out a snort of protest as he turned in a tight circle to the left, breaking stride. He slowed to a trot and finally a walk as he was pulled round in tighter and tighter circles.

"Let go of it!" Derek snarled. He was forced to release her for a moment while he leaned forward and pried her fingers off the leather. The horse straightened out his neck and stopped with a heavy sigh.

Keeping her wrists trapped in his one hand, Derek looked about him for a restraint of some kind. He pulled an extra leather tie off his saddle and bound her hands. Wrapping his arm around her again, he kicked the horse back into a gallop. "Just settle down now," he remarked in a quiet voice. "I promise I don't want to hurt you. The less fuss you make, the better."

His words made Ivey even more afraid of the fate that awaited her in Flintridge. The town was nearing at a rapid pace. She screamed and renewed her struggles to get free of him. Derek cursed under his breath as he tried to calm the female in the saddle before him.

Finally he was forced to lay the reins on his horse's neck and untie the bandana around his neck. Whistling and clicking to encourage the horse to keep going, he gagged Ivey with the bandana, muffling her screams. Regardless, she continued to scream into the gag while he took up the reins and whipped the horse on to a faster pace. The horse snorted, annoyed by its rider's haste, but obediently stretched its legs out and sped up.

They tore into Flintridge and charged headlong down the main street. Townsfolk dived out of the way while other members of the gang jumped onto their horses and followed Derek, shouting cat-calls and whistling at Ivey as they rode up alongside.

The noisy, rowdy procession came to a stop outside the saloon. Ivey's heart was hammering in her chest. Once he got her inside, escape would be impossible. She had just one more idea to try.

Derek was laying the reins on his horse's sweaty neck when Ivey threw her head back with all her might, hitting him square in the nose. With a sharp cry of pain, Derek brought a hand up to his face. It came back bloody. He gripped his nose, trying to stabilize the break. "Whore!" he snarled, shoving her roughly from the saddle. She toppled to the ground and lay, stunned. Her wrists were still bound behind her and she feared she could not get up.

But when the outlaws began pressing in and Derek slid from the saddle, she found that she did have the strength and coordination needed to stand after all. She gained her feet awkwardly and made a run for it. One of the men caught her arm and flung her back, laughing cruelly. She fell into the burly arms of another thug, who ruffled her hair with his disgusting blackened fingers before passing her along to the next man…and the next…

Finally she ended up in arms that were vaguely familiar. She looked meekly up at Derek's bloody face. He grimaced down at her and shook his head. Taking hold of her hair, he dragged her into the saloon and threw her to the floor.

Trembling, Ivey dared not open her eyes for a long moment. What would come next? She shuddered to think of the vile acts these lawless men might commit against her.

Derek came to stand behind her shaking form. He rolled up his sleeves to try and cool off; he was sweating from his endeavors. While he had managed to clean some of the blood from his face, a slow trickle still came from his broken nose.

"Had some trouble bringing her in Derek?" one of the men seated at the nearest table remarked. Derek nodded minutely in acknowledgement of his boss' comment.

"A mere woman did that to you?" The other man asked in amusement.

Derek swiped the blood from his lip. His forearm smarted and was already bruising, a result of Ivey beating him with her fists. He heaved a sigh, already in a foul temper and not appreciating the jokes made at his expense. He dared not speak his mind, however.

Pistol Lawson threw down his hand of cards and stood. He took the cigar from his mouth and exhaled a cloud of smoke. His unkind stare trained itself on Ivey, still lying on the floor with her eyes clenched tight. "I take this to mean you did not find her husband at home?" he asked of Derek.

The gentlemanly bandit snorted quietly, winced, and tried to speak despite the pain doing so caused him. "Byrne wasn't there," he remarked in a strained nasally voice. The pain seemed to flare up again for he pinched his broken nose between his fingers and sought out a chair in which to sit.

"Girl, get our friend some whiskey," Lawson ordered of a nearby barmaid. She hastened to fetch a drink for the wounded outlaw. When she returned she handed Derek a full glass of amber liquid and a wadded damp cloth. The bandit took it with a nod of thanks. He threw back the whiskey in a few gulps and then pressed the cloth delicately to his tender nose. He leaned back in his chair and kept a sharp eye on the proceedings.

Lawson knelt by Ivey. She heard his motions and dared to crack an eye open; knowing nothing outside of sounds was far more terrifying than anything she might see. In her current position she could see only the outlaw's knee where it touched the rough floorboards and plumes of smoke drifting down from his cigar. Suddenly she felt fingers brushing the hair away from her face and she flinched, sickened by the touch of yet another strange man. Pistol Lawson laughed. "Pretty little thing, innit she?" He looked up at his companions for their opinions. Derek gave an awful sneer while Gravedigger pretended to ignore the question.

Ivey was trembling again, her breath coming in quick, fearful gasps.

"Sit up a moment," Lawson instructed. He did not wait for Ivey to comply, instead he lifted her bodily off the floor and planted her in a chair nearby. She was quivering, unable to calm her body. She shot furtive glances at the outlaw gang leaders, not daring to make full eye contact with them. Peripherally she felt the weight of Derek's stare. He was some feet away, seated at another table. She imagined that he was still furious about the injury she had caused him.

Lawson took out his knife and Ivey turned her head away, terrified at what he might do with it. He paced slowly around her, his predatory eyes weighing heavily on her. Then he seized her wrists and cut the leather ties that bound her.

Surprised, Ivey brought her hands in front of her and rubbed at her tender wrists. The leather had bit into them in the course of her struggles, leaving ugly red lines.

Lawson cast a judging look at Derek, clearly wondering how a woman with her wrists tied could have broken his nose and bruised him up. Derek pointedly ignored this look; he had closed his eyes and was trying to get a handle on the pain.

The rancher's wife held her chin high, refusing to meet Pistol's steely eyes when they returned to her. She laid her hands in her lap and sat up straight, the very image of dignity.

Lawson knelt down before her and looked up at her with what was, for him, a soft expression. "So, Derek didn't find your husband on his ranch I gather," he began, resting his hand on her knee.

She turned in her chair, pulling her knee from beneath his hand. Still she refused to look at him. "You will do well to allow me to go home immediately and discontinue this most unorthodox interrogation. If you do so I may conceal your indiscretion from my husband and save you a thrashing."

Lawson threw back his head and laughed raucously. Hayes chuckled against his glass of whiskey. Derek, out of sight of Ivey, shook his head mournfully. He knew she was treading a thin line. If she kept it up one of the gang leaders would lose his temper. At that moment he was too preoccupied with his bleeding nose to intervene.

Ivey took offense to the looks of derision on the gang leaders' faces. Her southern blood began to boil, lending her boldness she might otherwise have kept in check. She stood, heedless of her close proximity to Pistol Lawson. Ivey looked piercingly down at him, silently shaming him for his actions.

Just as she turned to make good her escape he caught her by the arm, whirled her back around, and slammed her back into the chair. Ivey looked at him in surprise; she had thought her arguments held sway. Apparently she had been wrong.

Lawson planted his hands on the chair seat, on either side of her thighs and leaned in close to her face. His breath reeked of alcohol, stale cigars and decay. Ivey twisted up her face, trying to avoid smelling the vulgar scent. This close she could see that his teeth were well and truly rotten, yellow and black, with several missing. Unlike Derek, he had not thought to replace his lost teeth with gold ones. He was dirty and smelled horrible, as though he had not bathed for months. She presumed that he had not bothered to tidy himself since arriving in Flintridge. She almost said as much to him but then caught herself. His rag-tag clothing concealed a muscular body and in that moment Ivey realized, with a sinking heart, that she would not be able to leave unless they allowed her to go.

Pistol Lawson bobbed his head, his lips coming dangerously close to hers. "Now what indiscretion of mine were you going to keep from your husband?" His foul breath brushed her cheeks and Ivey turned away, coughing a little. "I haven't done anything to you...yet." The words made Ivey's blood run cold. Her mind filled with images and ideas, all vile, of what might befall her in the coming minutes.

"Your husband poses us no threat, Mrs. Jameson," Gravedigger remarked stoically from his seat at the table. His voice was gravelly and painful to hear; she suspected it hurt him a great deal to speak, which might be why he let Pistol do most of the talking.

"That's right," Pistol added, picking up the new direction of conversation from his partner, "he can't do nothin' to us. We just like to keep an eye on the residents of our humble town." He emphasized his 'h', exhaling heavily in Ivey's face. She coughed again, unable to stand the vulgar smell of him. The bandit grinned, thoroughly enjoying tormenting her.

"Why Byrne in particular? You seem to be expending a lot of energy and resources to find out why he is not at home."

Derek shifted noisily in his chair. Ivey ignored him, keeping her attention focused on Lawson.

"Why Byrne?" Hayes laughed. "Because, that low-down scoundrel rode with us once."

CHAPTER FIFTEEN

"Byrne, that's got to be the craziest thing I've ever heard you say," Ty remarked. His brow was knit and his eyes worried. What the rancher had proposed was so weird, so backward, so, well, impossible.

"I absolutely refuse to be a part of this hair-brained scheme," Alexander remarked. He crossed his arms and turned his back on the group.

"Oh c'mon Alex, it's not like you're a sheriff anymore," Byrne remarked. His tone was good-natured but the words cut into Alexander like a knife. He whirled on the rancher, his eyes fiery and body tense. Byrne stared him down and the ex-sheriff's fury subsided a bit. He huffed and crossed his arms again. His face was a study in contemplative melancholy.

"I don't like it any better'n the rest of you, but what choice have we? We need guns to take on the Hayes-Lawsons - we all know even fully armed we'd be out-manned - but we have not the funds to purchase them. That leaves us with a bit of a conundrum, doesn't it? Not to mention the food we'll need to see us back to Flintridge. I don't know about you but I'd just as soon face the gang on a full stomach instead of fasting for three days before."

None of them could argue against his points. They were all valid, all miserably true. Ponder for long moments though they did, none of them could come up with a better alternative.

Byrne looked around the group at his comrades. He stared at each one until they reluctantly raised their eyes to meet his. Cody and Ty seemed to be resigned to following along with the scheme but Alexander still held strong reservations.

"I simply cannot conscience being a part of this," Alexander said with a tone of finality. He shook his head, still bewildered that such an absurd, lawless plan had been concocted by the seemingly upstanding rancher.

"I understand your position very well," Byrne remarked. "If you don't object, however, I do have one job for you - a fairly inactive role, mind, one that will not compromise your standing with the law." Alexander refused to answer, still indignant. Byrne continued anyway. "Obviously we do not want the boy involved in this. He's been enough of a problem already. I can see him getting overexcited and ruining everything. Could you be a chap and keep him out of the way?"

Alexander heaved a heavy sigh. He knew when he signed up with Byrne that he would have to do things that might go against his morals. This, however, had been one step too far. Still, he wanted to be of use in ousting the Hayes-Lawson gang. Since he refused to actively participate in the venture, he felt he must do something to help further the cause. Closing his eyes, regretting the words before he uttered them, Alexander acquiesced.

"Good man!" Byrne said quickly, clapping the ex-sheriff on the back. "Now, you can go find our little stowaway while we lay plans for the day."

Alexander sighed again and stepped slowly toward the door. "I just hope you know what you're doing, Byrne," he muttered listlessly. He did not even entertain the notion of talking the others out of the scheme.

Byrne waited until Alexander had left the room. He turned to the other two men and was rather disappointed. They did not quite resemble outlaws, though they had tried to alter their costumes a bit. So long as they kept their identities concealed, that would be enough. The rancher pulled his kerchief up to cover the lower part of his face. He double-checked that his gun was loaded and then looked to the others. They had checked their weapons as well and were just pulling their bandanas up to conceal their features. "Right then. Out the back way. If you have to talk, change your voice. Everyone ready?"

Silent nods were the only answers. Byrne nodded as well. There was a knot of excitement and concern in his gut. He thought he had everything planned out, but there was just no way of knowing what would happen. Pushing his worries to the back of his mind he led the way out, trying to hold his gun so that it was not obvious that he was armed.

Much to his surprise they reached the general store without incident. Byrne did not hesitate: he kicked the door open and rushed in, hefting his gun up before him and aiming it at the first person he saw. Cody and Ty were close behind him and followed his example.

Their arrival elicited screams from the patrons and everyone ducked for cover. Something stirred in Byrne, a memory from long ago, and he felt a sense of satisfaction. He hated himself for it.

"Out!" Cody snarled authoritatively, waving his gun in a wide arch.

Men grabbed their wives and children and slunk out, keeping wary eyes on the outlaws and their guns. When Byrne felt some were moving too slowly he stepped behind them and forced them on, waving his gun threateningly. They let out cries of terror and rushed out into the street. Even the shop owner abandoned his store in favor of saving his life.

Once they had the store to themselves the three tucked their guns away and began frantically raiding the place. They found burlap sacks and stuffed them full of food, guns and ammunition. Everything else they left. They only took what they would need to accomplish their mission. They worked in haste, knowing at any moment they might be caught and challenged; they were not real outlaws, they knew they could not hurt innocent people.

With their sacks full of supplies they finally made for the back door of the store, hoping to escape round the back to the stables and retrieve their horses. Then they would only need to find Alexander and make a break for it.

To avoid the townsfolk forming a posse and catching up to them they would have to ride hard until dark and hide away in the hills. Byrne thought, with a strange mixture of pleasure and bitterness, that they were becoming bandits themselves. But, unlike the Hayes-Lawson gang, they had a purpose.

They kept their bandanas up over the lower part of their faces, desperate to conceal their identities. Furtively, they slunk round the back of the buildings on the main street, wove their way down alleys and finally reached the stables. Fortune seemed to be on their side, for the stable attendant was nowhere to be seen.

Byrne found the whole business easy, maybe too easy. He felt certain the townsfolk would not passively let them go.

Loading the horses with their ill-gotten loot, Ty and Cody swung into the saddles. "What about Alexander?" Ty asked in a low, gruff voice.

"He's only half-dumb. He'll figure out that he needs to follow when we rush outta here," Byrne answered as if it were obvious that they would leave Alexander to fend for himself for a time. The others did not seem pleased with his decision, but they also could see no reasonable alternative that would not end in them being caught.

Byrne led Cowboy to the stable door. "Ready? Here we go!" He swung the doors wide open. Cowboy instinctively bolted for the outside, as Byrne knew he would, and the rancher leapt into the saddle as the chestnut mustang broke into a run. Ty and Cody could not hold their horses back; they charged out after Cowboy.

Out in the street Byrne turned Cowboy for the quickest exit. The mustang threw his head, excited to be running again. The trio plowed their way through crowds of people, slowing only enough so they did not injure anyone.

Byrne spotted Alexander standing on the veranda of one of the shops. He was watching them in open-mouthed shock. Apparently actually witnessing the act was more repulsive to him than talking it through had been. The rancher let out a sharp, piercing whistle, a cue he hoped the ex-sheriff would understand.

Leaving Alexander in the dust, they rushed onward.

As Byrne had feared, they were to be met with resistance. Just before they would have cleared the town a broken line of men with guns formed. All the weapons were aimed at the marauding trio.

His blood running high with excitement, Byrne drew his own weapon in answer. Unlike the men on foot he was not aiming to kill. As Cowboy ran blindly along, Byrne took aim at the ground just near the men's feet, intending to clear a path through which the horses might pass and cause some confusion among the ranks. He fired off all six rounds in his gun. The bullets peppered the dusty ground very near the feet of the men. Instinctively they leapt back and aside, letting out exclamations. The muzzles of their guns dropped for that critical second.

Cowboy was upon them. The sturdy chestnut knew exactly what he had to do. Holding his head high he ploughed past the men, clipping one with his shoulder. The other horses followed in a rough V formation, throwing more men out of place. A few guns went off in the confusion. Byrne did not look back. Looking back, he knew, could be a costly mistake.

By the time the posse had recovered enough to fire off shots properly the trio was almost out of range. Almost. The townsfolk fired after them. Spumes of dust rose around their horses.

Cody and Ty's horses threw their heads and screamed in terror, shying violently. Byrne called back to the men, encouraging them to force the horses onward. When the beasts remained stubborn amongst another peppering of shot, Byrne reluctantly swung Cowboy back around. Letting the mustang have his head, he allowed him to act the part of a herd stallion again, pressing the skittish horses until they got moving again. Cowboy then charged back to the lead and the others willingly followed him.

Byrne was concerned that some damage had been done in those precious moments when they dallied within shooting range. He could not look back to check on his comrades, he could only assume that since they were still in the saddle they were alright. Even if they were not, the group could not stop there, in the open, where they would be easily hunted down.

With Cowboy in the lead, drawing the others onward, the trio of robbers raced out into the desert-like flats surrounding the town of Glenn Rock. The horses ran willingly despite their extra load of weaponry and food. They sensed the urgency that drove their riders to spur and whip them and so they flew across the dry, flat ground.

When they were far enough from the town to be almost indistinguishable, Byrne turned Cowboy toward the distant mesas. There they would shelter for a time and wait for Alexander to catch up, if he was clever enough to find them. Before long the wind blowing across the plains would obscure the tracks made by the horses as they fled. While this would be a benefit to them, preventing the townsfolk from tracking them should they come after the thieves, it would make it more difficult for Alexander to determine at which point they had veered toward the safety of the hills. Byrne hoped the ex-sheriff was smarter than he gave him credit for; if they had to go against the Hayes-Lawson gang short even one man, they would stand no chance of succeeding. As it was they hardly had a prayer of success.

The horses were blowing and sweaty, exhausting quickly after their previous days of exertion and moderate food. Byrne allowed them to slacken pace just a little, dropping to a swift trot. They would cover ground while saving the horses a bit.

When they finally reached the shelter of the first low hills the sun was already halfway to the horizon. Byrne wanted to continue, to get further away, to hide in the twisting and turning canyons. However, he was forced to concede that if they did not wait for Alexander he likely would not catch up to them.

So, the rancher allowed them a rest.

Eagerly the men adjusted their outfits, pulling the bandanas from their faces and shaking off their heavy coats. The day was warm and they had been sweating in those dense coats for the majority of the sunlight hours. They were all red-faced and thirsty but had to share their meager water rations with the winded horses. Byrne made sure they all drank in moderation, favoring the horses over themselves. They unloaded their guns, putting the ammunition safely in their packs.

As Ty was loading his extra items into his saddlebag he looked aside at Cody and noticed that the other man was pale and shaking. "You okay there Cody?"

His question caught Byrne's attention immediately and the rancher joined the others, concern written on his features. Cody could only nod as he struggled for breath. "No you're not. Sit down." Byrne helped him to sit on a nearby rock, forcing the stubborn farrier down. "Where are you hit?"

"I tell you it's nothing. Horses have kicked me harder'n this and it's never slowed me up none," Cody insisted as he shoved Byrne's hand off his shoulder. Byrne saw the wound, then, and realized how close they had come to real disaster. The left leg of Cody's pants was rent on the outer side of the calf. The bullet must have flown mere inches from his horse's haunches; had it struck and lamed or downed the beast they would never have got away.

Byrne exhaled silently, grateful that it was, as the farrier claimed, no more than a flesh wound. "Bind it up all the same, you don't want to lose anymore blood." As far as the rancher was concerned, he had dealt with the crisis.

Leaving the others to follow his instructions, Byrne took it upon himself to climb the nearest bluff overlooking the desert and keep watch for approaching riders. He had not noticed anyone following them out of Glenn Rock but if Alexander found their trail, or guessed it correctly, he might be followed.

Such possibilities weighed heavily on the rancher's mind as he sat atop the bluff. There was so much that could go wrong and his mind kept replaying pessimistic scenarios.

The sun beat down mercilessly from overhead. Though it was sinking steadily with the promise of night at hand, it was morbidly hot and Byrne was sweating heavily. His eyes, narrowed against the blinding glare of the slanting rays of sunlight, were growing strained from their constant vigil. The wind, when it did blow, was not soothing. It brushed dust and grit into his eyes, making them red and itchy.

Peripherally he heard the small rustlings and hushed conversation made by his companions below. The horses stamped flies from their legs and let out tired snorts every now and again. Somewhere in the hills, far from them, a coyote made its barking howl and was joined by others. Despite the heat, the sound sent chills up the rancher's spine.

He continued to visually search near the town of Glenn Rock, almost invisible on the horizon, for signs of a horse and rider. As time dragged by he began to have his doubts. Had Alexander deserted them? Would he follow? Had he been detained for some reason? The image of the ex-sheriff's disapproving look at them as they had ridden out of town surfaced in Byrne's mind and he began to fear that they had committed a grave error in leaving Alexander to his own devices. What would they do if they really were short a man? Should one of them go back to Glenn Rock and fetch Alexander?

Just as his fears were reaching a fever pitch a small black dot appeared on the horizon, moving away from Glenn Rock. Byrne's breath hitched in his chest. He squinted at the speck, focusing with all his distracted concentration. For certain, it was only one horse and its rider. It must be Alexander. No one from the town would ride out after outlaws alone.

Byrne turned and called over his shoulder to the others. "I think Alexander's finally making his way," he remarked, just loud enough to be heard. If he was wrong, and it was not Alexander, it would do no good to risk giving away their position. He would wait until the rider was closer, until they were sure of his identity, before summoning him.

It was rather a long wait. Dusk settled and the rider was still quite a ways out. They were moving at a trot, whereas Byrne and the others had been riding at full gallop. Clearly, this man was in no hurry. The wait made Byrne antsy. He really had wanted to get further from Glenn Rock before dark. There was no hope of that now.

As night settled in and the last remaining vestiges of light faded away, Byrne lost sight of the horse and rider. When last he saw them he thought they had been about to turn off on the track leading into the hills but he could not be sure. Pounding a fist in the gritty dirt, he debated silently with himself.

At last his impatience won out. Slithering down the loose scree bank, he gained his feet and walked straight to Cowboy. The intelligent stallion turned to look at his master, seeming to sense his intentions. Byrne swung into the saddle, ignoring the strange looks given him by Ty and Cody.

"You're going riding? Now?" Ty asked incredulously.

"Only to bring Alexander in. I doubt he can track in the dark."

"What about the terrain? Aren't you risking a lot?"

Byrne shook his head in the negative. Instead of answering, he patted the mustang on the neck and let him step out, away from the others, and they disappeared into the night. His voice floated back to them. "Don't light a fire, mind, we don't want to give any searchers a beacon."

CHAPTER SIXTEEN

Ivey's breath caught in her throat. She stared hard at the scoundrel Pistol Lawson, trying to read his lined, ugly face. His mouth was turned in a cruel sneer, his dark brown eyes flinty and hard, stained teeth showing. "You're lying," she insisted, trying to hide how shaken she was by his statement. It simply could not be true. Her husband, her Byrne, would never in his life have been a bandit. It simply was not in his nature to be as bloodthirsty and cold-hearted as the men that held her hostage.

"Don't you wish I was?" The bandit laughed again. "Your husband's a lowlife, just like us." He stood and stretched, casually, depriving her of the additional information she clearly wanted to hear. His statement had stung her badly but she was dying to hear more, to try and find a flaw in his tale that would disprove the whole thing.

"Clever mind he has. It were a shame when he went off on his own, or so I keep hearing. He planned all the best and cleanest robberies. Never lost a man under his leadership - or so I heard." Lawson shot a glance at his co-leader, Cliff Hayes, who had not moved.

Ivey practically jumped in her chair. Matters had become worse in those few sentences, much worse. Byrne had had a leadership role amongst the bandits? Catching herself on the verge of an outburst, she reined herself in and refused to allow herself to believe the lies of a lowly convict.

Still, as she turned her head away with a distrustful frown, she could not wholly convince herself. She put up a good show for the bandits but the seeds of doubt had been planted and were already growing wild in her mind and heart.

Pistol laughed, his foul breath brushing over her fair skin. Ivey shuddered, abhorring his presence. "Stew on that awhile, girl," he advised. He paused then, his eyelids twitching briefly as he took a long, calculating look at her. Ivey tried not to tremble in indignation and fright. The look in his eyes made her skin crawl.

When he touched her, trailing his rough fingers along her collarbone and around her neck, she could not hold back a shudder. His hands trailed lower, nearer to her bosom. She let out a strangled sound of protest.

"Please, have a little decency," Derek murmured from his chair. He still had the cloth pressed to his bloody nose. The skin around his eyes was shaded now, with grotesque pinpricks of darker bruises. Ivey was shocked that he had spoken up in her defense. She was very grateful.

Lawson paused his groping. "Still here Ward? I'd have thought you'd go get that looked to. You being such a fancy sort, can't have a crooked nose, now can you?"

Derek took the hint and fell silent again. Still, he did not leave, and that oddly gave Ivey a bit of comfort.

"Your strange manner of charms won't get her to talk, Pistol," Gravedigger remarked with a touch of humor in his scratchy voice. Lawson turned to his partner with a sour look. "Besides, we don't want to rouse Byrne's temper by molesting his wife."

"You said yourself we have nothing to fear from Jameson. Who cares if we do what we want to her?" Pistol's dark eyes refocused on Ivey and there was feral lust burning in them.

Derek, still seated and pretending to tend to his nose, tensed almost imperceptibly. He held still, listening intently.

"You weren't with this outfit when Jameson was," Hayes snarled back. "Even to a cold-blooded killer like me, there was something not quite right about him." He seemed to notice the intensity of Ivey's stare, then, and settled back in his chair, feigning at being dispassionate about his words. He realized he had said too much in the wrong company.

"At any rate, she's not ready to talk just yet," he added, shrugging to hide his concerns. "Give 'er a few hours, maybe even a day. If she stays quiet, well, we may just have to resort to less kindly pressures than merely asking questions." Gravedigger gave her a pointed look, getting his message across through the tone of his voice and the expression on his face. Ivey sucked in her breath.

Pistol heaved an annoyed sigh. He was the younger of the two gang leaders and, though he was a hot-blooded, eager man he knew when to listen to the counsel of the wiser Hayes. Reluctantly he took his hand off the beautiful woman, denying his lust for the moment. He knew, and Ivey feared, that that was not the end of their encounters.

"Where're you going, Ward?" Pistol asked, turning to face the gentleman bandit.

Derek had stood, leaving the bloody cloth on the tabletop, and was heading for the door. He stopped when addressed and turned slowly around. The dark circles around his eyes altered his appearance entirely and for a brief moment Ivey regretted her actions that had injured him so. "I thought I'd take your advice, Pistol, and get this," he pointed to his nose, which was smeared with dry blood and obviously out of place, "tended to. You do not need me for anything here just now, do you?"

"Nah, off with you," Pistol said with a dismissive wave of his hand.

Before Derek stepped out into the street he shot a subtle look back at Ivey. She thought she read in it the promise that he would return, that he would let no real harm come to her.

Then, as the door closed behind him, she realized he had left her alone at the mercy of the two most repulsive men in the West. Dismissing her hopes as the imaginings of a desperate mind, realizing that she was completely alone, her heart sank.

She thought longingly of her husband and prayed that Byrne would return soon.

~~~~~~~~~~

Byrne and Cowboy set out from their encampment in the hills. The night was so completely dark, with the stars covered over by clouds, that the rancher could see almost nothing. He trusted his horse's night vision to be better than his and to guide them safely across the terrain. He did not rush Cowboy but let him travel at a cautious walk. Each hoofbeat sounded deafening in the still silence of the early night.

When Cowboy kicked a rock, sending it clattering off into the night, Byrne flinched. Though he felt fairly confident it was Alexander who rode toward him in the dark night, he would not know for certain until they met.

Thus, the rancher rode tensely through the quiet night. He kept his eyes focused on the expanse of darkness ahead, straining to make out any shape.

Finally, after what seemed a very long time, he heard the ring of a shod hoof on stone. Cowboy stopped in his tracks, his muscles suddenly going tense. He listened for a moment, pricking his ears to focus on the direction of the sound. Then he let out a welcoming nicker as the other horse drew nearer.

"Byrne?"

The rancher let out the breath he had been holding. "Alexander," he whispered gratefully on the exhale. He turned Cowboy and let the mustang lead on back to their camp. Alexander brought Duke up alongside so they could have a hushed conversation. "So what took you so long to get out of there?"

"Jesse was being a bit of a handful. I figured we did not want him following us into battle."

"Indeed not," Byrne agreed. He could only imagine what trouble the ex-sheriff had been put to in order to rein in the energetic and eager youth. "So what did you end up doing with him?"

Alexander was hesitant to answer. Byrne could not see his face in the dark but he suspected the other might be stifling laughter. Finally, Alexander got breath enough to speak. "Found him a suitable - or perhaps not so suitable - mistress and locked them in together."

Byrne yanked Cowboy to a stop, utterly flabbergasted. He had never in his life expected to hear such an answer, much less from the man who had tried to end the prostitution business when it sprang up in Flintridge. The rancher shared Alexander's dislike for the whole dirty affair and so he was astonished at the ex-sheriff's words.

Duke stopped in turn, missing his equine companion and leader. The rancher let Cowboy step on. Byrne was still working his jaw silently, completely at a loss for an intelligible response. "You did what?" he finally managed, in a voice choked by bewildered laughter.

Alexander laughed outright. He caught himself quickly and lowered his voice.

"Thought that would get you. Of course I did no such thing."

"That's a relief," Byrne replied, and meant it.

"I tried all I could to talk him into staying in Glenn Rock willingly, even offered him what little money I had left. That did not have the desired effect. He would have run out into the street at the first sounds of the raid. I had to do something. So..." Alexander trailed off self-consciously.

Byrne turned to look at him but could only see a blurred motion in the darkness. It looked like the ex-sheriff was rubbing the back of his neck nervously. "What? Get on with it."

"So I, uh, I..." He trailed off, mumbling incoherently.

Byrne sighed, wearying of the charade. "Just say it!"

"I hit him over the head, tied him up, and locked him in the room we hired at the inn." Alexander had spit the whole confession out in one hasty breath. He inhaled deeply, fearing retribution. When the rancher stayed silent for a long while, the ex-sheriff grew more nervous.

Byrne's hearty laughter broke the silence. He wiped a tear of mirth from his eye. It was all too ridiculous: the one-time lawman had done something so against his morals, and to a youth at that! Byrne found it highly amusing.

When he managed to quell his mirth he apologized for his outburst. "Sorry about that. I really never expected you would need to take to violence. Then again, Jesse is awfully determined. Hopefully that will hold him long enough for us to lose him."

"He knows where we are headed, Byrne. He will come after us, no doubt about it."

"You don't think your, er, actions made it blatantly obvious that we do not want him along for the ride?"

"Really?" Alexander's tone was flat, disbelieving. "After all the straight talk we gave him at the start that did not deter him one bit, you think something as trivial as being tied up and left behind will stop him from following us?"

Byrne snorted in amusement. "Point taken. Ah, here we are. Evening, gents," he greeted the others as they finally rode back into the safety of their group.

After the briefest of greetings and sparse conversation, the tired men settled down to sleep away the rest of the night. The horses dozed, although their sleep was interrupted frequently by the yaps of coyotes in the hills. The men thought the canine voices sounded close, perhaps too close. None of them slept well.

At dawn, without even pausing to brew a morning pot of coffee, they set off. None of them was inclined toward conversation. They were all thinking days ahead, to when they would arrive back in Flintridge. Having little else to distract their thoughts, they thought of their families and friends, pets and homesteads, wondering how their actions would affect them.

In a few days' time they might all be dead. In a few days' time they might be heroes, having freed Flintridge from the yoke of the Hayes-Lawson gang. There was just no telling what would happen.

Byrne, in particular, was feeling insecure. He thought longingly of Ivey often, of the miracle growing in her womb, and dreamed of the life they could all have together. He knew that standing up to the outlaw gang might bring to light information about his past that he had kept secret, even from his wife. He had wanted so badly to start over, to leave his sordid legacy behind, but now it had caught up to him and was forcing him to stand and face it. The very idea made him edgy and bitter.

Cowboy picked up on his rider's stress and was fidgety and balky, throwing his head and kicking up his heels for no apparent reason. If the others noticed the change in the rancher they said nothing; in fact they were so absorbed in their own musings that they missed Byrne's increasing unease.

Without thinking of it, Byrne led them back into the canyons and hills outside of Flintridge. In the back of his mind he had planned it all, knew where they could hide out until they were ready to strike. He led his crew to this place, a small canyon sheltered in the bluffs. A stream ran through the place and there were three trails leading in or out. It was the perfect location for bandits to hole up.

The first thing they did was lead the horses to water and let them drink their fill. They unloaded their supplies, stashing them in a pile and covering them with rocks. It seemed they had made an unspoken agreement to wait until all of them were in the right frame of mind for the venture they were about to undertake. After all, if they all survived it would be nothing short of a miracle.

Conversation was sparse, only fulfilling the most basic needs of communication. They ate together in silence, tended their horses, and napped away the day. As evening fell they spread apart, each seeking their own brand of solace.

Byrne was the only one who paid much attention to the actions of the others. He was on alert, looking for any sign that any one of them might be having second thoughts. He would not blame them, not really, but he would have to find a way to talk them around, for all their sakes. They could not stand up to the Hayes-Lawson gang with less than four men. Absently he wondered if they had made a mistake in denying Jesse a part in their scheme.

Darkness fell. The creatures of the night began moving around, making their furtive scuttling sounds. The men were so self-absorbed that they hardly took notice of the animals. The night wore on without incident, though the tension at the small encampment hung thick in the air. Byrne kept a close eye on the others in case one of them decided to make a run for it in the night. They all knew they were coming close to action and nerves were bound to fray.

Eventually even the alert rancher calmed down enough to sleep. He lay propped against the saddle, hat pulled down over his eyes. The few hours he managed to rest were plagued with fearful dreams. Byrne jerked and turned in his sleep, trying to escape the thoughts tormenting him.

He woke with a start, just before dawn, his heart pounding. He was gasping for breath and sweating, with fear jolting his heart. His dreams had showed him his wife, showed him horrific things done to her by the Hayes-Lawson gang in his absence. He was furious with himself, knowing his dream-fears were well-founded. He had known those men, years ago, known what they were capable of. Why had he left Ivey?

Byrne struggled out of the wool blanket that had wound round him in the night and stood. He took in deep gulps of the crisp morning air, trying to calm himself. He tried to reason with himself, to convince himself that his plot against the gang had been a well-kept secret, that they would have no reason to retaliate against his family. Not yet. He would need to get Ivey safely tucked away somewhere until everything was settled.

"What are you up to, Byrne?" Alexander asked drowsily from where he lay. He had just woken and was rubbing the sleep from his eyes.

The rancher picked up his saddle and approached Cowboy. "I have some business to take care of in town," he remarked.

"What kind of business?" The ex-sheriff was now wide awake. Disturbed by the hushed conversation taking place at such an odd hour, the others were beginning to stir as well.

"You may as well come along too, Judge," Byrne said as an afterthought. "You're the only other one of us who has family still in Flintridge."

"Family? What do you—oh. Oh!" Alexander was on his feet in an instant. The rancher's hint had sunk in and made Alexander's heart go cold. "Would they really...?"

"Absolutely. Those men are hardened killers. Murdering innocent women and children means nothing to them." The rancher spoke from experience. A bit more emotion than usual entered his voice, but the other men were quick to dismiss it. "Cody, Ty, wait here. Alexander and I will return as soon as our families are settled somewhere safe."

Alexander followed the rancher's lead, hastening to saddle his mount. They let the horses drink at the stream once more before departing.

CHAPTER SEVENTEEN

Ivey sat in the chair she had occupied the day before. The tavern was empty, the hour being early. Pistol Lawson and Cliff Hayes had retired in the wee hours of the morning, drunk almost off their feet. Before they had left they had tied her to the chair, ensuring she could not escape. One of the tavern maids had taken pity on Ivey and offered her a glass of water and a few scraps of bread, but even her kindness was tempered by fear of the outlaws.

So the rancher's wife was left, alone, miserable and uncomfortable. Her fine blonde hair had come loose of its neat bun; wayward strands hung down in her face haphazardly. She had not slept at all the night before, too afraid for her own safety to risk dozing off for even a second.

The extended time alone in silence had given her mind plenty of opportunity to wander. She had contemplated what she had learned of Byrne's past from every angle imaginable, but she still had difficulty reconciling her knowledge of his character with a man who could run with brigands. Despite her faith in his good nature, doubts still lingered. Without her realizing it, her idealized vision of him had been flawed in minute but important ways.

Also chief among her thoughts were the intentions of the outlaws who held her captive. She did not know why they were taking such a sudden interest in Byrne's habits. She herself knew nothing of her husband's intentions aside from what he had told her. She began to search her memory for any hint she may have overlooked. Had Byrne really gone hunting mustangs? Why had he invited the other men along with him? Were they planning something? They must be, else why would the Hayes-Lawson gang get their ire up?

Ivey both hoped and dreaded that her husband was up to something underhanded. If he and the others were planning to move against the Hayes-Lawson gang, they might just manage to free the town from the grip of evil. Still, they were only four men. While she had never had a chance to tally the numbers, she felt certain the bandits had more men on their side. What if something went wrong? What if Byrne were killed? Ivey knew she could not bear life out in the West without her husband's company and protection. Especially with their first little one on the way...

Not one to languish over that which she could not change, Ivey turned her thoughts to escape. She tested her bonds frequently throughout the long hours of the night, hoping they had come loose. She was always disappointed.

When the barmaid came by to offer her refreshment, Ivey tried to befriend her. The girl was young, far too young to be in the life she led. Her age also made her timid; she would not make eye contact with the prisoner nor would she respond to Ivey's questions or attempts at conversation.

With her two best options for escape exhausted, Ivey resigned herself to wait. Until someone came into the picture that could help her, she was admittedly stuck. Resigned and miserable, she sat and waited.

Dawn came creeping in through the windows of the saloon, the light growing in strength and changing from gray to rose. Ivey hardly registered the change, though she had been sitting in the dark for hours. With the strengthening light, her mind began to race again, worrying over all the scenarios she could imagine. She knew not what the day held for her.

Over an hour later the first movements of a waking town could be heard in the street. Horses with their riders passed down the main road. Ivey did not turn her head to look at them. Men walked the street, talking in moderate voices, their words indistinct to the captive. She listened intently for sounds from the back of the saloon which might indicate that Pistol or Cliff were up and about. She sincerely hoped they would sleep in.

Out in the street a shout shattered her hopes. The man's voice drew closer, calling insistently for Lawson and Hayes. Footsteps sounded on the boardwalk a second before the doors swung open and admitted a rogue. He was rough-looking and travel-worn like all the others and he seemed to be in quite a state of excitement.

"Gravedigger! Pistol!" he shouted as he made his way toward the back of the establishment. Ivey flinched at the loudness of his voice. He hastened past without sparing her a second glance.

His cries brought the gang leaders from their rooms, looking very hung over. Neither of them was properly attired by any standard; Pistol was wearing only a shirt that was just long enough to cover the important areas, while Hayes was clad in only a pair of trousers and his hat, which he never seemed to be without.

Pistol grimaced as the man yelled again. The leader waved an angry, dismissive hand at him. "Shut yer trap, Brown." He swung his head around as if trying to loosen stiff muscles.

"Sorry Pistol," the rogue said with no real apology in his voice. He did, however, speak more quietly going forward. "You wanted us to tell you if we saw anything weird outside of town, right?"

"Well, get on with it then," Hayes ordered crabbily. He was rubbing his temples in slow circular motions. Like Pistol, he had a horrible headache.

"There's a fire out in the hills, bosses," the thug continued. He was still very excited and fairly squirmed in place with repressed energy. Ivey assumed he was new to all this, otherwise he would be able to handle himself with more decorum.

"Pistol go take a look," Hayes ordered in his low, gravelly voice. He gave his partner a hard look until he caved in.

Reluctantly Pistol nodded. "Alright, alright, I'm goin'. Let me just find mah boots." He disappeared from view. Ivey risked a glance at Hayes and was disturbed to see that the outlaw was staring hard at her, trying to read her reactions.

Minutes later Pistol came stumbling out of his room, swerving as if still drunk. He had managed to find his boots as well as a pair of pants. He followed Travis Brown out into the street.

Ivey watched through the big saloon windows as the two conversed. The man called Brown was pointing to a spot beyond Ivey's view. Pistol leaned forward, squinting, trying to make out details at a great distance. He thought for a long moment, exchanging murmured conversation with his subordinate. Finally Brown nodded his understanding and trotted off.

Pistol re-entered the saloon. He was still looking rougher than usual, but there was a new wicked gleam in his eye. Ivey did not like the look at all. Lawson's eyes trailed over her as he passed her by but he did not stop to molest her.

"What was it?" Hayes demanded. He had donned his shirt and vest during the interim. Ivey was ever so grateful that both men were now properly attired.

"Someone's got a camp out there in the hills. Brown saw the smoke from their fire."

Ivey's heart skipped a beat. She knew, instinctively, that it must be Byrne camped out in the hills. Help was so close at hand that she dared to hope for a positive resolution to the nightmare.

"Hmm," Hayes mused. He walked up to the bar and ordered two drinks, which the barkeep promptly filled. For the outlaws, the saloon was open at all hours.

Handing one glass off to Pistol, Gravedigger took his customary seat, not far from Ivey. Pistol made a slow circle around Ivey, looking her up and down in a predatory manner before taking his own seat. Upsettingly enough, Ivey was growing accustomed to his disgusting looks and was slowly becoming immune to them, so long as he went no further than looking at her.

The gang leaders leaned in close together and engaged in what they thought was a hushed conversation. They were such coarse men, accustomed to shouting at their followers out in the desert wilds, that they had not perfected the art of having a whispered conversation. Ivey listened with one ear, trying not to make it obvious that she was eavesdropping.

"I sent Brown and the lot out to the rancher's place," Pistol informed his colleague.

"Whatever for? Byrne's not there. He's in the hills."

"Just having them set up a little surprise for our old friend when he returns."

"If he returns. It's been nigh on a week. Maybe he up and left."

"Left his wife? What red-blooded man would leave a pretty little thing like that?" Pistol's eyes darted in Ivey's direction, drinking in her beauty at a glance.

Hayes scoffed, bringing Lawson's attention back to the point under discussion. "What are you having them do? Wait for Byrne to show up?"

"Nah. From what I hear, your precious Byrne is not so stupid as to fall into a trap like that."

"No," Hayes agreed in a level voice, not rising to take the bait.

"Well," Pistol breathed, looking askance at Ivey again, this time with a calculating look on his face. "Let's just say Byrne will find his homestead a bit empty when he does return." He had spoken a bit louder, making sure Ivey heard every word of the last.

The next hour or so passed in uneventful silence. The gang leaders sat at their table, drinking down shot after shot of whiskey. They did not speak further to one another or to Ivey. To order a fresh drink they simply raised their empty glasses overhead. By now the barmaids had learned to keep a sharp eye on the outlaws and to hastily fulfill their every wish.

Finally the silence was broken by footfalls on the veranda. The saloon doors swung open, admitting Travis Brown again. Now he was horribly dusty, his already rangy clothing ripped and torn. An ugly bruise was darkening one side of his face and there was an open cut on his forehead.

"What the hell happened to you?" Pistol demanded, rising.

"Shoot Pistol, you coulda warned us about the demon that rancher keeps in his pens!" Brown snarled accusingly, his excitable humor replaced with anger.

"What are you talking about?" Lawson returned, his own temper rising, fueled by drink.

Ivey chuckled inwardly. She still was not sure what Brown and the other men had been sent to do at Byrne's homestead, but she could guess that they had run afoul of the nasty-tempered stallion that her husband insisted on keeping. It seemed the untamable beast had come in handy after all.

"That palomino horse! He's the very devil incarnate!"

"Bull!" Pistol snapped. "He's just a horse, Brown." The gang leader caught himself on the edge of an outburst and sat down again, taking up his drink. "Anyway, if he gave you that much trouble I hope you put 'im down."

"We shot at the monster. Hit him, too."

"Good."

"But that didn't kill 'im Pistol! I swear it, Jarrod Cooke put a bullet in that stallion's heart but he kept on a'comin' and tearin' into us."

Pistol rolled his eyes over the rim of his glass. He had no sympathy for incompetents and he knew the younger man was embellishing the tale. "Never mind the stallion. Everything else get taken care of?"

"Oh, yessir."

"Good. Barmaid, a drink for my friend!"

Ivey watched the outlaws throw back their shots of liquor. Brown was not allowed to take a chair beside his bosses, but he seemed to be placated by the free drink.

"Now, go find Derek and send him 'ere," Pistol ordered.

"Sure thing, boss." Travis Brown whisked out of the saloon to do as he was bidden.

Pistol and Hayes returned to their drinks. Lawson noticed Ivey's curious glances that kept being thrown in their direction. He grinned. "I'll just bet you're burning with curiosity, eh girl?"

Ivey threw up her chin, defiant, and refused to answer him. Her actions elicited a chuckle from the outlaw leader.

Lawson's mirth dropped away quite suddenly as he thought he read something in her face that boded ill for him. Slamming his shot glass on the table, he stood and staggered toward her. "What's that look for?"

"Pistol, leave her be for now," Gravedigger ordered. He was ignored by his companion.

"Naw, shoot, look at her! She knows somethin'. I bet she's been holdin' out on us all this time," Pistol insisted, pointing a finger at her.

"You're drunk."

"Aye, and what of that? I can still see can't I?" Pistol was shouting now. Ivey sank back in her chair, wanting to put as much distance as possible between herself and the irate outlaw. She tugged at her bonds, desperately hoping they would give.

Gravedigger decided to leave the argument alone. He was deep in drink as well. He had decided that the girl knew nothing of Byrne's plans outside of what she had told them. For all he knew, she was telling the truth, that the rancher really had just gone in search of mustangs. Maybe all this time he had been reading too much into Byrne's absence. But, coupled with the disappearance of other men in town, it was too suspicious to overlook. He did not doubt, however, that Byrne would have wanted to protect his wife and so told her nothing of his true plans. If Pistol wanted to keep gnawing on this particular bone, Hayes did not care to stop him. After all, what value was the life of one girl?

The saloon door opened again, admitting Derek Ward.

CHAPTER EIGHTEEN

"Say Byrne, what is that?" Alexander asked, indicating a cloud of dust approaching them from the general direction of Flintridge.

The rancher leaned forward in his saddle, squinting to see against the early morning sunlight. The sun was at an oblique angle, shining directly into their eyes. Byrne tipped his head, trying to get the shadow from the brim of his hat to shade his eyes. "A horse would be my best guess."

"Do you think it is one of the Hayes-Lawsons?"

"Can't think of who else it might be." Byrne's voice was grim.

"What do we do?" Alexander was beginning to panic. He was intensely worried about the well-being of his new wife and family. If he and Byrne were apprehended by the Hayes-Lawson gang before they could overthrow them, what would happen to those they loved?

"Relax. Don't act like you have anything to hide. We're just riding back in after an unsuccessful mustang hunt."

"Okay," Alexander said in a shaky voice. He inhaled and exhaled deeply, trying to quiet his nerves. "Okay."

The pair rode on in terse silence. The cloud of dust came ever closer. The strange horse was galloping as fast as its legs could carry it. As it drew nearer they noticed something strange: the horse was riderless. In fact, it had no tack on it at all.

The wild horse raced toward them, snorting loudly as it approached. Byrne's eyes widened in recognition. "Beau!" he shouted as the palomino stallion rushed past them.

Cowboy swung round, expecting to be sent galloping after the escaped horse. Byrne held him back, utterly torn. Should he chase the escaped stallion he had worked so hard to keep? Should he ride on to Flintridge and take care of his business there?

Cowboy reared, screaming with excitement. He wanted to chase down the mustang. Byrne let him gallop a few strides, to try and work the thrill of the chase out of him. Alexander barely was able to hold Duke back, as the black horse

155

wanted to follow the others.

Finally Byrne was able to get Cowboy under control and turn him back toward home. His responsibility toward Ivey had won out. There would be time to chase Beau through the hills later, assuming they lived to see another day.

"How did he get out?" the rancher mused to himself as he rejoined his companion.

"Was that blood on his chest?" Alexander asked with a furrowed brow.

"What?" Byrne snapped out of his musings.

"It almost looked as if he had been attacked," Alexander explained. They were trotting toward Flintridge now, letting the horses work out their excitement.

"Hmm," Byrne pondered. His brow was furrowed as he thought the strange encounter through. A thrill of fear ran through him suddenly, a looming sense of foreboding. Whistling shrilly, he whipped Cowboy on. The mustang responded immediately, stretching out his legs and thundering toward home. Alexander was caught off-guard when Duke lurched forward and chased after his friend.

Byrne leaned forward in the saddle, letting Cowboy have his head. The mustang stretched out, taking long strides and covering the ground rapidly. Instead of running straight into Flintridge they veered off on the track leading to Byrne's homestead. As they came up into the yard, Byrne was horrified to see that, indeed, the Hayes-Lawson gang had struck.

Where once his corrals had stood there lay only broken spars of wood. Even the posts had been ripped from the ground and destroyed. The windows of the house had all been broken out; the front door stood open and one glance inside ensured him the place had been ransacked. At the moment he cared little about the physical possessions that had been lost.

He and Cowboy trotted around the property, seeking for his livestock and, more importantly, his wife. There seemed to be no sign of life left there. Distraught, Byrne stopped Cowboy as they rounded the house. He sat in the saddle, completely numb. He had been too late to save his wife and there was no way to tell if she yet lived.

Alexander and Duke arrived shortly and even the ex-sheriff's natural compassion failed to find the right words. He made his own pass of the property, searching more slowly than Byrne had done. As the horses mulled in the front yard and the men sat mute, they heard a low whine issue from the direction of the house.

"Sadie," Byrne whispered in a breath. He dropped out of the saddle and rushed up onto the porch. Into the house he went, making a wild search for the dog and calling her name. Another whine sounded, drawing Byrne back into the yard. He stood, chest heaving, and listened.

When the whine came again, he looked down at the boards beneath his feet. He jumped off the porch and went down on all fours, peering beneath the deck. Sadie looked out at him with sad, liquid eyes. He called her and she crawled out to meet him. Her fur was matted and muddy but she seemed to be unhurt, just scared.

"Good girl, good girl," he cooed, taking the dog into his arms and hugging her. At that moment she was all he had left of his former life. "I wish you could tell me what happened," he murmured into her fur. The rancher sat in the dust hugging the dog for a long while.

Eventually Alexander found his voice. "Byrne, what now?"

Reminded of his duty, the rancher opened his eyes. He let go of the dog and stood. There was a determined glint in his brown eyes as he passed the other man by on his way to his horse. "I have some business to tend to in town," he remarked with a cold, iron voice. He swung into the saddle and turned Cowboy's head toward Flintridge.

Alexander ran up to him and put his hand on the horse's bridle, holding the mustang back. "What are you going to do? Storm in there and take them on all alone? Do you even have a gun?"

Byrne reached into his saddlebag and drew out a pistol. He showed it briefly to the ex-sheriff before tucking it back into the bag for safekeeping. He gave Cowboy a kick and the horse lurched forward. Alexander grabbed the reins and pulled back on the horse's mouth, stopping him after a few jumps forward.

"Let go, Alexander," Byrne snarled. For a second his forceful temper, so rarely seen, set Alexander aback. The ex-sheriff released his hold and stared up at the rancher with sadness in his eyes. He knew the strong emotions that were spurring Byrne on, but he also knew the futility of confronting a group of outlaws alone.

Heaving a heavy sigh, Alexander admitted to himself that he could do nothing to stop his friend's suicide mission. He nodded once, minutely, and stepped back from the mustang.

Byrne kicked the horse and they sped off toward Flintridge.

Alexander ran to his horse and leapt into the saddle. He wanted desperately to ride into town as well, to see his wife and family safely into hiding, but now time was of the essence. If they were to have any chance of success they would need their full force. He gave Duke a sharp kick, sending him flying off toward the mountains where Cody and Ty waited.

~~~~~~~~~~

The rancher, his mouth set in a determined line, rode hard for the town he had founded years ago. The rogues, amongst whom he had once counted himself, had crossed a line. Taking over his town was one thing; Flintridge was inanimate, and the conflict over it could easily be resolved with an exchange of words or gunfire. Though Byrne loved his town, he could, in time, forgive those who had overrun it.

When they invaded his home and stole away his wife, however, that was a crime for which they would pay with blood. Every single one of them would suffer, of that the rancher was determined. He rode with one purpose: to see them all die. There was no room for sympathy or compassion in his heart.

Cowboy tore into the quiet town, raising a cloud of dust as Byrne jerked him to a stop outside the saloon. He had drawn his pistol on the ride in and so he was armed as he leapt out of the saddle. Without pausing for a second even to tie his mount, he sprinted up onto the veranda and pushed his way into the saloon.

The scene that met his eyes was not at all what he had been expecting. There was no one there to confront him and, lacking that roadblock, his ire faded somewhat. He let out a shaky breath as he spotted his wife, tied to a chair. Her head was bowed in utter defeat, her beautiful golden hair tussled. Byrne rushed to her and started on the knots that held her captive.

When she felt hands on her yet again, Ivey opened her eyes and lifted her head. She could not believe what she was seeing: her husband was there, finally. As he knelt before her, however, the doubts she had been harboring over the last several hours began to rise in her mind.

Without meaning to, she pulled away from him. He reached for her again and continued untying the ropes.

Finally Byrne freed her. He gently pulled her hands in front of her and held them in his, looking up at her with misty eyes. His brow furrowed and all sentimentality dropped away as her appearance hit him. She looked so frail, her eyes sunken and dark, her hair loose and sticking out at odd angles. Worse still, bruises and cuts muddled her fair skin. Byrne felt his temper rise anew.

Ivey regarded her husband askance, not certain if he could be trusted anymore. Her azure stare was guarded, uneasy. Byrne assumed it was because she was so shaken by her encounter with the Hayes-Lawson gang.

As Ivey looked at Byrne she saw that, beneath the wealth of sympathy in his eyes, there was something she had never seen before: a deep, unyielding hatred. She knew that emotion was not directed at her. It frightened her, however, for she had not thought her husband capable of that degree of ferocity. That look, so brief, had lent fuel to her doubts and fears about the man she had married.

A sound behind him startled Byrne and he turned, bringing the pistol up level in the same motion. His eyes were hard, flinty and feral; he was ready to kill at the slightest provocation. For a moment he was unable to determine from whence the sound had come. Then he rounded the nearest table and found the source.

Derek raised his hands in a defensive posture. He looked to be in a worse state than Byrne's wife. The gentleman outlaw lay on the dusty floorboards, his clothing badly wrinkled. His face was swollen and bruised, his lip was split. It seemed he was having a hard time drawing breath. "Please, Byrne, don't shoot," Ward begged breathlessly. His split lip bled freely and seemed to open a bit further as he spoke.

Byrne was unsympathetic. He thumbed back the hammer of the gun, pointing it downward and aiming at Derek's chest. The injured bandit sucked in a quick breath and then broke into a fit of coughing. He spat out a mouthful of blood and then lay more still, trying simply to get his breath back.

The rancher noticed then that Derek was clutching his middle and blood was trickling from between his fingers. Byrne's eyes narrowed for a second, and then he decided against action. "They turn on you? Serves you right, Derek." Byrne's voice was downright cruel. He turned his back on the injured man, having determined that he was no threat, and went back to tending to his wife.

Ivey was shaking with excitement and fear. Byrne tried his best to soothe her but he also knew there was no time to waste. He did not know where Pistol, Gravedigger, and the rest of the gang were lurking, though he was certain they were still in town and a very real threat.

"Please, love, don't be afraid. I'm here. I'll get you somewhere safe, I swear." Gently, he ran a hand down the side of her face. As he gazed at her his eyes lost their dangerous glint and for a moment it was as though nothing had happened. "Can you tell me where to find the men that did this? I imagine Derek was a part of it, but he has been dealt with. Where are the others?"

Ivey shook her head vehemently. She was in shock, unnerved by all that had happened, and unable to express herself properly. "No," she managed.

Byrne did not know how to interpret her answer. He did not know precisely why the gang had kidnapped his wife, but he intended to find out. His first priority, however, was ensuring that she was safe. He would find the outlaws and deal with them in due course.

Helping Ivey to her feet and supporting her wobbly legs, he began to usher her toward the door. He was not certain exactly what his plan of action was, but he knew he would protect her no matter what happened.

When she pulled up suddenly he stopped with her, though he was tense and eager to be on their way. He tried to remind himself to make accommodations for her, to relax and not rush her.

Still, she seemed to be perfectly able to walk. Why was she lingering? Byrne grew antsy again. He put his arm firmly around her and tried to steer her toward the door. She turned out of his grasp and stepped away from him.

Byrne looked at her in confusion. "Ivey? Is something wrong?" She did not answer. "Please, there's no time to waste," he insisted, keeping his voice low while communicating a sense of urgency.

"Just tell me it's not true," she whispered.

Byrne had to strain to hear her. "What's not true?" She was quiet for a long moment, giving him time to puzzle over her words. What had they told her? Obviously they had said something about him, otherwise why would she be acting so strange toward him?

Then it occurred to him and he felt ashamed. Suddenly he could not look at her. He cast his gaze aside in shame, his lips parted to offer an excuse but none was forthcoming. Having nothing to say to improve the situation, he gently reached for her. "Please, let us go."

"Not until you tell me the truth, Byrne. If they are to be believed, you are not the man you said you were."

Byrne exhaled tightly. There was no good way to enter into this conversation. "Explanations will take too long. Let me get you somewhere safe and when this is all over I promise to tell you everything." Still she hesitated, backing away when he moved toward her. "Ivey, how long have you known me?" He answered for her, not giving her a chance to speak. "Long enough, I hope, to know that you can trust me to protect you."

When she lingered still, undecided, he saw that he needed to be firmer with her. "Come with me now." He took her gently but firmly by the arm, drawing her toward the door. "Enough of this foolishness," he murmured, trying to keep his voice light.

"Wait, we can't just leave him," Ivey protested as they got to the door.

"Who?" Byrne had completely forgotten about Derek, lying bleeding at the back of the saloon. Now that he was reminded of the outlaw, he did wonder about the circumstances that had led to the injury. Derek was an essential part of the Hayes-Lawson gang, or so he had been when Byrne was one of the gang. He could not fathom what the clever gentleman-robber might have done to merit getting shot.

Returning to his purpose, Byrne tried once more to usher Ivey outside. "Don't worry about him," he advised unkindly.

"No," Ivey insisted, balking.

Byrne rolled his eyes. He was losing his patience. "Why? What is he to you?"

"He saved me," Ivey responded in a choked voice. She was pulling against Byrne, trying to get a look at the man she claimed was her savior.

Confused, Byrne let her go to him. She knelt beside Derek though she did not touch him. She seemed conflicted between her dislike of him as a bandit and her gratitude for his actions, whatever they may have been. Byrne felt the press of time. "Ivey," he begged.

She turned to face him and the look in her eyes was decisive, resolute. He knew she would not leave Derek.

Rolling his eyes, Byrne crossed back to where Derek lay. The bandit was barely conscious and made no struggle when Byrne unceremoniously threw him over his shoulder. Ward let out a strangled bark of pain as his wound was aggravated but he lacked the strength to put up a real protest.

"I'll be getting the full story from you later, dear," Byrne remarked dryly to Ivey as he led the way into the street with his cumbersome burden.

Their appearance did not go unnoticed. Byrne tried to progress like there was nothing wrong in the world. He carried Derek down the street, intending to leave him with Lucas Simmons, the town doctor. He hoped that act would satisfy Ivey so he could then get her to safety.

The curious stares of the passerby worried him far less than the whereabouts of the Hayes-Lawson gang. It bothered him a great deal that he had not seen any of them aside from the injured man he carried. Where had they gone? What had happened? If they did spy him aiding Derek, what would be their reaction? He guessed that there had been some sort of falling out that led to Ward's injury. Of course it was possible that some other force had fallen upon the Hayes-Lawson gang, but he doubted it. The timing would be far too convenient.

"Byrne," Derek choked out. His voice was weak, painful to hear. He fairly had to shout to be heard.

The urgency in the wounded man's voice caught the rancher's attention and he glanced over his other shoulder. He caught a glimpse of a man ducking into an alley not far behind them. Distinctly uncomfortable now, Byrne drew his gun from his belt and adjusted his grip on his burden. "Tell me when, Ward," Byrne ordered in a low voice, just loud enough to be heard by those close to him. He had no choice but to trust the invalid to watch his back. He only hoped that Derek did not pass out before they reached their destination.

"Now!" came the choked warning from Derek Ward. Byrne spun round so quickly that he almost toppled over, weighted awkwardly as he was by the bandit's body on his shoulder. The rancher raised the pistol, sighted his target, and fired a shot. The lurker ducked back into the safety of the alley, uninjured. Byrne had not expected to hit him.

Turning back around swiftly, he broke into a jog. Derek let out cries of protest as his wounded midsection was rammed against the rancher's shoulder. Byrne felt sorry for him but knew they could not afford to lag any longer. He made a dash for the doctor's office, ushering Ivey ahead of him so he could be sure of her safety. She held the door and he rushed in with Derek lying heavily over his shoulder. At some point, the rancher knew not when, Derek's weight had gone limp. Ivey ducked in behind her husband, closed the door and barred it.

Their sudden appearance had quite caught the surgeon unawares. He sprang up from his desk chair and stared at the strange group open-mouthed. "Byrne! Where have you been? I heard a shot but I assumed it was just the gang at their sport again—what happened?" He had spoken rapidly, barely pausing to take a breath. Belatedly he registered the body draped over Byrne's shoulder.

"Lucas, lend a hand here, eh?" Byrne ordered breathlessly.

"That's Derek Ward, innit?" Simmons asked warily. He seemed reluctant to offer his assistance. Though the outlaw was apparently helpless, he was an outlaw none the less.

"Yes, it is, now help me get him into the surgery." Byrne was not in the mood to be disobeyed. His tone relayed as much and Simmons reluctantly followed him into the side room. Together they laid Derek out on the table. He was unconscious.

"All yours, doc." The rancher turned to leave. The shoulder on which he had carried Derek was a gruesome sight, stained dark with blood.

Lucas Simmons looked the rancher over with a furrowed brow, utterly confused at all that was happening. He noticed the pistol which Byrne had tucked in his belt. "What are you going to do?"

"I'm going to run these varmints out of our town if it's alright by you," Byrne snapped back.

"Byrne, wait," Ivey begged, rushing over to him. She gripped his arm, trying to stay him.

He looked at her with a soft, loving expression. "Stay here with Lucas. I'll come get you when the dust has settled." He was careful not to give breath to the fear that filled them both, that he would not survive the encounter. Offering her as bright a smile as he could summon, he kissed her forehead. When he turned away she spun him back around and kissed him passionately. Lucas respectfully averted his gaze.

"I'll be expecting your explanation about him," Byrne added with a nod at the room where Derek lay. He grinned, the expression almost normal. Without further comment he ducked back into the street to face his fate.

Closing the door behind him, Byrne kept in the shade and shelter of the veranda overhang. He drew the pistol from his belt and double-checked the chamber. Five shots left.

Strangely, Byrne was at peace. He was not scared, nor was he apprehensive. He knew the odds were stacked against him but it did not bother him in the least. Of course he did not want to die, not so young and certainly not at the hand of his former gang. But, if this day were to be his last, he would accept his lot.

Refocusing on the challenge at hand, the rancher cast a furtive glance all around. The street was quiet, the townsfolk having deserted it when the first shot rang out. It seemed the only sounds were those of Byrne breathing and his heartbeat.

Creeping slowly out from beneath his cover, Byrne held his gun at the ready. He peered up at the rooftops, expecting to spot a sniper. Listening intently and hardly daring to breathe, he scanned the roofs of the surrounding buildings but saw no one. Still on high alert for danger, he stepped down into the street to get a better view. Everything remained still and silent.

Byrne knew it would not remain that way for long. The thug that had been lurking after him as he carried Derek was not an innocent. He had to be part of the gang, a new member, and had to yet be hunting him. It was not in Byrne's nature to sit by and wait for things to happen. In some instances he had to be the one to make the first move.

Boldly he stepped out into the middle of the street, making a prime target of himself. He prayed that Ivey had the sense not to be sitting at the window watching.

"Alright Pistol! Cliff! Get your sorry carcasses out here and face me like men!"

As he had expected, a peppering of gunfire answered. He sprinted for cover, choosing an alley further down the street from the doctor's office. The sharp angle would prevent Ivey from seeing events unfold if she were watching at the window. He felt certain she was watching and he did not want her to see him get gunned down if the worst should happen.

"Is that the best you scoundrels got?" he taunted loudly from his hiding place. "I dunno Cliff, old man, I think you hired on a pack of girls. They can't shoot worth—"

He heard just one footstep on the rooftop above and looked up. A mangy looking man was up there, aiming down at the rancher. Byrne swung his gun up, fired, and dropped the rogue. The body fell into the alley behind him.

"One down, Cliff. How many of these curs do you have to waste?" Four shots remaining. Byrne prided himself a good marksman but he knew there were more than four men left to kill. At least he would not have Derek Ward to contend with, for the gentleman robber was as fair a shot as Byrne.

"He's in the alley," one thug called to another. Byrne heard them making haste toward his hiding place.

"Fools, don't go rushing in!" Hayes' commanding, gravelly voice was easily distinguishable. Byrne tried to figure out from whence the order had come but he was distracted by the arrival of a pair of bandits. He recognized one of them as being Budd Stevens, the railway man who lost Emily Fletcher's hand to Alexander.

In the seconds it took them to come to a stop without running into each other and raise their guns, Byrne was already rushing at them. They had not expected a physical assault and were taken aback when the rancher fell on them with his bare fists, striking indiscriminately. Budd had the sense to fight back while the other simply cowered beneath the heavy blows.

Byrne focused his efforts on the one putting up a fight. Stevens was a younger man than the rancher, but matched him in strength. He landed several punches of his own and even managed to gain some ground. Struggling fiercely with Budd, Byrne barely managed to wrench the pistol from his hands and use it to whack him over the head. Dazed, the disarmed rogue backed away, clutching at his sore head. He cursed loudly at the rancher but, for the moment, was warded off.

The second one, who had been more timid initially, got his gumption back and stood a few feet off, his gun aimed at Byrne's heart. He was scrawny and cowardly, not one to risk a hand-to-hand struggle. Byrne turned on him in a slow, deliberately menacing way. The man's arm shook and he put both hands on the gun to steady it. "Don't you come a step closer, rancher!" he spat out in a single breath, trying to sound intimidating.

Budd was recovering from the blow to the head and Byrne knew his window of opportunity was about to close. He knew his options were limited. He chose to take the unexpected action: he stared the coward down for a long moment and then, without any warning, he sprinted out of the alley. Startled, disjointed shots rang out behind him but none came close to hitting him.

Byrne ducked behind the nearest building and ran along the row of structures. He was behind the establishments, with the wide plains stretching out to his left. How easy it would be to make his escape if only he had Cowboy with him. But then, he knew the wrath of the Hayes-Lawson gang would once again fall on Ivey and he could not stomach that happening again. No, he must stay and fight.

"Where'd he go?"

"Around that way, I think,"

The bandits' voices were muted by distance and the intervening structures.

As he turned another corner, Byrne found his way barred by a burly thug. Byrne skidded to a halt and paused, wiggling his fingers indecisively as if it would help him think. As the heftier man advanced, Byrne found himself backing up. He did not realize he was cornered until his back touched a wall.

The brute rushed at him with more speed than the rancher would have given him credit for. Byrne lost his breath in a whoosh as the man's fists struck him square in the gut, pinning him against the wall.

The rancher struggled but his actions were in vain; the other man was simply too strong.

Clutched in the brute's fist was a knife. Menacingly, the man brought the blade up to Byrne's neck, grinning with evil satisfaction. His silver tooth glimmered in the dull light in the alley. Byrne felt the touch of steel against his throat and swallowed tightly. His mind was racing, searching for a solution.

"You got 'im Zack?"

"You blind, Travis? Yea, I got 'im," the burly man holding Byrne growled in response. Budd and the cowardly bandit, Travis Brown, entered the alley. All routes of escape were blocked.

Byrne struggled in Zack White's grasp but still found himself held in place as if by steel bars. As the others approached he began to grow desperate.

"Alright, hold 'im there and I'll shoot 'im," Budd instructed, reaching for his gun. He drew it and opened the chamber, checking his shot count.

Brown, the coward, raised his own gun and pointed it at Byrne. Budd noticed and gave him a weird look. "What're you up to Travis?" Stevens shoved a few extra bullets in the chamber and spun it shut.

"What's it look like? I'm gonna kill 'im!" Travis Brown answered in his quavering voice. His arm was shaking with nervous energy.

"Why waste the bullets when I can do away with him?" Zack spoke up. He pressed the blade of the knife closer against Byrne's throat to emphasize his point. The sharp blade drew blood and it trickled down the rancher's neck.

"Hold up there, I called it first," Budd Stevens snarled, trying to take command. He was an ambitious man, and felt certain that disposing of the rancher who caused the gang so much trouble would advance his dubious career.

Byrne rolled his eyes and sighed, drawing all their attention. Ignoring the tense stares and guns leveled at him, the rancher feigned indifference. "Really, you all are so stupid," he remarked, emphasizing the last word on the exhale.

Zack tightened his grip on the rancher's throat uncomfortably. Byrne boldly slapped the hand and was rather surprised when the grip loosened. Evidently his brash behavior had convinced them to hear him out. He licked his lips and paused awhile before continuing. It would do no good to let them know they had him on the ropes.

When he did speak further, his voice was steady and derisive. "Did it never occur to you that Pistol and Cliff would like nothing more than to kill me with their own hands? If one of you idiots kills me first, do you really think they'll thank you for it?"

The three bandits exchanged glances. They were uncertain. Should one of them dispose of the rancher? Which of them should do it? Would Pistol Lawson and Cliff Hayes really be upset if they missed out on the murder? Was this a trick? What punishment might fall on them if they deprived their leaders of a desirable kill?

It seemed they were unwilling to risk the wrath of the leaders of the Hayes-Lawson gang. Zack roughly pulled Byrne away from the wall and shoved him down the alley, toward the main street. The hairy brute came up behind the rancher and caught him by the shoulder, forcing him to walk forward with the knife at his throat to keep him under control. Byrne went along quietly, using the interlude to complete the scheme taking form in his mind. Stevens and Brown came up on either side of them, pointing their guns at Byrne's head. He hardly registered the threat.

The trio of outlaws shepherded their captive out into the main street. They forced Byrne on, pushing him toward the saloon. Byrne walked on without thinking about what awaited him; he was racking his brain for a plan.

Then they crossed the invisible line where Byrne realized he must act or it would be too late. Zack turned him toward the saloon door and Byrne dug his heels in. He threw himself backward with all his strength, reaching up to catch the brute's forearm before he could press the knife back onto his throat. Byrne ducked down then, underneath that burly arm, effectively getting the pistols off his head. He made a mad dash forward, putting on all the speed he could muster.

This time the bullets that chased him caught him up. Byrne felt a searing pain cut across his upper arm. He dodged aside, hoping to stray out of the line of fire. The action proved to be a mistake, as evidenced when a bullet struck his leg, tripping him up.

Byrne fell forward with a shout and landed hard in the dirt. His pistol flew ahead of him, stopping several feet out of reach.

Panic seized Byrne. He scrabbled in the dirt, trying to force his lame leg to work. Unable to stand, he could only crawl forward, digging his fingers into the dusty ground to gain purchase. His fingertips brushed the barrel of the gun, but before he could get a grip on it a booted foot stepped down, pinching his fingers. Byrne drew his hand back with a hiss and looked up at the interloper.

The sunlight blinded him for a moment, but then the man looming over him moved and his shadow fell across the rancher's face. Byrne squinted up at Pistol Lawson. The rancher could scarcely steady his breathing but he tried, feeling undignified panting at the feet of his rivals.

Cliff Hayes came up alongside Lawson and the pair stood looking down at the rancher. Byrne spat at them. They laughed, the sound cacophonous and cruel.

Byrne's chest heaved with each breath, the pain from his wounds a mere background sensation. Adrenaline was humming in his veins. He knew his life would soon end.

"So what was your master plan this time Byrne?" Pistol jeered. He twirled a gun in his hand nonchalantly. "Huh?" He emphasized his word with a fierce kick that rolled Byrne over in the dust.

"Wow Cliff," Byrne coughed, trying to recover. He took a shaken breath, propping himself up on his hands. "Where'd you find this clown? Rather a step down for—" His words were cut off as Pistol kicked him square in the jaw. Byrne dropped to the dust, stunned. He spit out a mouthful of blood and felt certain one of his teeth was missing. Shaking his head, he tried to steady his vision.

Pistol grabbed the rancher's shirtfront and hauled him up onto his knees. The position strained his injured leg and Byrne yelped breathlessly. His vision still swam in and out of focus; his surroundings were spinning. He choked at the pressure on his throat.

"I'm a sight better'n you were," the bandit sneered into Byrne's face. "Much as Cliff praises your skills, you and I both know that I'm the better leader."

Though he was still dazed, Byrne's mocking spirit rose again. He grinned back at Pistol, the expression hinting that he would triumph through it all. The look fed Lawson's rage and he shook Byrne violently. "What's so funny?" he demanded hotly.

"Don't lose your head Pistol," Hayes advised in his gravelly voice. His voice was even, neutral. Byrne knew it would be much harder to push the older gang leader to losing his temper. "Put him down."

Pistol obeyed, releasing his grip on Byrne's shirt. The rancher dropped like a sack of bricks, hitting his injured arm hard on the ground. He rolled onto his back, coughing and wincing in pain.

Pistol brushed himself off, straightening his clothing and pretending to be unaffected by the rancher's inflammatory words. He turned away, giving Byrne a parting kick with the heel of his boot. "Whatever you say, Gravedigger."

As Pistol Lawson moved off, Hayes took his place standing over Byrne. The rancher gazed blearily up at the man with whom he shared a dark history. He knew he would receive no pity, no mercy simply because of those years of camaraderie. If anything, that familiarity gave him forewarning of the murderous, back-stabbing nature of the man he was facing. He stared back at Hayes, matching cold stare for cold stare.

"What happened to your shoulder, Byrne?" Hayes stepped forward, tapping the toe of his boot against the bloodstain on the rancher's shoulder. When the contact did not elicit a reaction, he drew back and contemplated the man lying in the dirt at his feet. "That's not your blood," the Gravedigger remarked suspiciously.

Byrne craned his neck around to get a look at the crusty stain, as if previously unaware of its presence. "No, it's not," he agreed with an infuriating grin.

Swift as lightning Hayes planted his foot on Byrne's chest, holding him down with very little effort. He leaned forward, putting his weight on Byrne. The rancher coughed and tried to squirm free but he was held firm. "What was this all for, Byrne?" Hayes kept his voice low, audible only to the man to whom he spoke. "This little stunt of yours?"

"Does it matter?"

Hayes shrugged and ground the heel of his boot down. Byrne winced. "I suppose not," Gravedigger agreed nonchalantly. He drew his pistol, opened the chamber and then spun it, toying with his victim. Looking down at Byrne through hooded eyes, he offered a grim smile. "Pleasure to have known you, Byrne." Snapping the chamber shut, he aimed the gun and thumbed back the hammer. "Shame you chose the wrong side in this."

Byrne closed his eyes tightly, dreading what was to come.

A shot rang out.

Byrne flinched, tensing up, but after a moment he realized that he had not been hit. Hayes cursed vilely and jumped back, removing his foot from Byrne's chest. Cracking one eye cautiously open, the rancher dared to hope that the tide had turned in his favor.

Wasting no time to determine what exactly had happened, the rancher scrambled across the dirt to where his pistol lay. Four shots. Snatching the gun up, he turned to face the action, ready to fire.

Pistol and Gravedigger were distracted, their attention focused on the far end of the street. Three horsemen stood there, all in a line, all armed to the teeth. Smoke drifted away from the barrel of the rifle held by Cody Harris.

For a brief moment there was a stalemate, utter silence in the street.

Then, all hell broke loose.

"Shoot 'em!" Pistol ordered, waving his arm in a wide arch, summoning the remaining bandits to battle. The echo of his voice had not faded away before a myriad of gunshots cracked deafeningly in the street.

Budd Stevens made the first rush, firing the two pistols he held indiscriminately at the horsemen. The shots striking all around them made the horses spook. They reared, screaming, and at least one of them kicked out at nothing. The men tried to quiet their mounts but the horses were inconsolable.

Cody and the others were forced to abandon the beasts, first using the animals' bodies for cover and then scuttling across the street, shooting back at the outlaws until they reached the cover of the nearest building.

Pressing his advantage, Budd made for Alexander's hiding place. There was murder in his eyes, a burning need to avenge the injury done all those months ago when he lost Emily's hand to the sheriff. He had joined the Hayes-Lawson gang in the hope of being given a chance like that. He did not intend to waste it.

Brown and Zack waited in the open for the other men to make their move. They were more than happy to leave the ex-sheriff to Stevens, knowing it was a personal matter. Cody and Ty slunk forward, darting from one area of cover to another. They fired intermittently at the two bandits stalking them, hoping to keep them on the defensive.

Pistol and Hayes kept up fire on both Alexander and the pair of interlopers, trying to intimidate them into surrender.

While the gang leaders were thus engaged, Byrne made his move. He began hopping away at an oblique angle from Hayes and Lawson. He kept a close eye on the two rough men, dreading the moment they discovered his absence. Because the gunfight kept the outlaws absorbed, Byrne was able to get away undetected. He kept limping away, trying to get to where he had left Cowboy. The trusty mustang mulled where he had been left.

Byrne gained the safety of an alley and whistled loudly. Cowboy's ears pricked and he turned, galloping eagerly down the street to where Byrne waited. The rancher hauled himself awkwardly upward, having to rely on the strength of his arms since his leg was useless. His cut arm threatened to give, but he managed to scramble into the saddle. Panting heavily to ward off the pain from his injuries, he took a second to get his bearings and adjust his grip on the pistol. Four shots...did he have time to reload?

Bullets thudded into the wood siding just behind him, giving him his answer. Hayes and Lawson had finally noticed that he had escaped and were refocusing their attention on him.

Leaning low over Cowboy's neck, Byrne kicked the horse with one heel and the mustang took off running. Letting the reins flop loose on the stallion's neck, the rancher turned in the saddle and rapidly fired off the rounds in his gun, aiming for the gang leaders.

Three...two...one... The gun clicked hollowly, empty. Bullets were still slicing the air all around him.

Byrne picked up the reins and directed Cowboy into an alley for cover.

CHAPTER NINETEEN

Alexander ducked and narrowly missed being shot in the head. The bullet meant for his skull burrowed into the wall behind him. The ex-sheriff was a bundle of nerves, jittery and paranoid. Timid as he was, he was running away from Budd Stevens.

"Stand and fight, coward!" Stevens yelled, firing another volley at Alexander's retreating form.

Alexander rounded a corner and slammed his back against the building. He fumbled with his gun, trying to reload it. Adrenaline was thrumming through his veins, making his fingers shake uncontrollably. His chest heaved with each nervous breath. He was panicked, rushing and failing at his simple task.

Finally he succeeded in putting fresh bullets in the chamber. Holding the gun tight, clinging to it as if it were his only lifeline, Alexander let out a steadying breath.

He jumped out from his shelter and leveled the gun at the other man's chest. Budd was not there.

Meanwhile, Ty and Cody stood shoulder to shoulder, placing their backs toward the nearest building. The farrier's leg injury had slowed up their movements; the makeshift bandage was stained darkly with blood. They held their weapons aloft: Cody had his rifle and Ty a pair of pistols. To either side of them stood Brown and Zack. Neither side exchanged fire for some time. They were all out in the open, all easy targets. The gunfight had devolved into a staring contest.

Nervously, Ty craned his neck to whisper at Cody. "They're out, right?"

The farrier shrugged. He had not been keeping count.

"Okay. I'm gonna reload. Cover me."

"With what?" Cody had spent his two shots.

Ty let out a strangled sound. He gritted his teeth, uncertain what to do next. Deciding to chance it, he tucked a pistol under one arm and opened the chamber of the second. He dug in his pocket, fishing for bullets, and came out with a fistful. He began jamming them into the chamber, shooting quick glances up at the outlaws as he did so. They, too, were frantically stuffing their guns. "Reload," he whispered to Cody. The farrier was already doing so.

"Go, go, go, go, go," Ty murmured to himself, his nerves fraying more and more with each second. Finally he finished loading his second pistol and swung both guns up.

The outlaws had beaten his pace. Ty found himself looking down the barrels of four guns. He swallowed tightly. His hands shook and his aim faltered. Repositioning his weapons, he clamped his eyes shut and pulled the triggers.

After the deafening sounds of the shots died out he risked opening one eye. Both bandits lay on the ground. Ty let out a shaky breath. He looked over his shoulder at Cody who gave him a congratulatory nod. Ty nodded back, stunned into silence. He was breathing hard, still haunted by the near-death experience.

The farrier moved cautiously toward the bodies, his rifle at the ready. Ty wavered in place for a moment and then his knees gave way. Cody jumped at the sound of a body striking the ground.

Having waited for the gang leaders to reload their weapons, Byrne tried to refill his only to discover that the mechanism was jammed. He shook it, whacked it, tried everything he could think of to get it to work, all without result.

Taking advantage of the momentary lapse in fire, he galloped Cowboy out from cover and barreled down the street to where his fellows stood. Pulling the horse to a smart stop, Byrne tossed his dysfunctional gun down to Cody. "Jammed," he explained breathlessly.

"Right." Cody tucked the pistol into his belt and bent to retrieve one of the dead outlaws' guns. He checked to be sure it was loaded before handing it up to Byrne. The rancher tapped the brim of his hat in thanks before he turned his horse and prepared to face his foes once more.

Belatedly he realized that Ty was lying in the dirt, motionless. He shot a concerned, questioning glance at the farrier. "Fainted," was the answer. Satisfied on that point, Byrne focused on Hayes and Lawson. Cowboy danced in place, ready to charge, but the rancher was shocked to see the street deserted again.

Shots rattled back and forth somewhere in the town, disclosing the general location of Alexander and Budd. Pistol Lawson and Gravedigger Hayes were nowhere to be seen. Byrne looked around frantically, expecting an ambush.

"Byrne, best get that leg fixed up. You're losing a lot of blood," Cody remarked with some concern. The gaping, bloody hole in the rancher's leg was far worse than the graze wound the farrier had received.

Byrne did not even hear him speak. He had spotted the gang leaders. "No time," he hissed as he kicked his mount forward. The mustang almost trampled Cody in his haste to obey his master.

Cliff Hayes stood on the veranda just outside the doctor's office. Pistol was nearby. Hayes turned to his companion, spoke to him, and the younger man nodded. He ducked into the building where Ivey was holed up. Byrne's blood ran cold in his veins. He found himself filled with an untamable rage, the cold-blooded desire to make the gang leaders suffer. Cowboy charged on, ears laid back against his neck, mirroring his rider's hostile thoughts.

As Byrne drew nearer, Cliff gave him a mocking sneer of a smile, his silver teeth glinting in the bright sunlight. The rancher did not even wait for Cowboy to stop before sliding out of the saddle. He landed on his bad leg and it buckled, dropping him gracelessly to the ground. He lurched and stumbled his way up the stairs and into the doctor's office, knowing he was rushing straight into a trap. All he could think about was his wife.

~~~~~~~~~~

At the other end of town Alexander ducked and dived around stacks of crates and wagons, using everything he could for cover. He was on the run again, being chased by that madman Budd Stevens.

"If only Emily could see you now!" the irate railway man barked loudly. "Would she still choose you over me?"

Alexander knew better than to answer. He took a few seconds to catch his breath and try to steady his nerves. He was shaking uncontrollably. He had never before been in a fight like this, and did not know what strategy to employ, how best to protect himself. It was a miracle that he had not been hit yet. He was running out of places to hide.

"Actually," Stevens muttered loudly, his voice turning thoughtful.

Panting, unable to hear anything beside his labored breaths and panicked heartbeat, Alexander waited. Looking around he could see nothing, but he knew Budd was not far away. He did not think the bandit had seen him tuck into this latest hiding spot but he dared not count on it for long. He also did not dare to make a run for it without knowing just how close his enemy was.

Budd overturned a barrel just on the other side of the one against which Alexander was leaning. The ex-sheriff panicked and fled, flushed from his safe place. The outlaw was ready for him, firing wildly at his retreating form.

Alexander twisted whilst he ran, shooting backward. His shots went wide, far off their marks, though they did succeed in making the outlaw flinch. Enraged and completely beyond reason, Stevens charged after the ex-sheriff with a loud yell. He fired his gun as he ran.

One of the shots struck the dirt just beside Alexander's ankle. Startled, he jumped sideways, lost his footing and fell. He scrambled wildly, trying to gain his feet before the other man was upon him. Budd Stevens was a fast runner.

Then, Alexander's world went dark.

When the ex-sheriff came round, he was where he had fallen, in the alley, somehow still alive. The back of his skull seared with pain. When he rubbed the sore spot his fingers came back bloody. In his fogged state of mind, it took him a moment to realize that he was not alone.

Budd Stevens stood over Alexander, his shadow falling over the downed man ominously. Wrapped in one arm he held Emily Fletcher, his hand over her mouth. She looked down at her husband with tears in her hazel eyes. Stevens had his gun leveled at the ex-sheriff's chest; his hand was steady. "Finally," he panted with a satisfied smirk, "the real man wins."

Emily squealed in concern, the sound muffled by Budd's hand. She fought his hold and he had to take his hand from her mouth to hold her tight. Alexander looked up at Stevens like a cornered rabbit. He completely forgot about the gun in his own hand.

"Hold still you little wretch," the outlaw snarled, giving Emily a violent shake.

Then, suddenly, something snapped within Judge and he acquired the cool detachment that had possessed Byrne earlier. He spat at Budd's boots and scowled up at him. "You'll never have her. She is too wise, too good and true for the likes of you. Kill me, if you must, but you will never be happy."

"Alexander," Emily murmured, touched by his words. She tried to go to him but the villain had a firm hold of her.

"We'll see." Budd did not seem shaken at all by the prediction. He thumbed back the hammer and tightened his finger on the trigger.

Emily grabbed hold of his gun hand and fought him for the weapon. For a few seconds they wrestled, and then the man overpowered her. As he was throwing her off, Emily made a final lunge for the gun. In the struggle Budd pulled the trigger and the shot rang out deafeningly.

~~~~~~~~~~

Byrne shouldered through the door of the doctor's clinic. He was horribly unsteady on his feet, scarcely able to put any weight on his right leg. Haltingly he entered, gun ready, listening carefully for any sound.

He did not see anyone in the outer room. Then, he heard Ivey's muffled cry from the next room.

"Leave her alone Hayes, Pistol," Byrne ordered sternly. He hopped closer to the threshold and paused, waiting for them to make the first move. The sound of his breathing seemed impossibly loud in the confined space.

"Come on in Byrne, we need to talk," Hayes' gravelly voice invited.

"No tricks?"

"No tricks."

"Pistol?"

"Aye, no tricks," was the grudging reply from the younger gang leader.

"I'll just bet," Byrne murmured under his breath. Having no other options, he proceeded, but cautiously, knowing the men would not keep to their word.

The scene that met his eye was, on the surface, comical: five people crammed into the surgery area, which would normally fit two comfortably. There the amusement ended.

Derek lay stretched out on the table still, apparently unconscious. His shirt had been removed and his midsection was wrapped in bandages. Lucas Simmons, the surgeon, was pressed into the far corner, cowering.

Pistol was immediately to Byrne's left as he entered the room. Hayes was on the other side of the operating table, holding Ivey in a tight grasp. The side of her face was freshly reddened and tears streamed down her face. She was so distraught that she could hardly make a sound. When she saw Byrne's condition, bloodstained and hardly able to stand, she let out a little gasp. In her eyes he saw reflected all the fears that had haunted him for days.

Pistol Lawson covered the space between them in one step. He snatched the gun out of Byrne's hand and laid it on the surgery table. Byrne curled his lip at the bandit but knew better than to resist. Hayes had a knife pressed tight against Ivey's pale throat.

"Let her go."

"Oh no, can't do that Byrne ol' man," Hayes ground out in his painful voice. "It's personal now."

"I think it was personal when you first involved my wife in this." Byrne tried to stand tall, tried to play down how much his injuries were paining him. He could not show weakness.

~~~~~~~~~~

In the alley, Budd was hopping on one foot. When the gun had discharged, the bullet had hit him in the foot. Cursing, the outlaw tenderly held his bleeding foot, not giving a consideration for the actions of the others.

The pistol lay where it had fallen. Emily, thinking faster than her stunned husband, made a grab for it. Alexander sat, bewildered, in the dust. His face was blank, his mind struggling to comprehend all that had happened.

When Emily leveled the pistol at Budd Stevens, Alexander came back to himself and realized he had to intervene.

Stevens glared at Emily. "Go ahead, pull the trigger. I don't think you have the guts, wench."

Emily was shaking with fury. Her eyes were hard, her golden brown hair disheveled, making her look like a wild woman. Slowly, her finger began to tighten on the trigger. She approached the outlaw, emboldened by her possession of the weapon, and pressed the muzzle to his heart. Budd sneered down at her.

"Emily, no," Alexander warned, a moment too late.

Without warning, Stevens grabbed hold of the pistol and wrenched it from Emily's grip. He seized her arm, twisting it round behind her. Emily cried out in pain and shock as she was forced to her knees. Budd threw her aside and Alexander went to her aide immediately. He helped her to sit up, wiped away her tears.

"What a touching sight," Budd drawled snidely. "I had intended to kill you, sheriff, and keep her for myself. But now, I think it would be best for you to die in each other's arms. It's more poetic." He snorted, showing them what he thought of the sappy sentiment. The gun was aimed at Alexander first.

Before Budd could fire, Alexander made a move. He hefted Emily to her feet and shoved her toward the mouth of the alley. "Run!" he shouted as he threw himself at Stevens. Emily knew better than to disobey; she ran for the safety of her mother's home.

Alexander and Budd grappled. The outlaw still held the gun, which he tried to use as a club. The ex-sheriff was wise to the trick and ducked as the heavy stock was swung at his head. Gripping Budd's gun arm with both hands, Alexander dug his fingers into the tendons in the outlaw's wrist. The pistol fell to the ground. Alexander kicked it well out of reach.

Giving Budd a mighty shove, the younger man ran for the mouth of the alley. Just as he emerged into the main street he was tackled from behind. Alexander hit the ground hard, knocking the air from his lungs. He coughed, trying to regain his breath, as he struggled to free himself from the weight on his legs.

Budd took command of the situation by grabbing hold of Alexander's clothing and dragging him backward. Once he had the ex-sheriff where he wanted him, the maddened brigand began throwing punches. Each time Alexander tried to retaliate or get away he was foiled.

Hoofbeats sounded, approaching rapidly.

Alexander hardly heard them, so absorbed was he in the intensity of the struggle. He was fighting for his life and feared he was losing.

The next thing Alexander knew, a horse galloped past him, its hooves crushing into the dust dangerously close to his head. Something knocked Budd Stevens to the ground.

Dazed, Alexander sat up and looked over at the two men struggling and rolling about in the dust. It took him a long while to realize that the newcomer was familiar to him and obviously much younger than Stevens.

"Jesse!" Alexander exclaimed in open surprise. "What the hell are you doing here?"

The youth did not hear him; he was focused on the wrestling match that he was rapidly losing. Budd flipped the younger boy onto his back and sat on him, holding him down with his superior weight. The outlaw punched Jesse several times, dazing the boy so that he stopped struggling.

Stevens lifted his fist for one more punishing blow but it never fell. Alexander whipped his pistol up and fired, emptying the remaining rounds into the crazed man. Budd's body jerked, blood welled up through his mouth. Finally he slumped sideways and hit the dust, lifeless.

Jesse clambered out from beneath the body. He was pale and shaking, his face bloodied, but otherwise he seemed alright.

"I, uh, I guess I owe you one," Alexander said awkwardly through panted breaths.

"And don't you forget it," the youth answered, gasping as well.

They sat for awhile trying to catch their breath. They exchanged glances, both showing uncertainty. Alexander was feeling horribly for his unkind actions toward the youth in Glenn Rock. Jesse was the first to offer a conciliatory smile. The ex-sheriff returned the gesture. They shook hands, both relieved to have survived.

~~~~~~~~~~

In the surgery room, Pistol stepped behind Byrne and shoved him forward. The rancher caught himself on the edge of the table. His right leg hung uselessly, too painful even to set on the ground. Byrne took in rapid, sharp breaths through his nose, unwilling to give the other men the satisfaction of hearing his pained cry.

Ivey stared at him with misty eyes, feeling utterly helpless. In her great concern for her husband she forgot about the knife against her own throat. "Byrne," she whispered, the word no more than a breath. Hayes gave her a rough shake, silencing her. The knife bit a touch deeper into her skin. Any further pressure and it would surely draw blood.

Lawson seized Byrne by the back of his shirt collar and forced him to stand. The bandit held his own gun in his left hand, pointing it across his chest at the captive. Byrne ignored the presence of the gun. He glanced surreptitiously around, looking for something he could use or turn to his advantage. The room was painfully, hopelessly bare. The only thing was his pistol, lying out of reach on the surgery table. He knew he could never reach it and get off enough shots to save himself and his wife in time.

"Pistol, take that gun off him," Hayes instructed.

The younger gang leader furrowed his brow. He looked from Byrne to Hayes and back again, confused. "Come again?"

"He's no threat. Do the polite thing and take the gun off 'im."

"What? I thought we was gonna plug him here in front of his girl. Wrap things up, ya know?"

"The plan has changed. Do as I say."

Lawson thought about it for a moment. He licked his lips as he contemplated his next move. Shifting his weight, he pulled Byrne a bit closer and pressed the barrel of the gun against his chest. "No. No, this ends here and now Gravedigger!"

Cliff took in a deep breath. His patience was running short.

"We can't let him live! You said yourself he's smart. He'll come back with more men and run us into the ground for—"

Lawson screamed, his voice deafening in the small space. Hayes had tired of his partner's arguments and thrown the knife, which was now embedded to the hilt in Pistol's shoulder.

Byrne stumbled away from his captor and then stopped. He looked back and forth between the two outlaws, bewildered. Pistol was gripping the hilt of the knife, grimacing as he tried to extract the blade from his flesh.

"You know I don't like no one talking back, Pistol," Hayes remarked with a cruel absence of emotion.

Ivey took her chance and broke away from the older bandit. She ran around the table on which Derek lay, intending to reach her husband. Hayes was the faster. He caught hold of her blonde locks and pulled her back into his arms. She struggled, thinking him unarmed. Her fists beating against his chest seemed to have no effect.

Since Ivey could not come to him, Byrne decided to go on the offensive. He began stalking slowly, limping, around the table toward Hayes. He moved with slow calculation, not wanting to startle the outlaw into doing anything rash; he was acutely aware that Hayes could snap her neck. His nickname, Gravedigger, had not been given him without reason.

Pistol let out an angry shout as he ripped the knife out of his shoulder. He threw it to the ground and advanced on his partner, face red with fury. Hayes held up a hand, stopping the younger man's advance. "Wait your turn Pistol. Old business first."

"Oh no, I'm sick of listenin' to you!" Pistol lunged at his companion one-handed, landing a grip on the older man's throat.

Hayes let loose his grip on Ivey in order to grapple with his former associate. He seized Lawson by the shoulders, digging his thumb cruelly into the knife wound. Pistol screamed in pain and tried to wriggle free but only succeeded in aggravating the wound. He reached for his gun only to find it missing; he had dropped it when he was stabbed.

Ivey rushed round the table, grabbed Byrne's pistol, and flung herself into the safety of her husband's arms. Her exuberant greeting almost knocked him off his feet. Before she could begin fussing over him he shoved her behind him, taking the gun from her in the same motion. "Run," he whispered urgently. He sent her off with another little shove. She knew better than to stay.

Lucas Simmons took his chance and ran out into the street after her. Only the outlaws and Byrne were left.

The pair of gang leaders wrestled in a tight grip for a moment before the older, uninjured man triumphed. He threw Lawson aside bodily. Pistol stumbled, lost his footing, and fell. His head smacked against the edge of the stout surgery table as he went down. The force of his body striking jarred the table and its contents. Derek's body jerked inanimately and slid a few inches nearer to the edge.

Lawson did not recover. Hayes gave his erstwhile partner a solid kick, ensuring he would stay down. Then the old, weathered outlaw looked up at Byrne, slowly, deliberately slowly. His eyes were devoid of light, gray and cold. "Now then. To old business."

Gravedigger shoved Derek's limp body off the table. It hit the ground with a thud and bumped against Byrne. Since the rancher was supporting himself on one leg he was quite knocked off balance and fell backward, rapping the back of his head against the wall as he landed. Stunned as he fell, he lost his pistol once again.

Boldly, Hayes jumped up on the vacated surgery table and drew his gun. He thumbed back the hammer and aimed at Byrne, his finger on the trigger. His eyes were hard, devoid of any emotion including hatred. It was as if he was acting on instinct, lacking any purpose beyond necessity. Byrne began to suspect he had gone mad.

The rancher craned his head back so he could meet that icy, inhuman stare. His mind was racing. There had to be one more thing he could do, one thing he had not yet tried. He had known Hayes very well in years past, almost well enough to have considered the cruel man a friend. Byrne recalled that the bandit he had known was one to respect bravery and was completely devoid of compassion. So, the rancher put on a brave face and stared Hayes down.

Gravedigger acknowledged the ploy with a mirthless grin. He dipped the muzzle of the gun in a mocking salute. "That's a nice thought Byrne, to try and bluff your way out of this," Cliff remarked. He shrugged as if shunning the idea. "It won't work this time."

Byrne raised an eyebrow, trying to appear perfectly calm and detached. "Worth a shot." Quickly switching tactics, Byrne struggled to free himself from the dead weight lying across his legs.

All at once the amount of blood he had lost hit him and he felt impossibly fatigued. He found his efforts growing weaker and weaker.

Hayes sat down on the tabletop, swinging his legs over the edge. He kept the gun trained on Byrne. The rancher looked blearily up at his captor. The edges of Byrne's vision grew fuzzy, rimmed with black. He blinked rapidly, trying to refocus. The outlaw leader clicked his tongue scoldingly. "It's no use, boy."

Byrne made one last great effort to stand but lacked the strength to achieve his goal. He subsided back onto the floorboards, breathing heavily.

Abruptly something changed in the outlaw. Byrne watched his features transform, the animalistic need to kill fade away. The weathered countenance took on a contemplative expression as Cliff gazed down at Byrne. Hayes lowered the pistol, apparently having a change of heart.

"Don't you ever miss it Byrne? The old days?"

Thinking he was going to die, the rancher saw no reason to lie. The words he spoke would never be heard beyond that room. "Occasionally I miss the money. Can't say I miss the rest of it much."

"Really? I can't believe that. You're not much different than me, Jameson. You're a leader, natural born. Clever, too. We made a good run of it." Hayes weighed the gun in his hand, thinking for a long moment before speaking again. "You know," he began, shooting a quick look over his shoulder where Pistol Lawson still lay senseless. "There is an opening in the gang. What say you come back and ride with us again?"

Byrne snorted dryly. He had been having an awful time focusing on the conversation at hand. He was tired, so tired. Still, he forced himself to keep up the discussion. "What about him?" He nodded in Lawson's direction.

"What about 'im?" Hayes repeated with a distasteful sneer. "That boy is too cocky. He's a loudmouth, not a leader. He'll get himself killed one of these days."

"By you?"

Gravedigger shrugged, indifferent. "What say you? Ready to live a real life again?"

Byrne shifted his legs, which were falling asleep from the weight of the body lying on them. For a brief second he thought that Derek might be stirring but then the gentleman bandit lay still again. "I say you might as well stop wasting your time, Cliff. I gave up marauding years ago and I don't plan on going back to that life."

Hayes shook his head with a grim smile. He had expected Byrne to say as much. He hopped down off the table. Stepping over Ward's body, he grabbed a fistful of Byrne's shirtfront. The rancher's heart sped as the outlaw pressed the muzzle of the gun to his chest. With each indrawn breath Byrne felt the cold metal press into his skin. Trapped though he was, Byrne could not find the strength to fight back. He had been a fool to leave his wound open and bleeding freely. Now he was paying the price.

"Shame that," Hayes remarked dryly. He did not seem overly upset. "It's because of that girl of yours, innit?" Cliff licked his lips, leaning in closer. "Not just her though. Oh, not to worry old friend, I'll make sure she's well taken care of. You won't have long to wait for her to join you on the other side." He smiled, showing his silver tooth in an expression that made Byrne's skin crawl.

Byrne jerked in response to the words, a feeble attempt to lunge at the other man. His strength failed him. The best he could do was glare at the other with seething hatred.

Hayes laughed at him, obviously enjoying the torment he was doling out. "You never did know how to take a joke," the outlaw remarked in his gravelly voice. "Thinking back, there were a lot of things not in your favor. You have morals, for one, and that just dunnit suit the life."

"It gives me something to live for," Byrne remarked hoarsely. He was scarcely able to speak. The darkness was closing in on his vision.

"It may have done, once. But now it's them very morals you hold in such high regard that are going to get you killed." Hayes shook Byrne to bring him back to wakefulness when his eyelids drooped. His finger began to tighten on the trigger. Byrne offered his best attempt at a glare, trying to be defiant to the very end.

The rancher jumped in surprise as another gun appeared, pointed at Cliff Hayes. Without hesitating, Derek pulled the trigger several times. His aim left something to be desired; he was bracing the weapon with both hands and his arms were shaking violently with fatigue. Regardless, one bullet found its mark, striking Hayes in the chest. The outlaw leader jerked with the impact and turned a murderous glare on Derek. The gentleman thief stared back, his bruised and cut features hard with a cruel expression.

Stunned, Byrne watched as the infamous Cliff Hayes wavered in place for a moment. He watched the spark of life melt from Hayes' eyes. Finally, after what seemed an impossibly long time since he was struck, Cliff fell to the side, dead. His steely gray eyes stared upward, unseeing. Byrne turned away.

The rancher exhaled the breath he had been holding. He dropped back against the wall, utterly exhausted. He lacked even the strength to thank Ward for saving his hide. Byrne closed his eyes, telling himself he would rest for only a minute...

When Byrne woke at the touch of a hand on his shoulder he was disoriented. His vision was faulty; the slightest movement sent the room spinning. He had no idea how much time had passed since he closed his eyes. With a groan Byrne tried to sit up but found that he lacked the strength. The hand on his shoulder tried to help him up but even their combined efforts proved futile.

It took a long moment for Byrne to realize that it was Derek's hand on his shoulder. The gentleman outlaw, looking very much worse for the wear, was kneeling beside him with his free arm pressed to the bandages covering his midsection. He looked as pale and shaky as Byrne felt.

Byrne gazed blearily at the other man, uncertain how to feel about him. He supposed he should feel grateful, since without Ward's intervention he would surely be dead. Still, he could not quite bring himself to think favorably of any man he knew to be an outlaw, no matter what their redeeming qualities.

Even as he tried to focus on the other's face he felt his head loll to the side and his eyes close. Derek gave him a rough shake, dragging him back into wakefulness. "Come on," he urged, pulling on the rancher's shirtsleeve. "We need to get out of here before Pistol comes around."

Derek Ward got haltingly to his feet, wincing at each little movement that aggravated his wound. Once up, he gave the rancher a small kick, encouraging him to stand as well. Byrne tried but he was far too enervated to follow suit.

Rolling his eyes, Derek threw his head, at a loss. "Fine then. But if they shoot me it's on you." He pointed his finger at the rancher, emphasizing his breathless words. Byrne's eyes were halfway closed and Derek suspected the rancher had not even heard him speak.

Forcing a tight sigh out through his teeth, Ward turned and gingerly made his way for the door. He himself was unsteady on his feet, still suffering greatly from his wound. But, being the better off of the two, he knew it fell on him to tie up the loose ends.

~~~~~~~~~~

Out in the street Ivey stood by, her eyes fixed intently on the door of the doctor's office. She had seen Lucas Simmons rush out close behind her, saw him run and find shelter in a different building. While her instincts had told her to join him in seeking safety, she could not bear to leave her husband behind. So she had lingered, listening with bated breath.

Alexander, Cody, Jesse and Ty had joined her at her vigil. The men were tired, winded from fighting, but still they were prepared to rush into the building to aide Byrne. Jesse, in particular, was chomping at the bit.

Ivey had convinced them to stay back, impressing on them the danger of the situation. If they forced the outlaws' hand, Byrne would surely die. They had reluctantly agreed to wait and the group mulled in the street, indecisive.

When the shots had rung out Ivey's blood had gone cold. She feared the worst, thinking how bad Byrne had looked when last she saw him. Still, until she knew the outcome, she could not leave the spot. The gunshots had startled the men and they paced about, wanting so badly to see what had transpired.

Motion just within the office caught Ivey's attention and she sucked in an expectant breath. Her hand went to her breast as she squinted, trying to make out the form of her husband through the gloom of the interior. "Byrne?" she whispered, hoping desperately that he had somehow triumphed.

"No," Alexander whispered, drawing his pistol, "it's not him."

The three men raised their weapons, aiming at the doorway. Ivey whimpered, unable to believe that Byrne was dead. She forced back her tears; she would not let herself believe it until she saw his body.

"Don't shoot!"

The men exchanged glances, silently asking one another if the voice were familiar. None of them recognized it. Alexander, taking the lead, thumbed back the hammer of his pistol and fired. The shot went wide, striking the threshold to the figure's left. The strange man leapt to the side. "I said don't shoot, damn it!"

"No don't," Ivey echoed, grabbing Alexander's arm and pulling the gun off its mark. The ex-sheriff gave her a confused look. Ivey did not even look at him. She sprinted the short distance to where the figure stood, clutching his midsection.

Confused, the men exchanged glances again. Cautiously, they lowered their weapons. Alexander strode forward to join Ivey and the strange man.

"No time, no time," the man was insisting in response to something Ivey had said. "Go find the doctor."

Alexander looked the other man over calculatingly. He was clad only in a pair of expensive pants. Without a hat holding his sand-colored hair in place, it dropped in unkempt clumps around his face. He had suffered badly, as evidenced by the bandages wound round his torso and the cuts and bruises mottling his skin.

"Derek, what happened?" Ivey asked urgently, laying a gentle hand on his shoulder.

The name struck a chord in the ex-sheriff's memory. "Derek Ward?" he asked suspiciously.

"Yes sir," the outlaw answered readily. "You may arrest me later if you really must, but for now send someone to get Simmons. The rancher is in a bad way."

"Byrne!" Ivey exclaimed, reminded of her husband's dire predicament. She shoved past Derek and disappeared into the surgery.

"Mrs. Jameson!" Alexander echoed, about to chase her in. He stopped short and gave Derek a hard look.

"I am not going anywhere," the gentleman outlaw assured him with a wry smile. Alexander glanced down at the bloody bandages and knew he was telling the truth. By the look of him, Ward would not get a mile out of town before collapsing. The ex-sheriff nodded minutely and followed Ivey inside. "I would tie Lawson up if I were you," Derek advised over his shoulder.

Eager to be of help, Jesse rushed in after the others. Ty and Cody waited out in the street, keeping a close watch on Derek Ward. Exhaling heavily, thoroughly exhausted, Ward leaned back against the wall and slid down until he was sitting on the veranda in the shade of the awning. "Well, is one of you going to go find Doctor Simmons?"

Ivey appeared at the door. Her face was pale and she was clearly shaken. "Please, make all haste," she begged of the two able-bodied men. Derek tossed his head, indicating they had better get moving. Ty took the lady's distress to heart and ran off in search of the surgeon.

CHAPTER TWENTY

A knock sounded on the door. Ivey answered and offered a smile to the man who stood on the porch. "Alexander, how nice to see you," she said genuinely. She was smiling openly, her azure eyes shining.

The ex-sheriff doffed his hat respectfully. "I hope I am not intruding. I was hoping to speak with Byrne, if he is feeling up to it."

"Of course. He's just out back. Come in and I'll go and fetch him."

"Already?" Alexander asked in surprise. "He was only injured two days ago."

"I have never known that man to stay still for more than five minutes at a time," Ivey joked as she led Alexander into the sitting room. Leaving him in a chair, she crossed through the dining area and poked her head out the back door. Alexander heard her yell for the rancher, heard the dog bark energetically. He tactfully waited until Byrne limped into the room and wrung his hand.

"Good to see you again Alexander," he remarked with far better humor than he had ever displayed before. It seemed a weight had been lifted from the rancher's shoulders.

"Same to you. You are looking well," the ex-sheriff remarked and meant it.

Byrne shrugged. Ivey pushed him into a chair. He offered a half-hearted argument but sat down anyway. "It was just a bullet. What would it do, kill me?" The rancher laughed heartily. His wife gave him a scathing look and he quieted apologetically.

"You gave me an awful fright," Ivey scolded. She took her leave of them, bustling into the kitchen and setting water on the stove to boil. "Coffee, Alexander?"

"Thank you Mrs. Jameson, but I do not think I will be staying that long. I came to ask a favor of you, Byrne," he added in a quieter voice.

The rancher sobered up and leaned forward, listening intently. He knew the request had something to do with the remaining members of the Hayes-Lawson gang. Cliff Hayes, also known as the Gravedigger, had been buried in an unmarked grave outside of town the day before. The bodies of the other men that had followed him and died were likewise disposed of. No one aside from those putting the corpses in the ground had attended the funeral, if it could even be called that. From Ivey, Byrne had learned that Pistol Lawson and Derek Ward were imprisoned in the old jail. He presumed Alexander had the key and kept watch over the prisoners.

"Ask away," Byrne invited. He leaned back in his chair and stretched out his legs, wincing as the motion strained his wound. He folded his hands and laid them on his stomach, waiting.

"Frankly I am at a loss as to how to deal with the captured outlaws. By rights they should both hang, each having enough sin on his head to condemn several men. Then there is the matter of my lack of authorization to act in any official capacity anymore. Without my commission I would be akin to a murderer if I were to string them up."

The rancher was shaking his head slowly. "I imagine Ward has managed to make the waters murky, too," he mused.

"Yes, there is that as well. You should hear the stories he has been telling me, Byrne," the ex-sheriff remarked. "If they are to be believed, I do not see how he can be sentenced to death."

Byrne shifted in his seat, becoming uncomfortable with the conversation. He had spent every minute of consciousness over the past two days going over and over the events of that afternoon, trying to find fault with Derek Ward, seeking for an ulterior motive for his actions. The gentleman bandit had to have one; he always did. Wrack his brain though he did, Byrne could not find anything from that day which might condemn the man. He knew well enough of Derek's past crimes, but if the villain had truly turned over a new leaf as he claimed...

Then there was the question of why Ivey was so quick to come to Ward's defense. Byrne had learned very quickly not to speak harshly of Derek in her presence, for she would not hear any foul word against him. The rancher had yet to learn the reasoning behind her behavior.

Alexander noticed the rancher's sudden silence, his contemplative frown. "What did happen that day, Byrne? You have not yet told me."

The rancher had not confided in his wife, either. "I think I will go into town with you," Byrne remarked, changing the subject in an attempt to avoid admitting his debt to Derek Ward, for it was a troublesome liability. He knew someday Ward would demand payment. It was not in the nature of an outlaw to be charitable, no matter how gentlemanly he was capable of acting.

"If you wish. I must admit, I expected as much. The trap is waiting outside, whenever you are ready."

"Did I hear you are thinking of going into town?" Ivey asked, appearing beside them with two cups of coffee. Her voice was hard, edgy. Though she knew matters were well in hand within the borders of Flintridge she had refused to allow Byrne back there. She herself had only returned once. There were so many bad memories, all far too fresh in her mind. She handed off the coffee and took the chair next to Byrne, laying her hand on his knee protectively.

"It'll be fine Ivey," the rancher assured her, rather sharply. He jiggled his knee, throwing her hand off. Alexander suspected they had had many conversations about the town and that Byrne was growing tired of his wife trying to protect him from imagined dangers.

Byrne stood, throwing back the cup of coffee in a long swig. Alexander sipped at his and gave Ivey an appreciative nod. His manners overshadowed Byrne's, per usual. The rancher handed the empty cup to his wife. "Thank you, dear," he remarked with a sickeningly sweet voice. She huffed at him, took the cup, and swept into the kitchen.

Hesitantly, as if walking on thin ice, Alexander set his half-finished cup down on the side table. He stood and brushed the wrinkles out of his clothing.

"You ready, then?" Byrne demanded. He was already limping toward the front door.

"Byrne Jameson you are not to leave this house without your cane," Ivey's sharp voice ordered from the kitchen.

The rancher rolled his eyes and grinned at Alexander confidentially. "Women. Does Mrs. Judge give you this much trouble?"

Since the events of two days ago, she did. Alexander was too proper to admit so, even to his friend. Domestic disputes were not a suitable topic of conversation outside the family.

"Thank you for your hospitality, Mrs. Jameson," Alexander called in farewell. It seemed that she would not come to see them off. The ex-sheriff followed his friend out the door. Byrne took some time negotiating the few steps down to level ground on account of his bad leg. Alexander waited patiently and descended after the rancher.

The house door opened and closed again. Ivey stepped lightly down the stairs and approached them as they were climbing into the conveyance to which Duke was hitched. She climbed up unaided and sat beside her husband without giving him as much as a glance. In her hand she held the rough-hewn cane she had found.

"Ivey, what do you think you are doing?" Byrne asked slowly, more amused than annoyed. He found her desire to protect him from the past very charming, if a little frustrating.

"I am going into town," she responded readily, still keeping her gaze focused straight ahead. She tried to push the walking stick into his hands but he would have none of it. Ivey held onto the cane, knowing he would have need of it at some point.

Byrne caught Alexander's confused look and shrugged. The trap seat was big enough to accommodate two comfortably. Three would be very tight.

"You heard Mrs. Jameson," Byrne remarked with a grin. He put his arm around Ivey's waist and pulled her tight to him. "Make some room for the sheriff," he whispered against her hair.

Reluctantly, feeling very self-conscious, Alexander climbed up and seated himself. He did not want to press against the rancher's wife, feeling it would be terribly improper. So, he sat on the very edge of the bench, hanging one leg out of the conveyance.

Taking up the reins, he started Duke off. The black gelding stepped up immediately and trotted out, ears pricked eagerly. The bouncing and jarring of the wagon caused Alexander to rattle about. When he almost fell off the seat Ivey caught hold of his coat sleeve and encouraged him to sit closer, putting her arm over his shoulders to prove he would survive the encounter. The ex-lawman offered a nervous grin and drove on, blushing.

No one spoke for the duration of the ride. Even Alexander made no effort at small talk, knowing it would only prove to be awkward. The married couple did not look at one another, though the rancher kept his arm around his wife. The tension between the two was palpable. The trio jounced and bounced along with the motions of the trap.

For his part, Alexander was burning with curiosity; he had gotten the impression that Byrne had some history with the outlaw gang spanning further back than the last few months. Still, he knew he could not press Byrne. Absently he wondered if Ivey knew the truth.

When they drove into town and their destination came into view it was a relief for them all. Alexander reined Duke in and assisted Ivey down from the carriage. He knew better than to try to help Byrne. The ex-sheriff stood by, pretending to busy himself with adjusting the horse's harness.

Ivey watched with a displeased expression as her husband made his descent. Byrne simply dropped down as he would have done were he fit, forgetting about his injury for a moment. His leg buckled with a spasm of pain. He cursed as he went down.

The rancher immediately picked himself up, gingerly putting weight on his bad leg. As he was dusting off his clothing he looked around, wondering who might have seen his undignified dismount. Wisely, Alexander averted his gaze. Ivey glared at her husband, silently berating him for his foolishness. No one else who was about seemed to have taken notice.

Byrne allowed Alexander and Ivey to precede him up the steps to the constabulary. As his wife passed him by she pressed the stout walking stick into his hand. This time he accepted the use of it, though he hated doing so.

Before unlocking the door Alexander paused, half-turning to address Ivey with a concerned expression. "Mrs. Jameson," he began, and got no further. Ivey's cold, pointed look reminded him that she had already seen horrible things and her mental stability would not be much affected by whatever scene awaited inside the jail. Reluctantly the ex-sheriff turned the key and held the door for the rancher and his wife.

It took a moment for their eyes to adjust to the darkness within. Being a jail, there were no windows in the front of the building on the main level. Black iron bars framed the hallway, forming two cells, one on either side. Byrne took the lead and he felt Ivey press closer to him. The rancher limped down the narrow corridor to allow room enough for the others in fill in after him.

He looked into each cell in turn, first the right and then the left. Pistol Lawson jeered up at him, his smile grisly when factoring in the scabby gash on his temple. His arm had been placed in a sling to avoid aggravating the stitched knife wound with unnecessary motions.

Eager as ever, the outlaw got to his feet and approached the bars, leering suggestively at Ivey. The lady pressed closer to her husband and clutched at her collar modestly. Byrne gave the outlaw a hard look and turned his back on him. He was easily within reach of the prisoner but he felt confident that even Lawson, sure of himself as he was, would not risk injury to his remaining good arm.

The cell to the left held Derek Ward. In sharp contrast to the jaunty, rude upstart imprisoned across the hall, Ward only looked up to acknowledge the presence of others. Even the slight movement of his head seemed to drain him; he breathed with hesitation.

"You've looked better Derek," Byrne remarked, not quite kindly. A smile flickered across the captive's face but beyond that he made no remark. Ivey gave her husband a reprimanding shove. The rancher's observation had been true. Derek's face was badly swollen and bruised, his skin had a ghastly gray pallor, and his wound caused him a great deal of pain. Even his breathing sounded sickly.

"I cannot argue with that statement," Derek wheezed in a hollow voice. He tried a smile but thought better of it as the expression stretched his bruised skin. His eyes flicked to Ivey and held her stare for a moment. "I do hope you will forgive me for not standing, Mrs. Jameson." A pang ran through his abdomen then, causing him to double over with a pained cry. Ivey shuffled closer to the bars but Byrne held her back. He suspected that the gentleman bandit was shamming, trying to drum up sympathy.

Derek began to recover from his fit. He tilted his head to the side and looked up at the people standing outside his cell, his features still contorted. "What kind of man brings his wife to see this?" he demanded, suddenly angry and self-conscious. "Take her away Byrne!"

The rancher was beginning to be of the same mind. He looked at his wife out of the corner of his eye and noticed that she had gone pale. His arm encircled her waist, lending her support. "Come away Ivey," he whispered, trying to draw her down the hall.

She shuffled sideways a few steps before planting her feet and refusing to move. "No," she murmured. Her voice was quiet but firm. She continued to stare at the outlaw, heedless of the strange looks given her by her husband and Alexander. Derek, too, seemed surprised that she refused to leave the unpleasant scene.

"No. Please." She turned to Byrne and leaned against his chest, looking up at his face with troubled eyes. "Please let him go." She included Alexander in the plea with a look over her shoulder. She was not sure on whom to focus her attentions, uncertain who had the most authority to act in this situation.

"Ivey, what—" Byrne shook his head, his brow furrowed, unable to process what his wife had said, with whom she was siding. At a loss, the rancher turned to Alexander for support.

"Why do you say that, Mrs. Jameson?" Alexander asked gently. He glanced at the outlaws listening intently on either side of them. He felt very uncomfortable discussing their fates in front of them.

"Because he...he..." Ivey's voice failed her as she began to sob. The memories of just a few days ago flooded back into her mind, overwhelming her. She relived the fear she had felt when she was brought forcibly to the saloon; felt the anger she had held for Derek when she broke his nose; the terror Lawson's fingers on her skin had raised. Then she was overcome with the startled gratitude for Derek which had been her chief feeling of him for the last two days.

Before she realized it, Byrne and Alexander were shepherding her down the narrow hallway, away from the fugitives. Lawson could not resist getting his barb in and he did so by swatting Ivey's rear as she passed. Ivey took in a sharp, offended breath. Byrne wheeled on the caged man, grabbing at him through the bars. Pistol danced back, grinning like a fiend. The rancher cursed Lawson loudly and swore that he would see him hang.

At Alexander's recommendation the trio went away, climbing the back stairs to the apartment above where they could converse in peace. Ivey was shaken all over again. Byrne followed her up, making sure that she had a comforting presence leading and trailing behind. He made good use of his cane as he slowly progressed up the stair.

Upstairs, Alexander found chairs for his guests and, lacking a third chair, stood himself. Byrne settled his wife in her seat before taking his own. He stretched out his bad leg, flexing the sore muscles.

"Now tell me Ivey," the rancher began, his voice a trifle hard with jealousy. He did not know her reasons for caring about the fate of Derek Ward but he intended to find them out. "Why are you of the opinion that we should spare ol' Ward from the rope?"

Ivey did not miss the tone in her husband's voice or the look in his eyes. Outwardly he appeared to be relaxed but she knew him well enough to be aware that he was very upset. "I believe you owe me an explanation as well," she remarked. If she could get Byrne on the defensive he might not be in such a harsh frame of mind.

As she had expected, the reminder tempered Byrne's anger. He licked his lips nervously, glancing between his wife and Alexander. Should he tell her the whole story then and there? What would the outcome be? Surely Alexander would not trust him once he knew the truth, and Ivey may just turn away from him forever. He was looking for a way to postpone the topic when Ivey spoke again. "Is it true what Lawson and Hayes told me? Did you really ride with those vile men?"

The cat was out of the bag. Alexander looked at Byrne in surprise, awaiting his answer as eagerly as Ivey.

"Ivey, I really do not think now is the time—"

"Go ahead Byrne. You are amongst friends here." Alexander leaned forward, encouraging the rancher to tell the tale. "I promise to make no judgments of you based on what I hear. Your actions have spoken for your character and I know you are a trustworthy man."

Relieved a little by the ex-sheriff's words, but still reserved, Byrne glanced at his wife. She was waiting, poised. There was no delaying the inevitable. Taking a deep, uneasy breath, Byrne launched into his tale. "Keep in mind that this was many years ago. But yes, I did ride with the Hayes-Lawson gang once upon a time. I regret to say that at that time we were known as the Jameson-Hayes gang. We numbered thirteen men at our strongest, back in 1827. Even though I was one of the youngest men in the band, a mere nineteen years old, I worked my way up in the ranks very quickly.

"Trust me, the competition was poor. Before I knew it, I was leading a band of plundering vandals alongside who I, at the time, thought was the greatest villain in the West, Cliff Hayes. We called him the Gravedigger because he was so quick to kill, utterly ruthless. He brought death down upon so many people. So many innocent people." Byrne's voice caught as a particularly unpleasant memory flooded into his mind, called up from the deep-slumbering past by the tale he told.

He sniffled once, fighting to keep his composure. The rancher glanced at his companions, who sat transfixed, listening intently.

The rancher cleared his throat and continued. "Hayes was a smart character. He recognized my potential, my ability to formulate plans and execute them almost flawlessly. I looked out for the men in the company and saved their lives on a number of occasions. All told, it was a thankless job. The men were like a pack of rabid coyotes, bound together by greed and quick to turn on one another.

"As I grew older I began to realize that the life of an outlaw was not all it was cracked up to be. It was a dusty, dirty life lived on the run and having to constantly watch your back. Even your own mates could not be trusted; they were likely to turn on you in a second if they thought it would serve their purposes. I can't even tell you how many gunfight duels I fought - and by necessity won - to keep the men in check." He took in a shaky breath. Reading a question in their eyes, he thought he knew what it was. "I'm sure you're wondering how many men I killed in that time. I was personally responsible for seventeen deaths. Each and every one of their faces is branded on my mind, something I will never forget. Three of those were men from my own gang that got too big for their britches. Had I not killed them they would certainly have killed me.

"The life became a whirlwind of death, paranoia and filth. Sure, we made a decent chunk of change robbing towns and trains and stagecoaches, but I felt as though I was paying with my very soul. When I turned twenty-two I decided that I had had enough. I told Cliff I was leaving the gang. Naturally he tried to stop me, but I was determined.

"They chased me across the plains, hunting me mercilessly. I finally found refuge in a hole-in-the-wall town on the border of Missouri. Hayes had taken his men back out West where they could find better spoils. I, in turn, sought to change my life. I put the years of riding in the desert behind me and looked to the future."

"We were married in 1833," Ivey mused in a quiet voice. She was still processing all the information she had heard. She did the math in her head. "You had been away from the gang for three years?"

"Yes. I had been rebuilding my life for years before I met you. Had I been where I was when I left the gang, I would never have trusted myself enough to seek your hand." He stood and hobbled over to her. When he reached her he dropped to his knees and picked up her hand, holding it between both of his. "Now you know all. I hope it will not prejudice you against me."

She looked at him with tears in her eyes. It had been a hard truth to stomach but she also recognized the great courage it had taken for him to share it with her. Even if her marriage had been built on a false pretense, the man she had married was still true to himself.

Ivey slid off her chair to her knees and hugged him tightly, crying quietly into his shirtfront. Byrne held her, pressing his face into her golden hair. Alexander turned a blind eye to the emotional display, fascinating himself by gazing out the window with his back to the pair.

Byrne's leg gave way suddenly, overburdened and overtaxed. The pair crumpled to the floor and lay there, laughing. Alexander turned around in response to the loud sound. Upon seeing that nothing was amiss, he smiled and went to offer the couple a hand up.

"Did Derek ride with you all those years ago?" Alexander asked once they were all situated again.

The rancher nodded in the affirmative. "He was a youngster like me. Rumor had it, he had run away from his fine family, or was kicked out of the house, something along those lines. We never could break him of those fine manners impressed upon him growing up. Of course, he was not too much a gent to abstain from the raids and murders," he added with a grim look at his wife. "So, my dear, I've told all. Now it's your turn. Why are you standing up for Ward?"

Ivey met his jealous look with a confidant stare. "Because if not for Derek Ward I would not be here speaking with you."

"What do you mean?"

Taking a shuddering breath, Ivey realized that she would have to elaborate, to tell the tale of what happened to her just days ago. The very thought of being a captive of the Hayes-Lawson gang made her shudder. Still, she knew she must relive those horrible memories in order to save the life of the man who had saved hers.

"Three days back Mr. Ward rode out to our homestead. He asked me what you were about, where you had gone, and the like. I told him all that I knew: that you had gone out to hunt mustangs with a group of men from town. He seemed to know otherwise and suspected me of lying. When I adhered to my story he - Byrne, do not get angry - he took me up on his horse and—"

Byrne slapped his leg and stood, his face a mask of fury. "That mangy cur! I'll strangle him with my bare hands!"

Alexander was quick to intervene. He grabbed Byrne's arms and held him back. The rancher put up a good struggle and would have got away but for the weakness of his leg.

Hastily, hoping to calm her irate spouse, Ivey continued. "Long story short he brought me into town. I must confess I got a trifle violent myself: when he stopped the horse I broke his nose." She blushed at admitting to having done something so unkind, even if she had been justified at the time.

Byrne stopped his struggles and turned slowly, still held by the ex-sheriff. His face was not angry, but perplexed. Suddenly he broke out in laughter. Alexander let him go in surprise.

The rancher had a good laugh. "You mean the," he pointed to his eyes, referring to the dark skin he had seen around Derek's eyes, "that was all your doing?" He let out another whoop of laughter and slapped his knee, doubled over in mirth. "Well done my love!" He caught her face in his hands and planted a kiss on her lips.

"Do not be unkind," she chided sharply, pulling away. "I was brought into the saloon and there I was held captive by those appalling men overnight. They drank heavily and interrogated me." She hesitated, watching Byrne's face closely. "They beat me."

His features hardened again. "Did they—?"

"No, thank Heaven," she answered quickly. There was venom in her voice as she thought of Pistol Lawson and Cliff Hayes. "The next morning, after they had sent men to tear down your corrals, they tried once more to glean information from me. I had none to give, but they would not believe me. They had summoned Derek - Mr. Ward - though I do not know to what purpose. Just as he arrived, Hayes drew a pistol and was pointing it at me."

"Bastard," Byrne spat.

"Language, Byrne!" Alexander admonished.

"Sorry."

Ivey closed her eyes, fighting back tears. "Thank God he arrived just then. Derek got into an argument with Lawson and Hayes. They wanted to shoot me, to teach you a lesson. Derek would hear none of it. He went for the gun and struggled with Hayes. In the process the gun went off and Derek was injured, as you saw.

"That murderer Hayes threw Derek aside and left him to die. Thankfully his intervention seemed to derail their plans for they left me alone after that. They left the saloon, though where they went I do not know. That's how you came to find me alone in the saloon."

"Hm."

Alexander turned to his friend. "You can hardly condemn the man that saved your wife's life, Byrne. I certainly could not." He spoke slowly, hesitantly, unsure if he was speaking out of turn.

The rancher stood with arms crossed and frowning features. He did not speak for a long while or make eye contact with the others. In his mind he was weighing Derek's crimes against his good actions. Reluctant though he was to admit it, Byrne realized that he owed both his own and his wife's life to the gentleman bandit.

"Byrne? What are you thinking? Speak, please, you are trying my nerves," Ivey said finally. She went to her husband, touching his arm to draw him out of his musings.

Byrne looked at her finally, his features hard and unreadable. Then he let out a heavy sigh and the fight seemed to drain out of him. "The truth of the matter is that I owe him my life as well. When Hayes had me trapped in the surgery with a pistol aimed, it was Derek who grabbed the spare gun and shot Cliff. I had been half-dead at the time, useless. If not for Derek I would have died then." He spoke grudgingly, unhappy at having to admit his own failings.

"I cannot cast my vote in favor of his death," Byrne concluded. "At first I thought I owed him only my life, but now that I am deeper in debt to him I see that I cannot let him hang. Very well Ivey, you win. That is, if the sheriff here agrees?"

Alexander gave him a wry smile. "I am hardly a sheriff anymore Byrne. You know my commission from the government has been rescinded."

"Still, you're the closest thing we've got."

"Well, if he saved the life of my friend I would say he has done enough good to offset his wrongs. I see no reason not to let him go free."

Byrne nodded. He was ill at ease with the idea of Derek Ward going scot-free but he could hardly demand that the man be kept a prisoner for the rest of his life. The rancher walked to the head of the stairs, relying heavily on his cane.

"Byrne," Alexander called, bringing him up short. The rancher turned and looked at the ex-sheriff. "What, exactly, did happen in the doctor's establishment that day? How did Lawson come to be injured?"

"Haven't you heard enough stories for one day, Alexander?" There was a playful note in Byrne's voice. He started down the steps slowly, making good use of his cane. The others followed him, Ivey keeping one hand on his shoulder in case he should be in need of aid.

When they descended to the main level Pistol backed to the rear of his cell, knowing that Byrne would not forget the little joke at his wife's expense. Derek turned his head to keep them in view but did not waste his energy trying to stand or even speak to them. The trio stopped in front of Ward's cell. Byrne pulled Ivey in front of him and held her there, safe from Pistol in the cell behind them.

Derek looked vaguely up at the three staring in at him. "I see you've decided what's to be done with me," he remarked. His voice was barely louder than a raspy whisper.

Byrne threw a nod at Alexander and the ex-sheriff unlocked the cell. Alexander entered and helped Derek onto his feet. Byrne held the cell door and waited at the threshold. Ward took a few hesitant steps, cringing at every movement. Alexander supported him to the door of the cell.

"You are free to go, Mr. Ward," the ex-sheriff remarked in a light tone of voice. "If you like, I will help you to the inn and fetch the doctor."

"Much obliged," Derek replied breathlessly. He gripped the bars of the cell, trying to support himself. He looked over at his sometime companion, sometime enemy and offered a pale smile. "Thank you Byrne."

The rancher was not to be won over so easily. "Why'd you do it, Derek? Save me, save Ivey?"

"Why?" Derek repeated with a breathy laugh. He winced and pressed a fist to his gut. "Because it was the right thing to do. Ever since you left the gang I've wondered how you were getting on. When I got my answer, I envied you." He paused to catch his breath, swallowing tightly and fighting back the pain. He wanted to share what was on his mind, to explain himself. "The gang was never the same after you left. Made me realize, I allow a little too late, that I am not cut from the same cloth as Hayes and Lawson. I did not want to be thrown in with their lot any longer."

"Hmph," Byrne said in answer.

"Can we be friends after all this?" Derek ventured uneasily. He was pale and shaking, obviously in need of medical attention, but he would have his answer first.

Byrne took in a long drawn breath and exhaled, looking carefully at the other man. "Can't say as yet."

Ivey elbowed her husband sharply in the ribs. She was tiring of his masculine pride.

Derek averted his gaze and gave a small nod. "Fair enough I suppose." His breath was wheezing.

Byrne leaned in close to the gentleman outlaw and kept his voice low, no more than a whisper. He did not want Ivey or Alexander to overhear. "I'll let you go this once, Ward. Cross me again and the result will not be so favorable."

"I understand," was the whispered reply.

"Come along, Mr. Ward, let us go to pay a call on Doctor Simmons."
Alexander pulled Derek's arm over his shoulders and assisted him out into the

street.

Ivey laid her hand on Byrne's chest. "What did you say to him?"

"Nothing to concern you with," Byrne answered tersely. He put his arm around his wife and started to lead her outside.

"Hey now, you're not forgetting about me are you Byrne ol' friend?" Pistol's snarky voice chimed from behind the pair.

"See you at the hanging, Pistol," the rancher answered without sparing him a glance.

CHAPTER TWENTY-ONE

With surprising rapidity things returned to normalcy in Flintridge. Pistol Lawson was kept under lock and key in the constabulary with men taking shifts watching over him. Alexander still acted as if he were a government-sanctioned sheriff, but he split his time between law duties and helping his family run the general store.

Work continued on the railroad just outside of town, bringing new men in regularly to bolster the economy. The townsfolk settled back into their usual patterns and felt more confident to go out since the Hayes-Lawson gang had been disbanded.

Whilst he was sidelined by the bullet graze to his leg, Cody instructed Jesse in the art of horseshoeing. The youth was still upset that he had missed out on so much of the action against the Hayes-Lawson gang, but he was willing enough to learn a proper trade.

A brief hearing was held in town which allowed victims to testify publicly against Pistol Lawson. By general consensus it was decided that he would be hanged for his numerous horrible crimes. The date was set, a week hence, and everyone went about their business lighter in spirit, knowing an evil man would soon be removed from the world.

Byrne finished rebuilding his stock corrals with help from local men. Frank the mule was seen home; Cody had found him burying his nose in a sack of feed at the local stable. The only horse still missing was the handsome but temperamental palomino stallion.

The loss of the golden mustang weighed heavily on Byrne's mind. It felt like a very personal loss, leaving a hole in the rancher's life. He knew he should be happy with what he had, should be focusing his energies on the new life that he and Ivey would welcome in a few months. Still, he could not help but think about that fiery-tempered horse and his longing to recapture it. Byrne bided his time, waiting impatiently for his leg to heal sufficiently for him to ride out into the wilds again.

He felt he must wait awhile, anyway. Leaving Flintridge and his wife alone whilst Pistol Lawson still lived made him uneasy. He knew the outlaw was imprisoned, knew he was no longer a threat, but still doubt and fear nagged at him. So he stayed, repairing the damages done to his homestead to while away the time.

Finally Byrne and Ivey were able to sit down to dinner with peace of mind. They knew that at dawn the next day Pistol Lawson would be hanged and trouble them no more. They exchanged friendly conversation, speaking often of the future. The natural light faded and they opted to go to bed early to save oil.

In the middle of the night they awoke to the sound of a galloping horse. At that hour it was a very unusual sound and it set Byrne's nerves on-edge. He gestured for Ivey to remain silent. The pair listened intently, staring at the patch of moonlight pouring in through their bedroom window. They held their breath and waited.

The hoofbeats drew closer and closer, louder and louder. It was only one horse, of that Byrne was certain. His stock whinnied out in the yard, startled at the appearance of the strange equine. The rancher heard them shuffling about, running up and down the length of their pens.

Then the sound of galloping hooves seemed to be in the room with them. The horse had to be just outside their window. Slipping out of bed, Byrne crept to the window and peered out. Why would a horse be out in the dead of night, galloping around a human dwelling? There had to be a rider. Byrne peered over the bottom frame of the window, out the lower panel.

A gun fired, the sound echoing eerily against the hills. The shot was positively deafening to the couple. Byrne ducked hastily, bowing his head just before the glass of the window shattered and showered down on him. The rancher shouted involuntarily, perhaps to warn Ivey to stay low.

No more shots came. The hoofbeats sounded again, this time fading away. Eventually only the normal night sounds were to be heard. Crickets chirped and coyotes howled in the hills. Byrne could scarcely hear them over the pounding of his own heart. He looked toward his wife, still lying on the bed. She was curled in a tight ball, shaking violently with fear.

"What was that?" she demanded in a harsh whisper.

"I think I know," the rancher answered with a grim tone in his voice. He stood and went in search of his clothes.

"Byrne, no," Ivey begged, realizing what he was about to do. "Do not go out after him. Please."

"I have to tell Alexander at least," Byrne replied as he pulled his pants on.

"Wait 'til morning. You can't possibly get a posse up and follow him in the dark."

The rancher was torn. He knew it had been Pistol Lawson who had fired into his bedroom window, endangering his wife and unborn child. He wanted nothing more than to hunt the fiend down and put an end to him. Still, he could not argue against Ivey's point, for she had the right of it. Reluctantly, he returned to bed.

~~~~~~~~~~

Next morning Byrne climbed into the saddle and rode into Flintridge. He had to go slowly because of his injured leg. Still, he set as fast a pace as possible, feeling that time was of the essence.

He arrived at the jail only to find a group of men standing on the veranda, mulling about. He did not dare to dismount and risk making a fool of himself so he stayed in the saddle and called out to them.

"He got out, Byrne," Alexander said with horrible disappointment in his voice.

"I thought as much. He paid Ivey and me a visit last night."

"What happened?"

"Shot out our bedroom window. Got clean away." The rancher's voice was hard with self-loathing. He had let Pistol get away because he was too much a coward to go haring off in the night. It was stupid, no one would have expected him to put his life on the line like that, but he could not help but blame himself.

"Not your fault Byrne," Cody assured him.

"But how'd he get loose? That cell was locked up tight," Ty said, scratching his head as he mulled the question over.

"The lock was opened. I did not see the key; mine is still in my possession," Alexander chimed in.

"If Ward had anything to do with this..." Byrne began in a low growl.

"I assure you, Byrne, I did not," Derek remarked with calm collection as he approached the group. As if set off by a trigger, the men wheeled on the approaching gentleman bandit and drew on him. Derek raised his hands in appeal. "Would I still be here if I had helped him get out?"

None of them could justify a scenario in which he might. Reluctantly they lowered their guns.

"Now, if I may have a look?" Derek asked as he pushed through the group and made his way into the constabulary. He moved slowly, still hampered by his wound, but he improved greatly since being released from jail.

The former outlaw took a look at the cell door, swinging it to test the hinges. He examined the lock and then entered the cell itself. Glancing over his shoulder, he saw that the others had followed him into the constabulary but remained in the hall. "Now don't go getting any clever ideas about locking me in here," he remarked, trying to lighten the mood.

Casting his gaze around, Derek let out a strained breath, thinking. He chewed on his lower lip as he examined the walls and floor. "Aha," he exclaimed mildly, and very carefully bent to pick up an item. Pinched between his thumb and forefinger was a bent nail. "Your 'key', gentlemen." He handed it off to Alexander as he came out of the cell.

The ex-sheriff held the object up for the others to see. The nail had been pried up from the floorboard and shaped so it could be used to undo the lock.

"So, do we go after him?" Jesse asked, joining the party late. He was eager to ride out again. He looked expectantly at Alexander, waiting for him to give the word.

All eyes, including Alexander's, turned to Byrne. They waited for his counsel. Byrne instinctively looked toward Derek, seeking input from the man who knew the most about Lawson.

Derek shrugged. "Go after him or not, I do not think it will matter much."

"Come again?"

"He is only one man, Byrne, and he is not the leader that Hayes was. No one will follow him. If he does get a gang together they will not last long."

"We can't just let him go!" Jesse exclaimed.

"In this case it might be better to let sleeping dogs lie, Jesse," the rancher said slowly. He was torn again. His heart told him to leave the whole messy business alone and stay in Flintridge. Perhaps if they did not bother Lawson he would not bother them. He felt that Derek was correct in his reasoning.

"You can't be serious!" the youth exclaimed, indignant.

Byrne looked around at the others. "What do you all say?"

They murmured, their responses muddled, but the general consensus was that it would be a waste of time to go after one man. The wind might have blown away all tracks and they did not know in which direction he had gone. As far as anyone knew he had only stolen a horse, no food or water, so it was unlikely he would survive in the wilds. They could spend weeks combing the surrounding hills without finding him. It would be more productive to stay in Flintridge and work to build a better life for the community.

CHAPTER TWENTY-TWO

A week later Byrne felt that his leg had mended enough for him to go out in search of Beau, the palomino mustang. At Ivey's insistence he invited Alexander along for the hunt. He still harbored suspicions of Derek and so invited him along as well, intending to keep his enemy close. They met at dawn in the yard of Byrne's ranch.

"Mornin' Byrne," Derek Ward greeted with a tip of his hat. He had purchased new clothes since last the rancher saw him and, for once, he was dressed more like a common man. Perhaps dressing fancy reminded him of his sordid past. Or, what was more likely, his pocketbook had failed him since they forced him to donate the lion's share of his ill-gotten money to the local church. "I would get down to shake hands but, to be frank, it was a trifle difficult to get into the saddle this morning."

Byrne noticed that the hand that did not hold the reins was pressed tightly to the gentleman's midsection. He had made a good recovery but the prospect of riding for days on end was somewhat daunting. Still, Derek had not dared to pass up the invitation.

"Not a whit," the rancher answered, turning back to his own preparations. "We're just about to leave. Ready Alexander?"

"Sure am, Byrne," was the ready answer. The ex-sheriff leaned forward and patted Duke's neck. The friendly black horse tossed his head eagerly.

Byrne swung up into the saddle. His right leg still troubled him some but he was almost back to full strength. Taking up the reins, he looked at each of his companions in turn. "Alright, we got everything? Food, fuel, water, guns?"

"Check, check, check and check," Derek replied. Alexander nodded in the affirmative.

Satisfied on that point, Byrne verified that they all had lassos lashed to their saddles. He looked at Derek closely. "Can you use that?" He indicated the coil of rope.

"I suppose you will have to wait and see," the gentleman outlaw replied with a mild smile. He nudged his horse onward and set off at a walk toward the distant hills.

Byrne, on Cowboy and Alexander, on Duke followed him. Though Byrne was eager to be on the hunt he was not unkind enough to force Derek to a faster pace, injured as he was. The rancher was rather impressed that Ward had agreed to come along.

Because they were moving slowly it took them the whole day to reach the hills outside of town. Byrne and Cowboy were in the lead, finding a path through the twisting canyons. Derek rode behind with Alexander, still distrustful of the ex-outlaw, bringing up the rear.

They went to the stream that Byrne frequented on such trips and decided to camp beside it for the night. Striking a fire, they prepared their evening meal and joined in some reserved small talk. Neither the rancher nor the ex-sheriff was entirely comfortable in Ward's presence. For his part, Derek tried to stay to neutral topics and tried to be likeable, knowing he was on thin ice as it was.

Next morning Byrne was the first to wake. He stoked up the fire and put on a pot of coffee. As he sat waiting for the brew to finish, Derek stirred.

"I did miss the smell of coffee in the morning," Ward remarked, rubbing the sleep from his eyes. Stretching, he winced as his still-mending wound was strained. He yawned and stood, then rolled up the wool blanket. His chore done, he approached the fire, rubbing his hands for warmth in the early morning chill. He had brought with him a tin cup from his saddlebag. "I do not suppose I could trouble you for a pour?"

Byrne glanced at him and, for a moment, he considered being rude. Then his better side won out and he nodded. Taking the kettle off the fire he poured a ration into the cup Derek held.

"Much obliged," Ward said genuinely as he took a sip. He gave an appreciative exhale. "There is nothing like good, strong coffee to wake a man up," he remarked.

They finished their drinks in silence, watching the murky gray light slowly strengthen on the surrounding bluffs. Alexander woke eventually and joined them in the morning ritual.

After a quick breakfast they saddled up and were off. They spent the day scouring the gentler sloping lands of the canyons and hills, searching for signs of wild horses. Always in the back of their minds was the possibility that Pistol Lawson was out there and that they might encounter him. They were all armed, though, and felt confident in their ability to take out a single man.

By the end of the first day of searching they had seen nothing to suggest wild horses existed in those hills at all. They had seen many other species, ranging from mountain goats, antelope and deer to small rodents, birds and lizards. Disappointed, they went to bed early. They woke before dawn, had their coffee, and set off again.

On the second day they found a pile of day-old droppings. There was no way to tell what horse had left them, but Byrne seemed hopeful that they would find the stallion amongst other horses. He found a mustang track and followed it.

In his excitement, Cowboy picked up his pace, drawing the others along at fast trots behind him. Derek's wound protested the jouncing gait but he did not complain. Instead, he encouraged his mount to break into a collected canter. It would tire the horse faster, but spare his wound.

They stopped beside a larger stream than the one at which they had camped before. As they stood watering the horses, Byrne casually looked about them at the high limestone walls of the canyon. It never ceased to amaze him how the open air tunnels had been cut through the land, how beautiful the red-buff rock was with its jade decorations of sage and other shrubbery. He inhaled deeply, savoring the fresh mountain air.

Atop the ridge to his right he thought he saw a flash of silver. Focusing on that spot, Byrne narrowed his eyes against the intense sunlight. Had he imagined it? Intending to find out, he threw himself into the saddle and tore off, leaving the others standing watching him in confusion.

"Byrne! Where are you off to?" Alexander called after him.

The rancher did not answer, nor even register that a question had been asked. He forced Cowboy through the creek, sending up showers of watery crystal as they forded through. His heart was racing with excitement as he turned his mount up the loose rock bank. Chips of stone cascaded out from beneath Cowboy's hard hooves as the sure-footed chestnut strained up the embankment.

They found solid footing and the mustang took off. The thrill of the hunt was flooding through them both again, banishing the bad memories of the recent past. Peripherally Byrne heard his companions trying to scale the shaley bank but he and Cowboy had left them well behind.

Ahead, a stallion's cry taunted them, leading them on. Byrne was certain the cry had come from the palomino. Cowboy made the agile leaps from foothold to foothold until they had gained the zenith of the cliff.

There the pair paused, looking about. Cowboy fairly danced in place as Byrne held him back. The chestnut mustang's nostrils were dilated, his eyes rolling white with excitement.

Far off, almost impossibly far away, Beau stood watching them. Byrne pulled his lasso free of its tether and prepared his coil, expecting to give chase.

The palomino stallion reared up, screaming his defiance of the man hunting him. Dropping to all fours, the horse turned and seemed to vanish amongst the tawny-colored rocks. Heat waves rose up from the land, distorting the vision, making it seem like the horse had been only a mirage, a phantom of the mesas.

Byrne held Cowboy back. He had been struck by the encounter and a realization had dawned on him. Coiling his rope, he held it in his free hand whilst he directed Cowboy off the promontory. The hardy chestnut mustang made the tricky descent look easy; Byrne leaned back in the saddle to keep them balanced.

Derek and Alexander stood at the base of the shale bank, having been unable to get their horses to climb it successfully.

"What was that all about?" Derek asked good-humoredly. "You were off like a bat out of hell."

"Was it the mustang?" Alexander asked eagerly, leaning forward in his saddle. Byrne nodded in the affirmative. "Where did he go? How will we catch him?"

The rancher grinned, enjoying a personal joke. "Some things lose their value once they are possessed."

"So you are letting him go?" Derek asked incredulously.

Cowboy landed the last jump down and Byrne led him to the stream to drink.

When the mustang had had his fill, the rancher turned him deeper into the hills. "I have yet to decide that," he said in belated answer to Ward's question. Grinning broadly, he led them off to continue their search. Even if the hunt proved to be fruitless, the chase kept them all alive.

A wild stallion cry echoed across the rocks. The horse stayed just out of sight. At most the men saw the swish of a silvery tail or the flash of a strong golden leg. They heard the clatter of the mustang's strong hooves on stone. Beau called again, taunting the men on.

The chase bound the unlikely group of men together, giving them a shared sense of purpose. All their differences seemed insignificant as they matched wits with the clever, indomitable palomino mustang.

The trio followed the stallion cries further into the mountains. Only a cloud of dust lingered in the air to mark where they had gone.

ABOUT THE AUTHOR

Ahi has been writing for approximately fifteen years, during the course of which she has started twenty-some-odd stories. *Flintridge* is the first to be published. Ahi has a degree in Accounting and works in the same field. Her two best buds just happen to be of the four-legged variety: Scout, her Quarter Horse, and Savvy, the family Cocker Spaniel.

When not with her critters or writing she spends her time at fencing practice, going out and about with her fellow pirates, watching rodeos, running agility, throwing knives, practicing archery, sewing new costumes, or playing online games. She has volunteered at a wildlife center working with wolves and other species native to the Midwest. Currently she helps out at a local horse rescue.

Made in the USA
Charleston, SC
05 September 2014